Yale Judaica Series, Volume XXX

In Queen Esther's Garden

In Queen Esther's Garden

An Anthology of Judeo-Persian Literature

Translated and with an introduction and notes
by Vera Basch Moreen

Yale University Press New Haven and London

Designed by Rebecca Gibb. Set in Cochin type by Keystone Typesetting, Inc. Printed in the United States of America by Vail-Ballou Press, Binghamton, New York.

Library of Congress Cataloging-in-Publication Data
In Queen Esther's garden : an anthology of Judeo-Persian literature / translated and with an introduction and notes by Vera Basch Moreen.
p. cm. — (Yale Judaica series ; v.30)
Includes bibliographical references and index.
ISBN 0–300–07905–2 (alk. paper)
1. Judeo–Persian literature—Translations into English. 2. Jewish religious poetry, Judeo-Persian—Translations into English. 3. Bible. O.T.—Poetry. I. Moreen, Vera Basch. II. Series.

PJ5089.I5 2000
892.4′08089155—dc21
99–044912

A catalogue record for this book is available from the British Library.
The paper in this book meets the guidelines for permanence and durability of the Committee on Production Guidelines for Book Longevity of the Council on Library Resources.

10 9 8 7 6 5 4 3 2 1

In memory of Martin B. Dickson (1924–1991)

The Sage is the ladder to Heaven

Jalāl ud-Dīn Rūmī, Masnavī, *v. 4125*

The true Zaddik unites the upper wisdom with the lower wisdom

Naḥman of Bratslav, Liquṭe Moharan *II, chap. 71*

Contents

Preface

The suggestion to write this book came to me from Leon Nemoy, whose *Karaite Anthology* (New Haven, 1952) has been a major scholarly achievement and a source of inspiration ever since it was published. Judeo-Persian (JP) studies, although better explored at this point than Karaism was when Dr. Nemoy published his book, are largely ignored by scholars of both Jewish and Iranian studies, and they are virtually unknown to the public. Significant publications touching on various aspects of Jewish life in Iran as reflected in JP texts have appeared sporadically in Hebrew and in a number of European languages since the nineteenth century, but knowledge of their contents remains the specialized domain of a small group of scholars. Yet there exists a large corpus of untapped JP manuscripts that, like the Judeo-Arabic texts of the Cairo Genizah, have the potential to shed considerable light on the ancient and vibrant Jewish communities of Iran—albeit mostly in their late medieval, early modern phase—since most of the surviving manuscripts date from the seventeenth to the twentieth centuries.

Judeo-Persian texts have the potential to enrich the fields of both Jewish and Iranian studies. They reward scholars of Jewish studies with variegated information about yet another Jewish diaspora community in a Muslim milieu. This milieu, by virtue of its being Shi'i from the beginning of the sixteenth century, adds a different dimension to our knowledge of Jewish survival in Muslim lands under conditions that were often less congenial than those prevailing in the Sunni world. Scholars of Persian linguistics, history, and literature can also find a great deal of useful information in JP texts. Because of the antiquity of the Iranian-Jewish community, JP texts are crucial to the understanding of the development of New Persian and its various dialects. Those JP texts which preserve historical (mostly Jewish, largely communal) accounts are also a valuable source of historical information, presenting a minority view of events that are barely alluded to or completely ignored by royal chronicles, the most important sources of Iranian history. In addition, by preserving many Persian classical texts (mostly poetry) in the Hebrew script, JP manuscripts constitute a potential source for refining critical editions of these texts. Finally, the original literary contributions of Jewish-Iranian authors expand the canons of both Jewish and Persian literatures. The strong reliance on and interaction with Persian literature of JP literature turns it into yet another branch of the prodigious, luxuriant Persianate literature, which flourished far beyond the borders of present-day Iran.

Stimulated by Dr. Nemoy's challenge, I undertook the task of compiling the present anthology of JP literature. It consists of annotated English translations of selections from some of the most important JP texts, preceded by brief introductions.

From the beginning I was aware of the numerous difficulties surrounding such a project. Two practical obstacles were the location of JP manuscripts and the lack of critically edited texts from which to make reliable translations.

There are several substantial collections of JP manuscripts worldwide, specifically, the collections of the Jewish Theological Seminary of America (JTS), New York; the Klau Library, Hebrew Union College (HUC), Cincinnati; the Ben Zvi Institute (BZI) and the Jewish National and University Library (JNUL), both in Jerusalem; the Library of the Oriental Institute (Institut Vostokvednya; IV) and the Saltykov-Shchedrin Library (SS), both in Saint Petersburg; the British Library (BL), London. The majority of these manuscripts are not catalogued. Three notable exceptions are Amnon Netzer's catalogue of the JP manuscripts of the Ben-Zvi Institute, Ezra Spicehandler's short descriptive list of the JP manuscripts of the Klau Library (see the bibliography), and Efraim Wust's catalogue in progress of the manuscripts housed at the Jewish National and University Library. I wish to thank all these libraries and their librarians, especially Robert Attal and Yosef Goel (BZI), Meir Rabinowitz (JTS), Efraim Wust (JNUL), and Nadezhda Ivanovna Nosova (IV), for their help and courtesy in providing me with access to the JP manuscripts in their collections. I owe a particular debt of gratitude to Oleg F. Akimushkin (IV), Saint Petersburg, for facilitating my trip to Russia and my visits to the libraries of Saint Petersburg. Special thanks are also due to Robert D. McChesney for drawing my attention to ms. 610 of Fond Vostochnykh Rukopise, Akademiia Nauk, Dushanbe, Tadzhikistan.

There are a significant number of privately owned JP manuscripts in Iran, Israel, the United States, and elsewhere that could not be considered for this book. I had access only to the collection of Efraim Dardashti (Merion, Pa.), which I gratefully acknowledge.

The bulk of JP manuscripts are literary in nature, reflecting the attraction for Iranian Jews of belles lettres, especially Persian poetry, rather than subjects of a halakic (legal), historical, mystical, or philosophical nature. (A separate study would be needed to establish to what extent these aspects of Iranian Jewry's legacy are represented by Hebrew texts produced in Iran.) Reflecting this inclination, the present anthology includes more poetry than prose. Naturally, the choice of texts and of the passages translated from longer works reflect my own taste. In general, I chose to translate texts that indicate the deep acculturation of Iranian Jews, as well as texts whose literary merit remained perceivable even after translation into English. I should point out, however, that these selections, while striving to be representative of JP literature as a whole, are not comprehensive.

Few JP texts have been translated into Western languages, and fewer still have been translated on the basis of critically edited texts. In compiling this anthology, the large number of manuscripts of many of the same texts precluded an exhaustive investigation of all available versions. In order to prepare sound translations for this volume, I edited, collated, or conflated several JP manuscripts for each selection, generally using at least two, and often more, texts. It is my hope that this anthology will spur the study of JP literature, especially the preparation of critical editions.

In Queen Esther's Garden has an important and inspiring precursor, Amnon Netzer's Persian anthology of JP literature, *Muntakhab-i ʾashʿār-i fārisī az āṡār-i yahudiyān-i Irān* (An anthology of Persian poetry of the Jews of Iran; Tehran, 1973). The aim of Netzer's volume was to introduce JP literature to Iranian audiences through the transcription of selected JP texts into the Persian alphabet. Although the present work attempts to do the same for an English-speaking audience, my selections, (partial) editions, and annotations differ from Netzer's more general approach.

I wish to thank the foundations that have partially funded my travels to see the various collections of JP manuscripts: the American Philosophical Society, the Littauer Foundation, and the International Research and Exchanges Board. A two-year translation grant from the National Endowment for the Humanities (1992–94) allowed me to concentrate on this project, and a Skirball Fellowship (1993) from the Oxford Centre for Hebrew and Jewish Studies at Yarnton Manor, Yarnton, Oxford, provided beautiful and peaceful surroundings for the most intensive stage of translation.

I would like to thank the following authors for contributing to this volume, either by providing reworked translations of earlier texts or by allowing me to do so. At the same time, I gratefully acknowledge the publications in which these texts first appeared and thank their editors for permission to reprint: Jes P. Asmussen, "Judeo-Persica II: The Jewish-Persian Law Report from Ahwāz," *Acta Orientalia* 29 (1965): 49–60; D. N. MacKenzie, "An Early Jewish-Persian Argument," *Bulletin of the School of Oriental and African Studies* 31 (1968): 249–269; Vera B. Moreen, *Iranian Jewry's Hour of Peril and Heroism: A Study of Bābāī Ibn Luṭf's Chronicle [1617–1662]* (New York: American Academy for Jewish Research, 1986); Moreen, *Iranian Jewry During the Afghan Invasion: The Kitāb-i Sar Guzasht-i Kāshān of Bābāī b. Farhād [1721–1731]* (Stuttgart: Franz Steiner Verlag, 1990); Amnon Netzer, *Sifrut farsit-yehudit. 2. Tafsīr-i midrash ʿaliyat Moshe le-marom* (Jerusalem: Ben Zvi Institute, 1990); Bo Utas, "The Jewish-Persian Fragment from Dandān-Uiliq," *Orientalia Suecana* 17 (1969): 123–136; David Yeroushalmi, *The Judeo-Persian Poet ʿEmrānī and His Book of Treasure* (Leiden: E. J. Brill, 1995).

In addition to the contributions of the individuals named above, many colleagues and friends have helped with the realization of this book. I would especially like to thank Tova Beeri, William Brinner, Efraim Dardashti, Abraham David, William C. Jordan, Daniel J. Lasker, Hava Lazarus-Yafeh (z'l), Bernard Lewis, Robert D. McChesney, Igor Naftul'eff, Ezra Spicehandler, Norman Stillman, Sarah Stroumsa, Ray Scheindlin, Wheeler M. Thackston, and Isadore Twersky (zṣ'l). I am also indebted to the unfailing help and courtesy of Gilad Gevaryahu. I would like to thank the librarians of the Annenberg Research Institute (now the Center of Judaic Studies of the University of Pennsylvania), especially Penina Bar-Kana, James Weinberger (Princeton University), and Heather Whipple (Swarthmore College), for facilitating access to many of the works cited. I thank Sid Z. Leiman, Ivan G. Marcus, and the editors of the Yale Judaica Series, and especially Susan Laity of Yale University Press, for their help in preparing this book for publication. Above all, I wish to express my profound gratitude to Dick Davis for his perceptive observations and corrections of my translations and to Grace Goldin (z'l), for her patient and generous aid in casting many texts into verse (she is in no way responsible for my failings); to my sorrow she is no longer with us to see their publication. I would also like to thank Judah Goldin (z'l) for helpful suggestions on questions of midrash. Last, yet always first, I thank my husband, Robert, and our sons, Gabriel and Raphael, for their love and patience during the long period of this book's gestation.

I am not indulging in Persian hyperbole when I say that hardly a sentence in this book was written without a keen sense of the loss caused by the untimely death of my beloved teacher and guide in Persian studies Martin B. Dickson, who encouraged this project. With trepidation, remembering his high critical standards, and the wish that I could have had the pleasure of continuing to discuss the book with him, I dedicate this work to his blessed memory.

A Note on the Text and the Transliterations

All Hebrew words and foreign words at first usage are italicized in every selection. All biblical quotations are from *Tanakh: The Holy Scriptures* (Philadelphia: Jewish Publication Society of America, 1985).

Names of well-known Iranian towns, regions, and well-known terms, such as "Sunni," "Shi'i," "Sufi," "mullah," "sultan," "hajj," etc., retain the spelling in common usage. All qur'anic quotations are from *The Glorious Qur'an,* trans. Mohammad M. Pickthall (New York: Mostazafan Foundation, 1984).

The texts in this book—particularly the epics—were often divided into chapters with descriptive titles. Those titles tend to be long, and for the reader's convenience, I have sometimes added short titles of my own. All the original titles are present; however, chapter titles in roman are mine.

The Hebrew and Persian transliterations have been made according to the following tables:

Table of Transliteration

Hebrew

Vowels

a	ַ
a	ָ
e	ֵ ֶ
i	ִ
o	וֹ
u	וּ
u	ֻ
e	ְ

Consonants

ʾ	א
b	בּ
g	ג
d	ד
h	ה
w	ו
z	ז
ḥ	ח
ṭ	ט
y	י
k	כ
l	ל
m	מ
n	נ
s	ס
ʿ	ע
p	פּ
f	פ
ṣ	צ
q	ק
r	ר
sh	שׁ
s	שׂ
t	ת

Persian

Vowels

a	ا
a	ی
u	و
i	ی
a	َ
o	ُ
e	ِ
a,e	ه
aw, ow	وَ
ay, ey	یَ

Consonants

ʾ	ء
b	ب
p	پ
t	ت
s	ث
j	ج
ch	چ
ḥ	ح
kh	خ
d	د
z	ذ
z	ز
r	ر
zh	ژ
s	س
sh	ش
ṣ	ص
ż	ض
ṭ	ط
ẓ	ظ
ʿ	ع
gh	غ
f	ف
q	ق

Table of Transliteration *(continued)*

Hebrew		*Persian*		
Vowels	Consonants	Vowels	Consonants	
			k	ک
			g	گ
			l	ل
			m	م
			n	ن
			u/v	و
			h	ه
			y	ي

Abbreviations

AO	*Acta Orientalia*
BL	The British Library, London
BSOAS	*Bulletin of the School of Oriental and African Studies*
BZI	The Library of the Ben Zvi Institute, Jerusalem
D	Collection of Efraim Dardashti, Merion, Pa.
EI (2)	*The Encyclopaedia of Islam* (new ed.), 1960–
EJ	*Encyclopaedia Judaica*
FVR	Fond Vostochnykh Rukopise, Dushanbe (Tadzhikistan)
HTR	*Harvard Theological Review*
HUC	The Klau Library of the Hebrew Union College, Cincinnati
HUCA	*Hebrew Union College Annual*
IOS	*Israel Oriental Studies*
IV	Institut Vostokvedenya, Saint Petersburg

JA	*Journal Asiatique*
JE	*The Jewish Encyclopedia*
JAOS	*Journal of the American Oriental Society*
JNES	*Journal of Near Eastern Studies*
JNUL	The Jewish National and University Library, Jerusalem
JQR	*The Jewish Quarterly Review*
JRAS	*Journal of the Royal Asiatic Society*
JSS	*Jewish Social Studies*
JTS	The Library of the Jewish Theological Seminary, New York
MGWJ	*Monatschrift für Geschichte und Wissenschaft des Judentums*
PAAJR	*Proceedings of the American Academy for Jewish Research*
REJ	*Revue des études juives*
SBB	*Studies in Bibliography and Booklore*
SS	The Saltykov-Shchedrin Library, Saint Petersburg
ZAW	*Zeitschrift für die alttestamentliche Wissenschaft*
ZHB	*Zeitschrift für Hebräische Bibliographie*
ZDMG	*Zeitschrift der Deutschen morgenlandischen Gesellschaft*

Introduction

Judeo-Persian literature is one of the most neglected areas of both Jewish and Iranian studies. Although JP texts, that is, New Persian writings in the Hebrew alphabet, date as far back as the second half of the eighth century CE,[1] and although they constitute the first recorded texts in New Persian,[2] they are still largely unexplored. There are two reasons for this neglect. First, most JP texts are available only in manuscript form, and these manuscripts are located in largely uncatalogued library collections.[3] Second, the study of JP manuscripts requires a thorough knowledge of several languages (Persian, Hebrew, and Arabic) as well as of Judaism and Islam, their respective religious and secular literatures.

Since the late nineteenth century, strides have been made in the study of JP texts.[4] Nevertheless, much remains to be done, especially in the realm of editing the texts, the first and most important step toward a comprehensive study. Until more scholarly editions have been prepared, our studies must necessarily be preliminary in nature.

Judeo-Persian texts include a large variety of genres: Bible translations, religious and secular poetry, chronicles, rabbinical works, grammatical treatises, translations of medieval Hebrew poetry, transcriptions of classical

Persian poetry, original epics. Many of these enrich both Jewish and Persian literatures. This wealth, as far as Persian literature is concerned, is best exemplified by the last two categories, that is, classical Persian poetry and original JP epics. Judeo-Persian texts could also further refine our knowledge of received texts and editions of classical Persian poetry as well as expand the parameters of Persian, especially poetic, literature.

In many ways JP literature is comparable to other bodies of Persian literature that flourished in the Persianate[5] world and outside the boundries of Iran proper (for example, at the Ottoman and the Mughal courts) in that it adopts and adapts Persian topoi and rhetorical modes of expression to traditional Jewish themes. It is the aim of this anthology to acquaint English-speaking readers with some of the most important JP texts, which are part of the literary heritage of Iranian Jews as well as of Muslims.

Most JP texts were, indeed, produced within the current boundries of Iran proper, especially in its central province, Fars. To the extent that we are able to determine their provenance, the bulk of JP manuscripts appear to come from the major ancient centers of Jewish population—Isfahan, Kashan, Hamadan, Kirman, Yazd. However, the number of Jewish communities in the Persianate world between the eighth and the nineteenth centuries, the time frame of this anthology, far exceeded the number of communities from which identifiable JP texts have survived. Many of these other communities were smaller; although we lack demographic information, we can postulate that they may not have had significant numbers of learned men. Jewish communities were scattered all over the map of the Persianate world, from the southernmost tip of the Persian Gulf as far north as the shores of the Caspian Sea, as far northwest as present-day Azerbaijan, and as far east as not only Bukhārā (the second–most important source of JP manuscripts after Fars) but well beyond, into the Caucasus Mountains, Afghanistan, Central Asia, and even China.[6] In fact, our earliest sources in JP are epigraphic, originating from locations along the Silk Road and thus suggesting that, as elsewhere in the diaspora, commerce played an important role in the spread of Persian-speaking Jewish communities.[7]

It has often been stated, yet it bears repeating, that the Jews of Iran constitute one of the oldest—if not the oldest—continuous Jewish diasporas in the world, as well as one of the most homogenous. However, their history is not fully documented, and there are many gaps in our knowledge. Here I shall attempt to sketch the broad outlines of this history, concentrating on the Islamic phase, the period which fostered the development of JP literature.

The origins of the Iranian-Jewish diaspora may well go back to 722 BCE, when the Assyrians deported a substantial number of Jews—the so-called Ten Tribes—belonging to the northern kingdom of Israel, and resettled them throughout their vast empire. According to Jewish tradition, these Jews eventually intermingled with local populations (2 Kings 17:27ff.) and adopted their forms of worship, so that, as far as historical evidence is concerned and despite numerous legendary claims to the contrary, they became lost to Jewish history.

It is more plausible to trace the origins of the Jewish diaspora in the Persianate world to 586 BCE, when Nebuchadnezzar conquered Jerusalem and sent many Judeans into exile in Babylonia.[8] Because the Babylonian Empire at its height included parts of western Iran, the early history of Iranian Jewry is linked with that of the Jewish communities of Babylonia.

It was an Iranian ruler who offered all the exiles in Babylonia, including the Jews, the opportunity to return to their homeland. In 538 Cyrus the Great, remembered for this in Jewish sources as "the Lord's anointed" (Isa. 45:1–4; 44; 25–28), issued his famous edict permitting the return that previous rulers had forbidden. As the Books of Ezra and Nehemiah testify, only a fraction of the exiles acted on this good news by returning to the Land of Israel. Although Cyrus gave the order to rebuild the Temple (Ezra 1:2–3), the actual rebuilding of the sanctuary occurred later, during the reign of Darius I.[9]

Jewish life in Babylonia flourished for a considerable length of time. This is not the place to review the well-known and extraordinary religious and literary accomplishments of Babylonian Jews, which culminated in the compilation of the Babylonian Talmud. Suffice it to say that Iranian Jews also contributed to those efforts.[10] Those achievements were made possible by the generally cordial relations between the Jews and their largely Zoroastrian neighbors.[11] We begin to hear about outright persecutions of Jews toward the end of the fourth century CE; they continued, intermittently, until the Muslim conquest of Iran.[12] Most of the time the persecutions resulted from political friction, such as when Jews sided with unsuccessful political factions.[13] Even though Zoroastrians generally did not favor proselytizing and did not use it as an excuse to oppress others, there were several instances of persecution which were motivated by excessive Zoroastrian religious zeal. One of the most devastating waves of anti-Jewish persecutions occurred toward the end of the third century CE and was led by Kartir, an eccentric Zoroastrian priest, who considered such actions part of a Zoroastrian's religious obligation.[14] More systematic religious persecutions took place in the fifth century, during the reigns of Yazdagerd II and his son Peroz.[15] Thus animosity against Jews and Judaism in pre-Islamic Iran is associated primarily with Sasanian, especially late Sasanian rule. Zoroastrian religious objections against the Jewish faith can be found in surviving polemical texts, which, although they come from the ninth and tenth centuries, may reflect earlier attitudes.[16]

The Muslim conquest of the heartland of the Sasanian Empire was not sudden, swift, or easy. It was actually a protracted undertaking that lasted from 637 to 644 CE, with distant regions added more securely into the Muslim empire as late as the eighth century.[17] The conversion of the local population to Islam was also gradual,[18] and we have no way of knowing how many Iranian Jews were involved at this early stage. There is little doubt, however, that the lot of the Jews improved as a result of the conquest, especially when contrasted with the hardships they had endured under late Sasanian rule. During the first three centuries of Islam, from the eighth to the tenth centuries, the great Babylonian academies of Sura and Pumbadita continued to prosper in tandem with the flourishing Islamic empire.[19] Jewish communities, like other non-Muslim groups, remained autonomous within the Muslim empire and were able to maintain to some degree (albeit with decreasing authority and jurisdiction) a form of centralized secular and religious leadership through the institutions of the exilarchate and gaonate, respectively, the former until the tenth century, the latter until the eleventh.[20]

In the eighth century, a time of great political ferment in the Islamic Empire, eastern Iran gave birth to several Jewish heterodox movements that appear to have been linked to similar trends in the Muslim environment.[21] They were led by individuals with pseudo-Messianic claims, such as Ḥīwī of Balkh and Abū ʿIsā of Isfahan. The latter's movement, the ʿIsāwiyya, became a significant schismatic movement, together with Karaism. The ʿIsāwiyya did not leave a lasting imprint on Judaism, and it is remembered chiefly from the accounts of Muslim heresiographers.[22] But Karaism, several of whose chief spokesman came from Iran, is still with us today. It received most of its early support from the Jews of Iran and "Babylonia" (Iraq), where some of the notable scholars of the movement were born.[23] It has been suggested, recently and intriguingly, that both movements "were formed in the same crucible that bore Shiʿism."[24] There has come to light a significant trove of Karaite texts in JP among the documents of the Cairo Genizah: deeds, personal letters, fragments of Hebrew grammar, and biblical commentaries (especially on the Book of Daniel).[25] It would appear that the Karaite community of Iran used JP extensively and that some of these texts fill a perceived gap in the body of JP literature between the ninth and fourteenth centuries. As Karaism itself began to decline in Iran after the ninth century, JP texts with Karaite content fell into desuetude.[26]

There is very little solid historical information about the Jews dwelling on the Iranian plateau and northeastward until the arrival of the Mongols in the thirteenth century. The earliest JP writings attest to the fact that Iranian Jews had the freedom to travel throughout the Islamicate world and to engage in commerce.[27] Most of the evidence for this comes from the Cairo Genizah, which appears to suggest a continuous move westward of those who had the means to do so. Iranian Jews came to the Mediterranean areas as colonizers, emigrants, and refugees from the turbulent political upheavals of ʿUmayyad, and later ʿAbbasid, policies.[28] Prominent in the Genizah documents are records of the commercial activities of the Karaite Tustarī family in the eleventh century, who, as their surname indicates, hailed from Tustar, a region in southwestern Iran famous as a center of the textile industry.[29] Trade in silk produced in Ṭabaristān, on the southern shore of the Caspian Sea, also involved Jewish merchants who had ties with the region.[30] According to Donald D. Leslie, the penetration of Judaism as far as China was achieved primarily through the commercial activities of Jews from the Muslim world, many of whom came from Iranian provinces.[31]

The success of such far-flung mercantile activities rested, ultimately, on the fact that the Jews of the Islamicate world did not labor under legal restrictions as onerous as those that oppressed their fellow Jews in Christendom.[32] In Muslim law Jews, along with Christians and Zoroastrians, were classified as *ahl adh-dhimma* (people of protection), or *ahl al-kitāb* (people of the Book [Scripture]). Laws discriminating against non-Muslims did exist; they are enshrined in the so-called Pact of ʿUmar. Attributed to the second caliph ʿUmar (r. 634–644), the pact, many of whose discriminatory laws derive from earlier Byzantine law, probably originates from the tenth or eleventh century.[33] Although Jews were subjected to the *jizya* (Arabic for "poll-tax") in return for *dhimma* (Arabic for "protection") and had to defer to the dominant faith in many other ways, their religious and mercantile activities were not severely restricted. Perhaps the greatest limitation they suffered was the prohibition to hold high office, but, as is well known, on rare occasions even this was disregarded in various parts of the Islamic Empire.[34] Except for a brief period under the Mongols (1248–1291), Jews in Iran proper did not occupy important positions at court. The astonishing career of Saʿd ad-Dawla, the Jewish grand vizier of the Mongol Il-khānid ruler Arghūn (d. 1291), is all the more striking because we know so little about the Jewish community from which he emerged. He rose to his high rank primarily because Arghūn had not yet converted to Islam and therefore had not yet learned to discriminate according to its teachings; in Mongol eyes all men belonged "to one and the same stock."[35] The fact that both ruler and grand vizier were eventually murdered and that the Jews of Baghdad were subsequently attacked indicates that his was an exceptional case in Persian, indeed in Islamic, history. Soon afterward, the Mongol ruler Ghazan (r. 1295–1304) embraced Islam, and Jews could no longer aspire to such high office. Ghazan's grand vizier was a Jewish apostate, the famous historian, physician, and statesman Rashīd ud-Dīn Fażlullah (d. 1318), who also met a violent death, partly because of his never-forgotten Jewish origins.[36]

It would appear that after the Il-khānid (1256–1336) and Tīmūrid (1370–1405) dynasties, until the beginning of the twentieth century, Iranian Jewry was almost always close to the bottom of the socioeconomic ladder, only a step above the much-maligned Zoroastrians and, in the nineteenth century, the Baha'is. As far as we can tell, Iranian Jews were primarily artisans, craftsmen, small-scale merchants, wine makers and wine sellers, brokers of medicinal drugs, and the like. Commerce was largely in Muslim hands, while "banking" (primarily money changing) was the occupation of a small number of Indians.[37] By the beginning of the seventeenth century most external trade, including the lucrative silk trade—which was a royal monopoly—passed into the hands of Armenian Christians,[38] and in some towns, such as Kashan, Jews were relegated to dyeing and weaving carpets using silk threads. This long period in the history of Iranian Jews remains obscure to a large extent because Iranian chronicles, the most important source of historical information, concern themselves with little besides the intrigues, feasts, and fights of royal courts. It is primarily through a few JP texts and the accounts of a number of European travelers and missionaries that we can fill in at least some of the lacunae.

Whereas under the reign of the Il-khānid rulers a Jew still felt free to write panegyrics in praise of a ruling monarch (perhaps even expected to be rewarded),[39] life must have become increasingly difficult for the entire settled population of Iran under the Tīmurīds and later under the rival Turkoman rule of the Qarā-qoyūnlū (Turkish for "those of the Black Sheep"; 1378–1468), and the Āq-qoyūnlū (Turkish for "those of the White Sheep"; 1435–1502), names derived from the groups' tribal insignia.[40]

A measure of political stability was introduced with the advent of the Safavid dynasty (1501–1731), even as this dynasty brought about a major religious upheaval. Its first monarch, Shah Ismāʿīl I (r. 1501–1524), began the aggressive conversion to the Shiʿi form of Islam of Iran's predominantly Sunni population. By the reign of Shah ʿAbbās I (1588–1629) there were few pockets of Sunnis left in the realm. Preoccupied with Sunnis, with various heretical Muslim groups, and with the prevalent mystical (Sufi) allegiance of their elite corps, early Safavid rulers seem to have paid much less attention to *ḏhimmī* minorities, such as the (Armenian) Christians, Jews, and Zoroastrians. But once the "Shiʿitization" of the kingdom was virtually complete, several shahs, beginning with ʿAbbās I, turned their attention to these groups. The Jews of Iran found themselves more isolated than in previous centuries—even from the rest of the Jews living in Muslim lands, not to mention from Jews living beyond those borders. Outbursts of anti-Jewish persecution occurred already during the reign of Shah ʿAbbās I, known as "the Great," because of his numerous accomplishments in practically every facet of Iranian life.[41] They culminated in the reign of Shah ʿAbbās II (1642–1666), when large segments of Iranian Jews, forced to convert to Islam between 1656 and 1661, continued to practice their Jewish faith secretly. Bābāī b. Luṭf, the first Iranian Jewish chronicler to come to our attention, described the events that affected Iranian Jewry in the first half of the seventeenth century in *Kitāb-i Anusī* (The book of a forced convert). His descriptions contribute a new chapter to the history of *anusut* (Hebrew for "forced conversion") especially familiar to us from the experiences of the Jews of the Iberian Peninsula in the fourteenth and fifteenth centuries.[42]

Though relatively short-lived, these persecutions and the failure of the

Sabbatean movement, which had affected many Jewish communities in Iran, had a general detrimental effect on the lives of Iranian Jews.[43] Thus, when the Safavid dynasty began to unravel soon thereafter, and the kingdom fell temporarily to the Afghans (1726–1736), "spontaneous" conversions to Islam occurred that were prompted by an overwhelming sense of fear and insecurity. Bābāī b. Farhād, Bābāī b. Luṭf's grandson, recorded these events in his chronicle *Kitāb-i Sar guzasht-i Kāshān dar bāb-i ʿibrī va goyīmī-yi sānī* (The book of events in Kashan concerning the Jews: Their second conversion), written sometime between 1730 and 1736.[44] The reasons for the persecutions vary, as can be seen from the texts translated below. However, it should be mentioned that even at their worst they seldom reached the level of persecutions that Jews experienced under Christendom.[45]

With the growing power of Shiʿi clerics during the Zand (1750–1796) and especially the Qājār (1779–1924) dynasties, the position of minorities deteriorated still further.[46] Already during the late Safavid period prominent theologians like Muḥammad Bāqir b. Muḥammad Taqī al-Majlīsī (d. 1699) were closely involved with wielding political power and felt free to promulgate, and probably to implement—at least in localities close to Isfahan, the capital—a host of anti-Jewish laws, many of which were merely restatements of the Pact of ʿUmar. However, some of these laws, especially those based on the Twelver Shiʿi concept of *najasa* (Arabic for "ritual impurity"), went further by declaring contact with all non-Shiʿis polluting.[47] It was undoubtedly this worsening social and political climate that led, at the end of the eighteenth century, to the continuous harassment of Jews in Azerbaijan and a devastating riot against them in Tabriz.[48]

The flow of information about Iranian Jewry increases as we get closer to the nineteenth century and contacts with Europe as well as visits by messengers from the Land of Israel intensify. Thus we know more about the last major outbreak of persecutions against the Jews of Iran, which occurred in Mashhad in 1839. Nādir Shah (r. 1736–1747), who favored rapprochement with Sunni Islam, had forcibly settled a number of Jewish families from Qazvin in Mashhad, an intensely Shiʿi city containing the tomb of the eighth Shiʿi imam. He may well have done so in order to dilute the Shiʿi character of Mashhad and thereby to plant a source of tension in the midst of the Shiʿi populace.[49] On the pretext that the Jews had insulted Husayn, the third imam of the Shiʿi tradition, the Muslim inhabitants of Mashhad attacked the Jews and killed about thirty individuals. In order to save itself, the Jewish community of Mashhad converted en masse. This tragedy, which came to be referred to among the Jews of Mashhad as *Allahdād* (God's justice or God's gift),[50] left a lasting mark on the community. For almost a hundred years the Jews of Mashhad who could not flee (and many did flee to Afghanistan) lived as *anusim* (Hebrew, "forced converts"), publicly Muslims and privately Jews.[51] By the end of the nineteenth century the Jews of Tehran were also harassed and forced to wear demeaning marks of identification.[52]

It is in the nineteenth century, owing to persecutions at home and a growing Zionist awakening, that many Jews from the Persianate world, especially from Bukhārā, emigrated to Jerusalem and began to establish a thriving community that clung to its JP heritage. The Jews of Bukhārā, whose history and cultural accomplishments are so closely linked with those of their fellows in Iran, deserve special mention. Their closeness diminished but was not entirely severed when Iran became a Shiʿi kingdom while Bukhārā remained under Sunni rule. A positive result of this separation may have been that Bukhārā's Jews were spared the waves of persecutions mentioned above. Yet the Jews of Bukhārā suffered their share of sporadic persecution. One such instance is described in *Khodāidād,* an eighteenth-century poem based apparently on a historical occurrence.[53] As forced conversions increased in number in the nineteenth century so did the number of anusim.[54]

Modernization, along with a strong attempt—enforced from above—to secularize, came to Iran with the advent of the Pahlavi dynasty (1925). This change brought to Iranian Jews and other minorities a fuller integration into the fabric of Iranian life. The development, together with the European influence that penetrated via the schools of the Alliance Israélite Universelle (which began to be established in Iran at the beginning of the twentieth century),[55] put a virtual stop to the creation, dissemination, and study of JP texts by Iranian Jews in Iran, although they continued for a while longer among the Bukhārāns living in Israel.

Judeo-Persian texts are written in the Persian language but the Hebrew alphabet.[56] Interest in these texts first emerged in the West among linguists who noticed that the earliest written traces of New Persian (that is, the written language in use since about the ninth century) actually appeared in the Hebrew script.[57] They also noticed that these inscriptions and texts preserved certain archaic linguistic features that were closer to Middle Persian (Pahlavī) than to later New Persian (Fārsī) in texts written in the Arabic script.[58]

Judeo-Persian has some interesting peculiarities that are difficult to understand without the appropriate linguistic background; I shall therefore limit myself to a few generalizations.[59] The idiom of JP texts tends to be colloquial, reflecting spoken Persian through such features as looser grammatical structure, the dropping of endings (especially in verb forms), the transformation of certain vowel sounds, such as "a" and "u," and the dropping of consonants, which last two practices tend to throw off the scansion in numerous poems. In addition, many texts, especially those written after the seventeenth century and those with a religious content, contain a substantial number of both Hebrew words and hybrid Persian-Hebrew (and vice-versa) words that are linked through the construct case. However, on the whole, JP texts testify to the fact that there never existed a single, unified, Persian dialect that belonged exclusively to Iranian Jews. In fact, a considerable number of Iranian-Jewish dialects existed because of the vastness of the Persianate world, but with the exception of the JP texts from Bukhārā, these did not leave appreciable traces on the corpus of literary JP writings that emerged between the fourteenth and eighteenth centuries.[60] Since JP texts tend to reflect the spoken language, their writers were not bound by "the orthographic and stylistic canons" of classical Persian literature. Through the use of the Hebrew alphabet, these texts also reflect "a totally independent orthographic tradition."[61] A curious, perhaps unique, hybrid language that was not unlike Yiddish did exist in all Iranian-Jewish communities; it was called *Loterā'ī*. This word appears to be descriptive, indicating that the language was *lo-Torah[i]* (Heb. + Pers. suffix *i* of abstraction), that is, "non-Torahic," because although it contained many Semitic (Hebrew and Aramaic) grammatical elements—such as the majority of verbs, nouns, and some prepositions—its morphological features (verbal endings, prefixes, suffix pronouns, and most particles) as well as its syntax were Iranian. Loterā'ī attests to the "antiquity of the Jewish settlements of Persia"; its use was intended to ensure private communication that would have been unintelligible to Muslims.[62]

Once the Arabic alphabet became widely accepted in Iran, we must ask the question, *Why* did Iranian Jews retain the Hebrew alphabet? The texts translated in this anthology suggest that the best Iranian-Jewish writers were familiar with the great Persian classics,[63] and in all likelihood with the Arabic-Persian script as well, at least to some degree. Although it may be valid to a certain extent to assume that Iranian Jews deliberately put a "self-imposed graphic barrier"[64] between themselves and their Muslim neighbors in order to ward off the Muslims' religious influence, it appears more likely that Iranian Jews simply retained their ancestral alphabet. For, like the Jews of medieval Europe, Iranian Jews were more literate than their non-Jewish neighbors because of their attachment to and ritual need of reading the Torah. This gap may have been even wider in Iran, where before the advent of Islam, the majority of the non-Jewish population was illiterate. As in most of the ancient world, literacy in pre-Islamic Iran was confined chiefly to the upper classes, to priests, scribes, some nobles, and merchants.[65] Pahlavi, the system of writing in use just before Arabic was adopted, was difficult to learn and cumbersome to use as it employed Aramaic heterograms and masks for the spoken Persian language. Knowledge and use of it was the monopoly of priests and scribes, who had an interest in limiting literacy as much as possible. This monopoly accounts for the relative speed with which the Arabic script, easier both to learn and to write, was adopted in the Persianate world.

Iranian Jews, whose literacy probably predates their sojourn in Iran, may simply have opted to retain their ancestral script, which they found adequate for the Persian (as well as the Arabic) language, rather than to switch to the Arabic alphabet. As noted above, under the Arabs, Persian (essentially the dialect of the central Iranian region of Fars) spread as far as Central Asia and the river Indus, becoming the lingua franca of a vast realm. Other minorities, notably the Christians of Chinese Turkestan, also experimented with writing Persian in a different script, in their case, Syriac.[66] Thus, as with other Jewish languages, in the case of JP it may be more appropriate to speak, at least initially, of a *retention* of the Hebrew script rather than a deliberate rejection of the Arabic alphabet. It cannot be denied, however, that this choice ended by becoming an effective but far from impermeable, orthographic barrier, as our texts show, resulting in the isolation of JP literature from the larger corpus of Persianate literature to which it rightly belongs.

Judeo-Persian literature is the product of the confluence of two mighty literary and religious streams, the Jewish biblical and postbiblical heritage and the Persian (Muslim) literary legacy.[67] The uniqueness of JP literature derives from the fact that it is a lovely amalgam in which the two streams, though recognizable, are strongly intertwined and interdependent.

The origins of JP literature may be attributed to the desire of Iranian Jews, as of the Jews in many other parts of the diaspora, to explicate, expound upon, and disseminate knowledge of the Torah. As was the purpose behind the creation of all Jewish languages, by translating biblical texts into the spoken Persian vernacular, Iranian-Jewish scholars, most of whose identities remain unknown, fostered both the study of Hebrew and at least some degree of literacy in the vernacular. Although very few grammatical texts[68] or dictionaries,[69] have survived, we must presuppose their existence at least to a certain extent.

Among the earliest JP texts that have come to light are fragments of commentaries on the Books of Ezekiel and Daniel.[70] An incomplete manuscript of the Pentateuch, copied in 1319 and probably composed earlier, shows the translator-commentator's thorough familiarity not only with the Hebrew text but with the Targums, Mishnah, and Talmud, as well.[71] Partial or complete JP renditions, some with commentaries, of a host of other biblical books have also survived to our day.[72] The Torah-centeredness of Iranian Jews, perhaps both cause and effect of Karaite leanings, is attested to by the small number of surviving halakic (legal) texts found among JP manuscripts, all of which tend to deal with practical matters, such as the laws regarding ritual slaughter and burial.[73]

The "bible" of Persian literature is the *Shah-nāmah,* "The Book of Kings," a massive epic completed around 1000 CE. Its author, Firdowsī (d. 1010), drew upon a substantial corpus of earlier layers of mythical, historical, and pseudo-historical materials; the *Shah-nāmah* is a "mytho-poeticization of the Iranian past and identity."[74] All later Persian poets are indebted to Firdowsī, whose work they mined for their themes, whose epic style they both imitated and consciously deviated from in the form of the romantic epic. They, as well as writers of shorter lyrics and mystical poems, alluded to the *Shah-nāmah* repeatedly, confident that its popularity would ensure that audiences would comprehend their allusions.

If we set aside the JP translations of biblical books mentioned above, and the earliest texts, which we may call literate but not really literature (see chap. 1), we come upon the figure of Shāhīn, the "father" of JP literature (see chap. 2). Like Firdowsī before him, Shāhīn probably had precursors, but their work has not survived. So we are presented with the apparent paradox that the first full-fledged poet of the JP literary tradition is also the best representative of that tradition. All later JP poets, like Firdowsī's successors, were deeply influenced by Shāhīn, and many generations of Iranian Jews lovingly preserved his memory and literary legacy.

Shāhīn shares with Firdowsī the transcendent goal of commemorating and glorifying his nation's origins, history, and ideals. For him as a Jew, the Torah, and especially the Pentateuch, was the source of his material, and he set himself the task of recasting large parts of it into a Persian epic mold. Shāhīn thereby made many of the Pentateuch's extraordinary narratives more accessible—and even more memorable—not only for his Iranian coreligionists but quite possibly for his Muslim neighbors as well.[75] Perhaps his wish was to demonstrate to everyone that the Jewish national heritage was no less glorious than that of ancient Iran.

Shāhīn did not versify the Pentateuch in its entirety and quite naturally (from a literary point of view) omitted its sizeable legal portions. Like the *Shah-nāmah,* whose most interesting narratives revolve around the exploits of heroes, especially Rustam, the central figure of Shāhīn's biblical epic cycle is Moses.[76] Similarly, because cycles of events in the *Shah-nāmah* are demarcated by various reigns, in Shāhīn's rendition of the Book of Esther (*Ardashīr-nāmah*), the action revolves around the royal house of Ardashīr (Ahasueros). The story of the Book of Esther is but one cycle within the broader saga of this reign. The "Esther cycle" actually culminates in Shāhīn's *Ezra-nāmah,* the short epic based on the Books of Ezra and Nehemiah recounting the rebuilding of the Temple and the deaths of Mordekai, Esther, and Cyrus.

Shāhīn's narratives fall within the tradition of the "rewritten Bible,"[77] but they are more than that: they demonstrate a deliberate effort to cast the biblical narratives into the Persian epic mold;[78] whether, or to what extent, he was successful is subject to interpretation.

The influence of Firdowsī's tragic epic, the *Shah-nāmah,* pervades Shāhīn's poetry. Undoubtedly he was also influenced by Niẓāmī's (d. 1209) romances and, to some extent, by the mystical epics of such Sufi poets as 'Aṭṭār (d. 1220) and Rūmī (d. 1273); the nature and extent of these influences remain to be investigated. Shāhīn used a certain amount of Muslim mystical (Sufi) language and imagery (not as much as his later imitators), and *Ardashīr-nāmah* in particular has many features characteristic of

Niẓāmī's romantic epics.[79] We have yet to find any evidence that the greatest Judeo-Persian poet knew or was aware of the lyrical poetry composed by Ḥāfiẓ (d. 1389), the greatest lyrical poet of Iran, who was Shāhīn's approximate contemporary and fellow Shirazian. However, unlike that of Hāfiẓ, Shāhīn's language, as befits a conscious imitator of Firdowsī, resembles the "pure," sparsely adorned "Khurasani" poetic language, which flourished between the tenth and twelfth centuries, rather than the more ornate poetic language, known as the "'Iraqi" style, of his time.[80]

At least four specific features contribute to the Iranian sensibility of Shāhīn's epics: descriptive passages of the natural and manmade environment; amplification of details beyond the biblical narrative; endowing biblical protagonists with characteristics typical of heroes and heroines in Persian epics; and inserting direct (or indirect) didactic comments on the fates of the heroes through their dialogues and speeches.[81] Shāhīn's syncretic style derives from a reliance on exegetical and legendary sources, both Jewish midrashim and Muslim *qiṣaṣ al-anbiyā'* (Arabic for "stories of prophets"), which amplify his narratives so that they appeal to both audiences. His knowledge of qur'ānic stories and their Sufi dimensions, such as the narrative of Adam's "fall,"[82] demonstrates the subtlety with which Shāhīn perused materials from both traditions. Unlike later Iranian Jewish poets, Shāhīn used few, if any, Hebrew words in his narratives, perhaps as part of his Firdowsian approach; Firdowsī had consciously shunned the use of Arabic words, which were increasingly popular in his environment.

If I have devoted a disproportionate amount of space both to introduce Shāhīn and to represent his poetry in this anthology, it is because he looms disproportionately on the horizon of JP literature. Later poets were not able to attain his rank, although many tried. His most successful imitator was probably 'Imrānī (1454–1536), a versatile and interesting poet in his own right. In obvious imitation of Shāhīn, 'Imrānī embarked on setting into Persian verse some of the biblical books that follow the Pentateuch, namely, Joshua, Judges, 1 Samuel, 2 Samuel (incomplete in surviving manuscripts), and the Book of Ruth, the aggregate of which he called *Fatḥ-nāmah* (The book of conquest; see chap. 2, below). 'Imrānī adhered closely to the biblical narratives and appealed much less frequently to Jewish, not to mention Muslim, legendary sources. His narrative style is more heavy-handed than Shāhīn's because it is more formulaic and, at times, more artificially fanciful. The Sufi element is more pronounced in 'Imrānī's oeuvre as a whole. In addition to his biblical epics, ʿImrānī composed versified renditions of midrashic and apocryphal tales, such as *Ḥanukkah-nāmah* (The book of Hanukkah; chap. 3), and set to verse both the mishnaic tractate Abot (*Ganj-nāmah* (The book of treasure; chap. 5), and Maimonides' "Thirteen Principles of Faith." A number of shorter, lyrical poems have also survived from his pen.[83]

Others have tried their hand at versifying post-pentateuchal biblical books. From among these, I include here an excerpt from Aḥaron b. Mashiaḥ's *Shoftim-nāmah* (The book of judges; chap. 2) composed in 1692, and Khwājah Bukhārāʾī's *Dāniyāl-nāmah* (The book of Daniel; chap. 2), whose work is also considered below in the context of the literary achievements of Bukhārān Jewry.

Like classical Persian epics in both the heroic and romantic forms, JP epics contain a strong didactic element that is often colored by Sufi expressions and sentiments, even though, as in the case of ʿImrānī's *Ganj-nāmah,* their chief source of inspiration is undeniably Jewish. One of the few JP works that can be strictly designated as a didactic work appears to be Yehudah b. David's *Makhzan al-pand* (The treasury of advice; chap. 4) written in the late sixteenth or early seventeenth century. It is modeled on an ancient Persian literary genre, although the Book of Proverbs may have influenced it equally.

Iranian Jewish poets were attracted to midrashic topics but, judging from the surviving manuscripts, not quite as much as to the biblical books themselves. Two examples of midrashic exposition are included in this anthology. The first is based on the Hebrew version, *ʿAliyat Moshe le-marom* (The ascension of Moses; chap. 5), which appears to have been popular among Iranian Jews, perhaps because it undermined Muslim claims of Muḥammad's ascension as the pinnacle of spiritual experience. The second, Amīnā's rendition of midrashic interpretations of Isaac's sacrifice, which is a central theme of the Day of Atonement, is included here in chapter 7, devoted to the religious expression of Jewish Iranian poets.

Although Iranian Jews appear to have referred to Shāhīn's biblical epics as *tafsīr* (Arabic for "commentary," "elucidation"), they are not biblical commentaries in the true sense of the word, which connotes the elucidation of difficult words and concepts, the making of connections between related ideas, and the like. It would appear that Iranian Jews did not write many biblical commentaries or, more likely, that very few have survived. Of course, the various works bearing the word *tafsīr* in the title (a word that for

Iranian Jews, as for Jews living in Muslim countries in general, meant *both* translation and commentary) often contain features ascribed to the commentary form. Still, the number of JP texts that can be recognized primarily as commentaries rather than paraphrase translations are relatively few. I include two samples, one from the pen of Yehudah b. Binyamin, who does not seem to have been particularly learned, and another from Shim'on Hakam (see chap. 6), the eminent Jewish scholar who hailed from Bukhārā.

Iranian Jews were deeply involved with the annual cycle of Jewish festivals and wrote many prose *derashot* (Hebrew for "sermons") as well as poems elucidating and praising the derashot's meaning; most of these appear to have been written after the seventeenth century (see chap. 7). Despite their intensely Jewish content, they were written in JP, not in Hebrew, and were clearly aimed at lay audiences whose knowledge of Hebrew was limited. A large number of sermons await careful evaluation.[84] They should provide valuable insights into Iranian Jewry's level of Jewish knowledge in premodern times.

Understandably, Purim, the Jewish festival that originated in Iran, has always held and continues to hold a special place in the hearts of Iranian Jews.[85] Two excerpts are included here, the first from Amīnā's versified retelling of the Book of Esther, the second a popular account of specific sentiments and customs that Iranian Jews associated with the festival (see chap. 7).

Iranian Jews bore witness to the historical developments in their midst, although, judging by surviving records, not as much as one would like. Their reticence accords with the trend observed among Jews in the diaspora in general. They tended to view history as a series of repeated divine patterns that went back to ancient (biblical) paradigms. These patterns were little affected by human acts and volition, and hence not particularly worth recording.[86] Nevertheless, two major waves of anti-Jewish persecutions in Iran, those of the seventeenth and eighteenth centuries, found eloquent commemorators in the chronicles of Bābāī b. Luṭf and his grandson Bābāī b. Farhād (see chap. 8). Whatever their shortcomings, the chronicles of Bābāī b. Luṭf and Bābāī b. Farhād provide valuable insights into the lives of ordinary Iranian Jews, a subject hardly ever touched upon by Muslim Iranian sources.

The hardships of anusut are also movingly described by Ḥezekiah, an otherwise unknown Iranian Jewish poet, while an outburst of persecution in Bukhārā was recorded in the short narrative poem *Khodāidād* (see chap. 8).

Perhaps even more scarce than historical texts are JP writings whose subject is philosophy and mysticism. The two philosophical texts included here, separated by some five centuries, share a polemical interest in their staunch advocacy, in the face of the constant glorification of Muḥammad, of the superiority of Moses and the laws revealed to him. Both writers appear to have been impressively learned. Yehudah b. El'azar, the seventeenth-century author of *Ḥobot Yehudah* (The duties of Judah), the most important philosophical text to emerge from Iranian Jewry, was well-acquainted with the works of earlier Jewish and Muslim philosophers and owes much to the thought of Maimonides (see chap. 9). The extent of *Ḥobot Yehudah*'s originality needs careful evaluation.

Iranian Jews became acquainted with Kabbalah at least by the end of the thirteenth century. We know of the contributions, in Hebrew, of one particular individual, Joseph of Hamadan, who wrote a treatise on *ṭa'me ha-misṿot,* the (mystical) reasons for the commandments and on the ten *sefirot* (emanations).[87] Kabbalistic allusions can be found in numerous Hebrew poems written in Iran, and many JP manuscripts contain popular formulas characteristic of practical kabbalistic practices. However, full-fledged theosophical kabbalistic texts are not well represented in JP manuscripts.[88] On the other hand, as I note throughout the anthology, the influence of Islamic mysticism (Sufism) appears to have been pervasive, raising questions about the nature and extent of Jewish involvement with this movement beyond the mere use of literary clichés.

Ḥayāt al-rūḥ (The life of the soul), by Siman Ṭov Melammed (d. 1823 or 1828), appears to be the most comprehensive mystico-philosophical work in JP. It is syncretic in the sense that it tends to express Jewish concepts garbed in Sufi terminology. But aside from its poetry, both in Hebrew and in Persian, *Ḥayāt al-rūḥ* is not particularly original. Like *Ḥobot Yehudah,* it relies heavily on the thought of Maimonides and of the Iberian Jewish neoplatonic mystic Baḥya b. Paquda (eleventh century). Melammed obviously believed that many Jewish and Muslim mystico-philosophical concepts were fundamentally identical, or at least overlapped considerably, and he therefore found nothing objectionable in using Sufi vocabulary and even writing a paean to Sufis. That his attitude was, nevertheless, not widely shared is demonstrated by an anonymous poem against Sufis (see chap. 10).

Fervent messianic hopes, which can be found in the mystico-philosophical texts mentioned above, also prevail in the religious poetry of Iranian Jewish poets (see chap. 11). Panegyrics honoring Moses, a subject often alluded to but seldom the theme of full encomiums in medieval Hebrew poetry, are fairly numerous in JP texts in a manner reminiscent of the numerous poems written throughout the Muslim world known as *nuʿūt* (Arabic for "attributes") that describe and praise Muḥammad's praiseworthy qualities.[89] Because Iranian Jewish poets appear to have written very few panegyrics dedicated to rulers or wealthy patrons, they honored their prophets instead, especially Moses but also Ezra and Ezekiel, whose not-too-distant tombs were destinations of pilgrimage.

Intense and moving *munājāt* (Pers./Arabic for "personal prayers"), such as those written by Binyamin b. Misha'el (known by the nom de plume "Amīnā," "the trusted," "the faithful") and Bābāī, probably owe as much to the Sufi predilection for the genre as to the Book of Psalms.[90] Themes connected with biblical history, such as are found in Amīnā's "A *Ghazal* on the Twelve Tribes," or devoted to philosophical concepts like God's attributes or those found in Shihāb Yazdī's "Almighty God Displaying Might" were also fitting subjects for shorter JP poems.

Classical Persian poetry, like the Arabic poetry it emulates, includes a large body of panegyrics to rulers and wealthy patrons. We find few such examples in JP manuscripts, eloquent evidence of the fact that Iranian-Jewish poets seldom, if ever, benefited from such patronage, even if they aspired to it.

The lyrical poetry of classical Persian literature is one of the great literary treasures of world literature. Iranian-Jewish poets were familiar with the genre in its various forms, the *ghazal* (a monorhymed poem 7–12 distichs long), the *rubāʿī* (quatrain), and the *qiṭʿa* (a fragment [of a *ghazal*]). Many Iranian-Jewish poets have tried their hand at these genres with varying degrees of success (see chap. 12). Because these forms are light, graceful, full of puns and alliteration, their efforts are even more difficult to convey in translation than the *masnavī* (discussed below). The themes of Persian lyrical poetry include unrequited love, the cruelty of the beloved, the beauty of the beloved, the (mystical) intoxication of wine, the deceptiveness of this transient world, and so on.[91] Lyrical Persian poetry developed a vocabulary all its own, even as it adopted and amplified the body of the rhetorical figures of speech of Arabic poetry. Many Persian poetic conceits became standardized. The prowess of a lyrical Persian poet was measured not so much by the originality of his themes as by his creative manipulation of standard ideas and images. Beginning with the twelfth century, this stylized form of Persian poetry became permeated with Sufi symbolism and thus acquired an additional layer of semantic richness.[92]

The JP lyrical poems included in this anthology are largely from the pen of Amīnā. He seems to have been a versatile poet, preferring the shorter lyrical forms of Persian poetry. Some of his *ghazals* are clearly based on standard themes. Other, somewhat longer poems like "The Story of Amīnā and His Wife," and "On Becoming Cold-Hearted Toward Women" have an autobiographical flavor that makes them somewhat original in content.

The body of both religious and secular JP poems is large enough and of sufficient literary merit to warrant further study. Albeit in the vernacular, in its use of Persian topoi and rhetoric, JP poetry compares favorably with the Hebrew poetry produced during the Spanish Golden Age, which also relied on Arabic poetical rhetoric.

The Jewish authors of Bukhārā probably deserve their own separate anthology.[93] They were active between the twelfth and the eighteenth centuries and often wrote JP manuscripts that included vowels indicating their dialectical peculiarities. In all other respects, these writers were influenced by Persian classical poetry. In this anthology I include a sample of their epic writing in the form of Khwājah Bukhārā'ī's *Dāniyāl-nāmah* (The book of Daniel; chap. 2) composed in 1606. Khwājah Bukhārā'ī undoubtedly knew the works of Shāhīn, and probably those of ʿImrānī as well. His narrative is richly adorned with midrashic elements.

Shimʿon Ḥakam was the greatest Jewish man of letters to hail from Bukhārā. He emigrated to Jerusalem in 1890 and established a JP publishing house through which he saved many texts for posterity by editing and disseminating them.[94] I include an excerpt from his pentateuchal commentary, which reveals his thorough acquaintance with traditional rabbinic sources (see chap. 6).

Khodāidād, bearing the name of its protagonist (see chap. 8), is a historical poem based on an incident of anti-Jewish persecution in the eighteenth century. It was probably written by Ibn Abū'l Khayr and provides a somber glimpse of Jewish life in Bukhārā. Yet this was far from a relentlessly oppressive environment, and Bukhārān Jews were close to their Muslim neighbors, shared their cultural tastes, and were recognized as excelling in certain arts, like music.[95]

Another poet from the eighteenth century, Yūsuf Yahūdī, the author of several JP works and of a lovely quintet in honor of Moses (see chap. 11), testifies to the religious fervor that flourished among Bukhārā's Jews, a feeling that led them to be among the first emigrants from the Persianate world to return to the Land Israel.

The Jews of Iran preserved their Jewish heritage in JP texts, in their own local customs and modes of prayer,[96] in artistic expression,[97] and in numerous Hebrew works, whose study falls beyond the ken of this anthology. There are other aspects of Iranian-Jewish literary culture that are not represented in this anthology because its exclusive concern is to give an overview of original JP belles lettres. If poetry is disproportionately represented here it is because poetry was, beyond any doubt, the favorite and most highly regarded mode of expression of Iranian Jews, as of Iranian Muslims. Judeo-Persian manuscript collections also include a considerable number of medical texts, based on the Islamic medical knowledge of the Middle Ages, as well as folktales, spells, and folk remedies, with which I am not sufficiently acquainted to discuss. Similarly, the large body of JP transcriptions of Persian and Hebrew classical poems needs a different mode of study than the one adopted in this anthology. Of course, without these additional dimensions, it is not yet possible to make a comprehensive assessment of premodern Iranian-Jewish cultural life as a whole. What I can state with confidence about the JP texts included here is that they constitute yet another chapter of Jewish diaspora literature similar in many ways to, yet distinct from, the literatures produced in the Hellenistic world, medieval Spain, and Renaissance Italy. Like these illustrious exemplars, JP literature attests to the phenomenon of deep Jewish acculturation without assimilation, a hallmark of most premodern Jewish diaspora communities. Thus JP literature enriches our knowledge of Jewish literatures in general while contributing to the vast and varied literature of the Persianate world.

In the translations that follow I strove to achieve a measure of literacy but not at the expense of the literal meaning of the texts. The *masnavī*, a narrative poem in rhymed couplets that was the preferred long poetic form of classical Persian literature for all types of contents—stories, didactic verse, heroic and romantic epics, even history and medicine—was also the vehicle of the JP epics translated here. For various technical reasons, rhymed couplets are difficult to reproduce in English. For most of the translations below I chose free verse as the most likely form to engage English-speaking readers. All translators, and especially those who translate from Persian into English, will undoubtedly sympathize with the various hurdles encountered in this process, while other readers, it is hoped, will be indulgent when wading into a tradition with which they are unfamiliar but many of whose literary conventions will become apparent to them through these texts. The task of translating was made all the more difficult by the tentative nature of the conflated editions on which they are based. Because I hope that this anthology will appeal to both Jewish and Iranian scholars and to general readers, I provide notes which may occasionally appear redundant to one or the other of these groups.

It is my hope that this offering of texts will stimulate further research in the field of JP studies and that future scholars will endeavor to correct my mistakes.

Earliest Judeo-Persian Texts

1

In his comprehensive *History of Iranian Literature,* Jan Rypka states, "It is a curious coincidence that the earliest records in the [New] Persian language are at the same time the earliest records of Judeo-Persian literature" (p. 737). In an earlier passage he notes that although these records cannot be classified as belles lettres, they are important "in virtue of their being the oldest first-hand documents committed to writing in the Persian language" (pp. 148–149). As such, they preserve many archaic features, both linguistic and lexicographic. Among the most important of these early Persian ("prose") records are:[1] a. the inscriptions found at Tang-i Azao (Afghanistan), initially thought to come from the mid-eighth century but more likely of considerably later provenance;[2] b. the letter of a Jewish merchant found in Dandān-Uiliq, northeast of Khotan (East Turkestan), dating from the second half of the eighth century;[3] c. the signature of witnesses on the Quilon copper plate in a church in Malabar, South India, ninth century;[4] d. a legal document from Hormshīr (Ahwāz) in Khūzistān,[5] and e. an undated commentary on Ezekiel.[6] Only the translations of texts b ("A Letter from a Merchant") and d ("A Legal Document") are presented here because they provide a coherent departure point for what will later develop into JP—and Persian—prose.

The JP fragment from Dandān-Uiliq (b) concerns, as its translator Bo Utas notes, "the trading of sheep and possibly also cloth[ing] and slaves."[7] Aurel Stein discovered the document on one of his expeditions, among the ruins of Dandān Uiliq ("the Ivory house"), a small community in which a minor imperial Chinese garrison was stationed. Dandān Uiliq, known to the Chinese of the T'ang period as Li-hsieh, was not on the Silk Road itself but somewhat to the north of it. Taking into account some of the observations made by later scholars,[8] Professor Utas kindly provided for this anthology both a word-for-word translation, to which I made slight changes, of the intelligible parts of the letter and a reconstruction of the entire letter. For the sake of coherence I include only the latter.

Professor Asmussen, who has worked on the letter from Ahwāz (d), also gave this anthology a full translation of the letter, refining the first English translation made by D. S. Margoliouth, whose notes remain valuable.[9] The document is the legal resolution of property taken unlawfully. The protagonists are vivid, but nothing more is known about them.

A Letter from a Merchant Translated by Bo Utas

[1] (*In the name of*) the Lord God, who shall be [our] helper.[1] Soon the day (*on which we have decided* [2] *will come;*) I wrote more [than] twenty letters, but y(*ou have not replied.* [3] *Please, obse*)rve with what my post (?) arrives and in [whose] hand (?) ([4] *it is found! And*) order [someone] to give [out] his three shares! My portion (*should be added to my account* [5] *and*) by this you should buy, until I have set out [and] gone down. (*If you arrange* [6] *all this in*) a good way, the Lord God (*will bestow*) on you good reward for it. (*As for* [7] *the cattle market,*) it was delayed until the ninth of the month, and until the tenth of (*the month I could not* [8] *find out what*) sheep there were. And they buy weaker, and the Lord God shoul(*d assist us! Regarding* [9] *the clothes*), he should ensure that not any of them is worn (?) because they (*were displeased in the last place* [10] *and*) the clothing that had been sold, that they thr(*ew*) in our face, (*so that in the end* [11] *very little*) was sold. There was (?) nobody; a hundred people of the town (*came together, however.* [12] *I am in doubt about those*) thirty jugs (?) which we should buy, and there is no nard (?) available. (*It seems that something of yours* [13] *belongs to me*) like something of mine to you. And I have a man, one (*who knows*) the work, (*who has done the accounts,* [14] *so that I shall*) know my profit and loss and nine *shabili (?) (*were counted*

to my credit. [15] *Try to find something li*)ke sheep to buy on my behalf, so that (*this will even up my account!* [16] *In your last letter*) you said thus: Rabbi, thirty (*pieces of those goods* [17] *were late*) to come and are heavily attended by loss. (*Will you, please,* [18] *give*) him (*the order to buy*) on my behalf seventeen bales (*of cloth and send them* [19] *together with the animals*) that you yourself bought and yourself sold and yourself dro(*ve to such and such place.* [20] *In this affair,*) if profit should be my share, I (*ask you* [21] *to take care of it,*) but do not take any trouble regarding a good count! (*About so and so,* [22]) you sent (*a message*), and he was not here, and the profit of the sheep [was] thus (*not*) correctly (*counted.* [23] *I hope that that agent*) of yours arrives, as God wishes, and [that] you personally (*will go*) to *Sababad,(?) (*and that* [24] *regarding that matter*) you will say thus to *Sababad(?): (*Bring*) me a harp (*and I have a girl!* [25] *If*) you bring the harp, I shall teach the girl, and [look] how fast (*she will learn!* [26] *What*) I (*wanted to*) find, I did not find, but from *Nurbak (*I got*) one h(*arp,* [27] *and that one*) I shall give [to him], so that he shall teach *Bagidi(?). The black eunuch (*will take care of the rest.* [28] *Be sure*) that I received your letter; but you said one thing better than that: (*if that is arranged,* [29] *then*) I shall work hard, so that the work which you ordered will be done. (*As for your fears* [30] *regarding*) my mind, do not suffer any anxiety that (*you will*) hurt my mind. (*As for the other matter,* [31] *know that*) I asked thus on behalf of *Angusht(?) *Robahah(?) [and] said (*that you must* [32] *certainly go*) to Parvan(?) and yourself make a request from that party regarding (*what they owe you.* [33] *Furthermore,*) in your letter you sent [the message] that to one hundred and fifty (*units there is consent* [34] *and that the buy*)er of that trifle of sheep (*accepts*) that (*price*) of y(*ours.* [35] *As long as*) you have not come out (*from the to*)wn, from the side of (*so and so anything may be expected,* [36] *so equip yourself*) suitably as regards saddle and stirrups and straps! (*Thus I wish you* [37] *the very best*) of everything [that comes] from the Highest!

Az-[38] -khar(?)

A Legal Document Translated by Jes P. Asmussen

"It was thus before us *witnesses,* whose signatures are written below this record: In Hormshīr [Ahwāz] town, which [is] among those of Khūzistān, which stands on the river Ulay, in the month of Shebaṭ, year 1332 *according to the [Seleucid] era of documents* [1021 CE], there were present before us

Ḥannah, daughter of Israel, son of Jacob, *may he rest in Paradise,* and she cited Daniel, son of Reuben, [son] of ʿAzariah, known as "Baby." And this Ḥannah bat Israel said thus: "This Daniel ben Reuben, my son-in-law, has gone without my order and without my desire and taken out of the purse of my brothers, who are in Egypt, six pairs of pearls and sold them for twenty-five dinars. And this purse was the property of my brothers Sahl and Joseph and Saʿīd, sons of Israel, son of Jacob, *may he rest in Paradise."* And the elders said to him: "You did wrong; you did this, that you laid hands on property other than your own, and you are in a state of lawlessness through this that you have done." And he answered: "I did it of necessity, [obliged] by my heart, for I was in great difficulty." And the elders said to him: "It is incumbent upon you, Daniel ben Reuben, to make recompense for it and to ask *forgiveness* from the owners of the property." And this Daniel ben Reuben said: "The thing which [belongs] to me is available to these [men], Sahl and Joseph, and Saʿīd, sons of Israel, son of Jacob, *may he rest in Paradise,* and I am content before you elders that you write it and rectify [the matter] against me, in that it became right, since I was agreeable. It is [so] that, in recompense for these pearls which I took, under their hands [as] recompense [there are] these dinars. I sold them and took twenty five genuine sultani dinars." And he was agreeable, and we took *the property acquired* from the hands of this Daniel, son of Reuben, [son] of ʿAzariah, known as "Baby," in [the form of] clothing. It is proper to take *property [so] acquired*—by *the laws of Sinai and the words at Horeb—with his approval and at his request.* And this Daniel, son of Reuben, [son] of ʿAzariah, abandoned all claim [on it] *to the end of all actions of protest.* And he wrote [this] and gave it into the hand of Ḥannah, daughter of Israel, son of Jacob, *may he rest in Paradise,* that it may be for her a discharge and a proof.

ʿAzariah ben Abraham ben ʾAmmar
Saʿdan ben Daniel ben Saʿdan.

Biblical Epics

2

Mowlānā Shāhīn-i Shīrāzī

The Jewish-Persian poet known as "Mowlānā Shāhīn-i Shīrāzī" (Our Master, the Royal Falcon of Shiraz) is both the earliest known and the most accomplished JP poet. His biography remains shrouded in obscurity. Beyond the fact that he flourished during the reign of the Il-khanid Sultan Abū Saʿīd (1316–1335), information revealed by the poet himself,[1] we know very little about Shāhīn. He appears to have been a near contemporary of Ḥāfiẓ (d. 1389), the greatest lyrical poet of Iran, who also lived in Shiraz.

Uncertainty about Shāhīn extends not only to his birth and death dates and his occupation but even to such fundamental information as his name and place of origin. It is not at all clear whether "Shāhīn" is the poet's first name or his *takhalluṣ* (nom de plume).[2] Bābāī b. Luṭf claims that Shāhīn is buried in Shiraz,[3] but some scholars believe that he may have hailed from Kashan.[4]

Shāhīn's surviving oeuvre consists of two major epic cycles: 1) a versification of selected narrative parts of the Pentateuch, *Bereshit-nāmah* (The book of Genesis; henceforth BN), *The Tale of Job*, and *Mūsā-nāmah* (The book of Moses; henceforth MN); and 2) the Book of Esther, *Ardashīr-nāmah*

(The book of Ardashīr; henceforth AN), and *Ezra-nāmah* (The book of Ezra; henceforth EN).[5] Of the two, the pentateuchal epics are the longest and constitute Shāhīn's magnum opus. Their first and only editor, the Bukhārān scholar Shimʿon Ḥakam,[6] named this biblical cycle *Sefer sharḥ-i Shāhīn ʿal ha-Torah* (The book of Shāhīn's commentaries on the Torah) when he printed them in Jerusalem between 1902 and 1905.[7] We do not know what Shāhīn himself called this work. Ḥakam's title is probably a reflection of the popularity of BN and MN among Iranian Jews.

The versification of MN preceded that of BN. It was composed in 1327[8] and it consists chiefly of the major nonlegal narratives from Exodus, Leviticus, Numbers, and Deuteronomy. The poem is approximately 10,000 distichs long and its meter is *hazaj mussadas makhzūf,* one of the simplest meters of Persian prosody and commonly associated with romances.[9] If MN was probably Shāhīn's first major work, BN appears to have been his last. Composed in 1358[10] in the same meter as MN, BN is somewhat shorter, consisting of some 8,700 distichs. The two parts, MN and BN, are sometimes copied in separate manuscripts. Rather than follow the chronological order of Shāhīn's compositions, in this anthology translations from Shāhīn's biblical epics begin with two selections from BN following the natural order of the Pentateuch. The first selection is on ʿAza'zel's (Satan) "fall" from divine grace and the second centers on Jacob's grief at Joseph's disappearance. Both highlight popular themes that also reverberate deeply in Islamic literature. The tale of Jacob's grief is part of the Joseph (Yūsuf) and Zulaykhā narrative, a favorite theme of Iranian epics,[11] and it is often found copied separately from the rest of BN. In both selections Shāhīn's interweaving of Jewish and Muslim legendary strands is particularly felicitous.

The selections from MN highlight Shāhīn's desire to turn Moses into an epic hero, modeling him on the great heroes of Iranian epics, especially Firdowsī's heroes in the *Shāh-nāmah.* In the process, Shāhīn glorifies Moses almost more than Jewish sources do, and thus contributes to a prevalent theme in JP literature,[12] the veneration of Moses, that was probably affected by a similar trend to venerate and praise Muḥammad in Muslim life and literature.[13]

Shāhīn gives short shrift to the legal and ritualistic contents of the four biblical books covered in this epic and centers his narrative around the "exploits" of Moses. In the selections that follow, Moses is depicted as a tender shepherd (which qualifies him for his mission as leader of the Children of Israel), a reluctant leader, a profound mystic and lover of God, a fair and implacable chieftain confronting Korah, and, especially toward the end of his life, a teacher anxious to instill God's message into the Israelites for all time.

At the end of BN, after a chapter on the descendants of Esau, Shāhīn appends a short (170 verses) versification of the Book of Job, motivated by the fact that Jewish and Muslim legendary sources place this tale similarly, after the death of Jacob's descendants, because they believe Job to have been either Esau's grandson or his great-grandson.[14] Shāhīn abbreviates the content of the Book of Job drastically, omitting two of its most important features, Job's dialogues with his friends and God's lengthy reply. He chooses to develop instead the insidious assaults on Job's faith by his wife, a subject referred to only briefly in the book itself.

Between his pentateuchal epics, in 1333,[15] Shāhīn wrote another complex epic consisting of a versification of the Book of Esther (AN) and a very free treatment of the prophetic Books of Ezra and Nehemiah (EN). *Ardashīr-nāmah* is 9,000 distichs long, and it is composed in a more complex variant of the *hazaj* meter.[16] The content of AN is not confined to the Book of Esther. It is distinguished by at least three major creative features. First, in addition to the biblical tale, Shāhīn also narrates the fantastic exploits of Shīrū, the son of Ardashīr (Ahasueros) and Queen Vashti[!]. Second, the narrative of AN is tied explicitly to Iran's national epic, the *Shāh-nāmah* of Firdowsī, by fictitiously identifying Shah Ardashīr with Ardashīr, son of Isfandiyār, one of the Iranian shahs mentioned in the *Shāh-nāmah*.[17] Finally, Shāhīn claims that Cyrus, the great Persian restorer of Jewish national sovereignty, was the offspring of Esther and Ardashīr's union.[18] He thus clearly reveals his chief literary model, the *Shah-nāmah;* he also intertwines the fates and histories of Iran and Israel, attesting to his love of both.

The translated selections from AN that follow describe scenes not found in the Book of Esther. They display Shāhīn's creative imagination at its best, such as in Ardashīr's difficult search for a lover to replace Queen Vashti, his courtship of Esther, Mordekai's role in the match, the royal wedding night, and the auspicious birth and childhood of Cyrus. Each of these themes is paralleled in both the *Shāh-nāmah* and in the classical Persian romances of Niẓāmī (d. 1209), whose influence is especially strong in AN.

Usually appended to AN and best considered a part of it—a sort of epilogue—is *Ezra-nāmah* (EN), a short versification (about 500 distichs) superficially connected with the Books of Ezra and Nehemiah.[19] The translated selections highlight Ezra's efforts to bring about the rebuilding of the Temple. In the process, Shāhīn polemicizes against the Muslim attitude toward the role of Ezra in the preservation of the correct copy of the Torah.[20] The relation of this epic to AN is made clear by the narrative describing the deaths of Mordekai and Esther, once their divine "mission" has been completed. Following the earlier description of Cyrus' birth and youth, we here have the moving account of his death, typical of a description of the death of a hero in JP (and Persian) epics. The deaths of these three protagonists close the second cycle of Shāhīn's biblical epics and reveal the poet's view that these heroes strove to fulfill through their lives God's higher purposes.

Shāhīn's epics have not yet been studied to the extent that they deserve. The most comprehensive study remains Wilhelm Bacher's *Zwei jüdisch-persische Dichter Schahin und Imrani*, a work frequently cited in this anthology. In addition to establishing basic information about the contents of the epics, Bacher also drew attention to Shāhīn's rhetoric, the manuscripts known to him, and the sources of literary influence, both Jewish and Muslim, on the poet (pp. 71–117). All these areas can and need to be studied more thoroughly. Here I confine myself to some general observations.

Shāhīn's poetic diction, his use of the Persian language and grammar, and the rhetorical forms he employs are typically those of classical Persian poetry. Among his most pronounced grammatical peculiarities is the frequent use of the colloquial forms *-imān* and *-idān* for the first person plural. But Shāhīn's language does not reflect a dialect. Manuscripts of his epics, and even more those of his successors, reflect many more colloquial features connected with the popular, spoken language of Iran, whereas classical Persian literature consciously avoids doing so. Shāhīn's use of Hebrew words and Hebrew rhymes is much less frequent than his successors'. Like many other Jewish writers from the Muslim world, Shāhīn refers to well-known biblical characters by their Muslim names: Ibrāhīm (Abraham), Mūsā (Moses), Qārūn (Korah).[21] When he refers to less well-known people, he uses the Hebrew forms. Shāhīn must have been among the first JP writers to use the construct *-i* (*iżāfa*) form to link Hebrew and Persian words. The fact that many verses in Shāhīn's epics do not quite scan properly is more likely due to the corrupt state of the manuscripts than to the poet's inability to write in the correct meter; hence the urgent need to establish critical texts in order to determine correct meanings.

As far as poetical rhetoric is concerned, Shāhīn's epics reflect his thorough knowledge of classical Persian forms and conceits. Like his Persian models, he uses rhetorical artifices, such as *tanāsub* (Ar./Pers. for "harmony of concepts"), *tażādd* (contrast), *ḥusn-i taʿlīl* (the beautiful explanation of a cause), *ishtiqāq* (paranomasia), and many others, to achieve the aesthetic peculiar to Persian poetry.[22]

Shāhīn's epics show that he was an erudite poet, acquainted with many Jewish and Muslim religious sources. Among the former, Bacher notes the Babylonian Talmud, the Targums, and many midrashic works, such as Bereshit Rabbah, Shemot Rabbah, Va'yikra Rabbah, Midrash Tanḥumah, Pirke de-Rabbi Eliezer, and quite possibly Saadiah Gaon's Arabic translation of the Pentateuch.[23] Preeminent among his Muslim sources are the collections of popular tales known in the Muslim world as *qiṣaṣ al-anbiyā'* (Arabic for "stories about prophets"), especially the Persian collection of Ibn Khalaf al-Nīsābūrī compiled sometime before 1100. He also displays some knowledge of the legends related by al-Ṭabarī (d. 920) in his famous *Tā'rikh al-rusūl wa'l mulūk* (The history of prophets and kings). Shāhīn appears to have had some acquaintance with the Qur'ān, which may not have been direct and could have been obtained from *qiṣaṣ* collections and from al-Ṭabarī. Many of these stories circulated in oral form, and there is no need to assume that Shāhīn's information came from books; quite the contrary, since books were scarce in his time. Above all, Shāhīn was undoubtedly well-acquainted with the great classical Persian epics—again, perhaps orally—composed between the turn of the millennium and his time. It is from them that he may have absorbed not only the nuts and bolts of his poetic craft but also much of the legendary Muslim lore that is found in his epics.

We do not know whether Shāhīn himself considered his biblical epics, especially those based on the Pentateuch, to be *tafsīrs*. This Arabic word has multiple, often overlapping meanings—"explanation," "commentary," and frequently, especially in the Judeo-Muslim context, "translation."[24] It would appear that for Iranian Jews, Shāhīn was more than just an imitator of classical Persian poetry. They apparently considered him a biblical commentator. The number of the surviving manuscripts attests to the popularity of Shāhīn's epics, but it does not reveal the extent to which Iranian Jews considered him a reliable transmitter of Jewish tradition. As the translations that follow indicate, Shāhīn did not hesitate to interweave in his narratives many details that originate from Muslim legendary sources. Unfortunately, we cannot determine to what extent his Jewish audiences were aware of this fact nor how it may have affected their view of Shāhīn's status as biblical commentator.[25] To us Shāhīn's work appears to be mostly literary because it lacks the traditional features we associate with the word "commentary," such as verse-by-verse clarifications, philological explanations, elucidations of difficult passages, that are associated with a more scholarly approach, such as is found in Rashi (Rabbi Solomon b. Isaac; d. 1105), in the Ashkenazic world. Unlike Rashi, whose commentaries expound on almost every verse of the Pentateuch, Shāhīn was eclectic in his choice of biblical episodes. He had no qualms about skipping over substantial parts of the Pentateuch, for example the legal parts, which held little dramatic interest from a poetic point of view.[26] As far as Iranian Jewry's regard for Shāhīn's status as a poet is concerned, we are not in doubt, for his work has been lovingly preserved and, as this anthology attests, frequently (if not always successfully) imitated. Shāhīn's great skill rested in fusing classical Persian prosody and poetical rhetoric to Jewish themes, culled, primarily, from traditional Jewish sources "leavened" with just those Muslim tales that would have been familiar to both Jewish and Muslim audiences.

Although he wrote excellent classical Persian verse, Shāhīn is not mentioned by any literary historian of Iran, medieval or modern, because his poetry was apparently not known beyond the confines of the Jewish communities. If his poetry was originally set down in the Hebrew script, this may explain its inability to penetrate the Iranian literary environment.[27] I hope that the translations that follow will reveal fully the close kinship Shāhīn's works bear with classical Persian poetry.

Bereshit-nāmah (The Book of Genesis)

The Fall of ʿAza'zel

The Description of ʿAza'zel's Greatness

ʿAza'zel[1] ranked among the celestial elite
Most learned, a teacher of the angels;[2]
Everything they knew came from him;
He lit the very lamp of grace.
No angel was greater than he
Who seemed kneaded out of Mercy itself,

Always obedient, forever bent
On increasing his service.
The heavens were his place of worship;
Perpetual service was his only task.
Faithfully he served for countless years,
Hoarding a boundless capital of obedience.[3]
He was unaware of the Most Merciful's decree
Although he knew that among palace intimates
Damnation could strike one suddenly.[4]
He was exceedingly exalted
Among the intimates of the Royal Falcon.[5]
But as for bowing before Adam, he refused,
Denying him any authority.
Still, accompanied by other angels
He set out joyfully flying to earth
Like the wind, alighting before Adam's form[6]
Suddenly, full of pride but curious
To know who the accursed one might be,
What he was like who was subject to no commands.[7]
Arriving, he stood at a distance;
Through his neglect he became himself unjust.
Angels kept flying in in troops
Surrounding Adam row upon row. Then
At the Pure Almighty's command,
They bowed down, rubbing
Their faces in the dust;[8] cheerfully,
One by one, they bowed before Adam
At God's command. 'Aza'zel alone hung back
Unmoving in his place and did not bow.

His Excellency Addresses 'Aza'zel

His Excellency then called out, "'Aza'zel,
Why are you standing bewildered, indolent?
Come, bow down, for such is my command,
Or else misfortunes await you in ambush."
Hearing God's command, 'Aza'zel replied:
"O Creator of the elephant and of the gnat,

Who is like me, possessor of such a capital,
Carrying out orders for years, obedient?[9]
Why should I bow before a lump of clay?
O Pure Almighty, should this be lawful for me?
He is made of earth, I of pure light;
I should not have to bow down before earth!"
The Almighty replied: "O foolish ignoramus,
Such is My command; don't disobey it!
I did not ask you to explain its roots and origins;[10]
Whatever I command you must obey.
What is your business with either earth or fire?
The latter burns, the former is foundation.
Do not imagine that fire is superior to earth:
Without a doubt Adam's clay is pure light.
Though Adam's light is not everlasting,
In him the earth becomes transmuted.[11]
Fire has no relation to the earth;
It is poison; earth is the antidote.
O unlucky one, fire is not superior to earth;
Ignorance prevents you from perceiving this.
With might I created four jewels:
Nothing is better in the world than these:
First wind, then fire and water,
Fourth is the pure earth, that limpid jewel.[12]
These four are the world's fortune;
The magnificence of each is well known."

. . . .

281 Then Iblīs said again: "O Pure Almighty,
Flaming fire is not inferior to earth!
What is a lump of earth in the world
That it should be superior to fire's essence?
I do not wish to bow down to it;
Why should I humble myself on its account?
Better than Adam am I in every respect;
Why should I grovel before him?
I will bow before none other than You;

I do not even contemplate such thoughts![13]
O Exalted One, beyond imagination, I will not
Bow before Adam even on Resurrection Day!
I will not yield this sign of servitude,
For Adam is not worthy of prostration.
You alone are the object of praise and bowing,
Not I, not Michael, and not Gabriel."
The moment he digressed from God's command,
That unlucky one became an infidel;
Iblīs' glory departed because of His curses
For no one should dispute with God.
With all his former acts of obedience,
Hidden and open, great and small,
The Incomparable Almighty struck his face:
"Take your obedience, O vile accursed one!
Since your back is loaded with obedience,
You escape My wrath and get off lightly.
I curse you till the Day of Resurrection:
You will be a source of calamities, a mine of evil;
You will stray throughout eternity
Full of anger, toil, suffering, and pain.
I will call you Shayṭān the Damned;
I will turn all your prayers into insults."
Beholding all his work destroyed,
Shayṭān replied: "O Praise of Praises,
Chasing me away from Your presence,
This is the greatest calamity of all!
It comes to me by way of Adam. I am
Trapped forever in the bonds of grief."
He pleaded once more: "O You
Who are One, Generous, Pure, and Judge,
Oppression and injustice are not among
Your attributes; You are the source and quarry
Of justice and mercy.[14] I deserve no evil;
For a mortal's sake do you humiliate me thus?
O You who are superior to imagination,
Is this how you wish to repay my countless years

Of service, to pay off your debt to me?"[15]
Then the Almighty said: "Vile cheat,
What recompense do you desire for that work?
Tell me, and I shall grant it to you;
Injustice is not one of My attributes."
Shayṭān replied, "O Generous One,
Since this befell me on Adam's account,
Hand him and his descendants over to me
That I may debase them through sin.
With trouble I will tempt them day and night;
So that they will remain forever far from mercy;
Befriending sin through me they will become
The very warp and woof of vice.
I will carry them with me to Hell;
They shall be my army and my troops.
I will never let them rest in peace;
I will turn all their gains into losses,
Ambushing them from right to left;
They will be in perpetual want."

The Debate Between Almighty God and Shayṭān

Again, the Judge responded to Iblīs:
"O you repulsive, sinister, unlucky infidel,
I will grant your wish concerning them;
Distress no further your sinister mind.
But O unclean one, over saints and prophets
You shall not prevail; they will break you![16]
I watch over their every state,[17] for they are
The quarry of every treasure and good fortune.
Upon them I bestow abundant favors
Because they labor for My sake."
Iblīs replied: "Day and night I will
Demean devotion in their sight;[18]
They will grow weary of service and devotion,
Deliver themselves from Paradise to Hell.
No longer will they rejoice in Your bounties;
I will convince them that sin is good;[19]

Each one of them separately will I trick."
The Almighty rejoined: "O tyrant,
If you demean devotion in their sight,
I will not abandon them in that hardship;
I will deliver them from it with ease.
I will make them repent; I'll soothe
And blandish them till they return."
But Shayṭān persevered, saying: "O God,
Through their sins I will make them tongue-tied;
One by one, I will keep them from repenting;
I will keep such thoughts out of their hearts."
The Almighty replied: "O sinister one,
You do not know the extent of Our mercy,
That I am the pardoner of servants,
The guide of all the weak and helpless.
Do not imagine in your sinister heart
That you can hold Us back from mercy."
"I did not know," Shayṭān replied, "that You
Have such an immense amount of grace for them . . .
My tricks then cannot work;
Your favor renders me impotent.
I have no remedy for this;
You've trapped me in great pain.
Strange! I know they will be my enemies,
Adversaries of my soul, my foes,
Vindictive against me for Your sake
They will seek only to harm me.
Thus will they be: they will not turn away
From striking an alliance with me,
Yet they will emerge victorious.
I am surprised that You will show them mercy;
I would show them nothing but sorrow and trouble."
The Almighty then said: "Since those dear to Me
Love Me, that which is difficult becomes easy.[20]
I will overlook their sins one by one;
I will rain Mercy upon all their heads.

Through My Grace I will bring them to Paradise
And I will keep them there for all eternity."
By the will of the Almighty, who is
Without friend or companion,
The Lord of Above and Below,
The Lord of the Green Firmament,
The Generous Master of Generosity,
The Lord of Truth, the Kind
Merciful One, the Absolute Sultan,
When He finished cursing Shayṭān
He cast a glance at Adam's frame;
Caressing him with His bounty's light[21]
And out of His mercy, He created
A shadow over that earthly creature.
When He endowed him with a living soul
The earthly Adam suddenly leapt up.
He bowed before the Universal Monarch
Rubbing his face into the dark earth,
Saying: "Praise be to God! O Lord,
I testify to Your oneness for You are
Lord of the created and uncreated,[22]
Lord of heaven and earth;
You have been and will exist forever;
The sun and the moon are lit by Your light.
Suddenly You brought me forth from earth;
You breathed a pure soul into my body's frame.
It is most fitting that You are the supreme God
For You are omniscient, intelligent, and my guide.
I fully acknowledge Your might;
You are the creator of day and night."
By God's decree, of a sudden Adam grasped
Every form of knowledge and all mysteries.[23]
All knowledge He made evident to him;
Thus Adam, through grace and knowledge,
Came to apprehend the whole world.
He came to know God's most exalted names;[24]

God preferred him above all other creatures.
355 He nourished Adam with generous favors
For He created him for the sake of good deeds.
God said to Adam: "O pure servant, you
Have I chosen from among the celestial innocents;
I created the entire world for you;[25]
I drew your stature like that of a cypress.
Wild and tame animals, birds and fish,
Cattle and lambs—whatever you would want—
Dry and moist fruits of the world
I created for you; eat in good health!
360 From your progeny I will bring forth
A multitude of peoples; with them
I will fill the entire world
That they may rejoice and delight in it.
All comforts have I created for their sake;
Wet and dry are meant to please their souls.
No prayer of your progeny will be in vain
Even if it must traverse the Earth's circumference."
O Shāhīn, whomsoever the Almighty Himself
Favors even a little, such a one
Becomes the favorite of both worlds;
O Lord, have mercy on my state.[26]

Jacob and the Wolf

Jacob Becomes Aware of Joseph's Disappearance

They carried out the fell deed suddenly,[1]
Flung Joseph, Jacob's son, into the well.
Quickly they slew a kid[2]
And kneaded its blood into Joseph's coat.
Then they came before exalted Jacob
Bareheaded, with torn coats, weeping.
Each one grieved separately,
Each one shed copious tears.
5 Jacob, that clever man, leapt to his feet
Bewildered, before his tent,
As he beheld his sons upon the way[3]

Come nearer, nearer, sighing and lamenting.
From far away he saw at once
That they were barefoot, weeping and forlorn.
The sound of their laments rose up to heaven.
Anguish pierced Jacob's heart as he thought,
"Some accident, some great calamity,
Has befallen Joseph!"
As they came nearer they cried very loud,
Justly lamenting their own evil deed.
Jacob addressed them thus: "My dear ones, oh
Why do you strew dust upon your heads?
Your torn coats and your cries, what do they mean?
Tell me, whom do you mourn in such a manner?
Where's the light of my eyes? He is not with you.
Is he in heaven, for here is not his place?"[4]
They answered: "[We mourn] for that shah of beauties:[5]
The lamp of the assembly, radiant sun,
Celebrated Joseph, crown of our heads,
Younger but better than ourselves,[6] who
Was suddenly slain by a wild beast's[7] claws;
Abruptly has his day turned into night.
He was among us, that heart-dazzling one;
He was in charge of all our flock today.
To him we entrusted it but for a while
And went joyfully into the desert.[8]
A wolf ambushed him from a hidden place
Like a lion, rushed upon him suddenly,
And carried off that rose-cheeked beloved,
Monarch supreme over idols of Rūm and Chīn.[9]
He pulled him down, trampled, tore him apart,
Killed and devoured him in his affliction."
When Jacob heard this news, his heart
At once became inhabited by grief and sighs.
Roaring, he collapsed; he fell
Unconscious, unable to move, astounded.
For a while he was completely out of this world,
Turned for him upside down.[10]

Jacob Laments His Separation from Joseph

After a time his consciousness returned;
Passionate love for Joseph seared his heart,
And he cried out, weeping in his grief:[11]
"What shall I do, what's left for me to do?
What have you done with my sun of beauties?
My Canaan's moon, what has become of him?
Where did you take that beautiful face?
Where did you carry off that heavenly moon?
Where did you take that sunny face?
Where did you carry off that curly head?
Where did you take that mine of modesty?
Where did you carry off that treasury of gifts?
Where did you take that weeping lion?
Where did you carry off that Yemenite pearl?
Where did you take that soft-spoken youth?
Where did you carry off that graceful cypress?
Where did you take that fierce lion?
Where did you carry off that sugar of the lips?
Tell me what happened to Joseph, tell me the truth;
Do not distort, my dear ones, do not embellish.
You mean to keep me in the dark[12] about him,
Intoxicate me with the cup of ignorance."[13]
Then Levi said to Israel, "O father,
What can be done against God's own decree?
The Almighty inscribed this on his brow;
Fate[14] itself stood in wait to ambush him.
He was trapped by the wolf's claws;
That jewelled treasure passed away.
We saw footprints of the wolf in the desert
And long ran after him,
Troubled all the way and full of grief,
But spied no trace of that moon-visaged one.
Then at the foot of the rocky mountain,
We saw his cast-off tunic soaked in blood."
Before Jacob he placed it and he said:
"This is the sole token of that beloved friend."

Jacob recognized the shirt on sight
And seizing it at once he addressed it thus:
"O shirt, where did your friend go?[15] Where is your master,
Who gave you little trouble, where did he go?
Where did your chosen intimate friend go?
Where did that moon-browed beauty disappear?
Certain it is you did not leave me singly;
Why are you single now, not paired with him?
Why are you far from your beloved friend,
And distant from the one who shared your griefs?
Why are you far from that bedroom candle,
And distant from the garden's box tree?
Why are you far from that radiant moon,
And distant from that brilliant sun?
Why are you far from that moon incarnate,
And distant from that honored chief?
Why are you far from my hair's musky noose,
And distant from my tall cypress?
Why are you far from that summit of the age,
And distant from that peerless moon?
Why are you far from that shepherd moon,
And distant from that sunny countenance?
Why are you far from my dear friend,
And distant from my beautiful standard?[16]
Why are you far from my protector,
And distant from my sun and moon?
Why are you far from my peerless pearl,
Distant from that kind boon companion?
What did you do to Joseph? What happened to him?
In whose claws did he fall down helpless?
What wild beast dared to fight him?
How did the wolf shed Joseph's blood?
Tell me the truth, what happened to Joseph?
How did the wolf eat him? He is not a deer!
Who dipped you in this blood?
Tell the truth, the truth; drenched with blood,
Joseph's shirt is no longer beautiful.

Why did you turn blood red?
You used to be [snow] white; this red,
You make me despair of my child.
You went off looking handsome;
Why did you come back ugly?
You have soaked yourself in blood.
Of Joseph you deprived me suddenly;
Alas, a hundred times alas for that moon face!
Now you're my only memorial of him,
Truth's intimate companion in sorrow.
Is it right that you should kindle a fire
And in this grief consume my heart and soul?
Is it right that you appear here without Joseph
And show me instead his blood?
Blood is no substitute for Joseph;
One never sells one's child for blood.[17]
Whoever heard such mysteries?
Blood cannot cut me off from my sun![18]
If I had seen this in a dream,
I would have died at once.
Confused, I know not what to do;
Grief came upon my soul so suddenly.
Joseph went out to play all unaware,
Left me behind in eternal sorrow.
The souls of the weak cannot be revived;
May no one ever suffer as I do now!
But how can I live without my life? O Lord,
Take my life from me now.[19]
Abruptly night and day have become one
For me, dawn turned into darkest night."
Uttering this, he lost his strength and sense
And fell, once more, unconscious to the ground
Like one utterly weak or suddenly dead.
Then once more he began to cry and groan.
His neighbors[20] came, and they encircled him
While he went on lamenting:

"Explain,
Dear friends, acquainted with every mystery;
Why did I not perish before him?
Why am I not carried off today?
He quit this life so young,
His spring turning to autumn suddenly.
Did I not fear the Most Generous Almighty,
The Lord of the Assembly and Resurrection,
Lord of both wound and salve,
I would kindle a strong fire right now,
Leap into it, and burn from head to toe.
Better a hundred elders like unto me should die
Than that one youth should lack a strand of hair!
Now the youth perishes, and the elder survives;
Who can explain this mystery?
Would that You, O Lord, had taken me in my wretchedness
Before Joseph, beneath the ground!
I'll guard his shirt as long as I'm alive;
I'll never wash out the blood
But I will keep it, seeking my child from it.
I'll rub it on my blind eyes day and night;[21]
I'll carry it, blood and all, into the grave,
I'll bring it with me on the Day of Judgment
To the Judge's palace, soiled with blood;
May He grant me justice from that wolf,
And mark him quickly, even in my day.
O God, is it right that a vile small wolf
Should shed my child's blood upon this countryside?
Exact justice for me from him, Lord;
May he dwell in misfortune day and night!"

Jacob's Debate with His Sons

All ten of exalted Jacob's sons
Stood bareheaded and disheveled before their father,
Reuben, and Naphthali, and Asher,
Zebulun, Gad, and leonine Levi,
Judah, and bold Issachar,

Also Simeon, the brave and valiant hero.
In private they confessed: "We are the wolf;
We have all sinned; the fault is ours."[22]
With pained hearts they lamented
That ugly, villainous deed.
Their father, seeing the grief and agitation
Rising from the depth of their souls, and their burning hearts,
Addressed them thus: "What is the use of lamenting
Now; what should have never been has come to pass.
It would be better that you act like men,
Sustain each other in this suffering.
You were and ever shall remain far from him;
The wolf vanquished him suddenly.
On Judgment Day, God will inquire after him
And will require something for his blood.[23]
You will be brought before that council;
The Almighty will not neglect injustice.
Each of you is in possession of such strength
That you can break the necks of lions, yet
A wolf outfoxed you, like a Turk or Tāzī.[24]
What a treasure you have cast into the winds!
Through carelessness you've pulled up root and branch.[25]
Spread out his shirt for me; show it again.
Contemplate how he was killed in grief;
Were his arms and back broken?"[26]
Then Levi opened up the tunic,
Before Jacob displayed it once again.
No part of it was torn,
Neither the collar nor its back;
No trace of the wolf's claws could be seen,
Nor of their deceit.[27] Jacob said to himself:
"There is a hidden mystery in this;
None but the Glorious One divines its meaning.
My sons were simply sporting with him,
But me they cast into a burning furnace.
The story of Joseph and the wolf is a lie,
Exceedingly brazen, a patent lie.

No wolf knows anything of Joseph;
The story of my darling sons is just not true.
Can a wolf burst into the midst of a flock,
Leave lambs behind and steal my Joseph?!
They're tearing me apart with their lie's claws,
Untouched the truth of Joseph and the wolf.
My shepherd, truly a bloodthirsty wolf,
Guards my sheep on the plain day and night.
Never have I had troubles from wild beasts;
No wolf has ever eaten from my flock.
How did the wolf tear him apart
And leave the entire flock behind?!"[28]
Then to his sons he said aloud:
"Inform me of this mystery,
I want to examine it thoroughly;
Speak nothing but the truth:
How did this unjust disaster befall Joseph;
How was he caught in its clutches?"
They once again replied: "O clever one,
May Resurrection's King be ever your help.
We went to play for a while,
We were simply fooling around;
We raced among the flowers and the green,
Picked roses, sweet basil, and hyacinths.[29]
He did not come with us to play;
We pressed him, but he would not come.[30]
So we left him with the flock for a short while;
We thought he would be safe.
We stripped off our clothes
And left them with that handsome one.
We neglected him for a while,
And thus he came to grief.
The wolf ambushed him from a hidden place
And like a lion pounced upon the flock.
The wolf ambushed him unexpectedly,
Carried him off by heaven's own decree.[31]
He took him away and ate him suddenly;

Killed and devoured him quickly.
When we returned from our games after a while,
We ran looking in haste toward the flock.
Seeing no trace of Joseph, we cried
And felt we were losing our minds.
We knew at once a wolf had carried him off;[32]
Hard-hearted, had killed and eaten him.
We ran looking for that wolf in every direction
But found no trace of Joseph or the wolf.
At last, and to our sorrow, we found this tunic
At the mountain's base, smeared with blood.
We have no other information;
All of us grieve and cry for him."

Jacob's Argument with His Sons Regarding the Fact That the Wolf Did Not Eat Joseph

Clever Jacob responded to them thus:
"All that you're saying is a complete lie:
If by heaven's decree Joseph fell captive
Into the clutches of a bloodthirsty wolf,
Where are the marks of the wolf's claws,
The paw prints, and the traces of his bites?
And if the wolf ate him without his tunic,
Why is it thus drenched in blood?
And if the mad wolf ate him with his tunic on,
Where are the tears of his fangs on it?
All that you utter is a lie, deceitful;
Deceit shackles your feet, each one of you.
If I could see that wolf in person,
He'd tell me about Joseph face to face.
Certain it is that a wolf did not eat him,
Nor treated him unjustly.
You're not telling the truth about him;
The lie within this tale is evident.
The truth is that a wolf did not devour him;
My child did not perish by the wolf's claw."
But his child's condition was not clear to him;

For God's gift of prophecy had left him then.[33]
He thought, "They've killed him
And smeared his shirt in blood;
If they did kill him, the Almighty will
Cause them in time to perish in affliction.
Then their long abode will be under the ground,
And their place under the dirt forever."
Once more he addressed the shirt and cried,
"Where did your royal master go?
Where is your friend, your heart's beloved?
Where is your elegant radiant embracer?
Where your rose-cheeked heartbreaker?"
He spoke thus and tore his hair,
Replaced his clothes with a coarse mantle;[34]
His sons wept, seeing him wrapped in the mantle,
And strewed dust upon their own heads.

Jacob's Sons Capture the Helpless Wolf and Bring Him to Their Father

Again his sons addressed the prophet, saying:
"O dear, exalted father, we will run quickly
Out to the desert and try to find the wolf."[35]
In agitation, they left Jacob's side
Barefooted and bareheaded, crying loudly.
Roaming the desert for a while,
They came upon a small and solitary wolf.
Cutting off his flight on every side,
They quickly captured that innocent beast.
Like thieves, they collared him,
And with a staff broke his back and flanks,
Bloodied his muzzle and paws; those "brave" ones[36]
Rendered him utterly helpless. They dragged him along;
They brought him back to Jacob, saying,
"May you come to a good end!
We bring the shameless wolf who devoured
Joseph, the offspring of Jamshīd;[37]
Ask him: Why did you commit this unjust act;
Did you rejoice in killing my son?

Why did you go after him, O wicked one?
What grudge did you bear against that moon-cheeked son?"
When Jacob, crazed with grief, beheld that wolf,
Covered with blood from head to toe,
Caned almost to death, blood flowing
From his throat and back, he said:
"This wretched wolf is innocent,
Although he is a vile and predatory beast."[38]
Then he prayed silently to God
To grant his hope, a wish:
"Release the wolf's tongue from its bonds
That he may tell about these awful wounds."
Quick as a flash the Almighty God accepted
The prayer of Canaan's sage; the wolf
Began at once to converse with Jacob;[39]
His tongue took to it rather nicely.

Jacob's Debate with the Wolf and His Querying of Him

Jacob addressed the wolf: "O tyrant,
Why did you set my soul on fire?
O wolf, have you no shame before God?
Why did you kill Joseph so wretchedly?
Why did you eat that soul of the universe,
Why did you devour that princely youth?
Why did you act so unjustly toward him?
Why did you deprive me of his company?
Tell me, O villain, what harm did Joseph
Do to you that you attacked him?
Why did you uproot my cypress tree,
Impale my heart upon a roasting spit?
You've robbed the boy of life and father;
Has this ever been done to the shah of beauties?
Did Time[40] drive your heart to such vengeance,
Or insane rage possess your head?
My heart's lamp you have extinguished,
Making the world appear perverse before my eyes;
You dared deprive the world of such a prince,

Who was the glory of the human race!
Why did you cast the die crookedly,
And burden me with pain and sorrow?
Were there too few flocks on the plain and mountains
That you had to aim at those sunny cheeks,
And eat Joseph instead of a lamb?
Did you think you were eating bread and herbs?
Was there nothing better to eat than my Joseph,
Not enough fat and lovely lambs around?
You've set fire to a world of good fortune;
The world is on fire by reason of this plunder.
How did you tear him apart with your claws?
Did you not see the beauty of his face?
Bitterly you robbed him of his sweet soul,
And me you flung into a burning fire.
Where did you eat him, tell me;
It may be I can find a strand of hair,
That would become my sweet companion and my friend;
My heart and soul I'd bind with that one strand.
One of his strands of hair is worth two hundred lives;
The eight heavens are of less value than such a hair![41]
That strand would keep me company in the grave,
Even on Resurrection Day; to me it would impart
Forever the scent of my beloved Joseph.
Though you had died ravenous,
You should not have harmed him.
No mercy came to that moon face,
None to his lovely black eyes.
No mercy came to that meadow cypress;
None to that moon of Khotan.[42]
No mercy came to that tranquil soul;
None to that soul of the universe.
No mercy came to that sugar bundle;
None to that jewelled necklace.
No mercy came to that treasury of gifts;
None to that brilliant light.
No mercy came to that fierce lion;

None to that living soul.
No mercy came to that sunny child;
None to that happy boy."[43]
Thus did he keen and rain forth tears
On his cheeks like a spring shower.
The pain that racked Jacob's grieving breast
Filled the heart also of the wretched wolf;
For the old man he cried profusely,
As if he had been struck by an arrow.

The Wolf's Debate with Jacob, by God's Command

The wolf then, by God's decree
Launched into conversation with Jacob.
He said, "O prophet, for the Almighty's sake,
Beware, bear not a bad opinion of me.
How could I shed a prophet's blood;
How can I contend with God's own prophet?
How can a beast devour a prophet,
A great man, a prince, acquainted with the Lord?
The prophet's blood is forbidden to us;[44]
I do not even know who Joseph is.
How does a beast rate against a prophet,
To dare attack him, O wise sage?
Beware, bear not a bad opinion of me;
Seek Joseph in other quarters; of these charges
I am innocent; God knows my inmost thoughts.
Had I seen Joseph, I would have laid my head
Down at his feet; tender respect and honor,
Caresses, hundreds, would I have shown him.
In all this time no wolf has dared
To hover round your sheep;
Should one so do, he'd merely frighten them;
You know their habits all too well.
And if all of a sudden a wolf should see
One of your stray sheep upon the road,
He'd drive and chase it away,
Sending it back to your flock

Without even smelling it for fear of you,
Even were he to expire from desire;
How then would he dare hunt down your Joseph?
Which wolf would dare to play that game?
Around your flocks, the wolves are shepherds,
Endlessly watching over them. No,
I know nothing of Joseph; and God knows
My inmost and my open thoughts.
Since one can't hover round your flock,
It would not be easy to devour Joseph.
Seek your Joseph in another place;
He was not harmed by us."
The innocent wolf's tale made Jacob suffer;
He asked him once again: "O beast,
Of Joseph's blood I know you're innocent
And now I do apologize to you.
But tell me, what did happen to him;
Who dared inflict on him such unjust cruelty?
Who blackened our day so suddenly?
They've killed him swiftly, in affliction;
No friend came to his rescue."
The wolf replied: "O honest lord,
Who but the Mover of the celestial spheres
Sees the invisible? But know, exalted prince,
One should not draw the veil aside like a spy.
I did not eat him; so much is certain;
The Lord of the Throne knows the rest."
Jacob then knew the beast spoke truly,
Pursued nothing but truth. The sons' falsehood
Needed some looking into;
Not one of their words was truth;
Out of their lies they wove
A deep, dense night. One cannot hide
The sun with dirt; water cannot be hidden
Under fire, the moon by a fish,[45]
Nor can blackness be washed out of the night.
Jacob said in his heart: "If things stand thus,

My sons have been deceitful, that's for certain;
I must suffer the pain with red eyes, yellow cheeks.
I will not find out the truth about him from them;
God knows they brought this evil upon me.
Their own misfortune they have bought with gold;
They have disgraced themselves in haste.
This they made plain by bringing here the wolf,
And now, alas, they are entirely disgraced.
The thoughts and acts of each are in God's hands;
Hidden secrets are manifest to Him.[46]
They have diminished their own stature,
And are bound intimately with their deed.
In the end, He will return those gone astray,
Whoever bears guilt in this matter.
This tale will come to light;
I'm confident of God's decree."
The moment he heard about his child,
Prophecy left that sage at once.[47]
As long as he knew not what became of him,
He endured the calamity and injustice.
But pay close attention to the games
The Judge plays with His prophets.

Jacob's Second Debate with the Wolf

Again Jacob addressed the wolf: "O beast,
Why are you now so drenched in blood?
Where have you been; what did you graze upon?
What prey did you tear apart today?
Was it beast or human being? On whose life
Did you wreak your oppression, your injustice?"
The wolf replied, "O lion of God,[48]
I am bewildered, wounded, and fatigued,
And I have wandered far away from home;
I am a stranger here, helpless and weak.
My habitation used to be in Syria;[49]
My permanent abode was in its mountains.
There in the mountains, plains, and forests,

Ferociousness prevailed.
In my lowliness I had only one child;
The dust of his paw prints was my diadem.
He wandered off from me suddenly;
He tore apart my sore, afflicted heart.
Ten days it is that I've been cut off from him;
Not one of these days has been good.
By evening I was headed toward the desert,
From Syria into Canaan, weeping,
Bewildered, and distressed.[50] I questioned
Every beast, good or bad, on every bypath
About my child and suddenly arrived here
In this valley and saw what I ought not to have seen.
I chanced upon these ten youths,
Nimble and strong, rough champions.
They cut my way off right and left; it seemed
The Day of Resurrection had arrived for me.
They trapped and collared me firmly
And with a stick broke both my arms and legs.
I fell into these straits, O wise sage,
Suddenly, through the grief I bore my child."
He said this, and from his eyes shed
Copious tears like pomegranate seeds.
His bewildered heart was so much on fire
It could have kindled a fire on its own.
Jacob said: "He's looking for his child,
Just like me; two streams of tears of blood
Flow from his eyes; without doubt,
He is afflicted, just like me. He is mourning
His child; he is stunned and afflicted."
Aloud, he said: "Come, let us cry together,
We have both lost our beloved children."
Then he commanded that they remove his collar
And give him food to eat aplenty.
The wolf heaped blessings on Canaan's sage,
Turned, and took off for the desert.

Jacob Argues with His Sons and Laments

Jacob turned to his sons and said,
"O twisted children, you are all sinners,
One and all, and you know it;
Your destiny is from the Almighty.
He made you guilty and sinful;
He made you acquainted with villainy.
The Almighty knows the secret you are hiding
For in the invisible He knows all secrets.
O God, may you experience my misfortune![51]
God grant me patience to suffer this pain;
He must make me patient.[52]
The day will come when I shall see my child's face,
I will happily sit in my Joseph's presence.
Should my time be up before then, I accept the order,
And I will die in separation's pain.
What can one do against the Lord's decree?
I would simply go helpless into the ground."[53]
This he said and began crying again.
The hearts of all present were aflame.
Children, women, men came and surrounded
Canaan's sage, lamenting in his pain.
They mourned his grief and in their turn
They grieved: sad, weary, and afflicted.
When Jacob lost Joseph so suddenly,
He gave up all his wordly tasks.
He sat in a dark house all day long,
Dressed in sackloth, his only occupation
Wailing and sighing, lamenting,
Like a prisoner inside a well.[54]
The sighs he uttered could smash
Iron hearts forged upon anvils.
When pain for Joseph made him sigh,
The cheeks of young and old turned pale.
He could if he so wished set fire to the world,
And then what straw he'd scatter to the winds!
Mourning, he dwelt within his house,

Grief's bread and water were his only food.
He rested on no couch other than on his knees;
He did not sleep by night nor rest by day.
His strength was lost in sleeplessness;
Much did he weep and greatly longed for death.
Blindly he cried, full of affliction,
Within his house, grieved, facing the wall,
Day and night bearing his sorrow
Which did not diminish over time.
His tongue uttered no word other than "Joseph,"
For Joseph was his strength of body and soul.
He lived with the memory of the boy's appearance;
Other than mourning, he had no occupation.
He allowed no one in his presence
Save those who like himself sighed and lamented.
And if his tongue did not call Joseph's name,
His mouth would fall silent at once.
Day and night Jacob lived with his sorrow;
None could converse with him.
O Shāhīn,
The sorrow of the ages prepares
The arrival of happiness' new shoot.
Dark night ends in a bright morning;
Day always follows a dark night.

Mūsā-nāmah (The Book of Moses)

Moses and the Burning Bush

God Manifests Himself to Kalīm Allah for the First Time

One night,[1] when Moses once again
Happened to roam the desert,
Walking round and round his sheep,
Night's face was veiled in darkness,
A sense of dread stirred discord in the heart.
Black *dīv*s[2] were lurking everywhere; it seemed
That turning Time itself was plotting ambush.
The world plunged into crow-black mourning,

And morning's neck was broken.
Fish and fowl were both asleep on this
Malevolent night full of foreboding.
The world was crying but the heavens smiled,
Displaying starry teeth upon the firmament.
Below, the prophet hovered in the desert
Around his flock of sheep.[3]
Suddenly,
A lamb jumped out before him, running madly
Away from the flock into the desert,
Dashing into the darkness of the night
Like an arrow shot from a bow.
The prophet, seeing this, ran quickly
After that beloved son.[4] And when between them
But a short distance remained, renowned Kalīm,
The sun of all creation, saw of a sudden
Flames enveloping a tree, resembling a pavilion,
Leaping from there to diverse other trees.
From far away, God's interlocutor
Was unable to see that the fire was,
In truth, nothing but light:[5]
It kindled not a branch. Boldly
Kalīm Allah walked in its direction,
Not knowing that the fire was but light,
The site of God's manifestation.
Courageously and quickly he moved forward
After the lamb[6] in hot pursuit.
And then he heard a voice:
"O Moses, Moses,
Remove your sandals quickly as you move;
This is a chosen spot; do not come[7]
So flustered, beside yourself![8]
Know that the flames you saw from far away
Are nothing but pure light."[9]
As God's voice
Was absorbed by his soul's ears, Moses replied:

"Here I am,"[10] then lost all consciousness of self.[11]
When by the command of Time's Creator
'Imrān's[12] son removed his sandals,
He was addressed again:
"Moses, know well
That I am the lord of your fathers
And forefathers. Toward Egypt make haste[13]
For there the Israelites are in torment.
I harkened to their cries and lamentations;[14]
The time has come to rescue them. Long ago,
I entered into covenant with the forefathers
Of this friendless folk, with Abraham,
Wise Isaac, and prudent Jacob, pledging that Canaan
I would return to them and would defeat
All their enemies—Canaan, that land
Flowing with milk and honey,[15]
By God's divine decree. Its excellence
Of vegetation can be matched
Only by the Garden of the Ṭūbā tree;[16]
Its air and water cannot be compared
With those of any other land;
Its breeze revives the dead; its gentle air
Relieves all grief. In all the world
No other place like this, a shady, pleasant place.
I send you quickly now
Off to Egypt like a flying arrow.
Carry my message to Pharaoh;
Give it to that unlucky, accursed infidel:[17]
"Let Jacob's offspring leave your realm
Such is God's perfect command!"
That luminary of earth's pedestal, Kalīm Allah,
On hearing the command of the Pure Judge,
Replied: "O Knower of all mysteries,
Ancient, Potent, Omniscient, Veiler,
Do not, O Generous One, entrust me with this;
This mission, no, I am not the right man,

I cannot carry it out;
A man more eloquent than I is needed,
One who can speak strong language
Before the oppressive pagan.[18]
Might and miracles are needed;
What am I saying? You know it all.
What might and miracle can I display,
And how dislodge the state crown from his brow?"
Having confided thus in God he banished
Speech into the birdcage for a while.[19]
Then the command came:
"Throw down your staff!"
He did so. Suddenly a snake appeared
Through God's power, showering sparks of fire
From its eyes. Beholding this,
The prophet lost his breath,
His soul lept to his mouth.
The call came once again:
"Grasp it by the tail; why are you so afraid?
Don't run away from the staff!"[20]
Made bold by God's command the prophet wheeled
Like a male lion upon that fierce creature,
Grasped its tail; and instantly it turned
Into a staff again; such was God's pleasure.
Came another command:
"Now place your hand
Into your bosom," and so Moses did.
The call pursued: "Now take it out."
Obeying, the brave prophet saw
His hand had turned all white; despair
Seized on him at the sight.
Again a call:
"O bright-faced man, once more
Place your hand in your bosom!"
The prophet once again obeyed
Intoxicated by these mysteries.
And when the command came, "Now take it out,"

He did and saw his hand quite healed.
Then God addressed him further:
"Glorious chief, the Hand of Might
Will keep you company. My Majesty will be
Your companion. When with the staff
You strike water and fish,
Myriads will die. Your staff
Will fill the waters of the Nile with blood,
Red blood will be its color."
But Moses spoke and said:
"O Mighty, Living Omnipotent,
Send someone in my place;
Conceal my person from this evil man's eyes;
My speech is not up to the task
As You, knower of secrets, know too well.
How can I be a messenger to Pharaoh,
And carry your message to that villain?"
But he was told, "I rule over your tongue;
I nourish you, body and soul. Why do you fear?
I Myself am your friend; grieve not,
Even if Fate should oppose you.[21]
You must set out quickly;
You do the going, I will display the might.
Your brother will come to meet you on the way;
He will carry out your wishes. At every turn
I'll be along with you and be your guide
On and off the path."
(Listen
And learn from me the mystery
Of Him who bade Moses remove his sandals.
The unperceptive disciple[22] does not know it;
This language is not known to every bird.
He meant: "You will no longer be around women,
To win the [polo] ball on the field.")[23]
When once again Moses glanced at the trees,
He saw the light no more and set out on the road.
He grabbed the sprightly lamb and quickly

Traversed the plain. Bringing it to the flock
He kept kissing its eyes and cheeks; then
75 A portion of the night, until the smile of dawn,
The prophet spent communing with the Lord.[24]
That night He spoke with him tumultuously,
One to one, till dawn. Intoxicated,[25]
By the night he had spent, the prophet headed
Toward the sage Jethro; lambs skipped before him;
That free cypress brought to the meeting place
The flock at the appointed time.
80 Kalīm the glory of the human race,
Came before the sage and told him
About his journey and shared with him
Those mysteries.[26] When he heard everything,
The thought of separation sparked turmoil
In famous Jethro's heart. But instantly
That prudent sage readied provisions
Of every type on hand. He gave
Fleet handsome beasts of burden
While grief tugged at his heart.
85 Beholding him intent on leaving, swiftly
Jethro adorned the prophet's mount.
Moses bade him farewell and he, in turn,
Assured him of the trust of times gone by.
Although he had had from the beginning countless sheep,
For each a thousand more had come to him
Through Kalīm's good fortune. The Perfect Lord
Gave him so many sheep that only He,
Their true provider, could count them now.

Moses' Vision of God

Kalīm Allah Beholds God's Countenance

Thus did Kalīm lament,[1] and said: "O Immortal
One, I have a wish: for Your mercy's sake
Reveal Your face to me from behind the veil;
Show me just once a vision of Yourself,
For I so long to see You. The pain of this

Great longing grieves my heart." Thus
For this vision's sake the prophet kept lamenting
Before God, rubbing his head and his white beard
Into the dust.[2] A voice called out: "O Kalīm,
Whoever sees Us must perish that same moment;
He endures not in the world but must, that very hour,
Relinquish his sweet soul; the mortal eye cannot
Endure so much light; only from far away
Can it behold My face and My eternity.
But do you now send Joshua, son of Nun, away,
Happy and cheerful toward the army;[3]
Once there, tell him to seek out all the people
And warn them that tomorrow at dawn no one
Except Aaron[4] should dare to leave his home.
Let them guard their flocks also within folds,
And let none of the people venture forth
From their own dwellings.[5] Such, O Kalīm,
Is My command and My decree. And as for you,
Tomorrow night you should go cheerfully
Toward that high mountain made of emerald,[6]
An open site; you'll see a designated mound;
Go, sit there free of worry.
O Kalīm, be alert and self-possessed; know
That tomorrow I shall pass quickly by that place,
But you[7] will not see anything except My back
Even if you were made of iron, steel, or stone.
In order that you may endure in the world,
I make you full aware on all accounts."
Hearing this the prophet kissed the ground
And with happy rosy cheeks that man
Of pure descent quickly departed to where
Joshua, the son of Nun, was waiting.
He told him God's entire message
And sent him off toward the army.
Joining his friends, that brave man
Revealed at once the burden of his heart.
He warned each one in turn to beware,

For such was God's command: "Tomorrow,
No living being leave his dwelling,
Nor wander suddenly upon the plain; no humans
And no animals should be around Mount Sinai.
Beware, and heed the Judge's own command;
If you would remain safe and tranquil,
And not dispatch your souls from your bodies,
Do not in any way rebel against it."
As for his part the prophet,
That wise old sage, headed out in the deep
Of night toward the emerald mountain,
To where the Judge, the Ancient One
Of night and days, had foreordained. Upon the way,
Intense desire for union with the Friend
Burned within him.[8] Then, of a sudden,
He saw the world flooded in light:
Fire fell upon mountain and stone;
Heavy mountains were toppled.[9]
Heaven and earth, mountain and desert,
All trembled by the Judge's command;
The entire world was filled with endless light,
Which every moment increased. Then suddenly,
Kalīm glanced up from the path, beheld
The Majesty and took leave of his senses.[10]
That pure man turned entirely into spirit;
Being beside himself, he rent the garment
Of his soul. A cry arose from the lover
Now that he suddenly beheld his Beloved enter.[11]
He passed in front of him: the prophet looked
And saw Him, and in beholding
His dread, he passed out at once.
The prophet fell moaning upon his face,
Rubbing his own beauty into the dust.
He said: "O Hidden and Manifest Creator,
Ancient, Almighty, Omnipotent, Glorious One,
Forgive the errors of this sinful world;
Absolve all who are seeking Your pardon.

Forgive my people all at once; cancel
And cleanse them of their sins, their crimes."
As he cried thus to God, to the exalted,
The Creator's message came in glory; a voice
Declared: "O Moses, rejoice, and raise your head;
Rise, do not tear your face, nor cry!
I do forgive them all wholly; all those
Who are worthy, I fully pardon;
Know this, drive this care out of your heart,
Your mind. For with their ancestors I made
A covenant, gave them My word, upon My soul,
That I will entrust Canaan to them and rain
The fear of them upon their enemies.
I will drive out the Amorites and Jebusites;
Leave no Perizite in place; the Hivites[12]
And the Girgishites[13] of the realm, enemies all,
Will topple, and fulfilling the vow
Of My generous soul, I will give them a place
As lovely and as fresh as Eden's Garden.
But O Kalīm, as regards yourself,
Grasp well the inward meaning of this mystery,
For since eternity I have decreed it so:
You will yourself not set foot in Canaan;
From this, O son of ʿImrān, you are withheld."
On hearing this the color left Kalīm's cheeks,
Tears abundant like the Oxus flooded his bosom.
Yet even as they flowed, Kalīm Allah
Thought in his heart: "Though I am not to see it,
This is no cause for grief; these my two eyes
Ought not to grieve, for when my people behold
That land and settle in it happily,
As You, O Knower of secrets, know full well,
It will be as if I saw it two hundred times!"
And when the prophet told himself this secret,
Good cheer returned to him once more,
A small, unfolding rosebud.[14]

The Killing of the Blasphemer

The Sons of Jacob Kill the Blaspheming Man

One day,[1] by fate's decree, two riders
In the glorious royal encampment
Fell into discord with one another;[2]
The hand of one turned out to be the stronger
And this he proved upon the other well.
He struck him down with a high blow
And gave no thought to helping him.
Upon receiving such a heavy blow,
This one then cursed his mother and his sister.
Then, full of enmity, he turned to God
And blasphemed with his tongue.
His mother was one of the tribe of Dan,
But his father was an Egyptian;
He had a father who was an infidel;
The jackal was now turned into a tiger.
His father's name was Hūrī of Sām;[3]
Shelomit was his mother's name.
When that accursed man vilified the Judge,
On hearing the curse, the army came running
From all directions toward that infidel.
They pressed around him firmly
And threw a rope over his neck and thighs.
Humiliating him thus, they dragged him
Before Moses; then those chieftains
Told Moses and Aaron what the vile man had said.
Informed of the man's blasphemy
Moses, that soaring royal falcon,
Angrily admonished the company thus:
"Do not associate with him;
Confine him to the prison until
I learn what the Almighty commands;
His way will come to pass."
According to the prophet's word
They threw him into prison, bound tightly,

Like an anvil. As if for a thief
They cleared a space for him in jail
And bound his feet in iron chains.
Kalīm Allah, having thus jailed him,
Received at once God's message: "O Moses,
Release now from your prison
That blasphemer, that cursed bad-tempered man;
Give orders to the army to bring him out,
Dragging him on the plain, and then
Let everybody stone him to death.
Let him embrace the consequence of his act
That others may take warning and shall know,
All who blaspheme shall in this manner die."
When Kalīm Allah heard from the Almighty
This mystery, he bowed and kissed the ground;
Apprised of God's command the prophet
Spoke at once to the assembled company:
"Depart from here quick as fire,
Relay this message to that infidel in jail;
Remove him from it, for such is the command
Of the Incomparable: let the army
Fetch him by dragging him out.
Let him be stoned to death so that
The world will heed this lesson
And hold its tongue in check."
When the army heard that mystery,
They hastened gleefully to the sinner's side.
They dragged him terrified out of jail,
Out of his mind, an iron collar
Fastened around his neck. The Sons of Jacob
Surrounded him and said, "O perverse sinner,
Did you not know not to contend with God?
You'll never rise from this calamity.
In this world such are your desserts;
Hell has been joined to your soul."
Thus spoke they to him and hauled him out
In humiliation, dragging that vile man.

And having brought him out, the army
Dug a circle on the surface of the plain
And then those famous men, all of one mind,
Seized him and stood him up within the circle.
They buried him up to his waist in dirt,
While from the ditch he roared like a lion.
And then from every side and direction
Those famous men rained stones on him.
At the first blow his fortune came to an end;
Quickly his trunk fell over, quickly.
One whose race lacks stock and lineage
How can he rejoice at belonging to the human race?
This man was of ill-fated, topsy-turvy descent,
Egyptian, not of Jacob's progeny,
He made his stock and lineage
Known to all, high and low, so that
All were aware, and through his curse
Were not themselves destroyed.
Black never turns to white though you
Wash it in a hundred waters;
Of certainty a crow does not become
A parrot; nor will bad stock turn good;
A bead of clay does not a jewel make,
Gilt cannot become a pure turquoise.

Qārūn's Rebellion

Qārūn's Argument with Kalīm Allah

They hastened and went quickly to the prophet;[1]
Raising a mighty clamor they addressed him thus:.
"Why should you count for more than we,
Have precedence in every matter over us?[2]
We're greater than you in wealth and treasure;[3]
There's nothing in which you're better than us;
You're indigent, a dervish,[4] whereas we possess
Money and treasures beyond count. Tell us,
In what do you surpass us? Think and then
Tell us, just who do you think you are?

We're equal in nobility, we and you,
As we are one and all of Hebrew stock.
Won't you then tell us, O Kalīm,
Wherein lies your greatness?
How long will you look so severe?
How long will you keep on saying
The Almighty has commanded thus,
Causing such anguish to this multitude?[5]
Calamity has come to us from you each moment;[6]
You showed no mercy to our white beards.
From the time you carried us away from Pharaoh
On this "pilgrimage," we have not seen in the world
Anything good, nothing but trouble hourly.
You've turned our daylight into darkness;
You aimed to kill us with your wisdom,[7]
This was your intention from the start,
To annihilate the Hebrew folk. As for us,
Our rank and station surpass yours
As does our combined nobility.
And you, what have you done for us?
Have you not thought of what you've done?
You gave the priesthood to Hārūn[8] instead of Qārūn
And thereby plunged us into mourning:
Who more than Qārūn was worthy of the priesthood
In the world, O son of 'Imrān?[9]
As for the Levites, they possess such "courage"
That out of fear of you they breathe as one.
You've seized the entire world in your own hands;
You have disgraced whatever it brought forth.
Through treachery you have thrust yourself forward;
You've rent the very innards of the world.
A beggar claims now his share in meddling!
Your ignorance is written on your heart:
You're a mere dervish; off with you to a retreat!
We don't need a beggar for our leader. We take
Precedence over you, whatever you say;
Our combined nobility surpasses yours."

When God's lion heard this from oppressive Qārūn
And his tribe, he was dumbfounded. The prophet
Addressed himself to Qārūn thus:
"Talk alone
Leads to no real results.
My rank and station come from God. Pay heed,
Oblivious man, to my mystery.
Why do you strive with me in vain? I fear
Through this you'll shed your blood.
Since you've let loose your tongue in foolish talk
And set your foot shamelessly on this path,
At dawn tomorrow, come before me and display
Your own rank and station.[10]
Each one of you bring along his censer,
And we will show you up in your own business.
Let each of you put incense in his censer and,
O mad, oppressive tyrants, undertake to sprinkle.
If you would wear the priests' garments
Then relinquish all your worldly goods.
Hārūn will also take hold of his censer;
You, he, and Qārūn will be left alone.
Then go to the opening of the Tent of Meeting;[11]
I will not heed your cries and lamentations.
There will it be manifest who is truly noble,
And who strikes whom by right."
Hearing these words from him who was Time's glory,
They walked toward their tents well satisfied.
Kalīm Allah went into his own tent, where he sat
Angry and brooding over Qārūn's tyranny.
He dispatched someone to fetch Datan and Abiram;
That noble cypress ordered both be found.
When those two elders learned where matters stood
They went like night that covers
The Almighty's sun.[12]
Said the prophet to them:
"Tomorrow at dawn, do not follow, do not be misled
By Qārūn. Take not your own censers,

For you will burn, in truth, or die.
Qārūn's star is now obscured in darkness,
His horoscope's account is in a ruined state.
Tomorrow he will die among his chieftains;
Violence will overcome his soul.
What lot these are, the progeny of Jacob,
Stricken from moment to moment upside down!
Who else has such a people in the world?
Their iniquity has worn me down.
I've traveled the twisted path in the valley
And now arrive near the goal,
That place wherein, by divine decree,
The milk and honey flow. Of those
Whom I brought out of Egypt,
From before Pharaoh, from the blame
They heaped on me, none has survived;
The rest who have remained will stumble,
Every one of them, for lack of righteousness."[13]
The elders[14] who heard this from the prophet
Said nothing, good or bad; fell silent,
And left the prophet's presence;
Quick as the night they hastened to their homes.
All that the prophet told them
Flickered round them, as in a dome.
But they did not believe the words
Of God's lion, did not befriend good fortune.
They did not heed one little word of it,
And they forgot the prophet's speech.
They did not turn away from their pledge to Qārūn
Nor did they withhold their hearts from him[15]
One grain of barley's worth, so when
Misfortune rose all round them,
It scattered all their learning.
Fate veiled their learning,
And strove to bring about their death.
When night passed into morrow
Tumult and clamor arose among those chiefs.

Qārūn, that tyrant, rose up and came forth
Once more among his friends. All went
Toward the Tent of Meeting,[16] with music
And with their censers, cheerfully.
They filled their censers with a special incense
And gathered round Qārūn. In that hour
Qārūn built a well-proportioned altar,
Exceeding the required measurements.[17]
Upon it he prepared to offer
Several sacrifices. Just as the animals
Were placed on the altar, Kalīm Allah
And Hārūn arrived. Hārūn held in his hands,
Greatly delighted, a censer full of aloes;
The chosen chieftain, Hārūn,
Entered at once with Moses,
Into the sanctuary;[18] they stood
In worship with open hearts and souls.

Moses Petitions God to Split Open the Ground

A divine message came: "O Moses and Hārūn,
Depart at once from out of the midst of these
That I may rain fire over their heads;
I shall cast dire affliction on them all.
I will leave not one of them alive and well,
For they are all oppressors steeped in error."[19]
When Kalīm Allah heard this he was full of fear;
The awesome dread sent shivers down his spine.
He sat down on the ground and rubbed his face in dust;[20]
From heart and soul he cried out to God:
"O You Who uphold the nine[21] vaulted firmaments,
Patient and generous, incomparable,
You know full well it is Qārūn who has sinned.
Do not, O Gracious One, oppress the rest.
You are that One and Only Peerless God
Who does not link the crime of one to another."[22]
Thus for a time he lamented before God
And launched a boat on that vast ocean.[23]

A voice came once again: "O 'Imrān's son,
Drive out the people from before the Dwelling;[24]
Separate them from Qārūn's folk
So that they will not be buried with them."[25]
On hearing this Kalīm Allah hastened
And ran toward his gathered friends;
He bade them flee,[26]
Then took his stand within the Dwelling.
But none of Qārūn's folk heard this,
None feared the Almighty's wrath.
Suddenly Qārūn uttered a savage roar:
"Who are Moses and Hārūn in the world?
Two begging dervishes needing between them
But one loaf of bread, who speak
Contrary to God's command.[27]
Now will it be shown who is God's chosen;
Now will we soon weep over them."
Kalīm Allah
Then turned in wrath upon Qārūn,
Walked swiftly, furiously up to him,
And as he did so he prayed: "O Pure
Almighty God, Lord of the Firmaments,
Open this very moment the earth's mouth,
Let it drag down this misguided man, first
His home and all his property,
His goods and chattels, treasure,
Money, whatever he owns, from end to end,
Worth but a grain of barley.
Let it all be destroyed before his eyes;
And may his wishes turn to poison.[28]
Preserve neither his cash or goods nor his treasures;
Let not one barley grain survive,
That none may say that Moses coveted
His gold especially or set his eyes
On Qārūn's money and because of that
Suddenly destroyed Qārūn."[29]
When thus Kalīm, the moon-faced, sun of the East,

Entreated the Judge, a voice proclaimed:
"O Kalīm, treasury
Of mysteries, seek another wish from Us.
For this I did not plan at My creation
And in My council took no account thereof.
You who approach the sun in countenance,
Know that I made the earth without a mouth."[30]
The prophet cried out once again and spoke:
"O Creator, Displayer of Omnipotence,
I ask that through Your might You may
At once endow the earth with a mouth, wide open,
And that it swallow this malicious,
Seditious, rich, and utterly corrupt man
At once, and let the army heed this warning,
Assenting on the spot with all their hearts."

The Earth Swallows Qārūn, His Wealth, and His Companions

As Kalīm Allah thus entreated God
And sought this habitation for Qārūn,
The World Founder, Judge of the Universe,
Monarch of Being at once granted his wish.
The goods, chattels, and beasts,
All that was Qārūn's on the desert plain,
All that surrounded Qārūn there
Filling the desert and the plain,
All that he owned of scattered herds
Hidden on mountains and on plains,
Through a miracle of the Lord of miracles
Came walking toward him; of Qārūn's wealth
Nothing, not a grain of barley, remained behind.[31]
It was all there, surrounding Qārūn,
The earth not visible beneath this wealth.
Those who beheld it were confounded;
How would they ever sort it out again?[32]
God only knows the meaning of all this;
Whom can you turn to when the stars portend ill?
That's what they were saying to one another;

Taking refuge in friendship out of dread.
The earth then suddenly split apart
And swallowed all the longed-for treasure.[33]
When Qārūn saw this, dread filled him with fear;
Deeply distraught, he trembled like a willow.
That was his state when, in a moment,
The earth swallowed him also, by God's decree.[34]
Along with him it swallowed Datan and Abiram[35]
Like trapped game. Then of the others who died
Among all those who had followed vengeful Qārūn,
Seven hundred were swallowed all at once.
Thus did the earth seize them, spreading
General dread by the Creator's decree, while nearby
Stood a close-knit group joining Kalīm,
Full of suffering and care.[36]
When the two hundred and fifty bewildered chieftains,
With censers full of incense in their hands,
Saw Qārūn thus destroyed,
Beheld him perish suddenly,
They were much distraught for Qārūn's sake
And were in awe of what they had seen.
A fire came suddenly from above,
From the seventh heaven,[37] that high sphere.
Yet awhile it burned on the sphere itself
Then struck Hārūn's censer and lept forth.
A flame rose from it suddenly, like an arrow
Set loose by the archer's thumb-stall.
It moved and struck fire above them
And set the army blazing all at once.[38]
Not one of Qārūn's faithful was left alive
Full of awe for Moses and Hārūn;
Smoke rose from them to the emerald sphere;
They turned to ashes, one and all.
That night fourteen thousand Israelite[39] heroes,
Male lions one and all, allied themselves
With Qārūn's group seven hundred strong;
With all their hearts and souls they turned to Qārūn

Full of aversion for their oath to the prophet.
Once joined in a pact they broke away
From their allegiance of old to Moses,
Plotting, they said: "In the morning
We'll attack, exalt heroism and death;
We'll wash off all the water of shame,
And seek revenge for Qārūn's blood.
Why should we be oppressed on his account?"
Thus did they speak of Qārūn's fate.
When they had thus decided to rebel
Against Moses, the lion of God,
The sole Creator struck them down in anger.
That very night they all died on the spot
Relinquishing this way their souls to God.
Next day, when news spread of the fate
Of these denying, treacherous Israelites,
News that a group from their own midst
Had acted this way,[40] such fear and dread
Entered into the hearts of the Israelites that
The memory of joy fled from them at once.
They ceased their talking and, like the sea,
Each churned within from grief.
The prophet's wish having been granted
Qārūn's fortune came to an end.
Kalīm then stood and worshiped God;
He loosened his tongue in grateful praise
Launching a boat on the sea of grace;[41]
His sailor soul skippered it for a while.
Through grace the wind pulled him upward,
And in a moment he cut a path through that sea.
When Kalīm came out from that mighty sea
He walked gracefully, free from grief.[42]

God's Great Name

Kalīm Allah Writes the Great Name of God for the People

By the command of Him Who is Most Generous,[1]
At once Kalīm Allah set down that hymn of praise;

He lined up all Jacob's sons before him
To teach them from the beginning to the end
The praises of the Generous Lord. The prophet
Addressed King[2] Joshua: "Now all our goals
Have been attained; reflect and fear no man.
Be strong; your friend is now the Knower
Of [all] mysteries. When in the company of friends
You head to Canaan, that land the Judge
Himself, Lord of the Universe, has pledged,
He will protect you and destroy your enemies."
When Moses completed writing it he arranged
The Torah into sections, and then the prophet,
The chosen messenger and royal falcon of creation,
Addressed the Levites thus: "O you
Possessors of the Great Name, guardians
Of the glorious Torah, as you now receive
God's praise, accept it among God's commandments.
The Torah's fruits are beautiful,
And all its parts refresh the soul;
As long as it remains a sign for you,
It will bear witness to the state within your midst,
Providing you with many rites and reasons,
Though you are stiff-necked, inclined to treachery
And pretense. I comprehend your deeds;
I know and am aware of all your thoughts, that you
Will fall suddenly into crooked ways,
Yourselves will open wide the door to calamities.
Because I am aware of all your secrets,
Your plots, tricks, arts, and artifices,
And because you are today in this covenant,
Do not tomorrow cease to heed me.
For if you oppose the Lord's command,
You will fall into decrease and disarray.
If you busy yourselves with evil deeds,
God will reject you. And now, O wise
And learned elders, gather all the people
For whom these precepts are intended, that I

Myself may clarify these mysteries to them.
I will reveal to them God's mystery,
Make manifest to them His message.[3]
I will invoke as witness to you concerning them
The earth and firmament, heaven itself:[4]
So that you not bring evil upon yourselves
Nor suddenly don the garments of idolatry.
I know for certain that when I am no more
And remain no longer in your midst,
You will become wicked, stray far from the road,
Grow famous for your evil deeds. The mysteries
I've heard from God I will once more confirm
Their first fruits to you.
I know that you do not remember,
And transgress all those commandments.[5]
But if you walk in crooked ways, calamities
Will buffet you from every side;
However you twist, fore and aft, your sweet water
Will turn to poison. I will relate to you
The evil your bad deeds will engender;
Let not your hearts pursue Ahriman's[6] vision!"
On hearing all those mysteries from the lord
Of generosity,[7] all those wise men went
And brought the judges and elders before
That handsome man. Then once again,
Kalīm Allah began praising the Lord.

Kalīm Allah Explains the Great Name to the People

Thus did the prophet speak: "O pure celestials,
And you, illustrious earthly men,
Open wide your ears to knowledge,
Climb high upon the roof of justice:
Turn not away from His Law,[8]
So that you find life through justice.
Hear from me all these mysteries,
Follow the precepts of the Law.
Like rain I will shower my words; my precepts

Will fall like drops of dew or like the shower
That falls on verdure,[9] restoring its life and beauty,
Like a nourishing rain which revives
The wilted green. When I utter
The Name of the Incomparable Creator,
I will make you hear and remember His Name.
The earth, mountain, and sea will tremble,
Awestruck and full of dread.
Acknowledge His might, for He is
Omnipotent, Bestower, and Veiler.
His will and deed are revealed every moment;
He is the God of old, the long-suffering one.
He has shown us the way of truth,[10] the laws,
The wisdom, and the treasures of the path.[11]
He is gentle and just and knows no crookedness,
He is unique, and He remains with none.
Do you pursue justice as well that you
Die not heedless, like your ancestors.[12]
They did not follow justice and of the precepts
They did not heed one in a hundred.
Although I counseled them all the time,
It was to no effect, they paid no attention;
Of God's precepts they were heedless.
They were exceedingly stiff-necked;
They turned my heart into a storehouse of grief.
When they would hear of the Avenger's wrath
They would rebel at once;
This people was devoid of wisdom, learning,
Knowledge, and gratitude for blessings.
In forty years those champions[13] died on the road,
Everywhere, complaining and ill-tempered.
They did not act justly toward one another;
Their actions were all twisted. They tried
Their Lord; calamity's road they opened for themselves.
Beware, and be not like those errant folk.
Acknowledge the pure and peerless Lord;
Guard night and day against His wrath.

Acknowledge His might; ascribe to Him no partners;[14]
Do not deny Him in your hearts and minds.
He is merciful and compassionate, sustainer,
Munificent pardoner of sins. The world
He did create, a good and lovely place,
Laid out well and perfectly arranged.
You He created for obedience,
Whence you should build your capital;[15]
Were you to travel day and night,
Still your provision is eternal.
The generous Almighty has thus adorned you
And turned you into a mighty and prolific
People; you should be satisfied.
To you I have shown the edifice of faith;
All is for you, O faithful folk.
The customs of the law, the road to salvation
I have shown you so that you can attain salvation,
And when you appear before God
On Resurrection Day, they will be your stock,
Earning the profit. Your time passes in years;
What will happen through aeons of Time?
Question the learned and wise men so that
Happiness will befriend you.
They will reveal the secrets of the world,
Show you the bright path.[16] And when those
Honorable sages turn you to
The manifest God, discern the One
From all realities, do not abide
In the sleep of neglect and tyranny.
For He is One, without like, unique,
Munificent, alive, with no abode.[17]
Ease leads to nothing but corpulence;[18]
Turn from it and find a better state
Lest it should prompt you to forget your God
And come to disregard His precepts.
Stray not from the road, nor let
The darkness of idolatry confound you.

If you sacrifice to idols,
To Lāt,[19] to demons,[20] you will be accursed,
You will become strangers to God, a byword
Among the nations. But now once more you have
The chance to stand up tall and straight;
You are more learned on the path of truth
Than were your forefathers.
None of them were learned; they were contentious
About everything, completely ignorant,
Lacking discernment in matters of faith.
Neither king nor lowly doorman has ever heard
From them the likes of the commandments,
The Lord's precepts and His blessings.
Because they did not heed God's will and covenant
Did not believe His deeds and might,
The Avenger's vengeance broke over their heads;
They have rebelled and therefore have perished.
You should head like lions to that region,
That homeland, that so famous place, and beware,
O great men, do not grow suddenly arrogant in it.
When you behold the royal crown and throne,
Choose not the futile road, for if you do so,
Like the pagans, plagues will come,
You will die suddenly; you will be driven out
From that land, from one end of it to the other,
Your enemies will drag you out in affliction;
Captive you will fall into idolaters' claws,
And you will go astray consumed by grief.
Your homeland He will hand over to the enemy;
One by one He will destroy you.
When you've been rendered helpless through
Your schemes, you will be completely scattered
Over the world. Your enemies will encompass you
On every border, they will oppress you utterly
And continually; men and women alike will tremble
In fear and dread of the leonine enemy.
Youths, children, old men, even the newborn,

Will follow idols whoever they may be.
Affliction will prevail in that whirlpool
Impelled by calamity, toil, and grief.
God told me too, revealed this mystery
To me repeatedly, that the rash enemies will be
Victorious, impudent, and rude, claiming:
"It is we who have caused all this evil;
Pleasant and lovely are our ways and customs;
We are exceedingly mighty
We ourselves ruined the sons of Jacob."[21]
They will think those bad things
Came from them and not from Me;
The hands of enemies will press them hard.
But I will destroy them in a moment;
I will diminish their excesses all at once.
All of your evil deeds, O faithful people,
Are clear, each and every one,
Before the Judge. All that is hidden
Is manifest before Him; He is eternal,
Almighty, sustainer of all.
So you ought not to persevere in wickedness;
Don, all of you, the garments of obedience.
Take wisdom and learning as your models
That you not die of grief and heedlessness.
Take to your hearts the words of God so that
Good fortune will appear to you and be
Your main provision on Resurrection Day;
Your deeds will stand upright,
Your good and bad will stand before the Judge,
And what a Judge—He judges the sun of the East!
He is as bright as the light of the flashing sun,
Omniscient, Creator, and Sustainer.
He placed the sea[22] into His treasury,
Like a helpless ant buried under the ground.
Seek refuge in none but the World Protector,
For He is the creator of all that is created

And He is glorious. He alone grants and
Withdraws life. He wounds and sends the salve.
He has no blemish; no one should suppose so.[23]
He is generous, omnipotent, assisting,
Perennial guide of young and old."
Thus did the prophet sing God's praises,
Such were the pearls he scattered
Among his friends. And when that chief
Imparted the praise to all his friends,
He addressed them once again:
"O faithful friends, these are God's words;
Heed all these precepts; transgress not
Even a jot or tittle of it; bequeath them
Also to your children; the promise[24] must be
Constantly fulfilled. Show them the customs
And the laws, reveal their mysteries to them
So that they will preserve these stipulations
Until the Day of Resurrection. Do not
Despise the Law, do not rebel
Against God's command, for from it you
Derive eternal life, both strength and station,
The wishes of your hearts, the length
Of all your days—so long as you,
Like the queen in chess, do not deviate from it.
So long as you cultivate this way,
Faithful to custom, all will be well with you,
You will live untried, without hatred,
In that land the Judge grants to you,
A gift full of healing, which He bestows on you
In good faith. You will dwell in it for many years,
You will drive out of it all your enemies.
Your wishes will be fulfilled there
As they had been at the Reed Sea."
When the prophet revealed to them
Those hidden mysteries, he lit the lamps
Of their eyes through his teachings.

And when the sons of Jacob heard this from him,
One and all they chose the way of this path.[25]

The Tale of Job

Beginning the Tale of Job

A wise sage once related[1] that
Eight children were born to brave Nahor.[2]
'Uz was his oldest and firstborn,[3]
Greatest among his brethren;
The other name he bore was Job.
He was much loved by God,
An honored, God-fearing man,
His woof and warp.
The Almighty bestowed on him great wealth,
Livestock, estates, and money without count.
When that mishap occurred to Dinah
Through low-born Shekem,[4] they killed him;[5]
Of all his folk no child was spared.
Then some years after that, Jacob
Married his daughter to Job.[6]
And in due time that moon-cheeked one
Presented Job with many children.
Daily his wealth increased, while he
Held God dear in every way and was
Perpetually bound to praise Him,
Never diverging from this path.
Satan was jealous of him[7] for he
Deemed obedience[8] to God his chief occupation.
The Almighty said to him: "O malicious one,
You've set yourself on fire through ignorance,
And cast your acts of worship to the wind.[9]
Why do you pursue patient Job?
You can't deflect him from the path
Nor trap him in the claws of sin.
I gave him guidance worthy of him;
Beware, you will not turn him off the path.

He's my most devoted servant, a veritable
Storehouse of worship, gratitude, and prayer."
Satan replied to the Incomparable:
"O You who provide sustenance to
Sultan and dervish alike, you gave
To Job all that he needs and crowned him
With the turban of good fortune;
Why should he not excel in worshiping You?
He's merely peddling flattery and fraud
To Your Excellency. You'll know
His real devotion if You take back
His wealth and riches. Then You'll not see
From him half an hour's worth of worship
Daily, or even in a year. It was all due
To wealth; he loves the material gifts of Time."
Then the Creator said to Iblīs: "O you
Most wretched creature in the universe,
Whether he owns property or not, it is
His worship that strews dust into your eyes!"
Satan replied: "If You will make him poor,
And withdraw all You have given him,
He'll cease remembering to praise You;
He'll cast Your worship to the winds.
Entrust him to my claws and let me
Suddenly fling him into the enemy's mouth.[10]
He'll stop his praise and glorifying,
And will soon wash his face in sin's waters."
Then God,
The Almighty ruler of the universe,
The peerless deity, answered accursed Satan:
"I'll hand Job over to you now;
I'll place him in your clutches. Destroy,
At one fell swoop all of his wealth;
Leave not a trace of all his blessings."[11]
At once Satan girded himself for the task,
Plotting against the faithful Job.

35 First he turned his aim against the livestock
By casting pestilence into their midst
Until they all perished; from his
Accursed snare none did escape.
The shepherds went to Job and told him
About the massacre this way: "Your flocks
Have perished all at once
Through the Avenger's vengeance."[12]
But Job replied: "It is no cause for grief;
What comes from the Almighty is not unjust.
God gave it and it is His once more;[13]
This does not trouble me." And then
40 He bowed and kissed the ground
Offering thanks to God once more,
Increasing his devotion yet again.
Satan was overwhelmed by pain,
As if an arrow had pierced his heart.
In other ways he carried out his design,
Attacking Job with all the means he had;
Within a few days Job was poor,
But still his heart grieved not. His worship
Did not decrease by so much as a hairsbreadth,
And day and night he prayed to God.
45 His deeds astonished Satan;
He turned his face aside for shame,
And stood in wonder.

God's Discourse with Satan Concerning Job

The Almighty said to Satan: "O ill-starred
Villain, Job's worship has not diminished.
He is as he was before, with all his heart
He offers Us each moment hundreds of blessings."
Satan replied again: "O You who provide daily
For mankind, birds, and beasts,
Job's happiness comes from his children;
On their account his heart is bent on worship;
50 For their sake does he worship;

It is for them that he exerts himself.
If You take back his offspring,
Leaving not one behind, he will no longer
Exert himself in worship, he'll drink no more
From the goblet of yearning[14] for You."
The Almighty replied: "O black day, you are
Impure, malevolent tyrant of creatures,
I will destroy them on your account,
Inebriate them from the cup of death.
Yet Job will not remain without thanks
To me and will continue strewing the dust
Of *tawḥīd*[15] in your eyes."
Job had from Dinah
Three daughters and seven sons, each[16]
With a friendly face, clever and bright.
By God's command they all died within an hour
Entrusting their souls to Him.
On seeing this, Job cried and lamented, saying:
"What shall I do? What course shall I pursue?"
Again he increased his thanks and devotion;
Not one moment did he do without them.
Then God addressed Satan once more:
"You devious, accursed traitor,
My benefactor's thanks have not decreased;
He is worthy of Our mercy."

Satan's Debate with God Regarding Job's Health

Satan replied: "He is in good health,
That's why he perseveres with praise and thanks.
Once he fell ill his tongue
Would cease to utter further praise."
The Veiler[17] replied to Satan yet again:
"O you source of calamities,
Misfortune, and affliction, I grant you
Power over his body;[18] I open wide
The door of misery before him.
Go, try him

With illness and turn his body into
A storehouse of pain and tribulation,
But injure not, malicious, ignorant dog,
His life."[19] That very moment vicious Satan,
By God's command came before Job and
Of a sudden rubbed his hands on him.
Job cried out from underneath his hands,
Barbs then assailed his body; the rose
Of his pleasant life turned to thorns.
Fever racked his entire body
Making him cry aloud,
Blood flowed from his scratching nails,
From every part of his whole being.
His body was an open wound from head to toe
And full of sores. Then worms
Began to crawl over him;[20] blood and pus
Flowed from his every vein.
That pain and torment went on day and night
And yet time in, time out, he remembered God.
And when a worm would fall off its place,
He'd pick it up and put it back,[21] saying:
"God has made me your daily sustenance;
One should never let go of one's sustenance."[22]
Thus he endured the worms and the pain humbly,
Warm-hearted and in cold blood.

Dinah's Dispute with Job

His wife kept saying to him all the time,[23]
"My dear, it isn't appropriate
To offer thanks and praise; how
Can you be thankful now for wealth when
Not a barley grain of it do you own?
You have nor gold, nor children, nor your health;
Illness has turned your full moon into a crescent.
Seek all you may, your body does not hold
Good health the size of a fingertip.
Your body is a sieve full of holes,

Front and back; weak and exhausted by the worms
Your world has now become as small as an ant's eye.
For which of its boons can you be thankful?
The words of a strange, undignified old man!
Wherever your thanks to God happen to fall,
On that same spot they cannot endure.
You have no business thanking God;
In vain do you live on. Do you think
You can deceive God if you patiently endure
The grief and pain He has dealt you?
Many, and more devoted than you,
Has He killed. Desist now
From worship a few days;
Devise a remedy for your own pain,
Mind your own business for a while.
Praising God is of no use to you;
A sick man may be free from all such duties.
Do you not know that God pardons
The sick and afflicted from fast and prayer?"[24]

Job Answers Dinah, His Wife

Job answered his wife thus: "My dear,
Why are you so arrogant and thoughtless?
I was God's friend while in good health
For many long years. What if today
I have become poor and my heart is racked
By pain and suffering?
I despair not but that the Almighty will
Once more bestow His Grace on us.
He will once more raise my head up to the spheres,
He will set me free from grief and pain and sorrow.
Through His Grace I will regain my health
And find respite from illness and weakness.
He will rekindle the lamp of my good fortune,
Consume together all my griefs and cares.
I shall find a light out of this darkness;
I shall find release from grief and injury.

I despair not of the Almighty's mercy,
For suddenly He will light the sun for me,
Turn my dark night into a bright day,
And all my days to a New Year's festival.
For the Almighty fetters no one without
Opening for him a hundred better paths.
Whatever He does is just, and I
Have greatly benefited from it.
His acts are joined to Wisdom;
He the merciful, generous, and forgiving."[25]

Dinah's Second Dispute with Job

Dinah replied, "Gratitude has brought you
Nothing but sickness and bad luck.
Do you wish to regain good health
From this illness, weakness, and grief?
You're old and have one foot in the grave;
This time I know you'll die for sure.
In your old age are you wishing to regain
The strength and benefits of youth?
You once owned heaps of gold and silver,
Handsome servants, and swift horses,
And you gave thanks for them; foolishness
Makes you ignorant of what you're saying.
If you wish something from the world,
Stop singing God's praises. You'll see
Your goods and wealth back in dreams.
Don't be in such a hurry with your thanks;
Do you think you'll see anything again
Of all your fortune? Dream on!
Youth is gone, you are old and sick;
Your time has come, and you will die.
Desist from idle thoughts; you're sick,
How can your strength return?
Calamity and grief have turned you upside down;
How can you after this dream on
Of wealth and goods? Because you're patient

In grief and affliction, do you think
You can deceive God?"[26]

Job Answers Dinah a Second Time

Then Job answered his wife:
"O harridan, leave me to my pain and grief!
What do you know of my body's pain?
It's best for me to endure it.
You know I'm captive to this misery;
My captor is the Incomparable Himself.
That hour when I relinquish my breath
The time of death will have arrived.
My heart seeks nought but God's pleasure;
My tongue utters only His praise.
I hope that through His grace my pain
Will find a remedy. Beware, speak not
With me of things that you should not.
Stop trying to free me from gratitude.
I do not wish to utter one hairsbreadth less;
I praise the Almighty with all my heart and soul."
Thus Job endured all his misfortunes
And bravely bore the sorrow of his heart;
Never did he cry aloud from that pain,
And bore his pain with both strength and ease.
They called him Patient Job;[27]
Through patience he became world famous;
By God Himself he was called The Patient.
They say that for seven long years[28]
That brave man endured the agony of worms,
But in Scripture[29] it is said
He suffered only one year of grief,
Affliction, pallor, and broken health.
Humbly he put up with the worms
And tended each one with great care.
He nourished them like a nursemaid, sitting
Sometimes in the sun and sometimes in shade.[30]
He had no other friends but the worms,

No other companions with whom to share his grief.[31]
The heavenly elite were deeply grieved
By his continuous pain and fever.
They cried to Almighty God for his sake
And then the Almighty went into action.

Ardashīr-nāmah (The Book of Ardashīr)

The Courtship and Marriage of Esther and Ardashīr

Shah Bahman Summons the Maidens

One day,[1] the prince and monarch of Iran,
Kayānid[2] heir, refuge of lions,
The most noble Ardashīr Bahman,[3]
Sultan of ʻIraq, Rūm,[4] and Arman,[5]
Reposed among his fortunate lords
And sat like a lion upon his throne,
All smiles from good fortune and joy,
Flashing his teeth into his cup of wine.
Full of good cheer he quaffed date wine;
The rebec's sounds brightened his mood.
But when the wine rose to his head,
He removed the veil of modesty;
Patience, rest, and repose left him;
He squirmed; the air around him heated up;
When wine and warm air cheered one another,
Well gone in lust and ardor's fire,
The shah began to long for the confined idols,[6]
But he resumed decorum for reputation's sake,
He calmed himself, continued drinking,
And sat feasting until supper time.[7]
As soon as it arrived, he summoned Hegai[8]
And said to him: "Run, bring to my harem
In all haste one of those seven[9] graceful idols;
Let me investigate her good and bad,
From her attain my heart's desire."
When Hegai heard the shah's command,
He took a sweet-lipped, moon-cheeked girl,

Adorned her like Venus and brought her to the harem,
To the sun.[10] The dazzling charmer spent the night
There with the shah until daylight came round;
Time's lips broke into a smile; the bright sun
Laughed, its teeth displaying,[11] the shah was drunk
By his companion's side, roused by the scent
Of the grape's juice.
Lords usually entrust one special servant
To set the bait for them into the snare, thus
The shah ordered Hegai to bring to his harem
Nightly a different ravishing, slender beauty,
Of the six remaining graceful moon-faced idols,
Each one of them bright-faced, with curly tresses.
In a week, one by one, Hegai brought them all
To the shah's palace, as he had wished,
For seven nights entrusting to him
Sedition-stirring beauties with sweet lips.
But however much each night the shah clasped
The idols, Jupiter could not take wing.[12]
For among all these he did not find
His love, his houri, his heart's companion.
His horoscope confounded him; each morning
The shah drove away another from his presence;
And though compelled to drive each one away,
He brought in yet another to his chamber.
Although he greatly honored them,
With feasting, pleasure, and indulgence,
Each time the shah reached out
To a lovely idol with moon cheeks,
Cruel fate would thwart his heart's desire.
Like a green shoot, grief sprouted in his heart.

The Shah Calls Hegai and Asks Him About Esther

There is nothing better than a loving friend;
How can one live without a bosom friend?
Life in the loved one's company
Is better than eternal life.

With such a friend, a companion, life is good;
Without, time is not worth a barley grain.
When Hegai saw the shah so inflamed,
With such deep sorrow in his heart,
He understood how the shah felt, that he
Was looking for his friend, his true beloved.
He sought the hour to approach him and
Came one night unawares into the harem;
Like a lion, he made haste to serve the shah,
And thus disclosed[13] to him the secret of Esther:[14]
"There is a tender idol, exalted in beauty
And learning; the likes of her has never been seen
In the world, no, not even among the houris
Of Paradise. Should you but see her cheeks
One night, and only in a dream,
You would never again look at moonlight.
Compared to her full moon, the moon
Is but a crescent; next to her stature
The cypress appears bent.[15]
Rest tranquil, only take her into your arms,
And see what a fountain you will drink from!
In her embrace a thousand Vashtis become
As boats gliding on water.
In learning, beauty, and grace,
In wisdom, goodness, and eloquence,
She is peerless in this world; so,
Don't throw a pitcher on a hard stone.[16]
You do possess such a delicate houri,
You have the lovely one within your reach;
Say then, what worries you?
Why do you distress yourself so much?
I've been her teacher these ten long months,[17]
I've seen all her good deeds;
Nothing bad will ever come from her,
Nothing but learning and good deeds;
Not even as much as a cup of water did she
Ever request from me;[18] she's never troubled

Anyone; now that I've shared with you the secret
I've been guarding,[19] don't just sit there
Helpless. Get busy! Be at ease about her,
Lift up your head to the fourth heaven;[20]
Marry that lovely idol and imbibe
Comfort without grief, until
You repossess your peace of mind
And happily sit again in your wonted station."
Hearing this from the devoted servant,
So truthful and sincere, Bahman replied:
"You're right in everything you say;
You seek nothing but our peace of mind.
Rightly you speak; tomorrow
I will lay the foundation of my happiness.
I will take the graceful Esther into my arms,
And stop my delusions. I'll send her
Many assloads of gifts and jewelry,
Musk, and I myself will provide her dowry;
I'll drink the sweet draft of union with her."
Light from this talk rose to the spheres
And hurled uproar upon the world's inhabitants.
The mirror of grace made its appearance;
A flame flashed from the crystal goblet.
At sunset the shah sat upon his throne
Glorious; Venus and Mercury fled out of shame.
The world turned amber yellow; dust rose
From the world's rubbish heap.

Shah Bahman Sends Wedding Gifts to Esther

He Who knows the mystery of this tale,
He ordained guidance through Wisdom.
Since Bahman was intent on union with Esther
He made arrangements to attain his joy.[21]
He ordered the old treasurer to open,
Without regret, the doors of the royal treasury
That he might attain his goal,
And relish union in the rose garden.

Thus he commanded Fīrūz[22] right away:
"Today, out of my treasury and stable take
A hundred rare, beautiful gifts of fabric,
A hundred bolts of satin, silk, and brocade,
A hundred *manns*[23] of gold[24] as red as fire,
A hundred elegant, lovely Turkish slave girls,
A hundred elegant Turkish and Chinese slave boys,
A hundred swift mules with decorated saddles,
A hundred hidden royal jewels, a hundred
Rose-cheeked, well-proportioned eunuchs,
A hundred great horses, swift as the wind,
Royally harnessed, saddled, caparisoned,
A hundred strings of embellished camels,
Covered with ornaments, furnishings, and carpets,
Wearing anklets of gold and carrying
Loads of gold, sugar candy, and sweets;
Ten beautifully decorated litters
From the sweet-lipped ones of Qandahar.[25]
Prepare all this as quickly as a lion;
Pay heed, delay not in this matter."
Fīrūz, the faithful vizier, saw to it
That all was properly carried out.
Then he came to the shah, blessed him,
And said: "I have prepared everything
And hasten into the shah's presence;
Tell me what plans are you issuing from
Your throne, your signet ring, your sovereignty?"
On hearing this from Fīrūz, Bahman said:
"Wisdom and knowledge are learned from you.
Since you have prepared the gifts according
To the manner and custom of Kay Qobād,[26]
Take them and drive them swiftly on;
Go with them all to Esther, accompanied by
Banners, royal parasols, golden kettledrums,
Tambourines, trumpets, and brass flutes."
Fīrūz took leave of the shah
And set out with a retinue of warriors,

Heading toward that offspring of the moon.
The sound of trumpets and kettledrums rose upward,
The surface of the earth grew dark as night
From the dust of hooves and mounts;
The heroes all held mace and sword in hand
And rode their horses like wild lions;
Cheerful, and in high spirits.
They set out toward Esther; you'd say
The firmament itself might tumble from
The kettledrums' roar, the wailing of the flutes.
When these and all the trumpets blared,
They stirred up the inhabitants of Shush,[27]
Who ran to see the grand procession,
Lining up row upon row; the white chain
Passed with kettledrums, waving proud banners.
Boldly then Hegai[28] entered the palace[29]
And straight away went to the moon-faced sapling;
The presents, all the gifts brought, were given
To Mordekai on the dazzling beauty's behalf;
When Fīrūz had handed over the bridal gifts item by item,
He returned to Ardashīr, the exalted Khosrow.[30]
He drank with the king as his friend,
A boon companion of the prince.

Mordekai Advises Esther

When wealth and fortune act virtuously,
Wealth sews a cloak out of good fortune
For one who is auspicious, and for a while
He holds on to it; but when the time comes,
He must return it. When Mordekai saw all
The shah's gifts, their vast quantity
Meant nothing in his eyes.
"How far did Qārūn[31] go with his wealth?
How did he topple from greatness?
To me God's mercy surpasses gold and silver,
It is greater by far than treasures,
Signet rings, and thrones.

He who gave life to a weakling like me,
And gave me reason, eloquence, and wisdom,
He provides my daily sustenance,
And never diminishes our portion.
What have we to do with gold and silver?
This is now a great burden on my soul."
Thus musing he debated with himself a while
About those gifts and presents, then
He summoned Esther, the concealed;[32] he sat down
And seated her before him, saying:
"O lovely idol, how sweet you are,[33]
How seemly is your manner and deportment;
The World Keeper endowed you even as He
Endowed the nine revolving spheres.
Listen, and pay attention: I will offer
A few words of advice; pray, attend to them,
And if you heed them, surely you will remain
Immortal in both worlds.
God's light is manifest in your face;
Your sunny nature is visible from afar.
This, then, O child, is my advice to you,
A sweet, good, pleasant counsel;[34]
When you become intimate with the shah,
Take care not to forget it!
Guard carefully the spirit of wisdom
And the fear of God daily in your heart.
Beware, engage not in evil deeds;
Veil yourself from sin and crime;
Do not foolishly trouble anyone;[35]
Each day the world elevates a person,
Entrusting to him a new station, but
How can one's heart grow attached to it?[36]
None can reside secure in glory.
Behold the treasure that the oyster shell conceals
From the rain drops falling from the clouds;
When it plucks its chosen drop out of the air,
In the end, the melting drop becomes a pearl;

Then when the diver leaps into the sea,
Bringing out of its depths an oyster shell,
Much like a lion contending for his prey,
He scatters it upon the ground like sand.
The pearl is then pierced through its navel;
No shell remains on it; though it has nourished
Every pearl, it must relinquish each of them,
Teach them the joy of flight. Only for two
Or three days the shell enjoyed the pearl;
Another came and took it away from him.[37]
Since in the end the pearl could not rest
In the shell's mouth, in the depths of the sea,
Helpless, it donned the garment of patience,[38]
Enduring the while Time's violent sting.
Since throne and station abide with no one,
What can a person lacking experience understand?
Therefore do not consider the throne's station today;
Think of tomorrow. Soothe those who are fallen,
Do what should be done. Do not seek to oppress
The wretched; have little or nothing
To do with anyone; if you do nothing bad,
You will have nothing to fear from evil;
Be passive;[39] don't struggle with yourself.
I have one more piece of advice for you,
Which I've kept well hidden in my heart:
Beware, reveal to none your origins and faith![40]
Conceal your lineage. Comprehend this matter well,
Take it to heart, heed all my counsel:
The royal ruby lies in the stone's heart.
Be ever prudent in dealings with the shah,
Be gentle and obliging: his affairs
Are set apart from those of beggars, princes,
And gatekeepers."
Having thus counseled Esther
Fully, Mordekai kissed the moon-face
On both her eyes, her face, her pure countenance.
When morning came he made arrangements,

Busied himself on the veiled one's behalf,
Though while in repose a moment,
Poisonous thoughts filled his heart.
Early in the morning Hegai arrived
Swiftly, sent by the king.
He adorned graceful Esther according to Kayānid custom,
As the shah wished, and thus displayed
That hidden treasure while hiding her in jewels.
As morning donned its garment,
Fortune placed a crown upon her head.

How Shah Bahman Married Esther

When the shah assumed his throne
The sun rose from the well's depths;
Trumpets resounded, left and right,
The clamor of fierce thunder from the clouds.
Shush was in uproar, its people
Full of gossip and chatter.
Fīrūz, the son of Bīshūtan,[41] and the warriors,
Mīlād,[42] and the heroes of Iran's kingdom,
Left the shah's presence bearing gifts,
Scattering coins. Arrived at Esther's palace,
The princes formed two facing lines.
Esther, behind a veil, like Venus
Presented the visage of the bright moon.
Upon her face she wore a beautiful veil;
Down to her feet tumbled her lasso tresses.
Softly, with graceful delicacy, she walked
With measured pace, like a beautiful partridge.
When the nobles saw that concealed face approach,
At once they brought forward a litter;
The lady within sat accoutered in fortune
And happiness while moon-faced slaves,
Girls and boys, waited upon that heavenly image.
Accompanied by minstrels and mirth,
They neared the shah's gate,
Where ladies attendant on the shah,

Together with the wise *mobed* Hegai,[43] came out
To fetch that moon, that jewel of the crown,
Ornament, and magnificence; sprinkling musk,
Rose water, gold, and adornments, chattering,
Carrying jewel caskets, scattering,
Gold coins, jewels, over the shah's lady,
Asking her countless questions.
The lady emerged from the litter
Like the moon from behind dark clouds;
Accompanied by beauties with pomegranate breasts
She entered the royal bedchamber.
Once more the houris scattered coins on her
To express their veneration and devotion;
She was worthy of a hundred thousand times more!
Her good fortune and happiness were young.
Then the mobed gladly contracted the marriage
With the hero Bahman, the just shah.
Afterward the monarch sat upon his throne and drank,
Agitated, as he recalled that moon.
All evening long he did not put the goblet down,
Offering wine to nobles and commoners alike;
Then when the wine had settled in him,
Helpless, for he was drunk, he rose.

How Shah Bahman Went to Esther's Harem

Like a partridge strutting toward a peahen,[44]
The shah entered the harem and came to his wife.
Impatient to be united with her, this fortunate prince
Came toward that moon upon the throne.
Ladies-in-waiting all departed quickly
From the moon's presence, all except her nurse.
Smiling and full of cheer, the shah
Drew back the veil from the moon's face.
When he glimpsed her cheek like the night,
He lost his reason, fell down senseless
Into the well, a foreign traveler exhausted
By the road. The lady, seeing him all undone,

Placed his head upon her knee. Awakening,
Bahman perceived his head was on the beauty's thigh.
She rose then and sat down by his side;
He reached for the beloved's curls.
Then that dark night beheld the sun,
The beauty of Venus in evening's court.
He was astonished by her radiance
And called down blessings on her lovely face.
Through the entire night until daybreak;
He exulted on sleep's couch, with heart on fire.
Through marriage, love, and kinship, he attained
His heart's desire from that beloved idol.
When the sun's countenance broke into a smile
Upon seeing the world, flashing its teethlike rays,
The earth became a glorious garden,
Smiling and radiant, pure and bright.
The shah rose happy from Esther's embrace,
Not the least sated by his beloved's face;
Love for her had so distracted him,
He plucked the rose and never felt the thorns,
Thinking of her only as the moon,
Loving her cheeks more than his own soul.
A heavy, jewel-encrusted crown the shah
Placed on the moon's head, bestowing on her
Vashti's station and all her former titles.
He sought every moment to please her;
He made her empress of the world.
Since the beginning of his auspicious rule
Seven years had passed. Having married the moon,
In union with her the shah was satisfied.
If Vashti ever entered into his thoughts,
Esther would overtop her like a crown.
In sunlight who needs the moon? If crowned,
Who needs a hat? So night and day the shah
Burned with impatience to see that lovely image.
Six days he remained within the palace
With the rose-cheeked, dazzling beauty,

And on the seventh dawn, when he arose,
He pulled himself together and sat upon the throne.
Gold coins and pearls were showered on him;
The palace was filled with game.[45]
The victorious shah then threw a feast;
From the first day he laid the foundations
Of the edifice.[46] He invited all famous men,
Heroes and warriors, and all excellent horsemen;
Wine sparkled in their goblets like
The rubies and the jewels of Badakhshan.[47]
Date wine intoxicated all the guests,
They grew frenzied, conceited, laughing;
Wine went round the shah and the heroes
Twice, three times, scouring grief
From proud hearts, increasing mirth,
Good cheer, and pleasure. The sages say,
Drinking pure wine to the sound of *rūd*[48] and song
Is better than another life.
What a pity youth is cast to the winds!
The sound of the rūd players rose
In the presence of the shah and the nobles;
The lute and the drum, the oud and the flute
Wailed while Bahman quaffed the pure wine.
With *sāz*[49] in hand, having so happily plucked the rose,
He burst into song, a drunken nightingale;
All melancholy sounds were lifted away
From the exalted name of Ardashīr; each moment
The drum, the flute, the lute, and the dulcimer
Struck a different mode. When the shah saw
Good cheer drown out sorrowful tunes,
With the sāz, and happiness, he then commanded
The treasurer to bring forth at once
Assloads of treasures and coins,
And was promptly obeyed; the pen cannot record
So many belts, headpieces, and tunics.
Then the shah gave to each according to his merit
Gold, treasures, garments, and much money.

Then he addressed those inclined to pride:
"Desist from tyranny; strive to be fair and just;
Do not put on the garments of injustice.
Refrain from cruelty and oppression; beware
Indulgence in fancies. Let Iran and its frontiers
Be tranquil, known for their lion champions;
It is my command that anyone beware
Who takes unjustly even a barley grain's worth
From another; render injustice weak in cities,
On the roads and the byways.
I swear by the pure Almighty, Lord
Of heaven and earth's expanse, whoever
Pursues injustice toward a living being,
Will not be able to conceal his misdeed;
If he tries, upon my soul, he will not live an instant.
I'll bruit his name about in every region;
Before the princes he'll become a warning
Both to the common men and the elite;
His morning will completely turn to night."
The clever shah held forth on justice
The while the heroes all bowed down
And kissed the ground before him to approve
His words. Then they replied: "We all
Seek but to carry out the shah's will,
Pledging our armies and our allegiance;
If any should act unjustly, let none
Survive in the world." Thus they conversed
Till dinnertime with cups of wine and date wine
In their hands. The sun revolved within the dome,
Turned amber in the desert, and departed,
Along with the stars, hiding from man's sight.
Then all the nobles turned into night worshipers;
Intoxicated by pure wine, each one
Took leave of Bahman and went to his own palace.
When the shah saw that night was all around
He entered the harem and went to Esther.
Affectionate and tender, he loved her

By day and night; although he had a multitude
Of lovely, moonlike beauties, he was sated
With all of them and chose to unite only with Esther. . . .

The Birth of Cyrus

Esther Gives Birth to Cyrus

The Wise, Incomparable Creator, Lord
Of the Heavens, of commoners and the nobility,
He who creates offspring from royal seed,
Who creates roses and greenery,
None knows His hidden mystery,
And none remains forever happy or afflicted;
Sultans and beggars alike are His prisoners
None steps away from His door.
He aids His slaves' affairs, He strives against none
Unjustly.
When Esther became the consort of the king
Of kings, she found dignity and an exalted station.
That houri delighted the shah's heart;
He saw nothing but light from her two cheeks.
He spent his time with her in joy and pleasure;
He enjoyed her company and making passionate love.
Through the will of the Greatest Father, Esther
Became pregnant,[50] and when her time of birth came,
God opened up for her the gates of purity,
[And she gave birth] to a beautiful, sun-cheeked boy,
[Worthy] of the crown and throne of Jamshīd.[51]
The shah rejoiced at the child's birth;
He uprooted oppression from the world.
He rolled back the tax on caravans,
Distributed much gold and money to the poor.
Because of his generosity and gifts
No indigent remained in Shush.
The shah empowered the dervish, who
In place of grief,[52] now gambled with gold.
Esther rejoiced at her newborn,
And she offered thanks to God; she chose two

Lovely, loving nursemaids for the child,
To nurture and educate him,
Help him to grow into a tall cypress.
On the midwives she bestowed gold, silver,
And colorful garments.
When Cyrus turned
Four years old, his face was like the spring
And like a tulip; that exalted princely jewel
Indeed grew tall, a cypress. Without him,
At dawn and sunset, the shah found no repose.

Shah Bahman Gathers the Astrologers to Instruct Cyrus

One day clever Bishutan said to brave Ardashīr:
"The time has come for the prince's eyes to be opened
To knowledge, to know good and bad, more and less;
His days should not be wasted." When the shah heard
His grand vizier's advice, he deemed it just;
He summoned many wise men appropriate for the task.
He gave each one of the learned men gold, gifts,
And his child, that they should each and every one
Teach him what every prince, what every brave hero
And famous man should know, brighten his face
With bravery and knowledge. When he was
Fourteen years old, fortune spread its wings
Over his head: in all the cities of Iran,
At the courts of intrepid heroes, no one
Waged war like him; steel was like copper in his hand.
Lions avoided confronting him;
His arrows could pierce rocks.
Were he to attack an elephant,
It would be rendered abject in his grasp.
If he would topple a tower from a mountaintop,
Mount Alburz[53] itself would be crushed.
If he unsheathed his sword, no one
Could stand against him in battle.
If he ungloved his champion's claw,
Men were carried away by fright.

He became great and famous; in horsemanship
He was like Rustam, the son of Zāl.[54]

Ezra-nāmah (The Book of Ezra)

Cyrus Grants Permission to Return and Rebuild the Temple

A man engaged in ugly acts[1]
What are the acts that follow him?
God sets misfortune over his head,
Lets him endure injustice, violence,
And oppression; humbles him with affliction,
Abases him, drags him in blood.
A wise man long ago declared
That none can fathom the Deity's acts.
When the Temple, that Special Quarry,[2]
Was destroyed, the edifice lived on
In heroes' hearts. Kalīm's[3] people were
Laid low, afflicted in the end
Through their own deeds, for which
That Special House, site of divine rendezvous,
In ruins lay for seventy long years.[4]
Time came, and at long last
That Site of Mercy was set free
Of troubles and calamities.
Two prophets of God lived in those days,
As bright as the sun and the moon:
Ezra was one, the other Haggai,[5]
Who was the elder[6] of the two.
(No prince but Mattatiah[7] survived
Of the tribe and progeny of Judah.)
The prophet Ezra in appearance was
Exceptionally endowed and was most generous.
Often he proffered his advice to Kalīm's people
And greatly did he help them, warning:
"Heed God's own counsel; take to heart
My command. Strive to obey
His judgment lest you find yourselves

Drowning in raging, boiling poison.
Know that God is All Forgiving and All Pure;
Banish all evil from your hearts,
And turn yourselves into proud cypresses,
Become, each one of you, a hidden treasure.
Then you will attain your heart's desire;
Shining like Venus, the sun, and the moon,
You will radiate light."
Since Ezra often did advise them thus
They set themselves to work.
They turned away from ugly deeds,
Became steadfast in faith.
On seeing them, Ezra's grieved heart
Regained its peace. He took his place joyfully
In the people's assembly and hoisted
The banners of guidance. He said,
Turning to Haggai and to the leaders,
"Bad times have passed and are now gone;
Merciful times have arrived; those evil, ugly,
Difficult, and troublesome days are truly gone.
Be my supporters and my friends;
Be faithful to your own covenant so that
Like heroes we may present ourselves bravely
Before Iran's sovereign. We will reveal to him
Our wretchedness, unveil our secrets,
Until he understands our state
And sets us free from our torment.
He will restore to Canaan the Quarry,
That Special Site of divine rendezvous."[8]
The leaders listened to the prophet's words;
They took to heart his good advice.
That day passed and on the next
Ezra,[9] the great prophet, accompanied
By Haggai, Zekariah,[10] and Mattatiah, the great king,
Went before exalted Cyrus, the phoenix[11]
In the company of three royal falcons.
(There were still other learned, pious,

God-fearing men with Ezra.)
When God's lion[12] came from the road
Unto the palace gates,
Within the righteous portals there stood
Many a cypress-statured courtier, but
When the gatekeeper[13] saw Ezra and his men,
At once he inquired of their needs. Then,
Full of agitation, he went before the shah
And said: "O brave young hero,
There are two or three persons at the gate,
Brave and exalted heroes, requesting
An audience with you. Light radiates
From their faces; none matches the glow
Of beauty on their countenance."
Upon hearing this, Cyrus gave the command:
"Bring them to me at once!"
The gatekeeper ran to admit them; he opened
The gates to the three or four of them.
The shah rejoiced on seeing Ezra
In the company of Haggai and the freeborn chieftains.
But looking at their faces, his heart
Contracted with dread and distress.
Then Mordekai[14] addressed the shah:
"O brave, handsome, and exalted shah,
Know that these chieftains are esteemed;
They are good people, full of discernment:
Prophets, kings, and famous men,
They reign over the people of Kalīm."
He introduced each one by name;
Informed the shah of each one's worth.
Cyrus seated them all with flattery
And cleared the court of all but his intimates.
Then he addressed Mattatiah,[15]
That jewel of the House of Judah:
"Tell us, what do you wish from us
Out of the royal jewels and the treasury?
I will fulfill your wishes;

I know full well what your business is."
On hearing this Mattatiah, that prince of
Judah's House, answered the shah:
"O may your wisdom last forever!
Through you the world is joyful and in bloom;
There has never been a greater shah than you;
In you the state has found its crown and throne!
May neither throne nor crown
Ever be deprived of you;
May your fortune endure forever!
You have succeeded in your father's place;
May you live as long as clouds cross the skies!
Know, O shah, that Canaan's kingdom,
Has been our hearth and home
Since the time of Kalīm, son of ʿImrān.[16]
A divine gift, by the grace of God.
For as long as we were fair and just
In worshiping our God, we prospered:
We possessed treasury, crown, and throne,
As well as victory, might, and fortune;
But when we lost our way, became idolaters,
We sowed the seeds of tyranny and evil;
We were thrown out of our abode in pain;
We became a byword for every evil.
A base and evil man arose; he toppled
Our sovereignty. Seventy years have passed
Since the kingdom's destruction through injustice.
I wish that through your generosity, O exalted one,
We might reinhabit this land. You will thus
Preserve your good name in the world;
You will be remembered in all the prayers
Of Jacob's progeny." Then Cyrus said
To him and to all the chieftains,
Among them to Haggai: "You wish
That I should fulfill your desire; I too
Have a desire that I wish you to fulfill:
That from my own hands, willing or not,

You should accept a cup of wine.[17]
Then I'll fulfill your wish and turn your land
Into the garden of the Ṭūbā tree.[18]
I will restore it everywhere: its land,
Its dwellings, and the rendezvous site."[19]
On hearing this, Mattatiah said: "O you,
Whose generosity is like the waters of the sea,
Today I cannot do so. Neither choose nor strive
To break me. I will now go to my friends,
The leaders and our famous men, to see
What the divine Law rules[20] in such a case.
I shall return tomorrow morning and reveal
All hidden secrets." Having said this,
He and the heroes cheerfully departed
From the shah's presence. Mattatiah then met
With Zekariah, Haggai, and valiant Ezra,
Seeking a ruling on that matter
From the gathering of wise chieftains.
Ezra addressed him thus: "O servant
Of the Living, Unknowable One, the King
Who ever commands the forbidden
And the permitted[21] to Moses' people,
What the exalted shah demands you must perform;
You must drink the cup of refreshing wine;
Accept and drink a cup, lest you
Forfeit your life at the hands of evil men[22]
And so that the Special House, O wise man,
Should be rebuilt once more."[23]
When the sun, out of the lapis lazuli firmament
Showed forth its yellow cheeks, it plunged
Into modesty's ocean, like lightning
Drowning in the boundless sea;
The world lamented, mourned over the sun's loss,
Dressed itself in black from head to toe,
Wailing and sighing, full of pain,
Regret and sorrow, at this malevolent design.
When clear morning beheld the world this way

It struck modesty prostrate and rent patience;
It dressed itself in silver, abandoning all
Distinctions of good and bad, of this and that.[24]
Mattatiah arose from a sound sleep
And went before the shah with Zekariah,
Haggai, and two or three others,
Freeborn men, well-known leaders.
When Cyrus saw him, with flattery
He made room for him on his throne,
Seated him according to rule and custom,
As if he were the Khosrow[25] of Rūm, Hind, or Chīn.[26]
Then Cyrus handed him a goblet of pure wine,
Saying "Drink up!"—and found his wish fulfilled.
Mattatiah took from him and drank the cup of wine;
Finding no remedy for it, he sought none.
At once Cyrus gave the command
To rebuild the kingdom of Canaan;
And to rebuild that Special House,
They would donate measures of gold and silver.[27]
Kalīm's people rejoiced at this; they have
Survived the times of tribulation.
Bad deeds engender only bad; spinning,
The world returns to its beginnings.[28]

How Ezra, Peace Be upon Him, Wrote the Ineffable Name and Went to the City of Moses' People

Now Ezra the prophet saw that Canaan once more
Would flourish by God's firm command,
And Jacob's descendants would return
Full of joy, laughter, and good cheer.
But ever since evil Bukhtanṣar had burned it,[29]
There was no longer Torah in the land.
Ezra, however, had memorized it all;
Thus skilled through miracle and might.
He wrote it all down as it was at first;
Not a jot or tittle of it was changed; then
He gave this precious gift and offering

To Jacob's progeny. But Kalīm's people said:
"O moon-faced prophet, you made the Torah
Manifest to us through God's will and grace;
Might not an error, more or less,
Have crept in unawares? Seventy years have,
After all, passed by since that unjust king
Burned the Word. Since then the world
Has been bereft of Torah; none has recited it.
Yet all of it, the entire Torah, the words
Of the Living Judge, survived preserved
In your heart. But it may be
That you remember a little more or less,
O excellent man. Like a star or quicksand
You must journey to Rekab's land,[30]
To the progeny of God's lion,[31]
The descendants of Moses, son of ʿAmram.
They have preserved the correct Torah
And they will show it to you. Search closely
That it match your own copy, and then
Return it to us so that once more
We may become intimate with it."
When Ezra heard this from them,
He was distraught and grieved. But then
That great leader thought of a recourse:
He sat down and wrote out the Great Name.[32]
At once he flew off like the wind,
Toward the quicksands and the promised place.
When those chosen people beheld him,
They ran to surround him. Right away Ezra
Recited the Torah aloud to their wise leaders;
Verse by verse, he recited it all, leaving
Kalīm's progeny smiling: not even a dot's worth
Of difference existed between Kalīm's
And Ezra's versions. The leaders spoke to him;
That illustrious gathering addressed him thus:
"It is as if you were an angel,[33]

Kneaded out of purity and light;
How else by heart could you have written down
The entire Torah, omitting nothing from its proper place?[34]
In truth, this can't be done by flesh and blood,
O mighty cypress, moon-faced one." Ezra,
With cheerful heart, snapped up the words
And took off like the wind, flew off to Canaan
As swift as the phoenix, back to the people of 'Imrān;[35]
Kalīm's folk, like tall cypresses, met him gladly.
He came cheerfully to them but they all feared him;
They turned to invocation[36] and prayer,
Thankful to have survived destruction.
The celestial spheres heeded their wishes,
One firmament after another, all eight.[37]
Their revolutions brought nothing but gifts;
Even Time[38] seemed to grant them eternity.
As long as you possess knowledge of God,
And engage in worship and praise, your work
Will be successful; you'll be endowed with soul
From head to toe. In upright deeds,
Nothing excels walking the path prepared.
But is there an antidote without a sting?
Beware, don't ever be led by the nose![39]

Esther and Mordekai Have a Dream and Go to the City of Hamadan

When Canaan became reinhabited,
Adorned by God's will, once there,
Kalīm's tribe, the people of God,
Consulted with one another often.
Their work proceeded in order;
Fortune obeyed them all. Because their hearts
Were true to one another, happiness
Adorned God's chosen people.
Wherever they'd been scattered from their land
They now returned to their own place,[40]
To grow intimate once more
With prayer and invocation.

It happened that one day, in a dream,
Mordekai[41] saw heaven and earth shaking.[42]
An angel from the emerald spheres appeared
Before him, saying: "Know, O wise man,
The time has come for you[43] to return;
Time to return capital as well as profit.[44]
Your resting place will be on Mount Alvand,[45]
In Hamadan, O virtuous man. When morning comes,
Both you and Esther will joyfully depart
For Hamadan, as it has been arranged;
At nightfall you will go to Paradise."
Upon awaking, Mordekai's anguished grief
And sorrow increased. By God's decree, that night
Esther, the concealed,[46] had the same dream;
She did not hide it from the sage
But shared with him the contents of her dream.
Her ladyship prepared herself along with him;
She launched her boat onto the self-same sea.
Their thoughts sailed toward the moon's casket;
Both of them glowed like fire and water.
The lady gave up her rank and position;
The exalted sage gave up both throne and signet ring;[47]
Swift as the autumn wind that sun and moon
Came to the appointed place, joyful and glad.
When they arrived in Hamadan they did not meet
With any companions or friends. The sun
Had already crossed the heavenly sea
And sank downward from the azure dome;
The world was enveloped in deep darkness,
In crow- and snakelike blackness. Off the path,
The two headed straight to a synagogue,[48]
As eagerly as a seed seeking its soil.
On seeing Mordekai, so learned and illustrious,
The *parnas*[49] asked: "Where are you from?
You seem an old acquaintance."
Mordekai answered: "May your spirit remain
Forever joined to wisdom!

I am a stranger, passing through,
Come to these parts by chance;
I am far from my city and my realm,
Here with my daughter, strangers in distress.
Tonight we'd like to spend in the synagogue;
Tomorrow, at dawn, we will be on our way."
The parnas showed him much kindness
And made room for them in the synagogue.
When the night's first watch had passed,
He went to sleep in peace. Then Mordekai,
Awake, perceiving no one nearby,
Except the loving Almighty One,
Crying, addressed himself to Esther:
"Of us, of you and me, the world has had
Its surfeit. Take care, for I'm departing;
You stay, I'm passing on.
The time for decamping[50] is here; doubtless
The time for sleep and slumber has arrived.
This illusory world is no one's home,[51]
And none can know the secrets of Heaven.
Time's sweet is all poison and alloyed joy,
Devoid of righteousness, faith, and religion.
Power and wealth are of no account with it;
It weighs neither spells nor stratagems.
Time nourishes itself with affliction,
Raises its head when the body is distressed;
What is a shah or dervish in its sight?
Forever it remains a stranger to its kin.
My days have passed and so have all my nights.
Mourn and lament over my soul.
Of all my family and kin now
There remains but you; I am weak,
Without brother or sister. Alas!
The hour of death is here. Much have I
Struggled in Time with its revolving spheres
And quaffs of poison; but now,
Neither poison nor injustice remains,

Nor their antidote; neither bodily strength
Nor intelligence endures. Now I depart
Toward oblivion; helpless, my soul
Hangs on my lips. The illusory world
Hands me the cup with which I pass on
To face the divine Cupbearer."[52]
Having said this, his soul quickly took off.
He sighed, and bid it a last farewell,
Sprinkling his sweet soul upon the Friend;[53]
And in this way the age's perfection departed.
Greatly did Esther lament him, shedding tears
Like the clouds in Adar.[54] Her own soul
She relinquished amid tears;
The silvery cypress fell beside him.
Esther and Mordekai perished;
The world was left without sun and moon.
As long as the firmament arches over the exalted vault,
It is a tent, a palace, the wide horizons;
Except for oppression, mourning, and grief
Nothing else comes from it. Its temptations
Set souls on fire; it crushes bones
Into fine dust and collyrium. Alas!
Man has not turned out well; his watery flesh
Brings forth fire. Water is never extinguished in fire:[55]
Man cannot restore what is destroyed.
This uncaring inn of a world
Separates many a father and son;
None dwells in it happily;
Grief is every soul's portion.
Each moment it shows forth a new trick,
Its unlucky omens. Wise men have no need
For Time's[56] vicissitudes; they recognize
Its false, deceptive blandishments.
Whoever is attached to Time
Becomes its laughingstock.
Where are Adam, Seth, Noah, and Job?
Moses, Abraham, Isaac, and Jacob?

205 Where are ʿIraj, Kay Qobād, and Nozar
Or Jamshīd, Gīv, Qobād, and Qayṣar,
Where are Zāl's Rustam and Nīram and Sām?
Where Bizhan, Farīdūn, Ṭūs, and Bahrām?[57]
Each was a leader in his time;
A royal falcon each, a peerless hero.
On desire's wind they entered the earth;
Now all are sleeping in the dust.
Death turns everyone's morning into night;
210 It spares no one. But for their names
Nothing survives of these warriors;
Their realms and kingdoms have been laid waste.
Helpless flesh is made of water and dust;
The fire of grief ever sears the heart.
The bloom of each rose and tulip
That cheerfully opens is in the end
Washed in the heart's blood.
Each cypress that grows in the meadows
Is felled in the end; Mordekai prevailed
Over this implacable power
Through prayer and invocation.
215 They built an edifice over their heads
Where people came in earnest pilgrimage.[58]

The Death of Cyrus, the Son of Ardashīr

Each rose, unwelcome for its prickly thorns,
Loses its blossom, scattered in the end.
It lives one day, two, three, at the most;
But in the end, death settles its affairs.
Such also is the way of flesh; Time ever
Takes vengeance on it. That year,
Cyrus sat full of happiness
Upon the exalted throne of fortune;
220 He sat upon the highest of all thrones,
Never deprived of a sense of justice.
He guarded his patrimony while God Himself
Kept guard over him. The shah's glory

Was exalted; his prayers were fulfilled
Through the Almighty's mercy.[59]
When his cypress stature became bent,
He grew weary of his own company.
Anguish assailed the depths of his heart;
He melted away in grief's crucible.
One day he cried out in pain a few times;
Calamity kneaded him back and forth;
When its work reached his soul, he gave it up
And toppled like a tall cypress.
At once his soul fled from his body
Abandoning all good and bad, all this and that.
His affairs fell from his throne
Onto the burial plank;
He died, leaving behind his royal affairs;
They cleansed him and clothed him in silk and brocade.
They sprinkled musk on his head for a crown
And camphor on his ivory bosom.[60]
They passed his accoutrements from hand to hand,
And then they opened the crypt for him.
He died, as all those born are bound to die;
None can endure in this world.
We're made of earth; to it we shall return
Even were we to fathom the greatest mystery.
Beware of Time, for it must feed on man,
Just as it feeds on snakes and scorpions.
When will it be sated with blood? Cry out
Against the oppression of the revolving spheres!
Adam and Eve ate easily of the grain,[61]
Relinquishing their souls.
We cannot escape either and must die;
We cannot save ourselves.
Should you endure even a hundred years and twenty,[62]
Except for death and dying,
There is no other end. Even if you endure
A thousand years, still, in the end,
You will befriend the dust.

Neither king nor gatekeeper
Escapes death; neither fairy nor demon,
Neither bird nor beast.
The road to nonexistence is hard;
All are compelled to travel it.
Happy is he who has provisions;
He finds a sheltering corner everywhere;
He rests tranquil from the journey's travails,
Reigning over his own riches. Without food
And provisions, what is his worth in the eyes
Of the noble toll gatherers?[63]
The world is an illusion from end to end,
Impossible for the intellect to grasp.[64]
Its wealth consists only of snakes and scorpions;
It is a sea full of men's blood. Abstain
From the scorpion's bite and sting;
Withdraw from its common chatter.
All clever men flee from what is bad;
They quarrel with their own destiny.
Shun not the rose because it has thorns;
It still has companions and friends.
All kingdoms possess tulip gardens;
The tulip's color comes from imperial blood.
Consider a heavy jug, O noble man;
Look at the jug, at its hand, tongue, eye, and nose.
Do not look down upon this jug,
For it is worth no less than you and I.
Alas! Like this old pitcher we shall also break.
Man is the reason for the pitcher's breaking,
It is he who opens the door of this base abode.
If the soul's pitcher is struck by death's stone
Shouldn't the pitcher be upset? It cannot stand
The stone; it breaks and spills the water.[65]
O noble man, you will be full of dust,
Whether you are like Ḥātim[66] or like Zaḥḥāk.[67]
This world of ill-repute made Ḥātim of Ṭāyy's work
Virtuous, full of generosity and kindness,

While sinister, accursed, treacherous Zaḥḥāk
Was counted among the rebellious evildoers;
He was the friend of Ahriman,[68]
Never pursuing equity and justice.
Fortune favored him for a short time,
But in the end it shed his blood.
The world is not partial to either good or bad;
It plays tricks equally on both.
Go, watch out for tricks and gifts;
Do not injure yourself through carelessness.
Ever since God created the world
For our sake he set things up
Through the eternal covenant.
We became prisoners of annihilating Time,
Heedless of His eternal excellence.[69]
Being is the realm of annihilating Time;
Better transcend the worship of self![70]
Shāhīn, worship God and prosper; behold
With both your eyes the Artist and the art.[71]
If you know yourself all your life long,[72]
You will be saved; go, you are still alive!

'Imrānī

Like Shāhīn, the second-most-famous poet of JP literature is known to posterity only by his nom de plume, "'Imrānī."[1] He was born in 1454 in Isfahan, where he lived until his mid- or late twenties, when against his will, and for reasons that remain unclear, he was compelled to move to Kashan, a flourishing town. He died in Kashan at an advanced age, sometime after 1536, outliving many of his relatives, friends, and contemporaries. According to David Yeroushalmi, "a profound sense of exile and alienation prevails in the majority of 'Imrānī's works and this sentiment may, in part, explain the poet's essentially disillusioned and pessimistic view of man and society. To his larger awareness of the Jewish exile 'Imrānī adds his personal feeling of forced and unjust banishment."[2]

The span of 'Imrānī's life covers two turbulent periods in Iranian history: the end of the Timurid era (1453–1501) and the advent of the Safavid dynasty (1501–1722).[3] As in most periods of political upheaval in Islamic history, this time was full of religious and economic uncertainty, which affected most Iranians; however, ʻImrānī's works do not convey specific information about the living conditions and hardships endured by the Jewish communities of Iran. Although ʻImrānī witnessed a momentous change in the religion of the kingdom (from the Sunni to the Shiʻi form of Islam), which was accompanied by an especially intense period of forced conversion during the reign of Ismāʻīl I (1501–1524), the first Safavid shah, the repercussions of this event are not reflected directly in his verses. His apparent lack of interest in contemporary history may be a result of the fact that, as far as we know, the change in Iran's religious outlook affected non-Muslim minorities only about a hundred years later.[4]

ʻImrānī's surviving work bears testimony to his literary versatility. Among his compositions we count epics on biblical, historical, and legendary themes; works in prose and poetry based on Jewish historical and midrashic sources; and several strictly didactic pieces.[5]

ʻImrānī's longest, and probably his most important, work is *Fatḥ-nāmah* (henceforth FN; The book of conquest), based on the Books of Joshua, Judges, Ruth, I Samuel, and part of II Samuel, in which he versifies major biblical events from the time of Samson until Solomon's ascension to the throne. *Fatḥ-nāmah* is modeled on Shāhīn's versification of the Pentateuch. ʻImrānī's epic was apparently undertaken at the bidding and encouragement of a patron holding an official (communal?) rank bearing the inflated honorific title Amīn al-Dawlah (trustee of the state).[6] The poet began working on FN in 1474, but he appears to have been interrupted shortly afterward, when his patron died. The encouragement of a new patron, a certain Rabbi Yehudah, was not sufficient to keep him on course. ʻImrānī's life seems to have been in upheaval during the writing of this epic, as he became embroiled in a conflict with the Jewish community of Isfahan and chose to go into "exile" to nearby Kashan. He seems to have harbored such bitterness, hostility, and sorrow over this experience that its imprint is visible not only in FN but in most of his later works as well. Although his working conditions in Kashan were far from ideal, the new environment was more congenial to ʻImrānī's creativity, as his prolific writings from that period suggest.

At the beginning of the twentieth century, FN and *Ganj-nāmah* (henceforth GN; The book of treasure; see below, chap. 5) were the only poetic works clearly attributed to 'Imrānī.[7] Yet recent research has shown him to be more prolific and versatile than Shāhīn, his erstwhile model.[8] These two works epitomize, rather, 'Imrānī's successful melding of Jewish and Muslim themes.

Fatḥ-nāmah is a *masnavī* of approximately 10,000 couplets composed in the popular Persian meter *hazaj musaddas mahẕūf*. Like Shāhīn, 'Imrānī follows closely the prosodic, rhetorical, and stylistic requirements of classical Persian verse, although at times he is less skillful than his predecessor.[9] Apparently 'Imrānī's original plan also called for the versification of the biblical books of the Prophets and Writings but no trace of these efforts, if ever undertaken, has come to light. 'Imrānī is faithful to the biblical outline of the tales he narrates in FN, but in their development he appears to be more restrained in the use of details culled from midrashic and Muslim legendary sources than Shāhīn. Similarly, like Shāhīn's biblical epics, FN is heavily indebted to Persian epic poetry, especially to Firdowsī's *Shah-nāmah,* in language, imagery, descriptions of feasts and battles, and characterization of heroes. There are many specific references in FN to the heroes of the *Shah-nāmah,* as well as to Iranian and Islamic concepts, which are placed anachronistically into the biblical settings of 'Imrānī's tales.

All of 'Imrānī's work illustrates his penchant for didacticism—a principal characteristic of classical (especially Sufi) Persian poetry in general. Nowhere is this more apparent than in GN, probably 'Imrānī's last work, completed in 1536. It is a versification of the first four chapters of the mishnaic tractate Abot ([The wisdom of the] fathers), which was popular everywhere in the Jewish world. Since it does not discuss halakic (legal) matters but deals with general and fundamental ethical precepts, it is accessible to all, not only to learned men. "Consisting of sayings and epigrammatic teachings of the [rabbinic] authorities of the Jewish tradition, Abot has been defined as 'the nearest approach made by rabbinic Judaism to a philosophical formulation of its ideas.' "[10] A large number of JP manuscripts on Abot, especially in prose, attest to the popularity of the tractate in the Iranian world. The fact that its exhortations resemble the wisdom poetry of Iran, known as *pand-nāmah* (book[s] of counsel), probably enhanced the popularity of Abot. *Ganj-nāmah* is also suffused with a mystical Sufi outlook and is indebted to such writers and works as ʿAṭṭār (d. 1220), Saʿdī's (d. 1292) *Pand-nāmah,*[11] and especially the various didactic works of Saʿdī, such as *Bustān* (The garden) and *Gulistān* (The rose garden). Its poetic imagery also calls to mind the imagery of Ḥāfiẓ (d. 1389), the greatest lyrical poet of Iran.[12]

In addition to these two major works, several other compositions by ʿImrānī have survived. Among these is a short epic (almost 2,000 couplets) called *Ḥanukkah-nāmah* (The book of Hanukkah), also known as *Ẓafar-nāmah* (The book of victory; see below, chap. 3). It is based on the Book of Maccabees and describes the struggle of the Maccabees against the Greeks.

ʿImrānī wrote at least three compositions based on midrashic narratives. The first, *ʿAsara haruge ha-malkut* (The ten martyrs of the kingdom), written in prose interspersed with poetry, describes the well-known story of the martyrdom of the ten Jewish sages at the order of the Roman Emperor Hadrian (117–138 CE). The second, known both as *Qiṣṣe-ye haft barādarān* (The story of the seven brothers) and as *Musibat-nāmah* (The book of calamity), again intersperses prose and poetry. It is the tale of the martyrdom of Ḥannah's seven sons, who were killed for refusing to become idolaters during the Hasmonean revolt (168–162 BCE). ʿImrānī's third midrashic work, *ʿAqedat Yiṣḥaq,* although based on the biblical account of the sacrifice of Isaac, concentrates primarily on Abraham; it is composed entirely in prose.

Among ʿImrānī's didactic works are *Vājibāt va arkān-i sīzdahgāni-yi īmān-i Isra'el* (The thirteen precepts and pillars of the faith of Israel), a masnavī based on Maimonides' "The Thirteen Principles (of Faith)," and *Intiḥāb-i nakhlistān* (The best of the palm grove), a masnavī that consists of "religious, moral, and practical advice to members and leaders of the Jewish community."[13]

Among ʿImrānī's poetic compositions that do not have a perceptible Jewish dimension, the lovely *Sāqī-nāmah* (The book of the cupbearer) and a short poem known as *Dar setāyesh-i tahammul* (In praise of forbearance) have survived. *Sāqī-nāmah* appears to have been modeled on a similar work by Ḥāfiẓ (d. 1389). *Dar setāyesh-i tahammul* consists only of sixteen couplets extolling the virtues of patience.[14]

The large number of ʿImrānī's surviving compositions, the wide range of his themes, and his poetic skills merit closer study. They assure their author of a place at the top of the list of outstanding Iranian Jewish poets.

Fatḥ-nāmah (The Book of Conquest)

Joshua's Conquest of Jericho

God's Angel Appears to Joshua in Jericho by God's Command

When,[1] through God's guiding grace,
The prophet Joshua and the Hebrews
Encamped before the town of Jericho,
Besieging it from every side,
They worshiped God, full of devotion,
All night long, from dusk to dawn.
Not for a moment did the prophet grow
Neglectful, idle in God's service;
Only of His traditions did he speak
And throughout the night slept not a wink.
One night as that exalted cypress
Began to pray in prayer's tent,
Lamenting until dawn as was his wont,
He beheld at dawn a pure being,
Rooted in place like a steel mountain,
His stature shaming the tall box tree.
Light from his face filled the retreat;
His beauty, a model for the Universal Intellect.[2]
A drawn bejewelled sword was in his hand,
It scattered sparks instead of luster.
When Joshua beheld that vision,
He was afraid and asked him:
"O excellent, exalted man,
Did you come here to shed my blood?
Why do you grasp this sword?
With it you grasp our very peace.
Tell me, are you, exalted one,
One of us or a stranger?"
The angel answered thus:
"O wise man,
Fear me not, and rejoice, for I am
A friend of yours; no enemy am I

But the Almighty's faithful trustee.
God sent me to you this very moment
And gave this mighty sword to me
To guard you from the war and sedition
Of these infidels. Therefore will I guard
The Sons of Jacob and keep these infidels
Far from you. I'll be your chief commander,
Your tender, loving friend everywhere;
Wherever this brave host and army
Wanders, there shall I also be
Scattering dust in the eyes of their enemy.
Insofar as they are the friends of God
By His command they will triumph. On them
I will bestow favor and victory;
I'll drive away in warning fashion
The infidels before them.
With this sword's mighty blows in battle
I'll spare no enemy of this folk.
If they be God-discerning, truthful,
And turn their backs sincerely on hypocrisy,
They will not experience despair in Time;[3]
Their faces I will light up everywhere.
But if they should suddenly stray, assume
The tunic of rebellion and unbelief,
I will defeat them always, mar their work.
I'll spread the fame of these brave men
Among the peoples of the world;
This is the task for which God sent me,
The reason He gave me this sword,
That I should guard you always,
Day and night, openly and in secret.
Relate all this to your commanders
So that through constancy they will excel,[4]
Through righteousness, sincerity, and worship,
Become distinguished.
And as for you,
Choice in sincerity,

You must excel the most, but first
Remove the shoes from off your feet:
The land on which you stand, O wise man,
Is holy."[5]
Hearing mystery from the incomparable angel,
Joshua's cheeks turned red; at once
He bowed to the Creator, and when he lifted his head
The angel disappeared. Amazed, Joshua
Summoned the Sons of Jacob, one by one,
And told them what had happened.
The Hebrews rejoiced on hearing
The import of the message,
And they obeyed the will of God
At once, as if they were His prisoners.
Each one of them purified his abode,
And cleansed his heart sincerely.
Whatever Moses, God's messenger,[6] bade,
Joshua quickly carried out.
A few days after these events,
On Joshua God bestowed His favor;
Joshua's fame spread everywhere;
His name became as well known as the sun.
The hearts of infidels turned to wax
Because of him; the vile enemies were
Gripped by fear, but they held fast
To Jericho and its surroundings.
No one could leave or enter the town
Of those cursed men. Jericho's sultan
To his vile, infidel subjects proclaimed:
"Whoever leaves the town to tend his affairs,
His blood will be shed on the spot, whether on plain
Or in the desert." For this they were angry with him.[7]

The Message of God, the Mighty and Exalted, to Joshua Regarding the Conquest of Jericho

A message came from the God of the Universe
To Joshua the prophet: "O mystery and treasure,

I chose you from among the creatures of the world
To be prophet, shah, and leader; know
That I bestow on you Moses' rank and station.
I made you cross the Jordan joyfully
And freed your heart from grief; behold,
I now bestow upon you the realm of Jericho;
Its walls and towers I will level with My might.
You'll conquer that province from end to end,
Its sultan, heroes, army. Tell Jacob's Sons
That tomorrow, at the break of dawn,
They should put on the accoutrements of war
And shout resolute war cries.
Let whosoever is a hero, skillful and brave,
Possessing sword and dagger, issue forth
To wage war resolutely, color the earth
With infidel blood. Tell them, O glory of creation,
To take this besieged town quickly;
Those brave warriors should march all
Around the towers for six days,
Once every day. Choose seven leaders
From among the *priests*[8] who are skilled
At blowing the *ram's horn.*[9]
Let them pursue these infidels and blow
The Almighty's *horn* for their own sakes;
Let them this way walk around the town
Six days. To El'azar give the Torah quickly,
So he, that glory of creation, may obey and walk
Along with Phinehas[10] and the other priests
Behind this tribe and host.[11]
Tell them to remain silent for six days,
Reciting litanies and chanting prayers;
But on the seventh, at daybreak,
When day's armies triumph over night's,
Tell these people to come out once more
And go around the city a seventh time;
Then let the priests blow their *rams' horns*
Together; as they do, tell all the people

To roar like lions; let them cry out
To God with all their hearts and souls;
Let them, full of devotion, rub their faces
In the dust; let them, O exalted conqueror,
Clamor and pray and magnify Me.[12]
Then I will command the earth to split;
At once the towers will fall into it;[13]
The walls, the towers, all will topple
By the Almighty's decree. Such might
The Sons of Jacob will not behold again
Until the Day of Resurrection.
This will be a memorial
They will recall through Time.
When all the walls and towers fall,
A path will appear on every side.
Tell them to enter and refrain not
From capturing infidels. Let none survive;
Let them place bridles on every head:
Infants, children, youths, old men.
Let them kill all with dagger and arrow;
Let them wipe out the fields and homes of the infidels."
Hearing this happy news, the prophet Joshua,
Who received this token,
Sought out among the great priests
Blowers of the noble *ram's horn,* seven
Renowned, and told them of God's mystery:
"O skillful, glorious men,
You must now walk behind this brave people,
And when I tell you, blow together
The *ram's horn* of the Judge."
When God's elite received this order,
They rejoiced at His command. At once
They took up their *horns* ready to obey
God's word. Then Joshua, that wise sage,
Summoned the Sons of Jacob and told them
The command; they too rejoiced.
That day, until nightfall, the army kept busy

Fashioning swords, maces, and daggers.
Next morning, by God's command
Those faithful folk took up their weapons
And marched once round the city with Joshua
And with God's priests, as He commanded.
Warriors and braves marched in the vanguard,
Chief priests followed behind heroes,
Holding in their hands *rams' horns* divine,
Each one beside himself, absorbed in union,[14]
Uttering His praise and exaltation,[15]
The leaders[16] all in a state of ecstasy.[17]
Joshua followed those illustrious men
Gladly with the Ark; behind him walked
The Hebrews, rich and the poor alike.
That day they went round the city once,
As God commanded. Joshua said to the people:
"This, O chieftains, is God's command:
That you make no sound
Until the day I tell you to clamor
Before the Almighty with all your hearts,
So that you may attain the goals
And wishes of your hearts."
On hearing this, the Sons of Jacob held
Their tongues at once. Thus did they walk
Till nightfall; it was as if
The world received benevolence from the night.
At eventide they all returned and
All night long communed with God.
When from the East the sun rose brightly,
The world bestowed a mandate on the sun.
Once more those brave people
Went all together round the town;
For six days, every day, that victorious folk
Went round the town; behind them came
The priests blowing their *horns* together.
When the eastern sun brightened the world
With its beauty, on the seventh day,

By God's command, at dawn they came forth
Once again together, the army
With Joshua, the priests, and the Torah,
Guardians of the Ark of Witness.[18]
Around the city they marched seven times,
As God commanded. The seventh time,
The priests quickly blew their *horns*
Six times, and at the seventh,
By God's command, Joshua said:
"Now, you famed people, cry out all of you,
With all your hearts and souls,
And rub your faces in the dust in worship;
Pray, O chieftains, magnify[19] God,
With the youths, children, infants, and old men,
That God may give you this beautiful realm;
And know clearly that this entire town
Is forbidden to you; whatever money, goods,
Property, silver, gold, and all such
Found in it are consecrated to the Lord.
Whoever takes a grain's worth will be banned;
By my sword will he die. I warn you of this mystery
Lest you dare take a grain of barley's worth.
Beware, beware, abstain from it
Lest you be trapped by the ban.
Do not, through greed, lift up your hands
And bring calamity upon this host.
If you entrap the people in the ban[20]
God's wrath will flare against them:
Jericho's entire wealth
Is proscribed for the Judge's sanctuary.[21]
Whoever dares to misappropriate,
I'll shed his blood without hesitation.
As for all those who are alive,
Wild beasts, birds, and humans,
Male, female, shed the blood of each;
Carry this out, O glorious, faithful men!
Let none survive; rid the world

Of these villains, allow no mercy
To enter into your hearts;
Spare none of these strayed men,
Except Rahab and all her household,
For she has shown us benevolence and favor:[22]
She saved the messengers from death
And sent them safely back to us.
Therefore a messenger should be sent to her
To help her come forth from the midst
Of these strayed folk. Whoever
Is in the house of that fair face,
Her relatives and friends,
Guard them, O chieftains, for such
Is the command of the Almighty.
Harm none of them, neither youths,
Old men, nor children."
When the Sons of Jacob
Heard this from God's sage,
They rejoiced greatly.
With pure sincerity that princely folk
Cried out before the Judge's court;
With prayers, the clamor of supplication,
They recalled the Sovereign of this world.
Those faithful men cried out at once
Together before the Judge's court.
Their laments reached to the Pleiades;
It seemed as if the earth itself rose upward.
In that same hour, by the command of the
Immortal beyond compare, the Lord of the earth
And heavenly vaults, the Eternal,[23]
The One True God, the Sultan Absolute,
A sudden gust of wind arose,
And for a while darkness covered the world.
Then the earth split and swallowed
All the towers; by God's might and decree,
The towers disappeared both one and all.
When the towers and the fort toppled,

The infidels' hearts leapt in surprise;
That might terrified them; the color
Of their faces turned to straw;
Out of dread they expired on the spot
And from there hastened toward the Lord's palace.
For their part, the Sons of Jacob,
When they beheld the impact of that deed,
Loosened their tongues in prayer once again;
Their bowed heads touched their feet.
Then they drew out their swords
And ran at once toward the town.
In place of walls and towers,
Columns of lions circled it now.
They blocked all Jericho's exits
And went on killing those vile folk.
Joshua, that honored chieftain, found
Caleb[24] and Phinehas and said to them:
"O warriors brave, remember the oath
Which you have sworn to Rahab;[25]
You swore in God's name to extricate
Her and her family from battle.
Honor your promise; don't sin against her!
Free her from war's tumult
Lest you break our oath and thus break
Our hearts. Whoever is in her house,
Strangers[26] or relatives, guard all of them
With their property lest they be harmed,
As you have promised; such was the oath you swore
In the name of God.
In addition to what is hers, relinquish everything
To her lest anyone misappropriate
A barley grain's worth and thereby bring upon us
Trouble and grief. If suddenly you break
Your oath, God's wrath will flare against us."
When the glorious leader of the age said this,
At his command, the two set out at once
And quickly came to that distraught moon.

On seeing the sign of the scarlet thread
They ran joyfully into the house.[27]
(That sun-cheeked beauty had placed
A red sign on her roof, and from the day
The brave heroes had left her
That red sign was there for their return.)
When that moon was informed of the arrival
Of the faithful heroes, that houri-face
And all her kindred came forth in welcome.
They fell down before the heroes' feet,
And kissed the ground before them, saying:
"O glorious heroes, may you always be princes
In the world, through your good fortune
We're set free, severed at last from these
Accursed infidels." The heroes answered Rahab:
"O you the light of whose face
Puts the moon to sleep,[28] now is not the time
To tarry; come, let us get out of town,
For it will be destroyed entirely,
Such, lovely lady, is the Judge's order.
Go quickly with all your kindred
And join cheerfully our host, with whom
You can dwell happily, free from grief,
At rest from grief's sharp sword,
Lest you be torn apart suddenly in the midst
Of this clamoring calamity; come,
O lovely one, to our host and worry not."
On hearing such words, that ravishing houri
Set out quickly, cheerful and smiling,
With her relations and the famed heroes
And all her property and chattels, cows, sheep,
Horses, and mules, also the property
Of all her relatives; she brought them all
Without reproof into the army's camp.
For their part, the army of God's lion,
With spears and swords and daggers drawn,
Encircled the infidels, whose blood

Flowed like a river; men, women,
Youths, children, old men, grand viziers,
Kings, princes, and viceroys,
Wild beasts, birds, cows, and sheep,
They killed them all, by God's command;
They left no soul alive; all fell
By the sword's blow, all except Rahab
And those who were with her;
The rest were killed at God's behest.
Whomever the Sons of Jacob saw in that sea,
They cut off his head at once.
Women and babes were not spared;
All fell by the sword's blow.
Whoever had a soul, he was soon parted
From it. Old men and youths, males, females,
Children and nursing babes,
Camels and donkeys, all were dispatched;
They finished off the infidels
And seized the town with all its homes.
They plundered the infidels' wealth
And brought it before the commander.
When Joshua saw all those riches,
He rejoiced and laughed happily;
Then he said to the braves: "O famous men,
God's command is that you destroy
This town entirely, turn it into a thicket,
A dwelling place for lions. I curse
Until the Day of Resurrection
Whoever would inhabit it again."[29]
On hearing this from God's prophet,
They made ready huge maces
And toppled the entire town, uprooting
The fort, its soil, mountains, homes,
And then let loose upon them water and fire
And cast everything to the wind.
They leveled the town with the plain;
They left no footprint's trace.

220 Then they returned to camp accompanied
By victory and conquest, and there
Those brave lions rested.
Joshua took money and treasure
And carried them into the sanctuary
Of the Almighty.[30] He dedicated all
To the Almighty of the Universe;
What God commanded, Joshua carried out.
He then ordered Rahab to be brought before him
With her tribe, family, and kindred.
225 Kindly he questioned each and every one
And shared his mirth with them.
He opened his hands in largesse
To give each one a fitting crown and belt.
He related to them God's command,
Making each one aware of his spiritual neglect;
They then became servants of God,
Abandoning the path of unbelief;
God's oneness they acknowledged,[31]
Sobering up from their drunkenness.[32]
230 They accepted Kalīm Allah's[33] customs
And freed themselves of unbelief.
Joshua, the wise prophet, gave them a station
In the midst of Jacob's Sons, according
To birth and kindred, and right then,
In the midst of the tribe and companions,
Joshua gave Rahab to Caleb.[34] With her
Caleb had several children, each one famous,
Wise, and a hero; a large progeny
Came from them, all famous, mighty, faithful,
Many revered wise men of high rank,
Strong among the people, learned leaders,
235 *Righteous, pious prophets,* many attaining
To kingship in the world.[35] They gave the world
The enjoyment of justice and placed
The crown of lordship on their heads.

See, O wise man, how Rahab prospered

In the world through goodness;
It was through goodness she attained this,
Through goodness she ascended.
He who expresses goodness finds a place
Wherever he may be; he who accustoms
Himself to goodness crowns himself
Among the people; in every assembly he joins,
He'll be deemed righteous; wheresoever he goes
He'll find his worth; Time itself will follow
His commands; his statutes will be accepted everywhere.[36]
The world stands through the righteousness
Of good men; the firmament keeps in place
For the love of good men, so strive,
Day and night to do good while you are
Under the gilded azure cloak.
He whose calling is goodness,
What does he fear from Fate?
How well did that wise man say this,
No one has ever said it better:
"He who assents to goodness in his heart
Conquers the world; it does not conquer him."
They asked that dear sage: "What is better,
A good name or happiness?" The prudent sage
Gave a reply more precious than a hundred treasures:
"Certain it is that he who lacks a good name,
Cannot, in truth, have happiness."[37]
Happy is the man who has a good name;
Through it he attains his wish always!
He passes through the world joyfully
And has nothing to do with what is bad;
He is always free from grief and sorrow,
A leader among the progeny of man.
Through goodness man attains to eminence;
Human calamity comes from a bad nature.
When Rahab, that pretty chin, performed
Her good deed that night toward those heroes,
Helped them elude the officers of the shah,

She tore the ropes of unbelief.
Since happines was her companion that night,
Today good fortune is her servant.
Freed from the blows of the vengeful sword
She turned with her loved ones from grief
To happiness. Through her good fortune
They escaped; they all escaped only through
Her grace. If not for her, they would have
All been killed by those brave heroes' swords.
Instead, that moon and all her people
Dwelt happily among the Sons of Jacob.
So save yourselves through goodness
And you will bring others to good fortune.
O Lord, for the sake of our good names,
For the sake of all the imams and innocents,[38]
Keep ʿImrānī upon the good road,
Far from the bad, and always close to You.

The Book of Ruth

The Birth of Jesse, David's Father

When[1] at the Bestower's behest Naomi came
Into the desert of Moab, the world was still
Weakened by drought; seeds and grains were dear
Everywhere; wheat and barley that the farmer
Sowed into the earth had not yet sprouted;
A carpet of new greens spread over
The cultivated fields storing within
The promise of bounty at harvest time.
By God's will, when Nisan's grace arrived,
Land and fields turned into rose gardens.
And as they praised that blessed bounty,
Women and men cried out in happiness.
When moon-cheeked Ruth became aware
Of farmers storing the barley stacks,
That fairy-face said to Naomi, "I want to roam
About this field; if barley can be found,

I will obtain it, but if it is not permitted
We will be helpless. Whether barley be found
In desert or meadow, I'll bait it, hunt it down.
I will return at nightfall
To share your sighs and grief."
Naomi answered, "O dazzler of hearts,
Go, and may the Lord grant success and happiness."
On her approval Ruth walked toward the field;
Swift as the wind the maid left Naomi;
Alone she set out toward the desert
Arriving where the farmers gathered.
No water had she, nor bread, nor other source
Of nourishment; she gleaned some barley on the way.
That moon-face thus traversed field after field,
In perfect solitude, just like the sun.
She chanced upon a cultivated field,
A veritable meadow in the desert,
Everywhere full of busy squires,
Happy and smiling over the barley harvest.
The moon-cheeked Ruth asked one of these:
"To whom does this huge field belong?"
Replied a farmer: "O fairy-face,
This goodly plain belongs to Boaz.
He is a fine youth and renowned,
Owns houses aplenty, property, and storerooms.
He is of Elimelek's kin, and now he rules
In Bethlehem. His wealth and property
Are endless, he is most courteous to all,
Great, a prince of Judah's folk;
Sunlike, God's love radiates from his face,
His counsel is auspicious, like a king's;
In fortune he resembles the sun of the age.
His lips do not touch bread or drink until
He welcomes some poor men into his house.
He looks upon the people's needs with favor;
Noble, he gives each commoner his due.
He cheers the sight of the aggrieved; hope

He restores to orphans and widows;
None come before him whom he does not ease."
Thus they conversed as Boaz himself
Arrived and saw Ruth's beauty from afar.[2]
Several chieftains rode along with him
Each one holding a *sāz*,[3] for he was never
Without joy and the sāz; the lute and harp
Were heard wherever he went. Beholding Boaz,
The farmers one and all rushed out to meet him
To pay respects. They bowed their heads at his feet,
Invoked God's blessings on him.
Then from the road Boaz questioned a youth:
"When did that moon appear from its zodiac tower?
Who is this sun-faced woman with a visage
Brighter than gold, and what is it she needs?
Why is she here? Why is she wretched and heartbroken?
What does she want? What is her name?
I will fulfill her wishes on the spot."
The youth replied: "O Exalted one, this sun-
Cheeked beauty is Naomi's daughter-in-law,
Who from the desert came with her from Moab;
And she has no one, neither mother nor father.
They two live together; she has no friend,
No intimate, no husband. Fortune its faith
Kept not with her; it turns out beggars everywhere.
She travels far without provisions,
Plucking their gleanings wheresoever she goes;
At nightfall she returns, like fire,
And shares everything with that burned one.[4]
That moon, her waist is cinched like heaven's wheel
In service to Naomi, in city, in plain.
Naomi has no one, no other friend but Ruth,
With whom to share her sorrow."
When Boaz heard the young man's words,
His heart froze out of grief for Naomi.
Lamenting the injustice of heaven he cried;

His happy heart filled with sorrow.
Then he called to Ruth, made room for her
By his side, seated her and said,
"O houri, the likes of you cannot be seen
Among the veiled; hear me, O radiant moon:
Remain with us here in the desert; beware,
Beware, do not go anywhere else; glean here
Among the storerooms, linger near my farmers,
No longer solitary like the world's sun."
Thus he commanded the farmers:
"See she is kept in good spirits; do not offend her,
For she is poor; a poor person is not happy.
From now on give to that moon from my storerooms
That which she ought to have; withhold not from her
Your water, bread, whatever else you have.
She is a stranger and fallen on hard days; none
Should harm the stranger."[5] And when Ruth heard this
From Boaz and saw such favor, kindness,
And compassion, she fell down upon the dust
Bowing at once before his feet. Lifting
Her head she said: "Exalted one, may you live
As long as the moon and the stars; may the sun
Never shine without your beauty, and may
Your enemies descend into the grave alive.
God grant, so long as heaven and earth endure,
So long as day and night, month, year, the world
Itself endure, that you be always victorious
Fulfilling in this world your friends' best wishes.
Because you've made this slave girl glad,
May God fulfill your wishes and desires.
You've acted like a kinsman toward me, a stranger;
You have in your station done many deeds of kindness.
In turn may the World Preserver grant your wishes
And like the sun greatly exalt your name."
Boaz replied: "O heart-ravishing beauty,
Companion of the moon, none is like you

Among those veiled in the world; in Paradise itself
No houri is like you. Men and women
Have spoken much of you, O moon-cheeked one,
Tales they have told of you; true faith, kind manners,
Right custom, these have you, O lovely one,
Shown toward Naomi; you shine on life's royal highway
Like the bright moon, meriting praises by the thousand."
So the time passed and dazzling Ruth was busy
Day and night, in town and in the fields. Each day
Till nightfall spent she in the fields,
And when night came she returned to Naomi,
And with her all night long, till dawn,
Time in, time out, she wailed and sighed.
Daily she brought Naomi food and was
Her ever-compassionate nurse. When Boaz came
Into the field to oversee his lands and property,
He would glimpse Ruth near his farmers, her waist
Cinched up to work hard like a man. She was
So nimble in her fieldwork she appeared
To win the wager against heaven itself.
Alone she piled the harvested grain and sought
The company of none throughout the bright day.
Her beauty she concealed even from herself;
She spoke to no one an entire month.
When Boaz saw her beauty and her renown,
Like a perfect moon in all she did, he gave
His heart to that graceful cypress, for
In truth, to such a one the heart entrusts the soul.
He fell in love with Ruth; fire fell
Into the house of patience. Passionately
Did he love Ruth, so that, save for her face,
No other moon he saw.[6] The harvest
Of the wheat and barley came to an end;
Farmers moved out from their tents to their homes.
Fairy-faced Ruth, like fairy kind,
Departed, and a longing for her tore

At Boaz's heart. Daily his passion for her
Swelled, for such is the nature of love.
When he went helpless from not seeing her,
He called together a few famous chieftains,
Sat among them and bade them all sit down,
And spoke of many things. After a time he said:
"Know, O faithful, exalted, and wise elders,
That I would marry Ruth, to be her husband,
She my wife. Since Elimelek, Mahlon, and Kilion
Were my kinsmen but now are gone, by God's will,
Leaving behind some property and homes,
For these, by God's will, I sought out
A guardian closer than I am in kinship.
He did not want them, and after some talk,
He offered me his guardianship entire.[7]
Now their inheritance is mine: those closest
In kinship can by right inherit."
The sages replied: "In truth,
You are the rightful guardian by God's will,
You have the right to act as you have said;
Do as you wish." At that moment they
Summoned Naomi, told her of the matter.
With what they said her heart was pleased.
Promptly they found a judge in the assembly.
Thus they arranged the marriage[8] of Khosrow
And Shīrīn[9] and freed them from bitterness
And separation; those two lovers found comfort
In one another.

Some time passed, and by
The Almighty's will, the moon-faced,
Lovely-breasted beauty carried within her
A young cypress shoot from the garden of souls.
At the appointed time, she gave birth to a child
Of great beauty, who brought much joy to Boaz's heart;[10]
He straightaway named the child Obed.[11]
Naomi's joy was overwhelming;

She felt rejuvenated in old age;
That veiled one offered many thanks to God
And nursed the child contentedly.
Day and night she nurtured him, like a nanny,[12]
Sometimes in sunshine and sometimes in shade,
Knowing no exaltation save in his beauty.
Though he sat on her lap, he dwelt in her heart.
She nurtured him as if he were her own;
Out of her heart and soul he plucked all the pain.
It seemed to her and also to others
As if the departed had returned.
Yet more time passed;
Wise Obed grew to a young man
Whose beauty watered the soul's garden,
The violet bestowing radiance upon the hyacinth.
If you beheld his cypress stature, you
Would forget your own measure at once.
If a nightingale saw the rose of his face,
He would delight no longer in the rose.
Unique in learning, chivalry, and lore;
In goodness he was heaven's mate.
His beauty filled the sight with light
That even from far off taunted the moon.
When once he came to the harem to find a wife,
He saw a cypress vision, straight from the garden,
A fragment of the moon framed by chains of curls,
Sun-cheeked, angelic in appearance.
The heart of Obed rejoiced in that beloved;
Not for one moment was it free of her.
And so it came about that in nine months,
God granted him a longed-for child.
Obed greatly rejoiced and gave him a name
Full of happiness, Jesse. From Jesse's stock
Came several offspring, prosperous in the world.
One was the prophet David, one of God's elect;
To this day it is recalled
That the contract between moon-cheeked Ruth

And Naomi was the Almighty's will.
So you, 'Imrānī, ponder the fate of dazzling Ruth,
How through her goodness she prospered in the world.
Since she set foot on purity's path,
Through goodness fortune itself became her guide.
The world keeps measure of both good and bad;
But Ruth was free of all that's good and bad.
Whatever music you play on your sāz
Time will play back the same to you.
Don't call out any tunes in this assembly, lest
You be chased away in public from the feast.
The arrow finds its way into the heart
Only if sometimes it strays from its course.[13]

Aḥaron b. Mashiaḥ

Shoftim-nāmah (henceforth SN; The book of judges) appears to be the sole surviving poetic composition of Aḥaron b. Mashiaḥ, who lived in the seventeenth century and hailed from Isfahan.[1] At some indefinite point in his life he moved to Yazd, perhaps as a result of the wave of persecutions that swept through Isfahan in the mid-seventeenth century.

Shoftim-nāmah, composed in 1692, sets to verse the Book of Judges up to chapter eighteen. It is a relatively short composition written in the same *hazaj musaddas maḥzūf* meter as 'Imrānī's *Fatḥ-nāmah.* Aḥaron b. Mashiaḥ claims not only that he was inspired by 'Imrānī's works but that the older poet had been his teacher and spiritual guide. Since 'Imrānī died sometime after 1536, this claim can hardly be true, except in terms of literary influence. Aḥaron b. Mashiaḥ's composition is usually included in manuscripts of FN, probably because of the correct perception that Aḥaron b. Mashiaḥ consciously strove to continue 'Imrānī's work.

Amnon Netzer draws attention to the fact that Aḥaron b. Mashiaḥ may be alluding to events in his own times when he mentions that a man called Mattatiah was murdered in Isfahan along with four other individuals. It is likely that this Mattatiah was Matthathias Bloch, the messenger of Sabbatai Ṣevi (the false messiah) to Mosul and Iran, who remained active after Ṣevi's apostasy and was apparently murdered near Isfahan sometime after 1668.[2]

Shoftim-nāmah (The Book of Judges)

Jephthah Sacrifices His Daughter

Jephthah's Daughter Meets Jephthah with Tambourines and Flutes

When Jephthah set out for the road[1]
He did so full of happiness and joy.
He had a daughter,[2] a solitary cypress,
Her visage fairyborn; two curls
Upon her temples rested, two weeping violets;
Her cheeks were like two jasmines;
She was a graceful cypress.
Her eyes were subtle, her forehead
As bright as the moon; moonlike in form,
She was wholly delightful, with a slender waist,
High-spirited, prancing a partridge's gait,
Both eloquent and elegant in speech.
On hearing that her father had set out,
That moonlike sun, cheerful and happy,
Decided to go meet him.
She took along a flask of wine,
Came out with *sāz*,[3] flute, and tambourine.
As fate would have it, Jephthah's daughter
Was an only child; as she came from the house,
She plucked the sāz, showed off her joy,
When suddenly her father came in sight.
Jephthah, that wise and peerless hero, approached
Happy and joyful, full of contentment.
As he drew near his house in Miṣpeh
And was about to step into his home,
By the Incomparable's will, he saw his daughter
Who had come out to meet him. When thus he
Suddenly beheld that moon of Khotan,[4] he cried:
"O my heart-ravishing daughter,
You grieve me, distress me utterly."
Having said this, he sighed, cried out,
And tore at once the garments on his body;
Again he addressed his daughter thus:

"O comfort of my heart, frivolously
Did I open my mouth when I declared
If I should return to Miṣpeh safely,
After killing my enemies,
I would sacrifice to the Almighty Judge
Whatever first came from my house,
And now I see you here before me!"[5]
That moon replied at once: "O father,
Why do you grieve? Did not Abraham also
Take Isaac, the light of his two eyes,
By the command of the World Keeper,
To sacrifice him on His threshold?
Remove this grief and sorrow from your heart;
Whatever you have promised, you must do.
You were victorious over lawless infidels;
You ought now to rejoice and be happy.
I do, however, have one thing to ask:
I would like to lament over my fate,
I seek your permission and consent
To offer up the gift of my innocence.[6]
I know for certain I shall be killed suddenly;
Grant me a respite of two months.
I will go to the mountains with my friends
To grieve and lament over my fate,
Bewail my virginity with them."[7]
When Jephthah, the chieftain, heard this request
He gave permission to that eastern moon
To go with a group of friends to weep
And lament together.
                    Thus did they spend two months,
Crying and burning up with grief; when the time
Was up she came accompanied by friends;
That radiant moon hastened to her father.
And once again when he beheld his daughter,
Jephthah rent his garments and said:
"I have only this child; the thought

Of hurting her distresses me profoundly!"
He wept copiously until he took her
Helplessly away. He readied for her
A tomb and he conveyed the moon-face there;
He gave her an eternal resting place
Sealed over with bricks and clay.[8]
Then among Jacob's seed arose this rite:
To send their daughters there
Four times a year to grieve over her fate;
Such was the way and custom of those times.
But it has been said that in the end wise Jephthah
Did wrong concealing his daughter thus.
Phinehas, the leader, was not with him
To suggest a remedy for his daughter,
To counsel him according to religion,
So that he would sacrifice a cow or lamb instead,
Or give it to the priest to burn it
In her place.[9] For this they both lost
Body and soul. Though Phinehas and Jephthah
Both magnified God, they were afflicted in the end.
O friends,
In every matter of which you despair,
You must act wisely lest your work
Become too difficult; then you will
Pick with ease the fruit you merit.
O, Aḥaron, act wisely always, lest
You become confused or disgraced.

Khwājah Bukhārā'ī

Khwājah Bukhārā'ī's *Dāniyāl-nāmah* (henceforth DN; The Book of Daniel) is a *masnavī* of approximately 2,200 couplets.[1] It versifies the Book of Daniel and adds to it some details not found in the biblical account. The poem is divided into eighty-eight chapters, and its meter, although often defective in various manuscripts, is the ubiquitous *hazaj musaddas maḥzūf* we encountered in Shāhīn and 'Imrānī's epics. Khwājah Bukhārā'ī, "the Bukhārān

Master," dates his composition to 1918 of the Seleucid era, that is, 1606 CE.[2] Although we do not know his full name, his *nisba* (Arabic for "lineage," "connection"), "Bukhārāʾī," indicating his place of origin, as well as the pronunciation of certain words in DN that are characteristic of the Tajik dialect, confirm that he hailed from Bukhārā, one of the fabled cities of Central Asia.[3] That Jewish poets thrived in Bukhārā is attested to not only by the surviving works of accomplished poets like Khwājah Bukhārāʾī and Yūsuf b. Yisḥāq b. Mūsā (see below, chap. 11) but also by the inclusion of poets of Jewish origin in at least one official literary *tazkirah* (biographical memoir) written by a Muslim.[4]

Based on DN, Khwājah Bukhārāʾī should be regarded as a learned man, acquainted not only with the works of other Iranian Jewish poets like Shāhīn but also with the great epics of Iranian literature, especially Firdowsī's *Shah-nāmah*. In addition to being knowledgeable in the Torah and its principal commentaries, Khwājah Bukhārāʾī was familiar with midrashic and apocryphal tales, which he weaves into his epic. His creativeness manifests itself also in some of the original contributions he makes to the biblical narrative, such as the dialogue between Daniel and the lions (vv. 100–110).

No other works of Khwājah Bukhārāʾī seem to have survived, although it is apparent from DN that he was an accomplished poet. Nor do we have any other biographical information about him than what can be gleaned from this work. The verses of DN are imbued with a pessimistic, antiworldly attitude that characterizes much of classical Persian, especially Sufi poetry. Like Shāhīn and especially ʿImrānī before him, Khwājah Bukhārāʾī does not appear to consider the fatalistic, largely Sufi, outlook of classical Persian literature alien to the spirit of Judaism, perhaps because such sentiments had been expressed already in the Book of Ecclesiastes. Yet despite superimposing a Persian mood and mold upon a biblical theme, Khwājah Bukhārāʾī's fidelity to the details of the Book of Daniel reveals him as a poet deeply attached to his faith.

Like Shāhīn and ʿImrānī, Khwājah Bukhārāʾī employs the epic and mystical conventions of classical Persian poetry to convey moralistic teachings to be shared with the Iranian Muslim population at large. However, a Jewish feature unique to DN is its frequent expressions of messianic hopes. In line with these, Khwājah Bukhārāʾī blends and shapes the facts of

Persian history to suit his messianic theology. Amnon Netzer notes that "none of the Jewish writers of Persia ever inquired into or questioned the accuracy of dates, names, events, and the succession of Persian kings presented in their works. In *Dāniyāl-nāmah,* Cyrus (550–530 B.C.) is king of Persia and he is a contemporary of Darius (522–486 B.C.) who is king of "Irāq.' They combine their armies and fight Belshazzar, king of Babylon. After defeating Belshazzar, Darius, at the age of sixty-two, sits on the throne of 'Baghdad.' "[5]

In the narrative that follows, "Daniel in the Lions' Den," Khwājah Bukhārā'ī correctly identifies and embellishes the religious moral of the story, namely, that through Daniel's ordeal others, especially Darius, are shown convincing proof that the God of Daniel is omnipotent and worthy of being worshiped (6:28).[6]

Khwājah Bukhārā'ī's literary talents are especially vivid in battle scenes and descriptions of sunrises and sunsets, which, like similar passages in the works of Shāhīn and 'Imrānī, echo the language and imagery of the *Shahnāmah.* The feasts (*bazm*) that follow battles (*razm*) and the lamentations over the deaths of kings and heroes are equally inspired by Firdowsī's great epic. *Dāniyāl-nāmah* displays many of the rhetorical and stylistic features that were appreciated in Khwājah Bukhārā'ī's day and that characterized all Iranian epics, features that educated Iranians can still understand and admire.

Dāniyāl-nāmah (The Book of Daniel)

Daniel in the Lions' Den

How the Sages Exaggerated to the Shah, and How Daniel Was Brought and Thrown into the Lions' Pit

In that time,[1] a tribe of lost idolaters
Came before the king of kings;
They said to him: "O guardian of the World,
Your law and order are diminished
If over Daniel you do not reign.
When will you fully rule your kingdom?
O Khosrow,[2] if you deliberately change
The Law of 'Irāq and of Fars[3]
The state's dun-colored steed will weaken;

The kingdom's reins slip from the hand.
This counsel is a thousand times more strong
Than the rampart Alexander built."[4]
Thus did those men exaggerate in concert;
On their account the shah now felt constrained.
He saw no benefit in treachery and craft
And said: "Bring Daniel here at once!"
His Excellency's servants quickly then
Brought Daniel to the opening of the pit.
The shah's heart was on fire, a censer
Full of grief toward that aged prince.
However, he did recover sufficiently
To walk gracefully to the pit himself;
Coming forth quickly from his palace
He headed toward the lions' pit.
Once there, none dared to utter a word.
That very moment bold men flung
The aged prince into the lions' pit.
But by the Omnipotent's command, the lions
Huddled together, head to head,
At the wise man's feet, he who brought joy
To prisoners' hearts everywhere.
Though landing quickly on the pit's bottom,
His body was neither injured nor damaged;
Safe and unharmed, by the Almighty's command,
That man of good deeds descended into the pit.
The lions bowed their heads before his feet
And opened not their muzzles to cause injury.
As long as he dwelled at the bottom,
The pit was fully illumined by his light.
Many a wise and understanding man has said
That the Creator of the world, while creating,
Informed the lions thus, out of His grace:[5]
"One day, in days to come, and of a sudden
One of my elite will be flung by his enemies
Into your paws. Harm not nor injure him;

Guard him like the pupil of the eye."
O Khwājah, if you are virtuous and perfect,
You are among the slaves of the Almighty's army.
Should you then fall into lions' paws, into the pit,
May God of His grace preserve you.

How the Shah Cried out to Daniel from the Opening of the Pit, and How He Comforted Daniel

When that sage landed in the abyss of the pit,
The shah cried out to him from the top:
"O you who know the mysteries of the Living,
Immortal One, the God before Whom you have always
Bowed, let Him deliver you from this pit
To please your friends and spite your ill-wishers.
May you remain untroubled by these fierce lions;
May you dwell safely in the abyss of this pit!
As God's grace is eternally your friend,
What grief can come to you from the oppression
Of cruel enemies?"[6]
The shah then ordered that without delay
A slab of stone be brought before him
That he might place it on the opening of the pit
So none should strive against his purpose.[7]
The people rushed to find a stone measuring
Many parasangs, huge on each side.
They searched for it high and low, but
In the end, most stones fell short.
Then God called out to Gabriel:[8]
"Carry a stone from Zion to Baghdad;[9]
Though his ill-wishers cover the opening
Of Daniel's pit, their designs
Will not prevail."
When the command reached faithful Gabriel,
God's own instruction and address,
He pointed with his wing to a stone[10]
Incomparably heavier than all others.
He lifted it that moment into the air;

In an instant he flew like the wind
From Zion to Baghdad.
By the Omnipotent's command, of a sudden
The stone fell down near that pit.
On seeing it, the shah's officers resorted
To tricks, cunning, even sorcery,
And dropped that heavy stone as if compelled,
Upon the opening of the pit.
Then Iran's Shahānshah sealed off the area
With his ring and princely stamp lest, unawares,
Cruel enemies should throw the stone in
And kill Daniel, and so that the old sage
Would not suffer more from their torment
Nor be afflicted by the wishes of their souls.

How Darius Returned to His Palace and Went to Sleep Grieving

When the world wearies of day's golden egg,
Shabrang,[11] the dark bay steed, appears
From under the crow's wings. Did not Jacob,
That sage of Canaan, consort with sorrow
On account of Joseph?
As soon as they flung Daniel into the pit,
The shah set out toward his palace,
Depressed and weary on Daniel's account,
He rent the pocket of his heart,
The very shirt of his own soul.
So torn apart was the king's heart
That his wound's pain kept increasing
As he walked on. Upon reaching the palace
His ruddy face had turned yellow like straw.
Grieving for Daniel, he was unable
To sit still upon his throne;
Anguish assailed him so for the old man's sake
It brought the shah out of his own home.[12]
He remained sleepless, although in search
Of sleep he rested his head on the pillow.
Thoughts of the sage chased sleep away;

Restless, he tossed from night to dawn.
Not even briefly did sleep visit his eyes;
It fled completely from over his head.

How Darius Went to the Opening of the Pit in the Morning, and How He Called out to Daniel, Who Answered Him

When dawn heralded the loyal morning,
The zephyr wiped the rust off night's mirror.
When morning's light turned bright
Time itself rejoiced at the occasion.
The moon-cheeked shah arose then,
Also radiant, like the sun,[13] and headed
Toward the pit, followed by courtiers.
Full of pain, with royal gait he approached
And saw his seal unbroken all around the pit.
At once he ordered his officers:
"Lift that stone off the pit."
They obeyed and opened up the pit;
With effort they pushed the stone aside.
From high above over the people, the shah
Glanced into the abyss of the pit and said:
"O slave of the Most Generous Creator,
Answer me, for I almost died of grief.
If you are alive, God's and your slave
Am I and all the world's kings.[14]
I did not sleep a wink on your account,
Drowning in fire and water, grieving for your safety.
My heart and soul bleed for your sake,
For I know not what happened to you.
God, before Whom you daily bowed,
Whose attributes you extolled day by day,
Did He ease this hardship for you or not?
Did he save you from the lions' claws or not?"
Then out of the darkness the sage replied:
"O shah, may you endure forever!
May your enemies grieve, your friends rejoice,
And majesty befriend you in the world.

May the heavenly spheres watch over you
Always. God, whose creation I am,
Sent an angel to me.[15] He closed the mouths
Of the ferocious lions;[16] by God's decree,
I did not suffer the loss of one hair,
Nor any damage or injury from those lions.
My actions always have been pure before God
And thus the wishes of my enemies have come to naught.
Ever prepared in loyalty toward Him I always
Refrained from actions that would displease Him.[17]
I never followed my own desires;
Thus all that is difficult turned easy for me.
And now, O shah, at your palace as well,
I am found guiltless and without sin."[18]

How the Shah Rejoiced and Threw a Rope into the Pit for Daniel

Full of happiness, that benevolent shah
Nearly jumped out of his clothes.
His heart was free from the bonds of grief;
Cheer turned his countenance into a nosegay.
He ordered his messengers at once: "Hurry,
Bring a rope to him quickly!"
On hearing the royal command,
They ran like wild gazelles
And brought a well-twisted rope,
Whose every loop contained a knot;
Its many twists and folds
Resembled lovelocks of the fair;
Its many folded, curly, closed chains,
Were like Majnūn,[19] a weeping willow,
Or a hyacinth. With his own hands,
The happy shah passed on the golden rope
To silver arms, saying to them:
"O tender youths, each one of you is dear to me.
Look up to elders with affection
For your own youth will fade away.
As you rescue Daniel and bring him up

Carefully out of this dangerous pit,
Even if you were peerless in affection,
An accident could happen; so help him!"
At once those moon-faced, sweet helpers,
Hastened to throw the rope into the pit.

How the Lions Became Aware of Daniel's Departure from the Pit and Came to Him in Mute Language

When by the shah's command the silver arms
Threw that golden rope into the pit
The lions knew for certain then
That the afflicted sage would leave the pit.
His going affected them deeply;
The thought of separation made them sad.
Within the abyss of the pit the lions
Began to speak by God's command
(Know that they spoke in mute language),
Saying: "You cheered our hearts and souls;
Why did you dwell here to begin with,
If now you must leave our abode?
When one warmly befriends the evening guest,
Next day's separation does not come easy;
Why do you flee from us now?
We showed you nothing but our goodness."
Wise Daniel replied: "May God's will[20]
Be pleased with you! How long will you grieve
Over our separation? Let not your eyes
Shed any more tears for me; having fulfilled
The Incomparable's command, you clearly passed
His test. O lions, your goodness will endure
In the world until the Day of Resurrection."
This good deed needs no further explanation
For this tale has become fabled everywhere.
The lions were satisfied with his answer;
They were set free from the bonds of grief.
Then the sage bid them farewell, while they
Continued to profess their loyalty.

How They Brought Daniel out of the Pit, and How Spectators Gathered Around

When Daniel freed himself from the lions,
He set his mind on coming out of there.
The wise sage leapt forth with skill,
The golden rope tied round his arm and waist.
With hundreds of graceful signs the exalted sage
Beckoned that they should pull him up.
The youths, admiring his polished airs,
Pulled him up with hundreds of cheers.
Fulfilling his friends' wishes at last,
The sage with moonlike face rose from the pit.
His countenance illumined the world;
He shone over creation like the sun.
The slender body of that good-natured sage, indeed,
Was not damaged, diminished, by so much as a hair.
The pure being of that exalted sage
Was free of any harm or discord.
The lions did not wound his heart
Because of his belief in his Creator.
So many people came to the pit's opening
That travelers were delayed everywhere.
And when they beheld the mystery-knowing sage
They ran toward him from every corner.
His former enemies were all remorseful,
For now they remembered Resurrection Day.
Their hearts were so agitated that you'd think
Their souls were ready to depart their bodies.
They lost their tongue, their speech;
Their rosy faces all turned pale.
Rending the collar of violent desire,
They severed greed from their souls.

How the Shah Became Angry with the Enemies of Daniel, and How He Threw Them into the Lions' Pit

Beholding that miracle, the shah's devotion
To the sage increased a hundredfold.
He turned into a firm believer and felt

Compelled to gird his loins in Daniel's service.
Love for Daniel increased greatly in his heart;
Endlessly he offered thanks to God.
But when he saw Daniel's enemies
He turned suddenly into a roaring lion.
The shah's face was kindled by aversion,
As if forbearance's sapling burned within him.
When thus he adorned himself in anger's garment,
A great cry rose freely, even from slaves.
That moment the people's cries and their laments
Reminded one of Resurrection and Judgment Day.[21]
That same hour the shah ordered his officers:
"Go quickly to those who slandered Daniel;
Seize them and throw them into the pit;
Thus should one deal with ill-wishers.
Spare not their wives or children;
Withhold your pity from them;
Throw them into the pit upside down;
Let those evil ones be food for the lions;
Let their souls' phoenixes[22] move from the world
Of being to the nether world with hundreds of groans;
Let them be torn apart by lions' fangs
That they may know the fate of the afflicted!"
Warriors leapt from their stations;
They tied the enemies' abject hands;
You'd say they took their very lives away.
Greatly they humbled all those people,
Driving them one by one toward the pit.
They threw those evil ones into the pit,
Delivering the world of them at last.
Their wives and children were thrown in as well;
All fell into the pit that they had dug.
Ferocious male lions leapt from their place
And sharpened their teeth and fangs on them.[23]
When the brave one threw them in but halfway,
The lions' rule began at once:

They trampled them on the pit's bottom,
Their paws left imprints with their blood.[24]
Their claws tore out the hearts of their souls,
Sending them to roam the desert of nonexistence.

How Darius Sent a Letter to His Realm Regarding the Security of Daniel's People and in Praise of God the Exalted

When the shah's fury had subsided,
He summoned all his scribes at once:
"Compose a fluent decree on my behalf
And this shall be your subject,
For every nation in each and every region,
Wherever Law holds sway,
I rule today, Shahānshah of Iran;
I am the realm's protector,
The leader of its heroes.
I am the heir of Jamshīd's[25] kingdom.
Write the decree in my name, first of all,
With the following content: 'No one must dare,
In city or in countryside, to entertain bad thoughts
Against or answer harshly the people
Of Prince Daniel. None should molest them,
Their labor or its fruit.
Nothing but goodness should the people show them;
For what is better in the world than being good-natured?
None should divulge their secrets;
Let not a talebearer against them remain
In the world. Their God is the Almighty Creator;
His grace is ever joined to them.
Their God is the creator of sun and moon;
And He protects His people always.
His miracles are witnessed through eternity;
No one has seen a miracle that was not His.
He delivered Daniel quickly from the lions' claws
And from the dark pit.' "[26]
Having instructed the scribes this way,
They erased from their hearts all thoughts

Of periphrasis. That very moment, reeds ready,
They took down the letter with their own hands.
In it they first praised the Creator,
Piercing many a pearl of his attributes;
They wrote down what was in the shah's heart.
His wish fulfilled, the shah was now content,
He dispatched the letters at once
To the four corners of his realm.

An Apocryphal Epic

3

ʿImrānī's *Ḥanukkah-nāmah* (The Book of Ḥanukkah)

Among ʿImrānī's minor works we find *Ḥanukkah-nāmah* (henceforth HN; The book of Ḥanukkah), only 1,800 couplets long.[1] Composed in 1524, it is based primarily on the apocryphal First Book of Maccabees, which recounts the struggle of the Maccabees against the Greeks under the emperor Antiochus Epiphanes (d. 164 BCE). This *masnavī* is also known as *Ẓafar-nāmah*, "The Book of Victory,"[2] because it celebrates the Jewish victory of the Hasmoneans, led by Mattatiah and his five sons, against overwhelming odds.

The style and tone of HN are reminiscent of ʿImrānī's *Fatḥ-nāmah;* its martial content calls to mind, once more, Firdowsī's *Shah-nāmah.* Its meter, *ramal muqtażab musaddas maṭvī marfūʿ*, is complex and shows off ʿImrānī's poetic skills. A noteworthy feature of HN is its substantially larger Hebrew vocabulary than most other JP epics.

The Victory of the Maccabees

Bagrīs Deceives Daqiyānūs, Gathers a Large Army and Countless Elephants, and Leads Them

The shah was taken in by [Bagrīs'] deceit,[3]
And with his princes now sat down to feast,

Dispatching first a host of messengers
To right and left and over land and sea.
Wherever a brave leader could be found,
A powerful commander, lord, or prince,
He levied a large army without end,
Ill-tempered infidels all, like himself.
5 From Khaṭā, Chīn, and Barbar[4]
He gathered many an officer for the army;
He even sent a messenger to Hindustān,
One close to the troops there,
Desiring a white Mangalūsī elephant.[5]
He accoutered everyone with weapons;[6]
Nearly fifty thousand elephant drivers
Came for his sake from Hindustān.
On seeing the large army he had gathered,
The infidel ordered them tallied:
10 It was nine hundred thousand men strong!
Then he set out, unlucky; with his own feet
He ran toward the grave, for doom is blind
To fortune! And as for Bagrīs,[7]
That reprobate dog (may Nimrod be
The affliction of them both!),[8]
When they reached *Israel*'s borders,
Both *uncircumcised* men rejoiced;
First Bagrīs then Daqiyānūs[9] said:
"Don't worry, have no care, our army
15 Is numerous and mighty;
Our Lāt[10] is undoubtedly on our side,
Whereas I think their God
Is no longer their Friend."
When the exalted leaders became aware
Of those infidel dogs and informers,
They felt helpless for a while,
Each kept calling on the Almighty.
Mattatiah and his five sons were,
One and all, wise men.
There was a site

20 Of mercy near Miṣpeh,[11] a station
Meant for bowing and prostration;[12]
There the Israelites gathered
And chose their location.
They practiced *interrupted fasts,*[13]
Lamenting greatly, bareheaded
And with bare feet, with wounded hearts,
Dazed and distressed by grief
Caused by the infidels.
One month after these incidents,
The great calamity appeared.
25 Daqiyānūs' army suddenly came into view,
With princes, gilded parasols, and drums,
And Bagrīs, that reprobate infidel,
Headed in haste toward the *Temple*
Of the Almighty; he breached it
Thirteen times, revealing all its substance.
Then he, the reprobate, decreed
That all the city's ramparts be destroyed
Along with all the homes; and then
30 That wretched man came to Daqiyānūs,
Displaying all his skills, and said:
"O shah, Israel fled;
You have succeeded in your wish.
I have destroyed the choicest homes,
All ramparts and all towers.
I have attacked with confidence,
Turned my attention to every province.
Wherever Israelites are found,
We annihilated or turned them into heathens.[14]
35 This people's name we scattered,
Their heads we severed from their bodies."
When Mattatiah heard yet again
Of this army's tyranny and injustice,
He summoned his sons once more,
Seated them gladly by his side,
And spoke: "I've had another revelation;

The *divine voice* called to me thus:
"This army, all these princes, and this host,
None other than the shah has mustered.
Yet shall they all fall by the sword,
To find a resting place in Hell.
God's house will be restored, and soon
We shall be free of this grief and thrall.
The Almighty's friendship will annihilate
This futile might, the infidels' tyranny.
For God and the Prophet's sake, fight
Yet again the infidels like lions;
Arm yourselves; show yourselves victorious
So that these accursed infidels will know
There is no God but only the Creator.
Their star has turned choleric; truly,
You have nothing to fear from these malicious men."
Having said this, he blessed them,
Thereby dispelling the infidels' work.
He beseeched God on his sons' behalf
And blessed Judah first: "Be like the lion
In the thicket; fear not the business
Of malicious men. O Judah, you are
My firstborn; prove it, and make me happy!
If you'll remain a lion always,
Your heart will not fear these dogs.
Judah, you are like Jacob's son;[15]
May all your work succeed!"
Next he blessed Simon:
"May your face never grow pale,
And may God's blessing ever dwell in your soul;
May it ever rejoice in God's mercy!
Like Simon, who toward Shekem and Hamor,
Showed manly strength and bravery,[16] just so,
May the Almighty grant your wish
To scatter the dust of these dogs
Upon the wind! May all of you triumph quickly
Over the infidels, prevail over the enemy!

Whoever engages you in combat will end
With a sword thrust in his heart."
Then he blessed Yoḥannan: "May the friendship
Of the universal Lord be yours!
May God the Creator watch over you;
May your good fortune never decrease;
Your good works increase.
Be bold everywhere;
May you be like Abner, the son of Ner![17]
Like Simon you are strong and brave;
You leave no enemies standing.
May the Divine Friend's favor
Never diminish toward you;
If you will love Him, all will be well;
If you will trust in Him, you'll surely tread
Upon the heads of your enemies!
God is your overseer supreme;
May the Friend's largesse never leave you!
May God watch over you continually,
And never overlook your deeds and pleas!"
Then he blessed Jonathan:
"May the Universal Lord befriend you always!
May you never be absent from the world,
And may your foot never be caught
In grief and calamity's snare!
Be not diminished, but increase,
And be first everywhere.
May your victory resemble that of Jonathan,
The son of Saul, that great man,
Who struck the Philistines by sword
And rescued the people Israel from torment.[18]
May God help you the same way, and may you be
Quickly rid of this army, this host!
May you suffer no injury; may your Lord God
Set you free! May God's blessing, in season and out,
Accompany you eternally!"
Last he blessed El'azar:

"May your heart never suffer pain!
So long as God's pardon is your companion,
Your work will prosper every minute.
May your enemies never lord over you,
And may a diadem ever adorn your head.
You are like Phinehas in purity;[19]
May you never have grief, trouble, affliction.
May your heart be illumined by God's light,
Your work prosper minute by minute.
May you never lack friendship,
And may you quickly flay all enemies!"
On hearing their father's blessings,
The sons rejoiced; they donned their arms
In turmoil like the sea; they kissed
The hands and feet of their father,
And set out for war. Their faces looked toward
The infidels; their hearts held fast to God.
They gave up hope of life and did not swerve
From their forefathers' tradition.
They offered themselves in sacrifice,
Heart and soul, to God.
Reaching the infidels' camp, they drew
The sword of vengeance from their belts,
Opened their arms to war to prove
Once more their renown.
When Bagrīs heard of this, the cheating infidel
Almost died of fear.
The heroes joined ranks, shut off the enemy
In five directions, so that while the heathens
Were mounting their horses,
They killed almost sixty thousand men.
Then Bagrīs, that wretched dog, came to the shah
And said: "If you wish to save your honor,
Command the army to don their weapons
And strive together for the shah.
If you will capture these three or four men,
You will exceed in greatness even Alexander!

O shah, against these five men,
Choose five hundred thousand from among
Your fierce, bloodthirsty warriors; fewer
Cannot oppose them in battle!"
On hearing this, the wicked infidel shah
At once browbeat his cavalry and army.
They donned their armor and swore victory
To the infidel shah. Armed with maces,
Axes, swords, and bows, the infidel army
Attacked. The war's riot was great;
Clamor and cries rose to the heavens.
But those five heroes in the battle's midst
Set upon their work like fire:
Whoever came forth from the cavalry or army
Was destroyed, annihilated on the spot.
None could approach them and return
Whence he came, but all the time
Ten thousand more warriors would come
From right and left. At last matters
Turned hard: the enemy's number was greater
Than the leaves of the trees, and yet
The heroes, male lions, persevered in battle,
At all times aware of one another.
God the Exalted sent them succor;
Boundless and countless aid He sent them.
From morn till dusk they battled,
With blows of the sword and piercing arrows,
When by fickle fortune it came to pass
That mighty Judah became helpless.
His horse was struck by an arrow;
He fell and almost died on the spot.
When that young man fell to the ground,
He wished to rise again, just like the wind,
But could not; hundreds, tens of thousands,
Of infidels surrounded him. Cut off
From his brothers, in the end,
He was killed by tyranny's sword.

When his brothers became aware of this,
They burst into laments over him.
Afflicted, full of pain, dejected,
Weeping, and wailing mournfully
Over Time's sorrows, they turned homeward.
They set the infidels free, and on the way
Ceased not lamenting. The four appeared before
Their father and told him everything.
When Mattatiah heard the news,
He was deeply distressed and grieved
But then addressed his four sons thus:
"It is not proper to rest in prison.
You say Judah is gone; grieve not,
But rejoice, for there is no decrease
In your ranks; I'll ride with you,
I'll be a lion chasing prey.
We will defeat these infidels,
Melt them away like silver.
There are five hundred thousand more of them
Still in place, evil and vicious.
O tyrants, if we survive,
The good name of good men will not perish!
Why do you now lament for one?
Shame on you! Why do you wail?
Neither Ezra nor the *Temple* survived forever;
Say our Judah did not die in vain!
He gave his soul for God's sake,
For Whom all ought to sacrifice themselves."
Having said this, he donned arms and armor,
Preparing to enter the fray on God's behalf.
His battle cry: "For God eternally,
For His sake and for His pleasure!"
He was not sad, grieved not for his son;
He cut his heart off from his son and kindred.
(He who has not come to such a pass,
How can he guide others on this road?
He whose faith is not as strong,

Surely he lacks knowledge of true faith!
A man without pain is but a rubbish heap
Defiled by sin. Until a man is purified
Through the Law, how can he attain the life
Of those who are pure?
Through fraud, tricks, and deceit,
Ideas, fame, and honor are turned upside down.
It is surely a disgrace upon your name
To lack knowledge of your own faith!
O you, as precious as the eye itself,
Better open your heart's eye
Till you behold the path of the righteous,
Those who know and contemplate God.
Then should you experience oppression
For three or four days, yet in the end
You would behold God's mercy.
The prophets of the world experienced
All manner of injustice and oppression.
Oppression's result is more oppression;
How can the way of such words be ignored?
If you cleave not to His mercy,
How can you attain your heart's desire?)
When Mattatiah and his four sons
Turned their faces on to God's path,
And God, the Lord of all, the Just Creator
Of everything, beheld their way,
Certain of the sincerity with which
They called upon Him, knowing His path
Truly, and aware that they suffered misfortune
Solely for God, Faith, and Law,
He brought another army into being
Made up of avenging, fearsome angels.[20]
Each was armed with a fiery mace.
They came and hemmed in the infidels;
The angels were bent on *destruction,*[21]
Striking the infidels with *fire and brimstone.*[22]
They stood in rows on the field of battle

Encompassing the army round about.
When Mattatiah and his sons arrived
And saw those troops, he smiled and said:
"O dear sons, what do you see?
What do you gather from this garden?"
They answered: "We see a large army
Of faces full of light resembling
Fire surrounding the infidels.
This gladdens us and grieves us not!"
[Mattatiah replied]: "God sent this army
To aid us, to drive them all away;
The efforts of the godly man
Always and surely turn out well."
When from their father they heard
The explanation of this mystery,
The sons bowed their heads in prayer
To God and then began to fight,
Raining misfortune upon the infidels.
Those angels, by the command of the pure Almighty,
Struck down three hundred thousand infidels.
All the famed warriors of that army
Were burned and turned to ashes.
Out of grief, Daqiyānūs tore his garments,
Saying, "Where did the fire come from?
Whence came this calamity upon me?"
The infidel had a fair companion,
A friend of Jacob's offspring,
Who said: "O ignorant one, flee!
Strive no more with your God!
If once again you make a stand against
This army, you also will turn to embers."
On hearing this, that misguided shah
Set out on the road to flee;
Abandoning both throne and crown,
Like a madman he took to the road.
He felt such dread, was so beside himself,
He failed to bring his grand vizier along;

He saved only his own head, took off
As quick as smoke, all by his solitary self.
When Bagrīs looked out of a sudden
And saw no army, no princes, and no shah,
He thought, with heart on fire:
"The likes of me should not fall prisoner.
It would appear that it is true: *Israel*
Is the noble, choice people of *God*.
Whoever strives with them contends against
His own purpose; without a doubt,
He'll come to woe and grief;
Sorrow and affliction will overtake him.
He who becomes the enemy of God's friends,
Will quickly become like me. This army
Is with God and knows Him; truly this is
A divine host." The infidel mused thus
When he saw the entire army laid waste.
All perished through God's wrath,
And those who survived were sorely tried.
Then Mattatiah and his four sons—
A thousand mercies on them!—
Fell on the infidels and chopped off
Their heads. Like a crocodile in battle,
Mattatiah opened wide war's mouth and arms,
Raising a new riot every moment;
Its fiery rage melted everything.
Only some two or three thousand riders
Remained in place, like sick donkeys.
Thus Yoḥannan decided and said to Jonathan:
"Capture these dogs alive by the munificence
Of the eternal living One
That we may burn these oppressors
And strew dust upon their eyes!"
Bagrīs then tried to flee,
To escape from that calamity and torment,
But Jonathan, seeing him from afar, told Yoḥannan,
Who drove his mount toward him and

Swift as the wind felled him to the ground.
They tied him firmly and broke his head
In twenty places. Then Yoḥannan, the Sun of the Age,
Exclaimed: "O ignorant infidel dog,
Of all the wells you've dug,
You threw yourself at last into this one.
O tyrant of the oppressed, you enjoyed
Oppression and injustice,
Heedless of poor men's sighs,
Ignorant of their laments and plaints;
At last their sighs have destroyed
Those who spurned them.
Whatsoever you did, openly and in secret,
Time paid you back only for one in a hundred.
O overthrown infidel dog,
All the injustice you brought upon the Sons of Jacob,
God the Exalted has visited on you;
Upon your head he rained your own injustice!"
Then he cut out Bagrīs' tongue, gouged out his eyes,
And drove him onward in heavy chains.
They all returned from battle then,
All present except for El'azar.
For him they greatly cried and lamented,
Rending their clothes in grief,
Questioning countless soldiers.
One person said: "I saw him making haste,
Ripping an elephant's body with his sword."
Then Yoḥannan ran out with Jonathan
Toward that elphant. At last they found El'azar
Pinned under the elephant, lifeless and dead.[23]
Then all lamented over him with groans,
Sighs, and tears of blood. Yet
Since it was a day of victory,
They were cheerful and glad as well:
Though they might not be free of grief,
All hearts were checkered with joy.

The Gathering of the Community of Israel, *Their Coming to the* Temple *and Purifying of It, Their Needing But Not Finding Pure Oil Except for One Night, and Its Kindling and Burning for Eight Days and Nights Through the* Wonders and Miracles of the King of Kings, the One and the Unique, Whose Name Is One, God, Blessed Be He.

When they beheld all the *uncircumcised* ones
Annihilated, the Israelites gathered,
All thanking God; they buried the two bodies.[24]
Mattatiah and his three surviving sons headed
Happy and smiling toward the *Temple*
Accompanied by all of *Israel*'s wise learned men,
Rejoicing and lighthearted. God's house
They restored at once and made it even better
Than it was at first; the breaches Bagrīs had made,
That cheating and malicious dog,
They rebuilt to blind the eyes of infidels
And ignoramuses. God's altar they rededicated
And offered sacrifices to Him once more.
The people *Israel* rejoiced at having subdued
The *uncircumcised*. They laughed with happiness,
And they cried out to God with all their hearts:
"Over the wonders and miracles,
The redemption and the wars,"[25]
Which You have performed for the weak,
Turning to joy the hearts of the aggrieved.
A brave and mighty king, the supreme ruler
Of seven climes, wished to tear out our hearts,
Destroy us all, together with our faith and Law,
Preying upon our weak and helpless;
And he turned us from our faith,
Humbled us with the sword of vengeance;
He opposed us and he opposed You;
Endlessly he oppressed us: but You
Bestowed on us countless favors,
You were the friend, companion of the abject,
You remembered the covenant with the *Fathers,*[26]

And in the eyes of the enemy strewed dust.
When our torment and injustice mastered us,
You stepped in to bring relief.
You stood over the weak, You restored justice
To the poor man and the destitute;
You annihilated the impious and desired
Vengeance upon them for our sakes.
You have entrusted to the weak and wounded
A full, well-equipped army beyond count,
Made up of tigers, boars, hyenas.
You've granted unto a few men to destroy
The enemy's pollution; you've uprooted the unjust,
To cast them into the arms of pious men.
The infidels have all been vanquished,
Root and branch, like a toppled tree.
They were impure, malicious, idolatrous.
You upended them, turned them topsy-turvy
In battle with the pure; upon the *uncircumcised*
You've loosed Your rage so that they perish
In the arms of the faithful;
You've annihilated them, beholding Your grace;
They perished like clouds from terror.
You've done this favor for our sake,
For the *merit* and excellence of the *Torah;*
Out of Your endless kindness had You mercy
Upon the weak and indigent. Wherever
This event becomes known, You have ennobled
Your Own Name and *Temple.* Before You,
Chieftains, leaders, and princes bow down,
Acknowledging there is no Judge but You.
You are both Padshah and Grandee,
Pure and Unique, the Creator.
Had not Your grace befriended us,
Our name would have perished in the world.
You've granted us a victory
Which set us free from bondage;
You have delivered us from calamity;

We who were chosen are chosen once again.
The *Temple* which the accursed infidels
Closed and uprooted, You opened its closed doors.
Freedom you gave amid destruction,
So that we can once more enter
Your house with thanksgiving and praise.
At last we have restored the chosenness
Of the chosen *holy Temple.*
When You kindled our lamp, we became
Safe in the world; You've raised us
And burned down the enemy's house.
May it remain lit until the Day of Resurrection,
And may the enemy's portion and salvation
Always consist of Your wrath.
May whoever contends with us,
And sheds our blood, all who oppress us,
Have their roots and branches wither, even as
Israel's faith and Law increase
Through our just God. May all who battle
Against God with us grow thorns in their hearts
And may they be on fire in the world.
May worship of You endure, O Lord,
As long as Your firmament stands,
Along with Your pleasure and mercy!
You show favor toward *Israel,*
You are the *Savior* of each and every one.
But when *Israel* turned from obedience,
The *uncircumcised* infidels tried us sorely."
Then they hanged the survivors,
And turned again to God with thanks.
At once they reopened the *Temple*
And placed in it its special implements.
Everything was prepared except the oil,
Which could nowhere be found. A special
Olive oil was needed, no other oil was
Appropriate. After much searching,
They found a single flask of it;

The *priests* rejoiced at this, for they
Deemed it most precious. When Mattatiah
Beheld the oil, he lit the lamps at once,
But there was only enough to light
The Chosen House for one night;
Of this right oil there was no more.
From morning until evening and back again
To morning, the lamps continued burning,
While by the Incomparable's order
The olive oil lasted.
When *Israel* beheld these miracles,
God's power amazed them;
Inspired by it, they cried out
To Him with all their hearts;
They drew close to Him, bound themselves
To Him heart and soul with a great love.
And when Mattatiah saw that miracle,
He called together the *Bet Din*[27] again
To register on the twenty-fifth of Kislev,[28]
How God showed favor, endless generosity,
And grace; Israel was released from torment,
From the oppression of the *uncircumcised* dog.
They sent the scroll to every kingdom
To inform the faithful everywhere.
They set apart these seven days
From morning until night, and on the eighth
Decreed that all should rejoice greatly,
Strive to praise God for His gift.
Those who could buy it should drink wine,
Be satisfied with the word of God.
They should embrace their wives and children,
Aid the poor, help out the helpless,
Showing them great kindness. They should take care
Of widows, refrain from harming orphans.
They should keep no mourning and no fasts,
Lament not nor grieve.

Therefore shall you place at your door

Another lamp each evening.
But put no drop of oil in the lamp,
Until your heart itself is illumined
And you[29] remember the *Temple,* offering thanks
For the Friend's favors.
When this *scroll* about the Almighty's grace
Had visited every province, each site of pilgrimage,
The faithful rejoiced and accepted the new custom:
They thanked God and were cheered by the good news.
There was a *Bet Din* to judge that age,
Its members diligent, working in harmony
With the leaders of *Israel.*
Perfectly skillful and perfect,
All came before Yoḥannan.
Jonathan became king,
Simon commander of the army,
A glorious, exalted warrior.
From Arabia all the way to ʻIraq,
Their names spread to the horizons,
And everywhere this tale came to be known,
Fear of God's wrath prevailed.
All purged their hearts of enmity
And cast their hearts' idols into the fire.
Yoḥannan's name was known unto
The kingdoms and cities of the world.
Kings brought him tribute; sovereigns
Offered him crowns; while he with justice
Displaying just favors came to be known
Throughout the world.

Didactic Poetry

4

Yehudah b. David's *Makhzan al-pand* (The Treasury of Advice)

I have already drawn attention to the inclination of Iranian Jewish poets toward didacticism, an inclination firmly grounded in pre-Islamic and classical Persian literature.[1] Whereas this device is usually present in verses scattered throughout various *masnavīs*, *Makhzan al-pand* (The treasury of advice), probably modeled on Saʿdī's (d. 1292) or ʿAṭṭār's (d. 1220) *Pand-nāmah,* is a short masnavī of about 160 couplets in the meter *hazaj maḥẕūf,* devoted entirely to proffering advice.[2] Without a doubt this genre was also influenced by the Book of Proverbs. *Makhzan al-pand* is a mirror of the ideals of a given age and society; as such its value transcends its literary merits.

There is practically no biographical information available on Yehudah b. David, the author of *Makhzan al-pand.* The most frequent *nisba* associated with his name in manuscripts, "Lārī," indicates that he hailed from Lār, a town in the southwestern region of Iran; however, he is also referred to on occasion as Yehudah Shīrāzī, Yehudah of Shīrāz. Yehudah b. David probably lived in the sixteenth or at the beginning of the seventeenth century. Amnon Netzer doubts that he is the author of *Timsāl-nāmah* (The book of similitudes), also known as *Qiṣṣe-yi haft vazīrān* (The story of seven viziers), although Shim'on Ḥakam and some early scholars of JP texts have so identified him.[3]

By the Creator's order and through His grace[4]
I open the locks of "The Treasury of Advice."
Listen to me, think evil of no one;
Make the fear of God your custom.
Place worship ahead of other work,
So that your works may prosper.
If you wish to befriend good fortune,
Express your gratitude to the Almighty
Day and night; trust Him in every matter,
And He'll fulfill your wants and wishes.
Guard in your heart God's rites and commands,
So He, in turn, will watch over you.
Befriend the well born;
Never cross over to the indolent.
Cast your eyes upon the intelligent,
And always heed their words.
Never be jealous of another's wealth;
Envy turns the complexion yellow
And fills the eyes with tears.
Content yourself with salted bread and greens;
Eat not a morsel from another's table [un]invited.[5]
Avoid needing help from relatives;
Death is preferable to their taunts.
Why should you seek from those who are
Themselves in need? Seek your desire from God;
From the Almighty seek your daily bread.
O person in Time's grip, don't say,
"I'll do it tomorrow,"
For who knows what tomorrow brings?
Do not curse a *judge* and a wise man;
The kingdom stands through their decree.
Choose a youthful wife, a pleasing friend,
Who will always be your bosom's heart.

Don't let your wife be bold toward you;
A snake is always better in its hole.
And if she gives birth to your child,[6]
Teach him good manners[7] so he will prosper.
Buy him a few books, and let him learn wisdom
In school; pay the schoolmaster
So that he'll teach him well.
Beware, do not converse with foolish women;
Never befriend or associate with cheats.
Never befriend a foreign woman;
Guard yourself from their tricks and plots.
If your scales are weighted right,
You will never suffer loss in this world;
But if you take another's wealth unjustly,
One of its barley grains will make you lose
A hundred harvests.
If you have any business with your ruler,
Don't lie to him and be discreet.
If someone chances to be far from home,
Take care of him as if he were at home.
Dwell in your home in winter,
When the roads are full of water and mud.
Never travel in snow and rain but always
In the spring.
                    Guard your tongue from slander;
It brings you nothing but trouble.
Never strive with the powerful;
The weak falls prey to the wolf's paw.
Be humble and peaceful with all men
And they will be your servants.
Seek God's wish in everything you do;
Through much effort many of your wishes
Will be fulfilled.
                    If you hire a laborer
Or a servant, treat him as your offspring
Or even better; do not be angry with him
If he is indolent. Pay him his wages,

And treat him in a manly fashion.
Regard his experience and intellect,
For this world holds no one in high regard:
Sometimes you see princes in need,
Sometimes the mangy wear a crown and robe.
The world always demeans the great
And raises up the fallen. A pauper is held
In low esteem by his companions.
Everyone in the world befriends the rich,
And all forgive a rich man's ignorance
While they laugh at the pauper's
Intelligence and wisdom.
Reread everything you write
Lest you upset someone through an error.
Flee from shahs and lords;
Become a hermit when faced with an army.
Don't be their guest at gatherings,
For you will stray if you eat their bread.
If you have acquired a lot of wealth,
You have acquired anxiety and grief;
Eating a slice of barley bread in peace
Is better than having a platter full of food
But lacking peace of mind.
Don't travel with an ignoramus;
Journey with wise sages. Teach your children
A craft so that they'll always be free
From oppression.
The world is like a venomous dragon:
Sometimes its nature is poison, sometimes sugar.
Time is full of grief and pain;
No one quaffs pure wine from its cup.
How can one sleep at ease upon this road?
Fear of ill-wishers splits the heart in two.
If a friend finds eminence in this world,
Don't envy him, if you are wise;
Don't speak to him as if you were a pauper;
Don't think he outranks you.

A person who is indigent does not always remain so;
Sometimes he is raised high and sometimes humbled.
The world gives no one happiness only;
Sometimes it gives anger and rage, sometimes one's wish.
Perform good deeds and you will find deliverance.
Like a shadow our lives are transient.
Redeem prisoners from grief's prison.
Don't take advantage of the lowly.
If you have animals in your home,
Do not neglect them, do not vex them.
If you should overhear another's secret,
And you are asked about it, say,
"I have forgotten." Conceal within your heart
Like buried treasure the secrets of your friends.
Do not praise anyone and do not boast;
God alone is worthy of praise and epithets.
Cherish your friend as your own eyes,
Don't vex him, do not torment him.
Do not converse with your friend's foe,
For if you do, your friend becomes your enemy.
To repent of bad deeds in old age,
Is like sowing at reaping time.
Dying of sadness in a foreign land
Is better than coveting things of other men.
When a person departs this world,
Accompany him to the cemetery.
If you love someone in your heart,
His heart will incline toward you.
Do not befriend those who have gone astray,
And do not drink wine at their feasts.
Strive hard to acquire knowledge of God;
Don't leave the schoolhouse for the market.
Be content with your gain and profit;
Respect the poor and the dervish.
Always seek God's gifts and kindness
For the kindness of rich men is beggary.
Treat lawfully him who acts badly toward you;

Do nothing that God rejects.
Always associate with His creatures.
Be like onions and salt in every soup.
Deem yourself blessed and fortunate when friend
Sits with friend.
                    Women and children
Cannot be trusted; they cannot keep
Another's secret. Never be mild
With a child, for he will become rude
And shameless to your face.
When you fill your belly in your home,
Set aside a piece of bread for the poor.
Be courteous to all men; do not
Esteem one person lower than another.
Another's child deem as your own,
And if he has a father, deem him a crown.
Do not make anyone wait until tomorrow;
One cannot have trust in the morrow.
Befriend those dear to you;
He is no friend who merely talks of friendship.
Not everyone who greets you in friendship
Is true to you in friendship and in love.
He who is your friend in good fortune
Becomes your enemy in your misfortune.
Befriend religious men first of all,
Then seek to converse with great men.
If you hear one mention another's fault,
Act as though you've never heard of it.
When there is love among people,
What is there to lament?
But if it breaks, everyone scatters.
                    All those who tell you
About another's faults, find fault
With you in others' company.
Always comply with the wishes of masters,
For the business of the fortunate succeeds.
If your friend befriends your enemies,

Cease to reveal to him the secrets of your heart.
If you possess intelligence and judgment,
Don't eat a morsel without appetite.
Don't eat until satiety; you will only
Harm and upset yourself.
Do not speak foolishly
In every gate, and to your enemies
Don't tell your dreams. Don't go to war
Under the opponent's command, nor to sea
During a tempest. Servitude is not proper
To one who is not your friend or comrade.
Beware of men who are full of talk;
You'll gain from them nothing but trouble.
A simple, quiet mouth is better than
A glib, lightheaded learned man.
Do not go out at night alone for profit,
And also do not feel safe with every Jew.[8]
Many a person who appears in pain
Is like a scorpion, full of stings and bites.
That tongue is best which stays shut in the mouth;
Men deem that tongue worthy, so hold it like a lion
In chains; if not, like a lion you'll fall prey.
If you utter a word out of time and season,
You will be paired with madmen.
He who knocks on doors in this world,
Others will knock on his door.
Do not form partnerships with bosom friends;
With relatives have little give and take.
Beware, do not dwell in the middle of a river,
When it rains take shelter in hills and caves.
Perform good deeds if you love goodness;
You will no doubt reap the seed you sow.
Do not like the ignorant love exaltation;
Conceit and vanity hold nothing good.
Do not dispute or strive with women and children;
Rest firm, and do not compromise your worth.
If you desire intelligence and foresight,

Always converse with great men; seek learning
And direction from great men and serve them
Till you yourself become a master.
Verily, in wisdom lies the fear of God.[9]
The intelligent man severs himself from bad deeds.
If you are content with your purchase,
Pay the pledge to judge and magistrate.
Do not give anything to anyone without witnesses,
And you'll be free of argument and strife.
This famous saying circulates in the world:
"Going to a house of mourning is better
Than going to a banquet," so go, visit
The *mourner* and the afflicted,
Restore the hearts of the distraught.
Never reveal your secret to your enemy,
And do not harbor his. Flee from
The continuous strife of the quarrelsome.
Always distance yourself from evil men.
Honor and hold your father dear,
Deem all your relations a crown upon your head.[10]
If you have access to the shah,
If you can go riding with lions,
If shahs and grandees know you,
The people will truly fear you.
Do not be bold with bulls and lions;
Fear both stings and antlers.
Don't grieve if a daughter is born to you,
For joy is attached to a daughter.
Many a daughter gains a crown,
And before her stand a hundred needy sons.
On all occasions, in want or profit,
Say nothing but thanks to God.
A buried daughter is better
Than marrying her off without dignity.
Live with good neighbors and keep far away
From turncoat friends.

Mishnah and Midrash

5

ʿImrānī: *Ganj-nāmah* (*The Book of Treasure*)

We have encountered ʿImrānī previously as one of the major Iranian Jewish poets who focused on the Hebrew Bible as a source of inspiration. ʿImrānī was a prolific author whose works deserve closer study. Only one of these, his *Ganj-nāmah* (The book of treasure; henceforth GN), has received such attention: David Yeroushalmi edited, annotated, and translated the first two chapters into English.[1] The selection that follows is based on Yeroushalmi's translation and notes.

Ganj-nāmah is a *masnavī* consisting of close to 5,000 rhymed couplets divided into eighty-eight sections which strictly follow the order of the chapters in the mishnaic tractate Abot (Fathers) in different lengths; GN is essentially a *tafsīr*[2] on this popular ethical tractate. ʿImrānī tends to comment on the first two or three elements of the mishnaic chapters, ignoring the rest. He embellishes their themes freely in the spirit of ancient and medieval Persian books of counsel (*pand-nāmah*; see chap. 4) and many Sufi compositions. In GN, ʿImrānī gives full vent to his "profound inclination towards ethical contemplation and moral didacticism."[3] However, unlike his other works, GN does not contain tales that illustrate his exhortations. ʿImrānī uses many

Sufi technical terms, and the general weltanschauung of GN is equally compatible with Jewish pietism and with Sufism. As mentioned below (chap. 10), such texts raise questions about the poet's relation to active Sufism even as his Jewish themes leave no doubt of his strong Jewish allegiance.

Section 41

Rabbi Yose the Priest says:
If you wish not to depend on people,[4]
Become the crown of princes;
You must be trustworthy,
Incapable of treachery.
Whatever a friend entrusts to you
Protect it according to the Torah;
For it is trust that upholds the world
And the heart of him who is always,
Openly and secretly, mindful
Of the Living Bestower.[5]
He takes not a barley grain's worth
From anyone; he burdens no one.
The man whose dealings are clean,
Why should he fear plaintiffs?[6]
How strange if one mired in treachery
Should rise, for he has fallen!
The vile, unlucky *thief,*
Wretched on earth and in the Hereafter,
Will be despised wherever he goes;
Oppression's fetters will enchain him.
In the end he'll be the world's disgrace,
Base and reviled forever.
He will be killed; he'll forfeit
Life and soul. Therefore if you desire
God's protection, protect another's charge
As if it were your own;
Then you'll be worthy and will prosper,
A man held in esteem.
To free yourself from every harm
And save your soul, heed my advice,

So that your offspring also will be pure,
Free from earth's fetters; and no calamity
Will touch you. Like the soul itself
You'll find eternal life upon the earth.
You must never covet another's wealth,
For you will lose yourself as a result.
Don't tolerate another's loss,
Lest you become weak and ensnared.
Should anyone's property be plundered,
Through sin, crime, or confiscation,
Hasten as much as you are able,
Return the property to its owner.
Fail not, for in return the Living,
Incomparable One, will multiply and increase
Your wealth. But if you are negligent
With it, He'll trample all of yours.
Should he who is able to act justly
Fall short in this matter,
The ancient pure Judge says that
Evil will seize him because of it.
But for one who exerts himself for good,
God will increase His help.
Whoever pursues wickedness,
Fortune's arrows will aim at him.
If Time's tyranny you wish to escape,
Your resolutions meet with a good end,
All your acts be orderly,
And good fortune be your servant;
Then you must follow the Spoken Word,[7]
Be perfect in both Word and deed.[8]
Since you will be pure inside and out,
You'll never dwell in gloom and sorrow.
He to whom it has not been revealed
How to acquire the sciences of Torah,
What does he know of good and evil?
For him light is like darkness!
If Word and deed lack foundation,

Why did God send them to the world?
They came for man's sake, to make him
Precious and most noble.
When man is firm in the Word,
His actions will ennoble him;
Since the Torah's meanings are revealed to him,
How can he dare reject the Torah's Word?
When through these two[9] he comes to know
His God, he'll grow ever more thankful
And obedient. The world's afflictions
Will not fetter him; himself he will deliver
To his Lord. As he becomes a man of faith
And piety, he will surely have no room
For treachery. When the Torah becomes
His protector, his ways will never be evil.
He who does not engage in treachery
Has nothing to fear, suffers no penalties.
But he who is perverse, ill-natured,
Crooked-minded, who rejects faith's path,
He wastes away the substance of his life
And throws himself into sin's abyss.
Either vile avarice degrades him
Or his heart's cravings ensnare him;
Either he follows his base carnal soul[10]
Or he becomes wicked and unjust.
Since God's way he did not learn,
How can he walk with burning feet?
Listen and heed this counsel, which comes
From Solomon's knowledge and wisdom.
He whose soul knowledge does not illumine[11]
Is but a corpse; toss him into the furnace!
Through knowledge Truth can be attained,[12]
The rank of the exalted; within your powers,
Strive not to be without it, for it is life eternal.
If it can find no customers at home,
Don't take it to the market! Take heed,
Be not dull-witted, weak, or a mere

Imitator[13] lacking virtue and wisdom,
Sinful and treacherous; how can such a one stand
Before the king? Expect no restraint
From him nor trouble the physician,
For such a one is dead! O dear son,
Strive and make haste so that you'll pass
From this dust to that water.
If you drink but one sip of that water,
You will forget the memory of this dust.
He who has not performed ablutions[14] with it
Will wallow in the dust, impure.
But one who is discerning will find jewels
In the Torah's waters. This water
That keeps Khiżr alive,[15] come,
Get some sir, for I possess it.
Heed my advice, for there is fellowship
In learning; it adorns the pious, learned man.
Without it all is naught, for it alone endures.
Die not of thirst on the river bank;
Weary and thirsty, grasp this chance.
Take heed; say not, "My son studies;
He will earn credit for the father,"[16]
Or, "My father is a learned man;
My need for knowledge is already satisfied."
If you give in to this temptation,
You will forsake yourself and God.
For if knowledge could be passed on to heirs,
Who would then suffer for its sake?
Since Moses' sons were not fit for the task,
Joshua, the son of Nun, succeeded in his place.[17]
If prophets could not find [fit] successors,
They did not let their heirs succeed them.
O you who indulge in ignorance, ill-mannered,
How long will you boast of your father's knowledge?
The sage[18] expressed this thought most fittingly;
Sweet is his speech if you would but comprehend:
"Granted your father was a learned man,

How do you benefit from it?"
If you ally yourself with ignorance,
How shall your offspring prosper?
If you are pious, a man of heart,
And have without a doubt set out
In search of certainty,[19] then you know well
The mystery of faith and salvation.
Listen to words spoken out of affection:
Devote yourself to the divine sciences,
Set your face, heart, and soul, toward God.
Do not rely on your father's virtues,
For they are here today and gone tomorrow.
Nor set your heart on your son's knowledge;
Detach your heart from this abode of clay.
Flee ignorance and faithlessness;
Relinquish hypocritical worship.
Be in charge of your own affairs,
The rose and nightingale of your own meadow![20]
Release the treachery you harbor,
Hold fast to the trust you have.[21]
If you fulfill these two or three precepts
Yourself to God you'll be entrusting.
You will be treading on the right path,
And all your actions will be godly.
You will behold the Truth, know God
Whenever you call on Him.
He will assist you always and will reopen
That gate He never shuts.
When God's favor becomes your friend,
It will never let you become afflicted and abased;
You will become innocent and pure,
Bright like the sun and the moon.

A Midrash on the Ascension of Moses

The themes of descending into the netherworld (Hell) and ascending to Heaven (Paradise) are common in the apocalyptic literatures of many religious traditions, including Judaism.[1] Within Judaism these themes are developed primarily in a midrash that describes Moses' visit to Hell and Paradise during the course of the revelation at the Burning Bush.[2] There are three principal Hebrew versions of this midrash, known as *ʿAliyyat Moshe le-marom* (Moses' ascension on high) or *Ka-tapuaḥ be-aṣe ha-yaʿar* (Like an apple tree among the trees of the forest).[3] In addition to these, Ladino, Judeo-Arabic, and JP renditions have also come to light. The popularity of this particular midrash in the Persianate world is clear from the fact that it is included in at least sixteen JP manuscripts, although neither the date of the Hebrew compositions nor that of its transmission into JP can be ascertained. The earliest JP version is no later than the fourteenth century. Since it contains a reference to Maimonides' *Mishneh Torah* (Hilkot deʿot, 5.1), the earliest possible date for the JP redaction is the first half of the thirteenth century. Although the relation of the JP text to the Hebrew versions is undeniable, there are enough intriguing dissimilarities to raise questions about the influence of other texts on this version. Among these one may suspect the influence of Zoroastrian texts, such as the Middle Persian *Arda Viraz-namag* (ninth to tenth century), and of the Kabbalah, probably in its pre-Zoharic stage of *hekalot* mysticism during the ninth to twelfth centuries.[4] Inevitably, Western readers will identify this midrash with Dante's *Divine Comedy,* which is itself based on a long tradition of visionary literature.[5]

It appears that the JP rendition of "The Ascension of Moses," though based on the Hebrew midrash, possesses many original features, which could have been set down from an oral rather than a written version.

The JP midrash begins with Moses' ascension to Heaven, God's reward for his righteousness and a token of His great love for Moses.[6] The angel Metatron, the highest angel in the celestial hierarchy, is ordered to take Moses on a tour of the nine heavenly spheres during which he answers Moses' questions about the mysteries he beholds.[7] Afterward, God shows Moses the punishments of Hell and the rewards of Paradise.

The Sections of Hell

In that moment He commanded the angel Gabriel, "Go with Moses, show him everything." When Moses saw the blazing fire of Hell, he said, "I cannot go near this fire." The angel Gabriel answered, "Do not be frightened, for God commanded the fire of Hell not to affect you; even if you were to walk into it you would not burn." Then Moses entered Hell; its fire drew back from him. At that moment Nagarsi'el,[8] the guardian of Hell, approached him and said, "Who are you?" Moses replied, "I am the son of 'Amram." Nagarsi'el said, "Why have you come here? This is not your place." Immediately God commanded Nagarsi'el, "Take Moses and show him all the sections of Hell." The sages of blessed memory have said that the length of Hell is three hundred years' walk and its width is also three hundred years' walk. It has seven sections.[9]

The first section

Then Nagarsi'el took Moses into the first section. He saw several human souls fastened to fiery chains and hooks. Some were hung by their eyes, others by their tongues or by their hair, and some by their breasts or by their ears. Some were hung by their legs or by their hands or heads, others by their penises or by their toes, and some by their fingers. Moses asked, "What evil deeds have they committed that they are thus tortured?" Nagarsi'el replied, "Those hung by their eyes looked at married women; they saw learned men and did not stand up before them; they saw poor men and ignored them. Those who hang by their ears on fiery hooks inclined to slander and talked idly in the synagogue; they did not pay attention to the cantors and to the words of the Torah; they did not heed the lamentations of orphans and widows. Those who are hung on hooks by their tongues slandered others and ate carrion and nonkosher food. They ate the food of gentiles. They cursed the man whose bread and salt they ate. Those who hang on hooks by their hands committed robbery, theft, and bloodshed. And those who hang by their feet on hooks trod the path of sin and did not go to synagogue; they did not go there at the proper time for prayer, as it is said, *Their feet run after evil.*[10] And those women who hang on the hooks by their breasts exposed them to men when they suckled their children and thus seduced the men to sin; they cursed their husbands. Since they died without repenting, they are thus tortured."

And he also saw several empty fiery chains hanging there. Moses asked, "What are these chains?" Nagarsi'el replied, "Each chain is for a sinner, *Ah, sinful nation!*"[11]

The second section

Then Moses was brought to the second section. He saw several wicked ones hanging upside down in the air;[12] they were covered with black worms from their heads to their toes. They cried and yelled and begged for death, but death would not be granted to them; their torment only increased, as it is written, *To those who wait for death [but it does not come].*[13] Moses asked, "What evil deeds have they committed?" Nagarsi'el replied, "They are those who swore falsely; they profaned the Sabbath and the festivals, despised the learned, offended orphans and widows; they gave false testimony and belittled the Torah. This is why they are thus tortured until the time they will be forgiven." Moses asked, "What is the name of this place?" Nagarsi'el replied, " 'Aluqah is its name,[14] as it is said, *The leech* ('aluqah) *has two daughters, 'Give!' and 'Give!'* "[15]

The third section

Then Moses was brought to the third section, named Dumah.[16] There he saw several sinners standing, each with two black scorpions attached to his eyes. Each scorpion had seven thousand knots on its tail; in each knot there were seventy thousand pitchers of poison. They were stinging the wicked. Because of the pain, the souls of the wicked were leaving their bodies. The angel Ruḥi'el would come and return the souls to their bodies so that they would continue to suffer.[17] Their eyes were dim because of the pains of torture. Moses asked, "What is their sin that they are so heavily tortured?" Nagarsi'el replied, "They gossiped against Jews, committed adultery, and put friends to shame. They introduced fear into the Jewish community [of something] other than heaven. They surrendered Jews to the nations of the world, brought damage to Jews, denied the Torah and considered the universe ancient.[18] Because they died without repenting, they are trapped in such tortures."

The fourth section

Then Moses was brought to the fourth section. He saw several sinners sunk from the navel to their feet in mud and slime; from the navel up they were burning in fire. The angels of destruction were standing by, pounding them with fiery maces, hitting their teeth with fiery stones and smashing them into small pieces. When the teeth grew back, the same torture was repeated, as it is said, *You break the teeth of the wicked.*[19] (*Do not read* shibbarta [*Thou hast broken*] *but* shirbabta [*Thou hast lengthened*].)[20] Moses asked, "What evil deeds have they committed?" Nagarsi'el replied, "They ate carrion and nonkosher foods, the foods of gentiles, and meat with milk; lent money for profit;[21] laid heavy stones;[22] fixed cheating scales; did not cover their nakedness; profaned the day of [Yom] Kippur; and ate insects and reptiles. Since they died without repenting, they are tortured in She'ol."

The fifth section

Then Moses was brought to the fifth section. He saw several sinners with half of their bodies on fire, the other half frozen from morning till night. When night came they froze the half-burnt ones and burnt the half-frozen ones, so that their torment would increase. [The sufferers] cried out and their lament reached the end of the world. Worms crawled on their bodes, as it is said, *They shall go out and gaze on the corpses of the men [who rebelled against Me].*[23] Moses asked, "What evil deeds have they committed?" Nagarsi'el replied, "They slept with married women and frequented prostitutes; they committed idolatry, theft, incest, and bloodshed. This is why they are tormented at the hands of the angels of destruction in 'Abadon."[24]

The sixth section

Then Moses was brought to the sixth section. He saw several sinners boiling in a pot filled with their own semen and filth. They were crying and screaming; their cries and shouts reached five hundred years' walking distance, but they found no release. Moses asked, "What evil deeds have they committed?" Nagarsi'el replied, "They have committed sodomy; lain with animals; committed adultery; they spilled their semen in vain. He who spills his semen in vain, all his sperm become angels of destruction. Now [the sinners] are being interrogated; all these angels of destruction are sperm that was spilt. This is why they suffer such torments."

Then Moses noticed several souls and spirits standing and looking at the sinners. He asked, "Who are they who look at them?" Nagarsi'el replied, "They are those who in this world used to advise them, but [the sinners] did not listen to their advice."

The seventh section

Then Moses was brought to the seventh section. He saw angels of destruction standing there placing the wicked on red fiery irons; they were feeding them with boiling filth from morning till night. When night arrived, they fed them red burning coals. Their livers were on fire, but they were not given water. And they screamed with all their hearts, but their voices could not come out of their throats because their pharynxes were filled with burning coals. Since they were so heavily tormented, Moses asked, "What acts have they committed?" Nagarsi'el replied, "These are those who did not respect their parents and cursed them. They called people bad names and despised the poor. They did not accept the words of the learned; they humiliated them; and they did not utter *Amen, may His [great] name [be blessed]*[25] with devotion. Their hearts and tongues were not one; they introduced quarrels between Jews; and they ate before the morning prayer, that is to say, they ate carcasses. This is why they are tormented. For each of their sins they endure several years of torment until they receive their just retribution."

At that moment Moses stood up to pray, and said, "May it be Thy will and mercy, O Lord, God of my fathers Abraham, Isaac, and Jacob, that Thou mayest save Thy people Israel from these calamities of Hell." At that moment, a voice called out, "God says, 'You have seen the reward of the pious and the retribution of the wicked.' [God says, 'There is no partiality in me'], 'as it is written, *Blessed be He with Whom there is no unrighteousness.*[26] I have created two enclosures for flesh and blood: one is Hell and the other is Paradise; for everyone according to his deeds of good and evil. Whosoever performs good deeds goes to Paradise; anyone who does evil goes to Hell, as it is said, *I the Lord probe the heart.*' "[27] Moses said, "*Wondrous in purpose and mighty in deed.*"[28]

After that, the angel Gabriel said to Moses, "You have seen all the wonders of God; now see Paradise, which is for the pious, and I will show you the deeds of the righteous."

Paradise

The angel Gabriel and Moses went to Paradise together.[29] At that moment the angels of mercy approached and said, "Is it time for Moses to come to Paradise?" Gabriel replied, "No, but God wants to show him the reward of the pious." Then the ministering angels bowed and said, "*Happy is the people who have it so [she-kaka lo].*"[30] *She-kaka lo* in arithmetical calculation [*gematria*] equals *Moshe* [Moses].

When Moses set his blessed foot into Paradise, a pleasant fragrance enveloped his body. He asked, "What is this pleasant fragrance?" Gabriel replied, "This is the smell of pious women whose fragrance wafts to a distance of five hundred years' walk." Moses asked, "What good deeds have they performed?" Gabriel replied, "They lit the Sabbath lamps promptly, observed their menstrual period well, and respected their husbands. This is why they are adorned with such a good fragrance."[31]

When Moses entered Paradise, he saw an angel sitting under the shade of the Tree of Life. Moses asked, "Who is this?" Gabriel replied, "This is the angel whose name is Shamshi'el;[32] he is appointed over Paradise." [Shamshi'el] said to Moses, "Come, I will take you to show you all the people of Paradise." At once Moses, together with the angel Shamshi'el, set out and saw several distinct thrones,[33] all made of precious stones; the legs of the thrones were of gold. Moses looked at the Tree of Life and saw that seventy kinds of fruit were on it; seventy kinds of fragrance were wafting about there.

Several of those thrones were made of precious stones and emeralds mixed together. The width of each throne was seventy yards. For each throne there were sixty ministering angels. There were among them larger and better thrones, which were ministered by 120 angels each. Moses asked, "Whose thrones are these?" Shamshi'el replied, "These thrones belong to the patriarchs of the world, and to the prophets, the pious, and the sages. This throne, which is the largest, belongs to you."[34] Then Moses began to praise and thank God, saying, "Thou art the Lord alone and the One, as it is said, *Moses is happy with his portion*."[35]

When Abraham our father, peace be upon him, saw Moses, he said, "*Praise the Lord for He is good; His steadfast love is eternal.*"[36] Isaac our father, peace be upon him, said, "Praise be to the Lord of Lords; His steadfast love endures forever." Jacob our father, peace be upon him, said, "Give thanks unto the Master of Masters, for His steadfast love endures forever." Moses said, "He alone does great wonders, *for His steadfast love endures forever.*" All the other righteous men rejoiced at seeing Moses; they chanted songs and kept saying, "Is it time for Moses to come here?" Shamshi'el replied, "No, but God wishes to show him the reward of the pious and the retribution of the wicked."

Moses turned his face to the left and saw there several thrones, none resembling another. Some of them were made of precious stones, some of gold, silver, and copper. Several angels were ministering to them. Moses asked, "To whom do these thrones belong?" Shamshi'el replied, "This throne of gold belongs to those learned in Torah;[37] the throne made of precious stones belongs to the perfectly pious; the silver throne belongs to the sincere proselyte; the copper throne belongs to the wicked one whose offspring is pious. By the merit of his pious offspring the father gains salvation. If you do not believe this, look and see Terah, Abraham's father, who by the merit of Abraham the Patriarch, peace be upon him, is seated on the copper throne."

After that Moses drew near to the Tree of Life. There was a spring gushing beneath the tree and splitting into four parts: east, west, north, and south.[38] There were rivers of milk, honey, balsam oil, and wine preserved in its grapes. Each river split into several streams; all were flowing under the thrones of the pious, and the pious were benefiting from them, each according to his good deeds, as it is said, *so as to repay every man according to his ways.*[39] When Moses saw these wonders, he said, "*How abundant is the good that You have in store for those who fear You.*"[40] A divine voice called out, saying, "O Moses, my obedient servant, you have seen the reward of the pious and the retribution of the wicked, each according to his deeds." Moses replied, "Blessed be God who gives everyone according to his deeds, as it is written, *to repay every man according to his ways.*"[41]

Biblical Commentaries

6

Iranian Jews, like most of the Jews in the diaspora, interpreted biblical texts to the best of their abilities. One of the earliest extant JP texts is a fragment of a biblical commentary on the Book of Ezekiel.[1] Rather confusingly, JP texts, like kindred Judeo-Arabic texts, refer indiscriminately to translations, paraphrases, and commentaries, of biblical and nonbiblical texts, as *tafsīr*.[2] Numerous manuscripts of JP texts that claim to be tafsīrs of one sort or another exist, in both prose and poetry. Many of these are word-for-word translations of Hebrew or Aramaic texts, especially medieval poetry; others also include glosses or comments. The names of the authors of most of these tafsīrs have not come down to us.[3] Not surprisingly, a substantial number of JP tafsīrs are devoted to the Hebrew Bible, covering all its books. Several tafsīrs have been subjected to close scrutiny by scholars, especially for their linguistic aspects.[4] We lack a comprehensive scholarly work on the JP biblical tafsīrs that would shed light on the value of their contents from a broader Jewish intellectual viewpoint and compare them to works of similar scope from the rest of the diaspora. This made it challenging to select and translate exceptional passages for this anthology.

The two selections that follow are representative in a different sense:

they show the range of learning present among Iranian Jews in the late Middle Ages. The first text, chapter 4 from Yehudah b. Binyamin's tafsīr on Ecclesiastes, appears to indicate insufficient learning: the author fails to understand some of the Hebrew verses he is trying to comment on and resorts only sparingly to traditional commentaries that could have helped him. We know nothing about Yehudah b. Binyamin other than the fact that he hailed from Kashan, but we can guess that he lived in the late eighteenth century, after the level of learning in that community had declined as a result of the hardships it had endured.[5]

The second text comes from Shim'on Ḥakam (1843–1910), the famous Bukhārān scholar, who emigrated to Jerusalem in 1890. Upon establishing himself there, Shim'on Ḥakam embarked on preserving, through editing, composing, and translating, a large number of JP texts. No less than twenty-nine works can be ascribed to his authorship or editorial supervision.[6] As we have seen, Ḥakam had published a complete edition of Shāhīn's *sharḥ* (commentary) on the Torah.[7] In this edition, along with Shāhīn's retelling of the Exodus saga, Ḥakam included his own prose commentary on the Book of Exodus. As the notes to the translation indicate, Ḥakam's learning in traditional rabbinic sources was prodigious, yet he wore it lightly. He interwove his sources so skillfully that the resulting narrative resembles a well-told folktale in its dramatic presentation.

Yehuda b. Binyamin: *Commentary on Ecclesiastes 4*

It is the wish of *young* Ye[h]udah,[1] *the son of the honored Rav Binyamin, may he rest in Paradise,* to explain[2] for readers the Book of *Kohelet* [Ecclesiastes] for three reasons. First, since all its counsels are precious and admirable, even better than those of the *Book of Proverbs,* and since not everyone in the entire *holy congregation* of Kashan—*may God preserve it*—knows the Book of *Kohelet,* he will comment upon it [for the sake of] *one from a town and two from a clan* [Jer. 3:14]. And the rest [who are familiar with *Kohelet*] have been reading a different type of commentary, which none could understand and which was not at all appropriate.[3] I saw a person who was reading a commentary on *Kohelet* on the *verse the case of one who is alone, with no companion* [Eccles. 4:8], and claimed that *one* referred to the *the Blessed Name,* Who is One and not two and who has no nephew[!][4] But this is not correct; rather, this *verse* is about a particular man, as it will be explained *with the help of the Blessed Name.* I wrote this commentary so that the entire community could understand its meaning and could always read *Kohelet.* Second, [I wrote this commentary because] for some time after I wrote a commentary on the Book of Proverbs the scribes were all busy, but now they are without work. I said [to myself] that the scribes ought to be employed.[5] The third reason is that I wanted my humble name to become known. He Who *knows the secrets of the heart* [Ps. 44:22] is aware of how many evenings I have sat around idly, without work,[6] so that I could explain correctly the *views* of all the *commentators,* [including those of] master R. David Kimḥi, so that my humble name should become known.[7] Every scribe who copies [this work] but does not, out of *pride,* copy its preface, or abbreviates it, may the *Blessed Name* not diminish his sustenance, bestow no *poverty* upon him.[8] *Amen, may this be His will. . . .*

I further observed [4:1]. I also observed all the oppression that is carried out under the heavens: that tears flow from the eyes of the oppressed, that there is no one to deliver them from the hands of oppressors, that no one has the power to comfort them.[9] I deemed more praiseworthy those who died earlier, who are free of the torments of this world; they are better off than the living who still suffer coercion. Better off than both [groups] is the person who has not yet come into the world and has not seen these oppressions and these bad deeds which are carried out under the heavens. I have observed all the injustice that men perform, and that all the good and bad they do is on account of the jealousy they have toward one another. This too is vain, and [mere] flattery of self. An ignorant man is not a tradesman; he folds his arms [idly] and consumes his own flesh with worry.[10] It is better that a man should obtain a fistful of flour[11] in tranquillity than that he should obtain two fistfuls through contention and disappointment. I further observed the futilities carried out under the heavens: It can happen that a man is a bachelor, never married, so that he will never engender a son,[12] and he has no brother who could be his heir, yet he is weighed down by many toils and troubles.[13] It is also vanity that he engages no partner or apprentice who could help him and diminish his troubles.[14] His eyes are never sated, and he will never become sated with riches. He never says to himself, "Why do I want all this wealth? To whom will I pass it on?" This situation is worse than all others. It is better for two to be partners than to be alone; whoever carries out his work and is oppressed, [ultimately] receives his reward. For if one of them should fall, the other takes his hand and raises him up. Woe betide him who is alone; if he falls there is no one to raise him![15] Furthermore, when two persons sleep side by side when it is cold, they become warm,[16] but how does the one who sleeps alone become warm? If one is attacked, the other can fight and stand up against [the enemy] to fight on his behalf.[17] Three friends are like a threefold rope which cannot be broken.[18]

It is better to be an ignorant man[19] than one who is thoughtless and clever, or a silly old king who cannot be heedful. It is possible for a person to emerge from a dungeon and become a king, and it is also possible for a king to become a beggar.[20]

I contemplated all the creatures who walk under the heavens since the days of the Flood; none of whom could earn God's approval. But that second child,[21] Noah, came in their place and earned God's approval. They [Noah's sons?] had many sons, creatures beyond number, and all types of good were prepared for them. Also the later generation, that of the *division* [Tower of Babel], none of them experienced any happiness.[22] They were also vanity, futility, and [mere] enticement.

Guard your feet from going to God's house in order to cry, repent, and confess your errors to God for having been affected by misfortune, though now you offer [a penitential] sacrifice. He who has not *sinned* is closer to God's threshold than those ignoramuses who *sin* and then beg forgiveness, offer sacrifices, and are unaware that they are harming themselves.[23]

Shimʿon Ḥakam: *Commentary on Exodus 3–4*

As fortune would have it,[1] it was New Year's Day[2] and the season of spring.[3] Moses took his flocks to distant parts, to uncultivated pastures.[4] He arrived in the pasture at Sin Desert, at the foot of Mount Sinai, which mountain was known to the Midianites by the name of Ṭūr.[5] It was on the 15th of Nisan.[6] Moses, holding his staff,[7] walked around the sheep. Suddenly, a lamb became separated from the flock and ran off toward the mountain. Moses followed that lamb and entered the mountain area.[8] He saw from a distance that at the top of a wild,[9] thorny thicket a flaming fire rose up, yet that wild thicket never caught fire. "What sight is this? Let me get closer and take a look at this wonder." He approached, taking three steps forward; he was brave and unafraid. He saw that sparks rose from above the two parts[10] of that thicket.[11] And in the midst of that fire he saw a form of light which flashed forth lightning like a sublime, world-displaying mirror.[12] And that form of light was the angel Michael, who accompanied *the Shekinah, as it were,*[13] which was clearly present there.[14] And in that place there were also some men, shepherds, passing by, but that vision appeared only to Moses' sight, and others did not see it. *The Shekinah, as it were,* saw that Moses approached boldly and stood forward. She then called out in a voice resembling the voice of ʿImrān,[15] Moses' father, saying, "Moses, Moses." "Here I am, my father."[16] "Don't come too close." "Remove and discard the sandals from your feet, for this land on which you stand is sacred. I am not your father; I am the God of your father, the God of Abraham, Isaac, and Jacob." On hearing this, Moses removed and discarded his sandals and partly hid his face in his sleeve.[17] He stood with his head bowed, for he realized that this fire was the *Shekinah,* "and how can I look upon the *Shekinah?*" The Divine Call came again: "Moses, know that the grief, affliction, torment, and toils of my people in the realm[18] of Egypt are all known at My court and I have seen them. The cries and laments they utter at the merciless hands of tax collectors[19] have all been heard at My court. I know about all their pains and troubles. Now the time for the end has arrived, when I will liberate the *Children of Israel* from the hands of the Egyptians, and I will take them from that impure and defiled land and bring them to a chosen, spacious, and good land, a land flowing with milk and honey. I will give you a dwelling place in the land of the Canaanites, Hittites, Amorites, Perizites, Hivites, and Jebusites. I will fulfill that oath and promise I made to Abraham, Isaac, and Jacob.[20] Come now and go, for I have appointed you messenger[21] to Pharaoh, and you shall bring My people, the *Children of Israel,* out of Egypt. Moses [said], "O Lord, O God and Divine Call,[22] me? Me do you send? Who am I? What is my worth that I should be able to go before Pharaoh, the ruler of a kingdom? Of what worth am I that I should be able to bring out the *Children of Israel,* a large multitude, from Egypt? I am only a shepherd, a stranger."[23] The Divine Call replied, "Don't say this, Moses, and don't be anxious! I Myself will help you. You will gain victory and success; I'll give you a sign of these: When you bring my people out of Egypt, you will worship at this very place, standing on this same mountain, at my court, all together." Moses answered a second time: "O Master of everything in the universe, the people of the *Children of Israel* are wise and understanding and come from the loins of prophets; they will surely ask me, "Whose God revealed Himself to you? What is His Name? How shall I answer them?" The

Divine Call replied, "If they ask you My name, say to them *I am that I am,*[24] that is, that I will be their liberator from this *exile,* and I will be their liberator from other *exiles* as well."[25] Moses [said], "Master of everything in the universe, isn't the grief of the present *exile* over their heads enough that I should inform them of other *exiles?*[26] *The Holy One, blessed be He* [replied], "You do not understand the meaning of this. I will explain and reveal these words to you, but to them it is sufficient that you tell them[27] once "*I am,*" and to say to them 'the *Lord,*[28] the God of your fathers, the God of Abraham, Isaac, and Jacob, sent me to you. This is my name in the world; thus am I remembered from generation to generation.' The first thing you should do when you arrive in the town of Goshen is go to the elders, who are sitting in *houses of learning,*[29] and worship before My threshold. (Having seen the oppression and troubles of the community, they are busy with the work of the community.) Gather them all together and give them the following explanation: 'The God of your fathers revealed Himself to me and said, "*I have taken note of you.*" '[30] And when they hear these words they will believe you at once. Then [you and] these elders, accompanied by the entire community, will go before the king of Egypt and say to him, '*The Lord,* the God of the Hebrews, commanded that we go three days' distance into the desert and that we bring and perform sacrifices according to the ways and customs of our fathers. Give us leave and permission to carry out the command of our God.' It is clear and well known at My court that Pharaoh will answer you accommodatingly several times but will not grant you permission to leave. Hasn't it occurred to you that Pharaoh is violent and powerful,[31] and that I am thus obliged to send a messenger to him in order to elicit his answer and permission [for the Children of Israel to leave]? Know that all the mighty tyrants of the world are weak compared to My might; all famous [men] are absurd nonentities, and all the savants of the world are worthless and ignorant at My court. And it would be easy for Me, and I can do it, to turn Pharaoh and his kingdom upside down in a moment, as I did with Sodom and Gomorrah, and thus liberate the *Children of Israel.* But I wish to display My might to the entire world and turn the realm of Egypt into an example through miracles, pain upon pain. I will annihilate Pharaoh and the Egyptians with troubles, misfortunes, and calamities; and I will bring upon their heads the evils they have perpetrated against the *Children of Israel;* and I will extract the vengeance of My children from them and perform miracles on behalf of the *Children of Israel.* I will make My lordship renowned in the world. As for the

Children of Israel, I will not bring them out empty-handed but rather with full hands and hems[32] and much wealth, with glory and honor. For I will cast love for the *Children of Israel* into the hearts of the Egyptians[33] so that their neighbors, every Egyptian man and woman, will lend them whatever gold, jewels, and chattels, silver and gold, expensive satin and brocade clothes, that they ask for. So much gold and so many vessels will they be able to take that they will empty the realm of Egypt of its wealth by right of the wages [owed to them] for so many years of burdens and sorrows of working with clay, which was their occupation.[34] They will thus obtain their wages and rewards, and this is permitted."[35]

Moses objected a third time, saying, "O My Lord, God, and Divine Call, do not entrust me with this office. I can never go because I am bound by oath to Jethro, my wife's father, that for as long as I live I will serve him and dwell near him, never going to any other kingdom."[36] The Divine Call replied, "O Moses, don't give me such pretexts; there is a remedy for every situation and a cure for every pain! You're bound by oath; the remedy for an oath is *loosening* it.[37] I Myself will *loosen* [the oath], and I will cast the thought into Jethro's heart that he should give you permission and set you free with goodness and in good cheer."

Moses replied a fourth time, "O Pure Omnipotent King, all secrets and mysteries are known at Your court. You Yourself know that I fled from Pharaoh's sword out of Egypt and came to these parts; I am a hated man. You are telling me to go before enemies; You are entrusting me to the hands of [my] adversaries![38] This is unheard of! I can never go; leave me alone!"[39] The Divine Call replied, "On this account also you need not grieve. That Pharaoh and all your enemies have died; none of your enemies are alive."[40]

A fifth time Moses objected, saying, "O Creator of the Universe, O Generous Sultan, the nature and temperament of the *Children of Israel* is clear and well known at Your court, they do not believe quickly in worthless talk, and they will certainly say to me, 'You're lying; God never appeared to you! If you really want us to believe you, perform a miracle or wonder for us to see, then we'll believe.' Then I'll really disappoint them!"[41] The Divine Call said, "O Moses!" [He replied], "Here I am!"[42] "What is that in your hand?" Moses [said], "O Creator, You know better than I what this is; it is a staff, for You know that You have appointed it to be a staff."[43] "Yes, I know. I have no doubt about this whatsoever. I have no doubt that the staff is sufficient. You would do well to throw this staff on the ground." Moses threw the staff on the ground, and suddenly the staff became a large snake, loosened its mouth, and spoke.[44] Extending and contracting itself, it moved upon the ground. Moses was afraid of it and fled at once, retreating from before the snake. The Divine Call said, "Moses, why are you fleeing? Fear not.[45] Come forward and take hold of the snake's tail." Moses came forward bravely, stretched forth his arm, and grasped the snake's tail firmly. And all at once that snake became as it was at first; it became a staff. "Therefore," [said God], "if the *Children of Israel* say, 'We do not believe your words,' throw your staff down on the ground in this manner, so that it becomes a snake, and then they will believe and have faith." He also said: "O Moses, put your hand into your bosom." Moses did so. "Bring your hand out from your bosom." Moses did so. He saw that his hand had become as white as snow with leprosy; Moses was astonished. God said, "Return your hand into your bosom!" He did so. "Bring it out." He brought it out. [Moses] saw that [the hand] had returned to its former shape and bodily color. "If they will not believe that first sign, perform this second sign, and then they will believe." But if they should not believe after these two signs, take a small amount of river water and cast it on the dry ground. That water on the dry ground will turn at once into blood. I am entrusting these three signs to you so that your heart will rest tranquil."

Moses objected a sixth time, saying, "O Sole King of Kings, may I find eternal dwelling at Your court, do not send me on this mission, for I am not a gracious and bold man, and I am dull of speech. And it has already been more than sixty years since I left the realm of Egypt, and I have forgotten the language and speech of the Egyptians. And it is not easy to speak with a king. This job is for an orator, an eloquent man. Leave me out of it, for this is no work for me."[46] The Divine Call replied, "O Moses, don't speak to Me this way! Who has inspired the creatures of the world? Tell me, who has given them a mouth to speak and the ability to articulate speech? And those who are dumb and cannot speak, deaf and cannot hear, blind and cannot see, and those who are intelligent, can speak, see, and hear, don't you know Who created these? They all exist through My might and creation. So don't ever be upset on this account, for I Myself will help you and will put speech into your mouth so that you will be able to say pleasing and appropriate words to Pharaoh."[47]

For the seventh time Moses thought matters over quietly, and then he said, "O Lord, for this ambassadorship and messengership You should send a worthy man, one who has experienced prophecy before this.[48] Send such a man; leave me, for I am not worthy." Moses' intention and unwillingness, from the beginning to the end, were on account of his brother Aaron, who was three years older than he, and who was also a *righteous and pious* man; he had once prophesied in the realm of Egypt.[49] [Moses thought,] "How can I take his place? How can I be so lacking in civility as to take precedence over him?" On account of *his humble* and modest character he was willing to step aside, and that is why he did not accept. The Divine Call addressed Moses quickly, "All your thoughts and imaginings are known at My court. I know what you are thinking. I know your brother Aaron, the Levite, well, that he is *righteous, pious,* learned, and eloquent. But know and be aware that I have chosen you in prophethood, so you yourself must go. And I will inform Aaron of this as well, so that he will come out to meet you, rejoice at seeing you, and derive satisfaction from your becoming a prophet.[50] And you relate to Aaron all My words and My commission. He will act as your interpreter. You will speak to him, and he will interpret to the community and to Pharaoh. And although he is older than you, you will act as the chief, and he will be the deputy of the chief. I would also have charged you with the leadership of *priesthood,*[51] but owing to this speech of yours, I will give the *priesthood* to Aaron.[52] Enough now! Utter no more pretexts! Take this staff into your hand quickly and set out. Perform the signs and miracles I have entrusted to you.[53] Never fear and do not distress yourselves! I shall be a friend and companion aiding you."

And so at last Moses bowed his head to the ground and was satisfied. This conversation between Moses and the *Shekinah* lasted seven days and seven nights.[54] For the *Shekinah* spoke to Moses, *as it were,* and Moses, unwilling, found pretexts seven times not to accept [the mission], until in the end, helpless, he did accept. Moses lifted his head from the ground and saw that the flame of fire and the light had moved away from above the thorn bush; he no longer saw fire or light upon that mountain.

7

Religious Festivals in Sermon, Commentary, and Poetry

Among JP manuscripts we find many collections of *derashot* (Hebrew for "sermons," "homilies"). Most of these are on the themes of the *hafṭarot,* the additional texts from the Prophets that are read on the Sabbath and on the various festivals of the Jewish year.[1] Many of these texts, like the *derashah* translated here commemorating the calamities associated with the Ninth of Ab, although carefully recorded, have come down to us anonymously. They are no less erudite and eloquent for that, and a careful study of them would no doubt enrich our knowledge of Jewish sermonic literature.[2] Judeo-Persian derashot are difficult to date, although context, as in the present case, can be helpful. Since there are two references to Lurianic Kabbalah in the derashah that follows,[3] we can assume that it comes from the early premodern period, about 1700–1900.

The learned author of this sermon uses the classic structure of a Jewish homily.[4] He begins with a theme verse (*nose'*) from the Torah (Jer. 8:13) and proceeds to the *ma'mar,* usually an aggadic[5] passage (a midrashic comment), which at first appears unrelated to the nose'. In this sermon the ma'mar consists of Moses' argument with God to obtain divine forgiveness for his brother Aaron after the Golden Calf incident (*Wa-Yiqra' Rabbah* 10.5, 18.1).[6]

The resolution between nose' and ma'mar, saved for the end of the derashah, keeps the attention of the audience on the words of the preacher and focuses it on his erudition and clever juxtapositions.

The poet Binyamin b. Mishae'el, known by the penname Amīnā (the Faithful), is probably the most accomplished Iranian Jewish poet of light short verse. He was born in Kashan in 1672/73 and died after 1732; the Kashan of his lifetime is captured in the surviving JP chronicles from which selections are presented below (chap. 8). Amīnā even wrote a panegyric in praise of Shah Ashraf (chap. 12). Amīnā appears to have been an important member of the Jewish community of Kashan. Although we lack detailed biographical information, we know a little more about him than about most Iranian Jewish poets. He was apparently unhappily married (see his views on women in general in chap. 12), divorced his wife after some twenty-five years, and left her and his seven children to move, possibly to Hamadan.

Amīnā is the author of at least forty poems, most of which are not very long. The translations below are of two of his longer poems (300–400 verses) associated with the Jewish festivals of Purim and the Day of Atonement. In addition to these, Amīnā also wrote a poetic commentary on the *Azharot* (Commandments and prohibitions) of Shelomo b. Gabirol, the famous eleventh-century Jewish poet from Spain, and edited Khwājah Bukhārā'ī's *Dāniyāl-nāmah* (see above, chap. 2).[7]

We know nothing about Gershon, the poet who wrote a lovely ditty in praise of Purim. Probably this poem, which is more in the nature of a popular song, also originates from the premodern period. It is studded with descriptions of local Persian Purim customs, not all of which are clear to me. The fact that we have several copies of this poem attests to its popularity among Iranian Jews. According to Netzer, Gershon's poem is printed at the end of Shim'on Ḥakam's edition of *Targum Sheni.* Unfortunately, I was unable to consult this copy.

A Derashah on the Hafṭarah for the Ninth of Ab

I will make an end of them—declares the Lord:
No grapes left on the vine,
No figs on the fig tree

[*The leaves all withered;*
Whatever I have given them is gone.] (Jer 8:13)

That is,[1] in the end I will finish them off completely; and He said to them,[2] there is no grape on the vine and no fig on the fig tree, and the leaves[?][3] have become withered.[4] What did the prophet say, and what do we understand [from it]? I will overthrow the overthrown, said God regarding Israel; there is nothing good left. "There are no grapes on the vine nor figs on fig trees"; what does that mean? And what does "that leaf became withered" mean? Although the *sages* have given this *verse* several *interpretations* and meanings,[5] its explanation and manifold meanings have not been exhausted, but *the blessed Master Elijah* informed me (*may I be remembered for good*) of the *difficult* answer.[6] He informed me that in the *midrash* it is said that when *our master Moses, peace be upon him,* erected the *Dwelling and the Tabernacle*[7] and offered *sacrifices, the Holy One, blessed be He,* explained all the *sacrifices* to *our teacher Moses, blessed be he,* from the beginning of *parasha Wa-yikra'* [Lev.], which is the beginning of the explanation of the *sacrifices,* until its end; he wrote to distinguish in it only the name of Aaron, the priest. Similarly, it is written, *And Aaron's sons shall dash [its blood]* [Lev. 1:11, 3:8, 13), *And the sons of Aaron shall . . . ,*[8] *[And] the sons of Aaron [the priest] shall put [fire on the altar]* [Lev. 1:7], *And Aaron's sons, [the priests], shall lay out* [Lev. 1:8], *And Aaron's sons shall offer [the blood]* [Lev. 1:5]. *Our master Moses, peace be upon him,* petitioned the court of the *Holy One, blessed be He,* saying, "*Lord of the Universe, the well is hated, but its waters are good, You have apportioned honor [even] to woods for the sake of their offspring [fruits], then how much more [should You do so] for my brother Aaron?*[9] That is, *Lord of the Universe,* the well is bad, but its water is good; meaning that Aaron is bad because he made the [Golden] *Calf* for Israel, but his sons, El'azar and Itamar are good, for You have said, '*And Aaron's sons shall dash,*' '*And the sons of Aaron shall put,*' '*And let Aaron and his sons lay [their hands]*' [Ex. 29:15]. Did You not do thus only to distinguish Aaron's name? You forgave . . .[10] for You said that they should not bring the wood of the vine to the altar to burn on account of its fruits, that is, its grapes, for the wine that is brought to the altar is for libation, and [You said] that they should not bring the wood [vine] of the grape to the altar to burn because its fruit is the grape and it is offered as a *first fruits* [offering]. Therefore, since You showed mercy to the fruits of trees and benevolence toward their wood, why have You no mercy and compassion upon my brother

Aaron for the sakes of El'azar and Itamar, his *worthy*[11] sons, and why do You not forgive my brother Aaron's offense, and why are You [still] enraged and never mention his name?" At last, *the Holy One, blessed be He,* stirred His mercy toward Aaron for the offense of the [Golden] *Calf,* on account of his two sons, and afterward called him by name explicitly: "*Command Aaron and his sons*" [Lev. 6:2].

Moreover, we have a *law* that if the wood of the vine or of the fig, which produces grapes and figs, is *prohibited even* in these days when we have no *Temple,* then no one can cut down or topple these woods; but the wood of the vine and fig which produce no fruits are *permissible* to cut down or topple, the principal reason being that we have no *Temple.* Therefore, it is well known that during the time that the *Temple stood,* it was not permissible to cut down the wood of the grape and of the fig. They did not cut them down or burn them, either as *arranged wood* [upon the altar][12] or for another place, although there was no *prohibition* against it. Therefore we should understand that for the sake of good offspring, fathers and mothers are released from all *laws,* calamities, and [evil] *decrees.*

When the *Holy One, blessed be He,* wished to destroy Israel, the prophet Jeremiah petitioned at the court of the *Holy One, blessed be He,* and said, "*Lord of the Universe, You have apportioned honor to woods,* that is, on account of the fruits of the trees You forgave and had mercy on the trees that were their fathers and commanded that they should not be cut down or burned upon the altar. And now that You wish to finish off all Israel, why have You no regard for their offspring, for *priestly offerings* will come from them, and [why do] You have no mercy on them although they will be righteous? Have mercy on them and do not destroy them!" *The Holy One, blessed be He,* said, "*I will make an end of them,*" that is, I wish to destroy them utterly. Concerning them Jeremiah said, "Why did He say, '*No grapes left on the vine, / No figs on the fig tree*'?" That is, these Israelites that you see today are all *evil* and all walk in the midst of *dregs,*[13] and the *other side*[14] mired them into its pitch; whatever they produce is the property of the *other side.* They did not produce and will not produce any *righteous man,* because they commit *evil and sin* and are not worthy of My mercy for the sake of their offspring, as in the case of the wood of the vine and the fig. Rather, they are like trees that bear no fruit, which it is *permissible* to cut down, to destroy, and to burn; that is why Jeremiah said, "*I will make an end of them, declared the Lord: / No grapes left on the vine, / No figs on the fig tree.*" That is, God proclaimed concerning them, "I will destroy them utterly." If you say that they will produce good offspring, well and good. [But] *"No grapes left on the vine, / No figs on the fig tree. / The leaves all withered,"* means that the leaves they have will also be destroyed.

The fact is that we always supplicate at the court of the *Holy One, blessed be He,* saying, "O *Lord of the Universe, 'The green figs form [on the fig tree], / The vines in blossom give off fragrance'* " [Song of Sol. 3:13], that is, now we all *repent,* and all our offspring are *righteous;* we are all like the vine of the grape and the fig tree, which produce fruits, and therefore we should not be cut down, burned, or destroyed but are [deserving] of mercy for the sake of our offspring. Another [mitigating] fact is that in this *dispersion* the *sorrows* and humiliations that we have experienced and continue to experience have been too much for us; yet even in this state we have not relinquished Your *Torah* and have raised our children according to Your *Torah.* And now the time has come in which the *King Messiah* should appear, *as it is said: "Arise, my darling; / My fair one, come away!"* [Song of Sol. 2:10], O *King Messiah,* rise now and come, for we are dying from [the intense desire of] awaiting you: *"For now the winter is past, / The rains are over and gone"* [Song of Sol. 2:11]. When the mercy of the *Holy One, blessed be He,* will stir, He will send the *prophet Elijah,* and He will proclaim in the *four corners of the world* and say: "O Israelites, *'The blossoms have appeared in the land, / The time of pruning [or singing] has come; / The song of the turtledove / Is heard in the land'* " [Song of Sol. 2:12]. That is, the *Messiah, son of David,* and the *Messiah, son of Joseph,*[15] have arrived in the *Land of Israel;* the time of *singing and melodies* has come. Sing *in the honor of His Torah,* for what *merit* is like the *merit of the song of the turtledove,* which is the *voice of the Torah*[16] that the *King Messiah* will read openly? *May it be His will* that the *Messiah, the King of Kings,* should appear quickly, to redeem us from this *exile,* humiliation, darkness, and *poverty,* and [then] all the *dead* will *revive,* and we shall find relief at last.

Amīnā: *Commentary on the Book of Esther*

Recite this *scroll,*[1] dear friends,
And let God's miracles astonish you.
In the third year of his ill-starred reign,
Ahasueros, Shushtar's[2] infidel shah,
Planned a banquet which all the grandees
Of the state attended; on the seventh day,

Intoxicated by the wine he drank, the shah
Wished to show off his women to all the khans.
He sent a messenger to summon Vashti
Naked, to show herself before the men.
Vashti was thunderstruck by the request
And through her servants answered thus:
"You're drunk and don't know what you're saying;
You know no shame and lack a sense of honor.
You were a mere Master of the Horse at stables
Before you found the means to come before my door.[3]
You've grown deluded and confused in kingship
You have forgotten the felt cap and cloak.[4]
No eye ever beheld such a drunken camel;
How can your command be binding upon me?"
On hearing this barbed reply, the shah
Questioned his khans and princes:
"For spewing forth such words,
What recompense does she deserve?
She acted rudely toward both shah
And husband. Shall I kill her or burn her?"
Memukan,[5] the lowest of the chieftains present
In that assembly, spoke his sinister words:
"O Shah, in such a case killing is specified,
For she has overstepped feminine custom."
Full of anger, the shah drew back his bow;[6]
Naked, Vashti was killed on Saturday.
Once she was killed, it was recorded in the annals,
Proclaimed throughout the seven climes:
"All wives who thus rebuff their husbands
Will die like Vashti, by the dagger's blow."
When Ahasueros' drunkenness departed,
Still hung over he remembered Vashti;
Full of regret for his drunken killing
He struck his head in grief with both his fists.
When the khans beheld the shah so distraught,
They gathered all the fairy-faced maidens
Of Shushtar in large numbers, hoping

That one of them would please Shah Bahman.[7]
Among the gathered maidens there was one,
Esther,
Whose light blinded all who looked on her.
The Jew Mordekai guided her like a daughter,
Although Esther was only his niece.[8]
Graceful, coquettish, and attractive,
She pleased the shah; he clothed her
In royal garments and placed her on the throne
In Vashti's stead.
Esther sat on the throne
By God's command and through divine favor.
. . . .
The third fast[9] was the feast of Nisan;[10]
Full of dread Esther came before the shah,
Eyes full of tears and pale as straw,
Accompanied by two slave girls.
When the shah's eyes fell upon Esther,
First they were angry and then full of love.
He said, "Best of the choicest, O beloved,
You're more precious to me than a hundred lives!"
Having said this he took her hand in his
And seated her on the throne at his right hand.
He showered her with love, kissing her face:
"O Esther, ask what you wish of me,
Even to half of my kingdom . . ."
. . . .
When Bahman warmed to the assembled company,
He said to Esther: "O heart-ravishing beauty,
Tell me, my dearest, your heart's desire,
And I'll fulfill it on the spot were it even
Half my kingdom; I grant you whatever you wish."
Esther replied with trembling words:
"O Shah, may your soul ever be twinned with
Granting favors! What is the use of
Making a request now that you've commanded
The unjust to shed my blood? Not only mine;

You commanded that my entire tribe
Should perish. We were content in servitude;[11]
Unjustly we will perish by the sword."
When Bahman heard this from Esther,
He was enraged and questioned her again:
"Who says this?[12] What is his sinister name?
Who dares to overturn his doom?"
Esther replied, "It's this accursed infidel.
He, Haman,
Is the foe and enemy, the cruel adversary."
Furious and enraged the shah stepped out
Into his garden and there beheld
A host of angels in the guise of men;
Their occupation, uprooting trees,
Destroying Bahman's garden. He asked them,
"What are you doing? Have you no fear
Of the shah's fury?" They said to him,
"Beloved shah, Haman, your grand vizier,
Commanded us to move them from here
And take them into his own garden."[13]
The shah's anger increased; he turned,
And heading back, he glimpsed
Haman fallen in earnest supplication
In front of Esther, the cloth of his bosom rent,
Grief-driven to distraction.
Full of anger the shah addressed him thus:
"You wish to couple with Esther
Even while I am in the house?"
By the shah's order Haman's face was covered;
Toward him Bahman would never turn again.
Then Harbonah[14] asked Bahman, "O shah,
To hateful Haman what do you wish done?
He has built a gallows for the shah's well-wisher,[15]
His choice adornment and that of the world."
With a loud voice Bahman proclaimed:
"Hang him upon that gallows instantly
In great affliction." The king's command

Was carried out in haste;
Quickly and easily Haman was hanged.
The anger of the world's king abated,
The wrath of Shah Ahasueros.
The house of Haman he bestowed upon Esther[16]
That there she might regain her peace of mind.
Esther, in turn, appointed Mordekai
Head of the house and all its contents.[17]
Then once again she begged the shah,
Beseeching and lamenting greatly:
"O Shah, how shall I look upon my people,
Killed by the sword, affliction, and distress?"
Then Shah Bahman replied to Esther:
"Let me gladden your heart: I hereby
Appoint you and Mordekai my deputies.
Since my decree is irrevocable,
Whatever you deem appropriate,
Of the wishes of the Jews, carry out.
Decree and append thereto the royal seal
Of this auspicious ring." Having said this,
He handed her the ring, and Esther's heart rejoiced.
The scribes wrote letters by the shah's command
And sent them to every corner of the realm:
"Let the Jews kill their enemies;
Let them unite to kill their enemies!"
They sent a letter to every town,
A cup of poison for the adversaries of the Jews.
Then Mordekai donned royal garments,
Upon his head a royal cap and crown;
And all the Jews were merry and rejoiced,
With hearts serene and much relieved.
There was rejoicing not only in Shushtar
But throughout Bahman's realm.
Many infidels, Christians, and Hindus,
Turned Jew in dread of Mordekai;[18]
All the shah's khans showed great esteem
And much respect to all the Jews,

For Mordekai was chosen and preferred;
His fame was spread throughout the world.
. . . .
Ahasueros reigned with equity and justice.
He no longer took from Jews, near or far,
Neither poll tax nor customary tribute.
All his royal decrees were in accordance
With the ancient customs of Kay Khosrow;[19]
They were recorded in the book of annals,
As was the way and custom of the princes.
Mordekai the Jew was the shah's Āṣaf,[20]
The grand vizier of the palace elite.
He was the head and leader of the community
Of Jews, the world's most benevolent man:
A seeker of peace, a source of learning,
An adviser in all its trials.
  O Lord, Who have performed miracles,
  You are the Jews' refuge, patron,
  And intimate companion. Favor us
  Once again; command the *Messiah* to come.
  Let *Redemption* take place in our time;
  Let us read this *scroll* with happy hearts.
  Amīnā makes this pact with God:
  If he lives to see the Messiah's coming,
  He will be the panegyrist of the Mahdī.[21]
    By God's grace, might, and favor,
    If you are a Jew, say quickly Amen.

Mullah Gershon: *Purim-nāmah*

When the month of Adar,[1]
Spring's lovely season, comes,
Tranquillity into the world comes.
A hundred lights and couriers have come.
By the Merciful's command,
The scent of Tatar musk[2] comes,
Good fortune to pass,

The rose bud into bloom comes,
Misfortune ends.
With a thousand happy faces Adar comes,
With warm weather at last;
What happened to cold weather?
The lover to his beloved comes,
Prepared for her embrace.
Happiness two thousandfold comes;
Thousands of nightingales;
A hundred fruits to ripeness come:
Apples, pomegranates, and quince.
Happines to pass is here;
Beyond limit, beyond count, it comes.
Turtledoves to plane trees,
Storks to the lighthouse come.
Every lover to his beloved comes.
Drunks lapse into hangovers.
Lovers aplenty come
And turn every night into day.
Song to the turtledoves comes,
The camel to the mule;
Upon the horse the rider comes,
Upon the camel the load.
From Bandar-i Lār[3] it comes,
Without stirring up the dust;
Better this year than last it comes,
Toward Gulbār;[4]
Wheat into flour comes.
Time to hang the enemy,[5] the vile dog,
Upon the gallows comes.

May Purim be ever blessed!
We shall all kill Haman (. . .)
(One should do so every year! . . .)
Hang Haman upon the gallows,
Bring terror upon Zeresh,[6]
Hang Dalfon[7] upon the gallows,
Together with all his brothers.

Utter curses, two hundred, on them all! (. . .)
Utter *blessings* all at once.
[Spend time] coloring *eggs,*
Increase all the merriment;
May Purim be ever blessed!
Eat many a sweet thing
(Hang Haman upon the gallows!),
Drink many cups of wine,
Let it overflow the earth[8]
Knead the wheat of the fields
(Peace be upon their souls),[9]
Eat lots of *boghra*[10] and *polow,*[11]
Give donations without end,
Let them overflow the earth.
Give out many gifts as well[12]
(Hang Haman upon the gallows!),
Give everyone two *dīnār*s,
Give *charity* without end.
Act righteously before God,
And be all of you full of *joy;*
That which is hard in religion
Has today become easy![13]
Strike up *celebrations* everyone,
Be free of all thoughts of grief;
May your feet never grow weary,
And may you behold this week
The *Sanctuary* and its *sacred vessels,*[14]
Which have been taken from you.
Whatever you've lost, whatever way,
May you find it again this way.
May you be always full of joy,
Within the limits of courtesy.
Play with eggs and turtledoves,
Proclaim God's righteousness,
[How] we have easily escaped
From accursed Haman's hands.
O Lord, may all friends and relations

Come [now] to [visit] Gershon!
Make [tasty] rice halva,
Play with the eggs of turtledoves,
Sew new breeches and tunics (. . .).
Spend your days with *ḥalakah*
And your nights with *melakah.*[15]
Tonight is Purim's eve,
So take lute and flute in hand,
Young and old folks all alike,
With lute, tambour, and clarion;
Since [Purim] has come, drink wine,
Move to the sound of lute and flute.
Before the harvest of roses,
Sing, all of you, like nightingales;
Befriend each other [everywhere],
In meadows and gardens;
Be like nightingales when they behold
The amorous rose in the tree's shade;
Act like this and drink like that;
Know Purim['s customs] really well.
It's a *commandment* to laugh.
In the month of the New Year[16]
Find we rest and repose.

Amīnā: *On the Sacrifice of Isaac*

Then Khalīl[1] answered God:
"I have sworn an oath upon the Truth;
I will not hold back my hand from Isaac
Until my oath is carried out. O Lord,
My condition to desist is a witnessed covenant,
That when my offspring sin, entrapped
By evil, but come to You afterward
In supplication, truly to repent,
You will accept their repentance,
You will become their salve and remedy,
You will desist from further punishment

And not pry into their sins."[2]
The Merciful spoke again: "I accept your oath."
Khalīl was satisfied and loosened the ties
On Isaac's feet, and chancing to look up,
His eyes fell on a wondrous ram, its horns
Caught among branches. He was filled
With wonder. That ram, the only one of its kind,
Had been prepared from pre-eternity,
A substitute for Isaac's soul so that[3]
The heavenly lamp would not be extinguished.
Khalīl sacrificed the ram before God
In his son's place. Its hide he entrusted
To the pleasure of preeminent Khiżr,[4]
That he, like a panegyrist, should wear it[5]
On his shoulders day and night, morning
And evening. Its sinews he set aside for David
(Such was the Lord's decree), who made
Ten harp strings and who sang God's praises with them
In verse; accompanied by the *sāz*[6] and other instruments,
Daily at dawn he sang and praised in *song*.[7]
Its horns are for the Morrow,
Readied for Resurrection's time.[8]
But pay attention,
I have yet another tale to tell:
When Khalīl saw that ram,
That large, fat, masculine ram,
It fled before him; and Khalīl sped
After it, swift as a gazelle. Unable
To catch it, he saw the powerful ram
Blocking the entrance to a cave.
Khalīl entered that cave alone.
Abraham, that brave man,
Beheld a wondrous place, a bright,
Paradisal place, suffused with light,
A golden castle in its midst,
Filled with silver and gold, with jewels of rubies,
Agates that shone like the eastern sun,

Great heaps of turquoise, jasper,
Diamonds, and pearls. Its walls and doors
Were all adorned with festive scenes,
Mysterious, undeceiving, like the heavens.
Around that rose garden fortress
(May God make it the friends' portion!)[9]
On fruit-laden trees grew fruits of every kind
The heart desires, fit for a shah.
The birds chirped out thousands of melodies
In harmony with nightingales and parrots.
On every side there flowed a hundred springs
Of water with gemlike drops. The praises
Of such a brocaded place can never end.
When Khalīl's eyes beheld this site,
He cried to the Creator:
"O Lord of firmaments and of angels,
Tell me, what is this chosen, noble place,
The like of which cannot be seen in the world?
Is it the very mansion of the Lord?"
The sound of a reply then reached his ears;
From the unseen, the secret was disclosed:[10]
"O my chosen friend Berahīm,[11] know for certain
That this chosen site, this magnificent place,
Is an earthly paradise and like unto
The one in heaven, abode of the righteous,
Dwelling of the noble and the wise.[12]
Now catch the ram, for it awaits you."
Khalīl stood and worshiped;
Prostrate he bowed his head,
Praised the Almighty.
He caught the ram by force and offered it,
Sacrificed it before the Lord
In his son's place.[13]
This act completed, Isaac and Khalīl rejoiced.
Swift as the wind they then departed
Home, with good cheer.

Then He, the Author, Said, Giving His Reason for Composing This Book and by Way of Exhorting the World

O heart, you've heard this tale,
Do not fall short in devotion.
If sin appears, the oath to God
Cannot be reneged; *repent* for ten days,
Then carry out *commandments* every day,
Until the exalted, eternal Almighty
Forgives your sins and errors
Out of His mercy and eternal grace.
Upon you shines the light of His generosity;
It opens the gates of bounty, guides
The chattels of good fortune to you.
Whenever evil confronts you,
Cry out to the Almighty;
Shed tears, lament sincerely
Together with other Jews and say,
"O God, fulfill Your oath of Your own accord,
Absolve us of sins and errors;
Dissolve our problems as it were in water;
Deliver us from punishment.
O be a Refuge for him who seeks to know God.[14]
You are the deliverer of slaves,
Source of joy for the mournful
And their companion; grant the wishes
Of the destitute, heal broken hearts,
Be cure and remedy to the sick.
For today is the *Day of Atonement,*
All day, a flaming light.
Forgive the *sin* of everyone;
Heal everyone's pain.

This was completed in the year 5470;[15]
Our wish and hope was fulfilled.
Forgive all our sins
And send *Redemption* speedily.
Send the Messiah to us in all haste

That he may heal the wounds of our hearts.
This helpless slave Amīnā,
Ever in need of the *Shekinah*'s[16] favor;
He is a stranger in this world.
Misfortune ever deprives him of wealth.
May the Judge melt away his enemies
And upon him bestow His kindness.

Historical Texts

8

Bābāī b. Luṭf: *Kitāb-i Anusī* (*The Book of a Forced Convert*)

Bābāī b. Luṭf, the author of *Kitāb-i Anusī* (The book of a forced convert; henceforth KA), is the first known historian of Iranian Jewry.[1] He hailed from Kashan, where he recorded the sufferings of his coreligionists during the first half of the seventeenth century. We do not know the year of his birth; he died sometime after 1662.

Ibn Luṭf's fame rests primarily on KA, a "chronicle" composed in Persian verse that is more than 5,000 couplets long.[2] Its style and content imitate those of popular versified (*masnavī*) Persian chronicles.[3] However, unlike the latter, which are not concerned with Jews, KA describes the plight of Iranian Jewry during the reigns of three shahs: Shah ʿAbbās I (1571–1629), Shah Ṣafī I (1629–1642), and Shah ʿAbbās II (1642–1666). The height of anti-Jewish persecution in the form of forced conversions to Shiʿi Islam occurred in the third reign, between 1656 and 1661/2. It affected the Jews of such major towns as Isfahan, Kashan, Hamadan, Khwānsār, and Gulpaygan. Bābāī b. Luṭf provides detailed accounts of the circumstances leading to the forced conversions in each town, as well as of the manner in which the Jews regained their religious freedom. The persecutions occurred at the instigation of Muḥammad Beg, the grand vizier under Shah ʿAbbās II, and seem to have been primarily religiously motivated, although economic factors also played a significant role.[4]

In KA, Ibn Luṭf provides a precious eyewitness account of the persecutions. Although he had the opportunity to flee, he chose instead to record the suffering and deliverance of his coreligionists. The reliability of his account in KA, a work he compares in content to the Book of Esther,[5] when checked against contemporary Persian sources and the accounts of European travelers, is impressive.[6] Bābāī b. Luṭf's effort to integrate his narrative into the larger stream of Iranian history enhances the importance of the KA both for Jewish and Iranian historiography.

How the Grand Vizier Found a Pretext Against the Jews of Isfahan and Drove Them out of Their Homes

In the age of every ruler,[7] old and new, time and again some affliction befell us. But this one was greater than any other: in it hundreds of hearts and souls were torn. If evil befell us in former generations, it could be abated with our money and property. In this generation we were entirely devastated. Our religion and law were lost as well as our money and property. Would that our souls would depart the same way! We have never been so at the mercy of ill-wishers. When the shah gave Āṣaf[8] permission [to convert the Jews], he said, "May the Lord grant an opportunity [to carry out your task]!"

Come, listen and see what these afflicted [Jews] experienced and how they became Muslims. No previous generation has ever seen a day such as we have seen, full of hundreds of lamentations and sorrows. The Āṣaf of those times summoned the Jewish community of Isfahan and said, "You are all poor; you are unclean and impure as far as our faith is concerned,[9] yet your bodies come in constant contact with our own. You touch everything; is there no difference between wine and vinegar? The order of the shah, the Master of Favors, is that you leave the city on this very day. I will show you an empty place where you can build new homes." The [Jewish] community of Isfahan was deeply grieved on hearing this for it was innocent of any crimes. Afflicted and crying, the Jews replied, "We have all paid the *jizya;*[10] moreover, for several reigns now our homes have been in Isfahan. The Jewish quarter has remained as before;[11] it has seen no additional building or repairs these past few years.[12] Moreover, we pray for the shah and we always ask the Almighty to preserve his life." Āṣaf replied, "We know nothing of all this; we will drive you out of Isfahan. Whether you accept this or not, I shall expel you from your present area." When the community realized the worsening of the situation, it was decided that it was advisable and prudent to depart. The Jews said to Āṣaf, "O Great Protector, grant us a respite of two months so that we may put our affairs in order; there are hundreds of thousands of tasks before us. Come, show us some land with good air that we may build our homes there." Full of deceit and driven by the desire to afflict the Jews, Muḥammad Beg assigned them the mountain known as Kulāh-i Qāżī (The judge's cap).[13] That bad mountain was famous because it had always been the dwelling place of animals, wild and domesticated. There was no vegetation, water, or fresh air for ten parasangs around it; it was a dreary mountain. Āṣaf said, "Lay the foundations of your town here and call it Mihnatābād (Abode of sorrow)."[14]

The Jews went there at once but saw nothing except jackals, wolves, and hyenas. Men and women, one and all, became frightened and returned with hearts full of pain. They went to Āṣaf bewildered, crying and wailing, men, women, and children, saying, "The air is unhealthy there; show us a different site." Āṣaf replied, "Go then to the Takht-i Pūlād (Throne of steel) for that is a good dwelling site—it was a place full of corpses—you will never be lonely there, day or night."[15]

Then the community officials came forth and offered him a large bribe. When he heard the bribe mentioned, Muḥammad Beg became perplexed. He said, "I shall give you a place with the Zoroastrians. Come to me tomorrow and present your names. I shall go with you to Gebrābād (Zoroastrian abode)[16] and let you rent houses on a street like Qaṣr-i Shimshād (Shimshād's castle). Dwell there part of the year until I give you your own place." Next day the Jews set out as planned, but Āṣaf followed them like fire. They went to Gebrābād and rented a street from those ugly, afflicted Zoroastrians.[17] They leased it for six months, [thinking], "This is temporary, until the shah assigns us our own place." Those poor people took up their chattel and went and stayed overnight among their enemies, [the Zoroastrians]. When evening fell Āṣaf summoned all the Zoroastrians to him in a great hurry. Shrewdly, he said to them, "These Jews are unclean;[18] they are enemies of religion and they have denied, at one time or another, all religions. In the morning your entire community should come to the royal palace.

Stretch out your hands, shouting and wailing, and say, all of you, full of grief, 'O shah, we do not want these Jews; assign another dwelling place to this envious folk! This entire territory was given to us by the former, Paradise-Dwelling Shah[19] until the Day of Resurrection.' Cause an uproar; do not fear the council, for I shall take care of your affair." Such a trick did he devise on that night against the Jews, and such a thorn did he bring against the community.

The next day the Zoroastrians went to the palace of the World-Sustaining shah. They all cried out for justice, saying, "How can we go on living happily? How can we bear to see Jews dwelling among us wherever we turn? Since when can Zoroastrians and Jews dwell together when they don't even want to look one another in the face?[20] If the shah allows such a thing, we shall all kill ourselves in order to protect ourselves. For we are all like willows, and they are all like saws. We regard each other as the wolf does the lamb."

When the shah's Āṣaf heard this, he said, "Cut the story short; throw out the Jews!" The Zoroastrians rushed out at once and chased away the Jews. O poor afflicted folk! Because the Zoroastrians have hated the Jews throughout the ages, they did not give them a place among them.

Once again the community was in dire straits. With clamoring hearts they went to Āṣaf. Lamenting, they said, "Supreme Refuge, may the heads of the enemy fall in your snare like [polo] balls! The infidel Zoroastrians chased us out and tried to capture and grieve us. Where else, like the wind, shall we roam? Allow us to make for ourselves a corner as Farhād did."[21] The shah's Āṣaf replied quickly, "Go, all of you, to hell! Go wherever you want; no people will allow even one of you among them!" Having said this he chased them away from his presence, adding, "Don't come to me again in flight!" They left, crying, wailing, and with burning hearts; they headed toward the desert.

By chance, this happened on a Friday night. They were all crying in the vicinity of the Torah when in the city and bazaar a proclamation was heard: "All Jews, male and female, must leave quickly, tonight. Whoever is seen tomorrow will lose his head." When the people heard that proclamation so late at night they became greatly agitated. "What shall we do? Woe to us! If tomorrow arrives, we risk our lives staying here. The night is dark, and there are guards everywhere. We won't be able to see our way and will fall into the trap, suddenly, like helpless children." The men started up in confusion, carrying their wives and children on their shoulders. Thus in the dark night, fearing the sword, they took the road toward the tomb of Seraḥ bat Asher.[22] On the same Friday they arrived there, despairing of all hope of life. They were standing there crying, full of suffering, young and old, even children. Wailing in God's abode, they prayed continuously, "O God, turn this misfortune away from us!"

When Saturday morning came, all went to the synagogue. Āṣaf was informed of the situation and chose his most cruel soldiers, saying to them, "Bring the Jews to me at dawn, and bring their leaders to me again." By chance, the leader of the Jews of Isfahan during the reign of Shah ʿAbbās II was a good man, like balm to the soul. The name of that great man was Saʿīd. He was a friend to all, a jeweler by profession. The night on which Āṣaf said to the Jews, "You must get out of town," one group set out for the tomb of Seraḥ bat Asher, another became wanderers, and another group dispersed, crying, in great confusion. Instead of tents they sewed together old *chādur*s[23] and set up homes underneath them. It was Friday night when they did so, looking like corpses and the *chādur*s like shrouds. In great distress they kept on calling out to God, crowded six people to a corner.

All at once, on Saturday, they saw royal servants armed with bows drawn taut. They were leading a few Jews who were in deplorable condition, hands tied behind them ignominiously. The guards were after the leaders of the community: Saʿīd, Obadiah, and Sasson. After they found their dwellings, they seized them and tied the leaders' hands at once. They were dragged before Āṣaf in this condition and lined up in a row before him. Āṣaf said, "O dirty Jews, you all give me trouble! Go all of you, men and women, and leave your property behind. Leave our region and choose for yourselves another place, or become sincere Muslims at the hand of Shah ʿAbbās." When the helpless Jews heard this, they gave up hope of life. With hands tied behind their backs they went out, following the previous group of Jews. Thus on the Sabbath they too set out, stupefied, toward the tomb of Seraḥ bat Asher. The people who were already there suddenly heard a great clamor. When they saw Saʿīd and Sasson, they grew alarmed. Instead of the sound of Sabbath songs, wailing was heard, because of this day of sorrow. They mourned everywhere. The cruel soldiers killed many of them mercilessly. Like captive pigeons they were forced to relinquish their women and children. Such was the Sabbath they spent in that desert. Grieving, they set out once again.

They were brought to the palace in the presence of Āṣaf and the Shah of Shahs. When they saw the full council, they began to tremble like willows; it seemed as if the Day of Resurrection had arrived! Tears stained their cheeks, and fear reigned in their hearts. Āṣaf suddenly called out to Sasson, "I offer you an easy solution. Take all your women by the hand and leave this realm. Leave your wealth, property, and houses behind; go thirsty until you reach a shore with water. Or else become Muslims at once and sincerely; cease being hypocrites!" Sasson answered, "O Āṣaf, my refuge, know that I am powerless to decide in this matter. Saʿīd is a *mullah*[24] and learned, the teacher of our children. If he will convert now I will also embrace the new faith." Then Saʿīd was brought forth, and Āṣaf said, "O Jew, turn Muslim that you may find honor and hasten on the road to Paradise accompanied by friends. Become God's slave and our brother; you would be the best of Muslims!" Saʿīd said to him, "O light of my eyes, I cannot deny my religion. We are already Muslims in the Jewish manner;[25] we too know only one God." When Āṣaf heard these words he became angry and ordered his servants at once, "Take this Jew and tie his feet firmly to a camel. Tear up his belly; and say nothing of this to anyone." The servants took the old man and tied him to a camel, but God Himself became his shield. God inspired him to say, "Grant a respite until tomorrow." When the grandees heard this, they granted his wish willingly. In his distress, the poor man thought, "Perhaps tonight God, the Living Founder of the World, will grant deliverance from the hands of the council!"

O Bābāī be humble before God. Who else can grant you access to the Fountain of Intercession?

How the Grand Vizier Converted the Jews of Isfahan to Islam, and How He Bestowed Favors on Them

O Lord, by the God of the pure family,[26] by the Lord of those who suffer pain, by the Lord of the Prince who suffered the separation, by his migration,[27] and by the light of the Prophet,[28] may You send redemption to the world. Grant us deliverance from the hands of the oppressor! Come to our rescue in this exile; let no one remember this affliction. Many hearts have been wrecked in this exile; heart and soul, law and religion, have been subjected to torment.

When Āṣaf granted the respite, the famous Saʿīd foresaw the blows that would follow. Several servants were sent repeatedly to fetch him that day. They brought the learned man face to face with danger. He came before Āṣaf the next day and greeted that moon of the East.[29] Āṣaf said, "Welcome, O light of the eyes. Did you see ʿAlī in your dream last night?[30] Utter the profession of faith and you will behold its honeycomb; you will pluck hundreds of flowers from the garden of the world. Whatever you want can be within your reach: fine clothes, robes, money, and titles of honor." Saʿīd replied, "O Āṣaf, refuge, may you remain forever in the shah's good graces![31] Listen to my situation. I am old and my head spins like a compass. Grant me a worthy reward that would benefit me every day. I have no strength left in my hands and feet; all I want is to be allowed to sit in one place. I shall pray for the shah and make prayer and fasts my habit." They gave him a caravanserai so that he could stay out of mischief. He uttered the profession of faith and became a Muslim at once.

Then all the others uttered the profession of faith. First all the heads of the community went one by one and recited the profession of faith before Āṣaf. Then one by one the people also pronounced it, fearing the shah. But they sought a reward at the same time. One took money, another clothes. One said, "I want a slave girl to clean my house." Another said, "I have many outstanding debts; pay my debts and I shall convert to Islam." It was decided and duly registered that each man would receive one or two *tūmān*s.[32] They took five thousand *dīnār*s from the property of the foundation of the Fourteen Innocents.[33] It was also decided that the women would get fifteen thousand Tabrizi coins.[34]

When some who were hiding in corners heard this they came out to get the money; thus were the people led astray. For the sake of money they all relinquished their faith and opened the gate of suffering in every direction. Some, because they possessed homes, were unable to leave their nests. Others felt bound to stay because of wives and children. How could one's heart approve leaving town without them?[35] Some had many debts and obligations and were unable to set out without help. In other words, they were all trapped; they could not stir from the place day or night. By acting this way they gave Āṣaf an idea: "I should send the order to every region to arrest Jews everywhere, turn them into Muslims at once. They should become of one faith willingly or unwillingly." Āṣaf went to the World-Owning shah and said, "May the Almighty ever be your Protector! May He grant that you live in pleasure, feasting, and joy as long as the world endures. I have turned all the Jews of Isfahan into Muslims. I desire, for the sake of your ancestry, to brighten your lamp with our faith. I shall send soldiers to every town and proclaim to the infidels that whosoever is willing in the faith should at once, and with a sincere heart, become Muslim. Anyone who refuses the faith of Islam takes his life into his own hands and is lost." The shah gave him royal permission at once with the instruction, "I wish you to make religion flourish but you should not bring compulsion into this business in order to make them confess the Shi'i faith."[36] Āṣaf bowed before the shah, and said, "Rest your mind at ease!"

Then he left and wrote eighteen letters; you'd say he jolted the heavenly spheres! There was some delay caused by the making of the seal, but rumor of what was to come spread to every town. When this news arrived, hundreds of cries arose from all around. The Jews proclaimed many fasts, offered many sacrifices, and treated orphans and widows generously, like beloved sons. They blew the *shofar* a great deal and sounded the *teru'ah*.[37] But because of God's decree they were unable to contrive a plan before the shah.

O Bābāī, be mindful of preordained fate! Find some expedient to help you!

[Muḥammad Beg was unsuccessful in enforcing his decree of conversion throughout the kingdom. Some of the Jewish communities located closest to Isfahan, the Safavid capital—notably the communities of Kashan, Shiraz, Qum, and Hamadan—suffered the most, while others, among them Farahabad, Gulpaygan, Khurramabad, and Khunsar, showed heroism and remarkable initiative, as in the case of Yazd, described below. The Muslims' venality is offset by the possibly exaggerated description of their economic dependence on the Jews of Yazd.[38]

The period of forced conversions lasted from 1656 to 1661/2, after which the *anusim* (forced converts) of Iran were allowed to return to Judaism.]

The Zeal of the Muslims of Yazd: How They Went to the Royal Camp and Entreated Shah 'Abbās II, and How They Obtained Permission for the Jews of Yazd to Return to Their Own Religion

When the [Jewish] community brought forth the gold,[39] it interceded for them with the council [of Yazd]. For gold is like a sword, brother: if you strike it with a stone, it will show its edge. Do you know why the infidels pray to idols as part of their worship? Because master goldsmiths finish them in gold from head to toe. They love them for the sake of the gold and discriminate [in their favor], heart and soul. Such is [the role of] gold in the world; it settles all business!

Thus, when the Jewish people brought forth gold, the Muslims could not resist it. They all put aside the business of the world at once and became pursuers of vanity. They set out toward the city of Isfahan and took themselves to the palace of the council. They threw themselves on the second shah [ʿAbbās II] and called down upon him all manner of blessings. They carried with them a [request of] exemption to which all grandees had put their seal. Then all the *kadkhudā*s opened their mouths together,[40] at once, in praise of the just shah: "O shah of the world, for the sake of the Prophet, listen a while to this testimony, for we have traveled a long way for the privilege of kissing your feet, O wise shah."

When the shah heard this from the kadkhudās, he took the [request of] exemption from them and looked at it. Since there were numerous seals on it, the kadkhudās had written on the other side. What he saw written was: "O World-Conquering Shah, the whole of Yazd is upset by this grief, namely, that the Jews must leave the town this year and go far, to a desolate desert, or, taking their children by the hand, to another country. Know, O shah, that if they leave the province of Yazd, the Muslims will be in straits, like a limp donkey. They [the Jews] will want hundreds of thousands from us, which, by the God of the Friends,[41] we are unable to pay. All the business and important affairs of the Muslims prosper through them, O shah. We will be hindered for a long time; the business of the Muslims will be lost. All of us in the town of Yazd, young and old, are their apprentices in business, gardens, meadows, and homes, in silk weft, warp, and woof. Everything is set right by their hands; woe to us a hundred times if they leave.[42] Moreover, if they become Muslims, we will lose our faith at once because they do not believe, heart and soul, in God's Messenger. (Even if you wash a negro two hundred times, you will find no trace of whiteness on him.) There are many Zoroastrians in town; they have no religion or Scriptures; [they are] like infidels.[43] They are the ones who should be oppressed, the load of ten camels placed on their necks. As for the Jews, O shah of Duldul,[44] they should be set free by [your] magnificence. Now you should know, O shah, that if they leave Yazd, our entire Muslim community will have to follow them at once. Therefore, for the sake of the light of the Prophet, tolerate the Jewish community."

When that just shah heard this speech, he left and desisted from this difficult matter for a while. After an hour he uttered exalted words and said, for the grace of God: "Tell the Jews to remain in their own place, joyfully, with all of us. I have passed [a decree] regarding the [Jewish] community of Yazd that they may dwell safe from violence and oppression. Go back to your town, all of you; do not come before me again in flight."

When the kadkhudās heard this good news, they were made very happy by the decree. They blessed the World-Owning Shah: "Long may you live in the world! May you endure as long as the sun and the moon, together with the throne, signet ring, and station of Jamshīd.[45] May God be your friend and may Haydar [ʿAlī] ever stand behind you! May Zū'lfiqar[46] always rest in your grip!" Having uttered these blessings, they went on their way, sending a herald ahead. They brought the news to that [Jewish] community, and they were all made happy by that intercession. Now they remained in complete tranquillity; may they remain so until the Day of Resurrection!

O God, send redemption to every city and extricate them from violence. Forgive the sins of the Jewish people, particularly those of the people of Kashan, male and female.

O God, by the God of the son of ʿImrān[47] forgive your faithful Bābāī!

Bābāī b. Farhād: *Kitāb-i Sar-guzasht-i Kāshān (The Book of Events in Kashan)*

The second JP historical document that has reached us is *Kitāb-i Sar-guzasht-i Kāshān dar bāb-i ʿIbrī va Goyimi-yi Sānī* (The book of events in Kashan concerning the Jews: Their second conversion; henceforth KS), written by Bābāī b. Farhād, the grandson of Bābāī b. Luṭf.[1] Considerably shorter than Ibn Luṭf's chronicle, KS is only 1,300 verses long. It is also narrower in scope, concentrating primarily on the hardships endured by Iranian Jews, chiefly of Kashan, during the Afghan invasion of Iran (1722–1730). Caught between fighting Iranian and Afghan armies and suffering from the depredations of both, the Jewish community leaders of Kashan resorted in 1730 to "voluntary" conversion to the Shiʿi form of Islam. In spite of such precautions, they were not spared heavy taxation. The Jewish community of Kashan was permitted to return to Judaism seven months later.

Although Bābāī b. Farhād himself compares his chronicle to his grandfather's, such a comparison is not favorable to his own work. The style of KS is weaker than that of KA in both its literary aspect[2] and, especially, its historical content.[3] Nor can the voluntary conversions described in KS, which lasted some seven months, be compared to the forced conversions Iranian Jews endured less than a hundred years before, which lasted about seven years.[4]

Bābāī b. Farhād, like Bābāī b. Luṭf, tries to give a historical context to his short chronicle and thereby provides an interesting popular account of some of the struggles in Iran during the first half of the eighteenth century. These difficulties were not limited to external threats, such as the Afghan invasion of Iran and the simultaneous Russian and Ottoman forays into the kingdom, but were internal as well. The weakened Safavid dynasty was falling apart; a new dynasty, the Afsharid, replaced it in 1735.[5] Bābāī b. Farhād's chronicle provides further testimony to these turbulent times and illustrates the plight of the Iranian Jews caught in a complex political maelstrom along with the rest of the country.

The translation of the following two chapters from KS highlights the tensions within the Jewish community, which was caught up in the internal political events involving the two Afghan rulers, Maḥmūd (r. 1722–1725) and Ashraf (r. 1725–1730), and the latter's rout at the hands of Ṭahmāsp Qulī Khan, the future Nādir Shah (r. 1736–1747).

The Reign of Shah Maḥmūd in Isfahan: How Shah Ashraf Came out of House Arrest, Killed Shah Maḥmūd, Took His Place on the Throne, and Reigned

Come, O heart,[6] and proclaim a flood upon the world; no shah has ever completed his work. When Shah Maḥmūd sat upon the throne he conquered cities through luck and good fortune.[7] Whoever heard his name would start up, even if asleep.[8] His fame spread throughout Iran, from Ray to Rūm, from Khurasan to Gilan. He killed several thousand youths and old men, each one of them like a cypress in a rose garden. He had an envoy like Āyāz,[9] the noble whose nickname was "Almās" (Diamond).[10] Almās' command was obeyed throughout Iran; the shah's own command never lacked Almās' seal. He was froward with the shah, with the shah's permission; all his business was successful and opportune. (Whenever God hurls someone to the ground, He elevates him first, like the accursed Pharaoh.) All the nobles of Isfahan were under Almās' command. Whenever he would wait upon the shah he would have about fifty heralds. Whenever he would serve the shah he would first eat new fruits and whatever else he wanted. There was none smarter than he in the country; he was called Diamond, but he was sharper than that.

There were some people who feared the shah. They said, "We'll find a solution for this [fear]." They poisoned the food of the Shah of Shahs. Since they forgot to salt the food, [their trick was discovered and] they were doomed. When Ashraf found out about this affair, he set out like a lion on the track of his prey. He came to the Shah of Shahs and asked, "How are you?" Then he killed the shah suddenly.[11]

[Shah Maḥmūd's] soul departed to the ancestors of his native country, while Ashraf appropriated the land for himself. First he fought Almās and killed him because he wanted to be shah in his own right.[12] They beat the kettledrums in Ashraf's name; in that hour the world bowed to his will. He confiscated all Almās' property, although some relations appeared, right and left.[13] It then occurred to him suddenly to conquer Hamadan out of sheer bravery.[14] He conquered some other cities as well, all with the blow of the dagger.[15] It then occurred to that hero not to allow any gentiles to live in Isfahan.[16] First he killed the powerful princes who were the light of the eyes of the harem.[17] Each day he took some [Shiʿi] Muslims to the main square.[18] He would hang five or six, and he would kill all with arrows and rifles. If Mullah Żaʿfarān[19] had permitted it, no [Shiʿi] Muslim would have survived in Isfahan. While the impure [Shiʿis][20] were being killed, the Jews feared for their own lives.

As soon as Ashraf returned from Hamadan, it occurred to him to conquer the Mazandaran [Caspian] region. The Shah of Shahs came as far as Kashan;[21] sun and moon trembled out of fear. He had a few noble riding youths, each one worth a lion. They were carrying thousands of pieces of artillery, each one accompanied by special soldiers. He also had thousands of swift horses, as well as two pairs of male and female lions and tigers. A few bazaars accompanied him also lest his subjects suffer any deprivation. Shah Ashraf rode in the midst of the people [of Kashan] honoring them by talking to them. That shah possessed much dignity and was very generous toward the Kashanis. He gave them carpets and other things without them paying him one dinar. He left and stayed a while in Qum and Mahsam;[22] he had no rest day and night, not even for a moment. From there he went to Khurasan, arriving in Simnan and Damaghan.[23] He, like Pharaoh, fought a few battles, while Ṭahmāsp Khān[24] was like Farīdūn.[25]

Come, O heart, esteem the virtue of valor; follow it and educate yourself! May no good come to him who does evil in the world! Only bad rice can be set aside to die; a man of bad character and deeds cannot. If you have a lantern, send it forth [and light your path]. Know, O heart, whether or not you worship [only] God. Those who walk on the right path go to the halting place without stumbling. Those who think of deceit and mischief will always remain burdened. Happy is he who is successful; he does work which comes to fruition in the world.

Go rest, Bābāī, there is no craftsman like you. May the Life Giver light your lamp!

How Ashraf Fought in Khurasan, and How Ṭahmāsp Khān Appeared in Kashan and Found a Pretext to Convert the Nasi *and Ten Other Kashanis*

Listen again to a dirge about what happened to us in Kashan. Many youths died in the famine[26] and were buried with a thousand hopes [still] in their hearts. O Creator of the Firmament, although each one of them was like the rising moon and the branch of the box tree, he was carried off into oblivion. They carried sorrowful hearts into the grave; they left us in the claws of the oppressors.

It was in the year 5490 that Ashraf became shah.[27] He came to Kashan and went to war. He went to the Mazandaran via the road to Qum fighting the *qizilbāsh* and the lions.[28] First he fought because he had lost face, but afterward he had not a moment without fear. The kind shah [Ashraf] came as far as Kashan, not stopping anywhere even for a moment. He said, "I have no problem with the Kashanis, so don't play tricks on me. If you do, I will cut you up with sword, dagger, and the blows of the mace. Go dwell in peace in your own corners, and watch the outcome [of the struggle] from your doorways." He departed [as quickly] as fish in water and hurried off to Isfahan in a single day.[29]

The next day Ṭahmāsp [Khān], that clever man, arrived in Kashan. When he heard that Ashraf had taken off, he was very surprised and set out in pursuit like a yoked lion. He took off like a mortally wounded gazelle, collecting taxes and tolls[30] from every region.[31] By heavenly decree, he came as far as Kashan to carry off property and money from the *kadkhudās*.[32] May God have mercy upon Mīr Abū'l Qāsim[33] a hundred times; he was an intelligent man in Kashan. He went out to meet the general, who had an army numbering forty thousand men.[34] Such was the lot of the enemies on that day, but for friends it was like the New Year.[35]

David was *nasi*[36] in those days. He had seen much and had become sinful. When everyone went out to meet the general, servants[37] called out to him loudly, "All Jews are prisoners;[38] they must become Muslims at once. If not, we will kill them all. We will not leave a single Jew alive in the province!" [The Jews] were thus the khan's prisoners until the following day.

Come, ponder again the state of the households! Several servants were stationed in every house, all armed with guns, swords, and daggers. They struck and kicked the heads and legs of the unfortunate women and children. No one has ever seen such injustice in the world; such was the calamity that occurred in our generation. Then he [Ṭahmāsp Khān] also wanted money and tribute, as well as clean straw and barley for the horses. Such were the times; next they would demand women with lutes and wine!

Come, listen to what happened to the kadkhudās. They were rounded up together with the common folk. It was decided that the kadkhudās of the Jews would pay a few thousands.[39] The *nasi* drew up an account of what would be taken of the coarse and fine foodstuffs. Ashraf's money was dissipated;[40] you would say the world has turned upside down! Then the accursed ones set out in pursuit of Ashraf. But because of our sinfulness, they [the Afghans] did not win; otherwise we would not have feared them [Ṭahmāsp Khān and his troops] so much. As for the Multānīs [Hindus], they fared better than we. There were seven or eight such [families] there; [only] five hundred tūmāns were taken from them.

What shall we do, O God, what shall we do? We are all melting away like silver! God had mercy on all women obeying their husbands. If it had not been for them, we would have forfeited our souls.[41] How good it would have been if we had not given up our religion!

It was on a Friday evening, as we were longing for the Sabbath, on the eighth of Ḥeshwan.[42] It was like a weekday now for the Jewish people. The day turned upside down, as one would wish for one's enemies; several Sabbath prayers were thus profaned. The Jews had no possessions, no money, and no credit, while everyone else held swords drawn against them. Thousands of homes were destroyed; women and children as well as men were crying. In this manner [the khan's men] carried off money along with the *nasi* and some Jewish leaders.

The khan was at a banquet in the *Mīr*'s house while they were deliberating about the Jews. The kadkhudās were very upset; they did not have even one dinar in their hands.[43] Among those present were Binyamin, Khodādād of Lar, Mordekai, Rabbi, and David Shahriyārī, also Khwājah and Israel Gurgī, supporting each other like two towers; Misha'el Kohen as well as Mordekai Isfahani, who thought that they had been invited to the banquet! Zebulun had converted the previous Friday;[44] his relationship with Ya'qub was that of a cat to a mouse. Binyamin Shākshūl acted the leopard; he thought he could conquer both lions and crocodiles. He recalled the calamities that had befallen him, that his riches had been plucked away.[45]

Those were the individuals who went to that council. What a pleasant gathering it seemed! Suddenly another cry arose [in the assembly]: "Pay a hundred tūmāns, great and small!"[46] The *sa'īd*s[47] of the people of Kashan had arrived, causing an uproar, making everyone bow down [before them] in the dust, saying that the Jews must give them a few more *tūmāns*. The Jews replied, "We don't have the money; we might as well strew dust on our heads [in mourning]!"

A thousand curses on Satan! Know for certain that he was present in that assembly. For then Binyamin made an about-face, saying, "In the generation of this previous master[48] I shall reveal the *shahādah*[49] of Muḥammad's religion in Moses' words!"[50] *Nasi* David was an ignoramus, hasty in speech. When he heard these words from the kadkhudā, he said, "Give me your hand; let us swear allegiance [to the new faith], let us glorify all the Jews thereby." They made an agreement and set forth, entrusting themselves to the House of 'Alī. They said, "We are Muslims now; 'Alī has made us [zealous] like wolves. We gave money in offering to the shah;[51] we have become Muslims and we will not renege." Then the just khan said, "Moses was better than anyone else. He turned the dry branch green in the world. When he planted the branch he plucked roses from it at once.[52] So it behooves the followers of Moses to adhere to their religion just as Christians should not tamper with theirs. In your hearts you have not severed yourselves from your religion. I know this to be true even if you bring all the prophets before me. You should abase yourselves before us and give us the money."[53]

There were a few fools and opportunists there. When they heard this they raised a banner of protest. One of them was an exalted kadkhudā named Khwājah Binyamin.[54] He said, "We will become Muslims, heart and soul, as will the entire Jewish community as well."[55] The khan rejoiced when he heard this speech, saying, "Come forward, House of 'Imrān."[56]

They went and sat down in that assembly, shutting the door of happiness in their own faces. All present congratulated them. They ate, some without reciting the grace after meal. That very hour the khan issued a decree to this effect: "I exempt the new Muslims from the *jizya*."[57] They bestowed some robes of honor on the kadkhudās who had thrown themselves into Satan's snare. They came out with the letter [of the decree] on their heads,[58] thinking that they could still embrace the Torah.

O God, tell us what to do; we are melting away because of our sinfulness. We are disgraced at Your palace; we are no longer Your servants. What else will come from the turning of the world? The hearts of robbers [already] rejoice over us! What shall we do with ourselves and with those ten persons?[59] The hearts of robbers [already] rejoice over us! Once again an evil decree has fallen upon us. Give them a chance to return to their religion, that they may yet grow strong in Your Torah, day and night.

Grant Bābāī light, once again, for he is Your slave and You are the king.

Ibrāhīm b. Mullah Abū'l Khayr(?): *Khodāidād*

The JP literary legacy of the Jews of Bukhārā, like that of the Jews of the Iranian plateau, appears to consist more of various forms of poetry than of any other genre. Although we may yet discover texts of clear historical import, so far the only JP Bukhārān text of historical significance is the poem known as *Khodāidād,* after the name of its hero (Persian for the Hebrew name Natan'el). Neither the identity of its author nor the time of its composition is certain. According to Carl Salemann, the first scholar to edit and study the text,[1] *Khodāidād* may have been written by Ibrāhīm b. Mullah Abū'l Khayr,[2] the author of several other poems whose titles, at least, have survived.[3] Some of these were written at the beginning of the nineteenth century, leading Salemann to speculate that *Khodāidād* could have been written earlier, toward the end of the eighteenth century. Both Bacher and Fischel, on grounds that are not clear to me, state specifically that the author of this work lived in the second half of the eighteenth century, possibly during the rule of Amir Ma'ṣūm (d. 1802).[4]

Khodāidād is essentially a record in narrative verse (*masnavī*) of the martyrdom of an ordinary cloth merchant endowed with extraordinary faith, able to resist the persecutions of fellow Muslim merchants and the enticements of their overlords. The simplicity of the verse (in the *hazaj* meter) and of the diction (in the Bukhārān dialect) contribute to the poignancy of the content and are reminiscent of *seliḥot* (Hebrew for "penitential prayers") commemorating Jewish martyrdom in many other Jewish communities in the diaspora.[5] As was the case with KA and KS, I prefer to translate *Khodāidād* in prose, for its diction, like theirs, is not primarily poetic.

This is the Poem About Mullah Khodāidād

One of these days I will relate the fine tale of young Khoidāt.[6] By Providence, in the days of this age there was among youths one Khoidāt, of noble stock,[7] eloquent, and loving in carrying out God's commands. That wise man was wonderfully zealous, *blessed*, and a family man. (5) God's *blessing* ever rested on his brow; he was immersed in God's mercy.

If I were to describe him fully, this tale would never end. He was a distinguished and wise man, a lion at God's court. In agility he was like a falcon in flight; in verse, that distinguished man was well versed. He carried off the prize among his contemporaries; he could earn his fame in the twinkling of an eye. (10) Although he was not of the progeny of the great,[8] yet he was the king of youths. Whatever task he laid his hand to would become *blessed*. He never injured anyone; that chosen one was *humble*.

It happened that one day, having finished his morning devotions to God, this God-fearing youth went to the market, [full of] fear and apprehension. (15) On that day he needed some velvet,[9] so he went to the cloth dealers, may their names perish! A Muslim came and said, "Khodāidād," in greeting and inquired [after his welfare]; the latter answered him.[10] They grasped each other's hands politely, setting the hearts of the others on fire. They said, "O sinful Muslim, [already] early in the morning you shake hands with a dirty infidel?" Khoidāt's heart was grieved; turning pale, that moon-faced [youth] answered them at once, (20) saying, "O Muslims of the Shah, I have [already] said my prayers this morning. I am here in [a state of] ritual purity; why do you complain against me? We believe in the religion of His Excellency, Moses. You know [full well] that we know God and seek Him, so malign [me] not with your tongues."

His words made them angry. They answered, "Infidel, [you must] turn Muslim!" (25) The cloth dealers grabbed him by the collar, like a bird falling into the claws of a falcon.

This was a difficulty with no easy solution; they had made an insinuation which has no end. All the cloth dealers went to their leaders and repeated the conversation to the Falcon Keeper,[11] saying, "A Jew has turned Muslim, and we bear witness for the sake of the Praised One." They testified and swore [to this effect]; for certain they set their own [future] graves on fire![12] (30) They testified to a lie; how will they remove the blackness off their face?

They carried off[13] that youth, the eloquent, brave young man, in fetters. It was decreed that he remain in fetters in the hope that he would turn away from the religion of the *Torah*. . . .[14]

[The verses that follow (33–131) describe Khodāidād's resistance to conversion before the local grandees, his family's pleas to free him, Khodāidād's farewell speech to his mother, brothers, and children, and his entrusting the latter to the care of the former, as he continues to resist pressure to convert.]

They said, O infidel,[15] "Turn Muslim, or we will kill you on the spot!" Having said this, they brought him before the king;[16] they placed his litter[17] there. The king said, "O Jew, turn Muslim, and you will regain your youth and childhood![18] (135) Have mercy on your soul, O Khodāidād, or else like chaff you will be scattered to the winds at once! Present are all the witnesses, who testified that 'a Jew had turned Muslim.' They swore and testified before us at this exalted court. They testified and swore an oath; [if you refuse], you have no remedy but death. So come now, turn Muslim, turn away from the religion of Moses, the son of 'Imrān. (140) If you turn Muslim, you will become our brother; we'll cover your head and feet with crown and jewels. I will make you a tax collector,[19] I will give you silk clothes, a robe of honor, and money.[20] The nobles of the state will obey you and will honor you in hundreds of ways.[21] We[22] will give you a dagger to wear at your side, and some [men] to carry out your orders. (145) Come, grow gentle, be pliant,[23] lest we kill you like a beast. Why should you be deprived of home and hearth,[24] bereft of your children's love and delight? Know that we're giving you [good] advice.[25] The wishes[26] of the sultan's command [stand];[27] I speak to you kindly, dear [man]. I will issue an order at once concerning you; Why should you be your own enemy? (150) Right now, if you turn Muslim, we will make you rejoice and be glad."

Some more advice was offered by the lords without success;[28] the sultan's order remained.

The Debate of the Jew Khodāidād with the Shah

Then Khodāidād answered the shah: "O shah,[29] may you live forever! Allow me[30] to present my petition first: I have been greatly afflicted by the cloth dealers. I am a seller of kerchiefs, a weaver, engaged in business with the cloth dealers. (155) One day, having been kept waiting,[31] I went to the enemy cloth dealers and said, 'O wise men, give me the money [that you owe me]; I have been kept waiting long [enough for it].' I had no other other intention.[32] I said no more[33] than this—God be my witness, O brave shah! My asking for the money was their pretext against me, so they all united against me, (160) saying, 'Infidel, you have turned Muslim; we'll testify [to this effect] heart and soul.' They resolved to cast suspicion upon me; they testified, and burned their religious integrity.[34] They've made you surety for my blood; know for certain that they are not men of faith. They have cut me off from home and hearth, bereaved my children of me."

The shah replied, "O chosen man,[35] there is a way to deliverance even now. (165) If you, O infidel, turn Muslim, know for certain that you will attain a crown and diadem. We will bestow on you a high seat,[36] a riding horse covered in gold from head to hoof.

Khodāidād Debates Again with His Excellency the Shah for the Sake of the Religion and Law of Moses

Khodāidād said again,[37] "O shah of the times, may the Keeper of the World ever be your helper and friend,[38] before you give me up to the winds, I will tell you—pay heed!—a word from the Torah. From the time when the Merciful gave Moses the Torah on Mount Ṭūr,[39] (170) He gave signs, saying, 'Go and tell your people that if ever a day of false accusations befalls them, they must beware and turn not from [their] religion and customs even if [the enemy] split them in two with an ax. Let them stand firm in the religion of 'Imrān[40] and turn not away from it, even though a hundred houses be destroyed.'[41] On this basis, I do not turn away from my religion; I've been ever appointed to behold the Torah. Whatever God has decreed, no person can [re]arrange.[42] (175) He made me a Jew from the first; His decree can never be changed. Why do you raise your hand above His decree? Why are you heedless, and [why do you act] intoxicated? His decree cannot be changed! He wrote it down and such is His pronouncement. He made one man a God-seeking Muslim, another He made faithless and ill-tempered; He cast the waters of mercy on the head of one, and cursed another in a hundred ways. (180) He lifted the veil for some, and seized the crown off the brow of another. Such are His decrees in the world; whatever the Most Generous Creator wills, is. He created all of you Muslims; such was His decree for you. You ought to follow His decrees and judgment."

The shah grew angry at these words, and said, "The time has come to teach you a lesson!" (185) He cried out, "[Send in] a bloodthirsty executioner!" An executioner came at once. [The shah] said, "Remove this hard-hearted infidel;[43] take him and shed his blood on the gallows!" The wicked executioner took Khodāidād[44] and tied his hands in front of him firmly, like a thief. They dragged him under the gallows; many looked on from every side. Like Isaac, he stretched out his neck, saying, "Kill, O cowardly executioner!" (190) The executioner said, "O Khoidāt of the infidels, no work should be carried out blindly. I will be patient; maybe you will repent your deed and turn Muslim. Thus I will act justly, and you will find deliverance from your torment. Come, consent, O hard-hearted [man]; unfortunate one, have mercy on your soul."

Khodāidād answered at once, "O faithful one, faith in your prejudice is not advisable.[45] (195) Kill me, I said, bloodthirsty executioner; let me depart quickly from this treacherous world. Even if a man were to endure a hundred years, one thing is certain: in the end, his place is in the ground. Kill me, I said, for my soul is in torment; it would fly from this birdcage, although it is righteous. It is just that I should sit in the Garden [of Eden] among the rows of [righteous] souls, while angels wait on me whose brows are crowned with mercy.[46] (200) Such a place has been appointed for me. Let me be killed, and still I will not turn from my religion."

Matters stood thus when[47] a wise man clad in white appeared.[48] He said, "Kill him quickly, O perverse executioner! How long will you torment him? Kill him quickly: he is a Jew, become a martyr. Who is like him in the world?" On hearing this, the bloodthirsty executioner slaughtered him at the foot of the gallows. (205) With one blow of the sword that *ṣaddiq*[49] was felled; the face of that youth turned [as pale as] straw. . . .

[The poem ends (206–279) with the heartrending laments of Khodāidād's mother, brothers, and children.][50]

Ḥezekiah: *The Tale of the Anguish of the Community of Forced Converts*

This wrenching poem, a veritable dirge, comes from a Jewish apostate who deeply regrets his conversion to Islam.[1] Unfortunately, the poem is not specific enough for us to determine when it was written. Judging by its content, Ḥezekiah could have been a member of Ibn Farhād's community, or perhaps one of the *anusim* from Mashhad (see the Introduction). In both cases, Jews who did not or could not flee converted to Islam; in the case of Mashhad, many continued a difficult double life as crypto-Jews.

We know nothing about Ḥezekiah beyond what he reveals about himself in this poem. Clearly he was not the only convert of his town; his entire community appears to have converted to Islam. Judging by his accusations, it had not resisted conversion very strongly. Ḥezekiah's feelings of remorse far outweigh his poetical skills. Sincerity and remorse are the poem's hallmarks, as the poet expresses his regret and describes the devastating psychological consequences of the conversion upon the Jewish community in which he lived.

O Lord, You Who are One,
Peerless, and without compare,
Remove from our heads
This afflicting faith.[2]

O Lord, You Who are Provider,
Creator of all creation,
Make us not deserving of
This afflicting faith.

By the grace of Aaron's God,
Deliver us from this faith;
Our hearts are bleeding by reason of
This afflicting faith.

We are split into seventy groups,[3]
The crazed Mosaic nation,
Driven to madness through
This afflicting faith.

We're without synagogue and Torah;
Plunged into a state of sorrow;
We are struck dumb by
This afflicting faith.

We're without Sabbaths and *songs,*
Through this afflicting faith;
We're like trembling willows from
This afflicting faith.

We're without *peace* and honor,
Like grains caught in a snare;
Woe to us, we are hopeless through
This afflicting faith.

We're without schools and teachers;
We're like uprooted flowers,
Infidels gone astray through
This afflicting faith.

We're without faith and doctrine,[4] as if
We were new to religion;[5]
We deem ourselves unworthy because of
This afflicting faith.

We're without New Year, the fast;[6]
We weep day and night;
They told us not to mix[7] in
This afflicting faith.

We lack spiritual guides and teachers;[8]
We're without honor and guidance;
With hearts and minds unhappy from
This afflicting faith.

We're like the *gebr*[9] without our faith,
Lacking patience and strength;
We shed tears like clouds because of
This afflicting faith.

We're without veil and reputation,
Like roses without scent,
Forever mourning because of
This afflicting faith.

We're without hearth and home,
Bereft of all, like the wind,
For we have brought upon ourselves[10]
This afflicting faith.

We're without heart and soul,
Suffering, without guidance;
Doubtless we have become like beasts through
This afflicting faith.

We're without eyes and ears,
Both blind and deaf;
We have been poisoned by
This afflicting faith.

We're without rule of Law,
We've all left our faith;
Bright faces, bleeding hearts, from
This afflicting faith.

Outwardly we are all Muslims,
In our hearts we're Jews;
By God, may we not remain in
This afflicting faith!

We've increased Islam's riches;
We've no fear of fasting;[11]
We all constantly argue about
This afflicting faith.

Through Muslim ways we've lost our souls;
We are sick beyond repair;
We are all weak from
This afflicting faith.

We are weary and grieved,
Far from God's path,
Without moisture and light because of
This afflicting faith.

We're sick and helpless,
Sorely trapped; what a pity
We have entrusted our souls to
This afflicting faith.

O Lord, You Who are almighty,
The guide of every act,
It's time you brought us out of
This afflicting faith.

We hardly bear our suffering,
Throw ourselves into wells
And fires because of
This afflicting faith.

We're in debt up to our necks,
No longer worth a penny;
Like willows we tremble from
This afflicting faith.

We're like trees without leaves
That cannot cast a shade;
We are in search of death from
This afflicting faith.

We keep on lamenting,
Petitioning the shah;[12]
We don't accept for ourselves
This afflicting faith.

We slander Islam every moment,
A thousand times;
How can our hearts delight in
This afflicting faith?

When we left our town[13]
We entered our graves alive;
Woe to us, we are oppressed in
This afflicting faith.

We have lost everything, but
Torah still lives in our hearts;
Alas, a thousand times alas, for
This afflicting faith.

We've turned completely ignorant;
There is none more stupid than we;
By God, what I have said is true because of
This afflicting faith.

We've gambled our fortune away,
Having cast our own die,
And with our hands we've grasped
The Muslim prayer beads.

We spilled our faith upon the ground,
Like rolling grains of barley;
A tailless donkey we've become from
This afflicting faith.

O God, You Who are my life,
Who are the salve for my pain,
Ḥezekiah grasped the pen because of
This afflicting faith.

My name is Ḥezekiah,
I am a Muslim preacher;[14]
I am ashamed of what I've done for
This afflicting faith.

I used to drink cup after cup of wine
From the Jewish faith, but now
I drink cup after cup of poison[15] from
This afflicting faith.

Polemics and Philosophy

9

The text that follows is the earliest sample of JP polemical literature discovered so far. The fragment exists only in one manuscript (BL Or. 5446) and appears to consist largely of an introduction followed by a commentary on the subject of circumcision. According to scholars the document's chief interest, in addition to and perhaps even more than its content, lies in its linguistic features. Dating from the twelfth century or earlier, this text is written in what appears to be an archaic form of JP; its vocabulary preserves many words reminiscent of Middle Persian (Pahlavi) forms.[1] However, it is the content, especially of the introduction, that interests us here. In it the speaker (author?) presents a closely knit popular and polemical—rather than strictly philosophical—argument for the necessity of prophecy in general and for the incontrovertibility of Moses' prophetic mission in particular. He refers to the religious "confusion" of Christians, Zoroastrians, and Muslims regarding prophetic authority and appears acquainted with some of the tenets and rituals of the latter two groups. The tenor of this polemic is defensive, implying the existence both of pressures on Iranian Jews to convert (first to Zoroastrianism and later to Islam) and of some lively dialogue between the adherents of these faiths and Iranian

Jews.[2] Because the exact time and provenance of the text cannot be determined, however, we cannot speculate further on its historical background.

The short commentary on circumcision leaves little doubt that the author was a learned Jew. The first part consists merely of a JP paraphrase of the biblical verses he expounds. The second and more original part of the commentary indicates that the author was acquainted with such early midrash collections as *Bereshit Rabbah* and *Midrash Tanḥuma.*

The translation that follows is primarily that of D. N. MacKenzie, taking into account the emendations of Lazard and Shaked (see n. 1).

On Moses' Prophethood

(A) If one asks you, "How do you know that [Moses] was a prophet for the world, and what need was there of a prophet?" you answer, "He was a prophet for the world, for the world cannot dispense with a prophet because the management of the world rests on prophethood. For the God of the entire world is the creator of all things, and whatever He created, He did not create it to be despised, nor did He create it in vain (perish the thought!), for such is not in God's nature; He does not like what is vain or unworthy. He is a God who has foreknowledge of what He creates, and He creates support for everything before He creates it, knowing as He does (B) what is needed for its structure and support. And whatever He creates comes from Him and has the breath of life in it; He has created nothing greater than mankind. He endowed mankind with many qualities which He did not bestow on any other animals. For an animal or a bird possesses the ability to carry out its tasks without the teaching of a guide, and they know their function and what is or is not proper for them. Know that if you take an animal, young and small, just weaned, and abandon it on a plain or on a mountain, it will know what herb to go under, what will suit it as (C) food, and what will not. And this is true of both birds and animals. Know (also) that when you take [the egg of] a bird and place it in the nest of another bird until the time it moves and the chick comes out of it, the chick will know the way to its own tasks without the teaching of a mother or father, and it will know what is or is not necessary to do, and what food to eat and what to abstain from. Their support comes from the quality of the physical nature of their creation and from its essence; the movements of wild animals are also like this. And in another (example), if you take one of them and kill it in front of the others, they do not know what [killing] is and have no concern for it, because they (birds and animals) have no understanding in their nature, (D) nor do they experience sorrow or anxiety.

"As for mankind, its quality, essence, and nature have not been created in this manner, for man's innate quality is toward (giving) great thought to acquiring in advance. It is on account of (this) great thought that men fight with one another and out of anxiety and despair, lest something should (turn out to) be so or not, that the strong tramples on those weaker than himself and fears lest one stronger than he should rise up against him. And in another way, the quality of the physical nature of his creation is such that if you bring a human being, young but full grown, and put him in a garden in which there are various kinds of trees, some of which are safe for man to eat and suitable for him, and some of which are poison fatal to the human being you (E) have placed in the garden, and nobody teaches him, who will be his guide to teach him which of those trees it is suitable to eat from and which not? It is correct to say that he could learn from (such) a guide about what he does not now know. Know, therefore, that mankind cannot dispense with a person who is experienced and a guide and organizer. Now know, therefore, that the God of the entire world did not forsake the world, (leaving it) desolate and despised, for it would have been spoilt, and what would have become of it? But the God of the entire world, in order to be known and for the support of His creation, initiated the guidance and organization of men. And this is the answer of the question and support for the proof of prophethood."

(F) And if a questioner asks you, "How do you know who that prophet is on whom your religion is based?" you answer him and say, "His name is Moses." And when he asks you, "That man whose name is this—how do you know that he is the prophet of God?" answer also, "We know that he is the prophet of God by this, that the people of the world are in disagreement, and each basis of disagreement has a name, and it is a religion—one Mazdean [Zoroastrian], one Christian, one Muslim, and one Jew; if it were not for the disagreement of the four of these, they would all be one. The hearts of many people would not be in doubt, for they ought to know where the truth is, what it is, and with whom it is. But on account of those (people) who disagree (with them) each one says to the other, (G) "The truth is those things on which I stand, and the false is that on which you stand." For this reason heart(s) fall into doubt and search is necessary, but it is not necessary to travel the whole world (for it)! Now I thought to myself and debated with myself about this doubt in my heart: from which direction does it come? And I reached the head of the matter and observed that that doubt in my heart had arisen because of the disagreement of the people of the world. And then I observed and noticed that everything has an opposite: the opposite of night is day, that of darkness is light, and that of fire is water—and [I observed] that each opposite can be held (in check) by its own opposite. And then I said that the opposite of disagreement is [lack of] disagreement, and since my doubt came about through disagreement, (H) it would be excised from my heart by that which contains no disagreement. Now I asked the people of the world, those opponents who are in disagreement with one another, and each one maintains, "This is the truth on which I stand, not that of yours," and on examination of their words (not that it was necessary to assume their testimony as true), and inquiry into their words and answers, they all admitted, one by one, that God had a prophet whose name was Moses. And when I asked them, "Since you admit that God had a prophet whose name was Moses," I asked them, "How was the prophethood of this prophet, whom God sent to mankind at that time, acceptable to those men, so that they recognized that his prophethood was genuine? (J) For they all believed in the signs Moses performed, from among those God had vouchsafed him (and he gave signs to Pharaoh and to the people of Egypt), and all the signs and miracles that God performed through the handiwork of Moses in Egypt, at the (Reed) sea and in the wilderness, until the entry of the children of Israel into the land of the Temple. Since they all believed in these, the prophethood of Moses was confirmed by their agreement and belief."

And if he asks you, "Now that you have confirmed (the prophethood of) Moses, (what of) these matters which you say (are) by God's command, that is, some He has commanded, 'Do,' and some He has commanded, 'Do not'—how do you know the rightness of this matter?" you answer him, "Also by the belief of these opposites." (K) When I asked them, "What commandments did that Moses, a prophet of God, bring to mankind?" each one held the (following) opinion, saying, "He brought this to mankind: of the commandments of God there are (some) which are admitted by the faith of the Mazdeans, with their performance of *bāj*,[3] and by the faith of all types of Christians, namely, the matters of Sabbath, clean and unclean, quadrupeds, and (other) animals." (Some) of these (commandments) are [also] admitted by the faith of the Muslims—such as the Sabbath and the prohibition of fat and other things,[4] concerning which, when I asked all three opponents, "Since you confess that this matter has come from God to mankind by the handiwork of the prophet Moses, how is it that you do not act according to it?" they answered, "Someone came to us (L) as a prophet from God, saying, 'Leave that,' and he brought other (commandments) for us." And I replied, "You confess of the former to the truth of his coming from God; now, because of this person you say, 'We abandoned that one because another commandment came from God, saying: Cleave to the other'—where is your proof of this?" In this matter also which I examined, (I discovered) that none of the (people of) these religions believed in the other's, in the supporting of their words against one another, and that each one stood cut off, without proof.

And in another way I said to them, "Is not our Creator perfection in understanding, knowledge, and foresight? And moreover, He is the lawgiver, and confusion is not possible in His making of the law, (M) for He knew beforehand to what extent knowledge of each thing was necessary to mankind forever. His wisdom, law, and knowledge, are likewise this way, for He created one religion and commanded it for all mankind forever, so that it would spread and *progress and reach all (men as) one religion. It is not possible in the godhead that today He should command one religion and tomorrow He should change it. First, this would be lack of wisdom, and it would also be injustice, as men would be confused in (their) affairs because first there was a trust in the signs and miracle working of one who went about openly in the world for many years, and then (another prophet) raised his head in secret from (some) direction, to everyone's fear—(for) it is not possible to (N) recognize goodness in concealment—and says, 'God has sent me, so that you should abandon the thing which has gone on for many years openly, as well as that (prophet's) name and those wonders.' Does that accord with God? And what does this resemble? (It is like) a king who appoints a deputy over a city of men, and orders that city, 'Carry out the orders of this my deputy,' and he confirms that deputy over them by great works and signs and wonders in order to make that deputy known to them, commanding them, 'Everything this deputy orders you (to do) is my command, and do not be rebellious toward him; and in these commands which I command you, do not exceed or fall short, (P) for whoever falls short or exceeds is rebellious against me forever.' Now if it (should happen) that after affairs go on in this manner publicly and openly in the world for many years, a man comes and says, 'I am the deputy of this king, the lord of this city, who gave these matters into your hands,' (and) he says, 'He has sent me for this purpose, that I command you to change these affairs, and commit shortcomings and excesses in them,' is it right for them to accept? Should they not answer that man thus: 'This present state of affairs, which we did not accept lightly, and that deputy, whom we accepted over ourselves—we accepted these because of the great signs, wonders, and manifestations over the whole (Q) world. Now we shall not accept the word of anybody (else) unless he brings signs and wonders throughout the world, like (those of our prophet) or greater than his.' But know that this affair of the opponents is not and will not be a proof for them in any way or to any extent."

And I saw that the fourth (group), called Jews, (despite) whatever the opposing gentiles maintained, (namely) that "the nonvalidity of the prophet Moses had come from God," (the prophet) whom they (the gentiles) had abandoned, and (whose) commandments they did not observe, (yet) the Jews believed in him and carried out his commandments, because we recognized that these opponents are all broken and liars in their own faith. And they revealed their beliefs to the Jews, but the Jews persisted in their belief, saying, "This matter in which we believe is from (R) God," and they continued to act according to it. In this matter this people, called Jews, were upright above all (those) opposing peoples.

Now the prophethood of Moses has been established, as well as the commandments which Moses brought to the Israelites, by the acknowledgment of all four peoples[5] and by the fact that the three peoples upheld the truth of the Israelites, saying, "We have recognized that right is with the Israelites." But when we examined (the matter) we found them contradicting one another, except for one belief,[6] so that the Law of Moses emerged established to all. Now [thereofore], the Torah of Moses is confirmed with proof, in every way and to every extent, and there is no doubt in it.

(S) *Blessed is He Who was and is and shall be* [Ps. 33:4]. *For the word of the Lord is right; His every deed is faithful* [Gen. 17:10]. *Such shall be [the covenant] between Me and you:* This is My covenant, which you should keep between Me and you and your children [and those] after you; cut all males among you. (11) *You shall circumcise the flesh of your foreskin:* And cut the flesh of your foreskin, that it may be a sign of the covenant between Me and you. (12) *[Every male . . .] at the age of eight days:* And cut among you the boy eight days old, every male of your generation, homeborn or bought with silver, from all foreign boys, he who is not of your children. (13) He *that is homeborn must be circumcised:* Let the one homeborn and him you have bought with your silver be cut, so that my covenant may be in your flesh, an everlasting covenant. (14) *And [if any male is] uncircumcised:* And the uncircumcised male, (T) the flesh of whose foreskin is not cut, let that creature be cut off from his people, for he has not carried out my covenant.

And what is this "foreskin," and from where should it be cut? For as to this *ʿrl* (foreskin, uncircumcised), everybody mentions a (different) place as *uncircumcised lips*[7] and *uncircumcised in heart,*[8] *behold their ear is uncircumcised,*[9] and *uncircumcised tongue.*[10] How can I know from where He commands it to be cut and of what place He says it should be cut? But we know from this place, where it is written, *the uncircumcised male:* Cut the male foreskin, and not the foreskin of the female child, which is so that we may know that He speaks of the place whereby it is possible to recognize male from female. This is the male member, except for which it is not possible to recognize male from female. Now He says, *the uncircumcised male,* and *male* is the name of (V) *masculinity;* for the name of masculinity and femininity does not apply to any other member except to this place.[11]

Now from where to where is it necessary to cut? Joshua came and (God) spoke according to the teaching of Moses, and then (Joshua) acted, for it is written, [Josh. 5:3] *So Joshua had flint knives made:* And Joshua made strong knives and cut the sons of Israel at the hill of the foreskins. Has this "hill" been mentioned (in the Scripture) concerning the beginning or the end (of the cutting of the foreskin)? Now He enjoins (us) concerning that place which resembles a hill, and concerning the skin, as follows: Cut (the skin) until it reaches that place which resembles a hill. This is the limit of cutting. *(At the hi)ll of the foreskins,* not the place. . . . He would have said *bgvʾt* which (W) would have been "on the hill," for as to *bgvʾt,* "on the hill" is its explanation, (whereas) *el gvʾt,* "at the hill" is its explanation. This is the interpretation, namely *el* is "to," "at," as in *to Moses, to the land,* and many such. And if he had said of the place thus, "From such-and-such a place to such-and-such a place" (for it is possible [to do so] with [specific] words, as it is written, *from your native land and from your father's [house to the land that I will show you]* [Gen. 12:1]: from such-and-such a place to such-and-such a place), but he does not speak in this manner, for (it is) written [Josh. 5:3]: *And the Israelites were circumcised at Giveath-haaraloth* [at the hill of the foreskins]: he had the sons of Israel cut at the hill of the foreskins; and this is as it has been interpreted.[12] And as to that place having a name, for it is called Gilgal, . . . [Josh. 4:19] *The people came up from Jordan on the tenth day of the first month, [and encamped at Gilgal].*[13]

Yehudah b. Elʿazar: *Ḥobot Yehudah* (*The Duties of Judah*)

Ḥobot Yehudah (The duties of Judah; henceforth ḤY), written by Rabbi Yehudah b. Elʿazar in 1686,[1] is as far as we know the most important philosophical text to emerge from the Iranian Jewish milieu.[2]

A learned rationalist philosopher, Rabbi Yehudah displays a thorough mastery of major philosophical issues. His command of Hebrew, Aramaic, and Arabic, in addition to Persian, enabled him to consult a wide variety of Jewish and non-Jewish sources. About the author's background we know only what he chooses to reveal about himself in this work. He was a physician by profession and wrote, in addition to ḤY, an astronomical treatise called *Taqvīm al-Yehudah* (The calendar of Judah) and a short document on the dangers of wine.[3] Rabbi Yehudah lived in Kashan, the home of several other JP authors included in this anthology: ʿImrānī, Bābāī b. Luṭf, and Bābāī b. Farhād. In the seventeenth century, Kashan was a prosperous town famous for its commerce in silks and its weaving of textiles and rugs, activities in which Jews also participated. It may be that Rabbi Yehudah was the son of the Rabbi Elʿazar mentioned in Bābāī b. Luṭf's *Kitāb-i Anusī.*[4] In any case, Rabbi Yehudah was learned in his own right; Refu'ah b. Elʿazar Ha-Kohen, a fellow citizen of Kashan who produced a condensed version of ḤY soon after it was written, refers to him as *rabbi* and *dayyan* (Hebrew for "religious judge").

Rabbi Yehudah's Persian is "richly eloquent"[5] and shows a fine command not only of rabbinic sources (Talmud, Zohar) but also of Greek (Plato and Aristotle), medieval Islamic philosophy (al-Farabī, Ibn Sīnā, Nāṣir ud-Dīn al-Ṭūsī, al-Ghazzalī, and Ibn Rushd), and Persian belles lettres (especially poetry). He also refers to the New Testament, the Apocrypha, and the Qur'ān. Rabbi Yehudah's style is somewhat repetitious because of his paraphrastic method of translating Persian phrases into Hebrew and vice versa. Like many other Iranian-Jewish authors, he introduced Persian syntax into some of his Hebrew sentences, especially for words in the construct state. Rabbi Yehudah's Persian is heavily strewn with Hebrew words and quotations.

Ḥobot Yehuda deals with the principles of the Jewish faith as laid out by Jewish thinkers, especially Maimonides. Rabbi Yehudah appears to have been well acquainted with the works of all the major Jewish philosophers as well as of some of the Kabbalists.[6] He singles out for praise and response Maimonides (d. 1204) and David Messer Leon (d. 1526?). He quotes extensively, directly and indirectly, from their works and from those of other Jewish thinkers without indicating the exact source or location of his quotation, a common practice in the Middle Ages. He enters into lively debate with his sources, but the nature, extent, and especially the originality of his arguments remain to be evaluated.

The major themes covered in the eighteen sections and one epilogue of ḤY are: 1. the principles of the Jewish faith; 2. the existence and essence of God; 3. prophecy; 4. God's knowledge; 5. Divine Providence and free will; 6. the status of the Torah; 7. the Oral Law; 8. the resurrection of the dead; 9. creation and the Divine Chariot (*merkabah*); 10. and the essence of the soul and the intellect.

The translation that follows is from section 2, part 3 of chapter 3, "The Explanation of the Heavenly Torah." The theme of this section is undoubtedly polemical; Rabbi Yehudah probably experienced the forced conversions described in Bābāī b. Luṭf's KA, and he wishes to emphasize here the impossibility of conversion as far as Jews are concerned. In addition, in the larger scheme of ḤY and of the specific chapter, Rabbi Yehudah uses the topic of apostasy as yet another peg on which to attach his praises of the Torah.

On Whether Israelites Can Apostasize

It was explained earlier in part 2 that faith is [like a] *possession,* that is, it is a possession that belongs to man's soul, the way knowledge belongs to the soul of a learned man. Yet we see that these possessions, notwithstanding that they are impressed upon the soul, often become corrupt and enfeebled when a learned man forgets accidentally and becomes ignorant: *Joseph forgot his learning because of oppression; he fell silent before you.*[7] So it is with a *believer.* It is possible that he can lose his faith and become a nonbeliever on account of an accidental occurrence. But the *sages* said that *the Children of Israel are believers* even if they remove the *yoke of the Torah* and abandon [their] *faith* in God. They cannot belong to another faith and religion because, whether they change their religion willingly or are forced to do so and have no escape, they still remain *Children of Israel;* whatever affects the *Children of Israel* for good or ill befalls them also. About those who abandon their religion it is written: *Even though he sinned, he is an Israelite.*[8] [Similarly], the prophet said: "*When you say, 'We will be like the nations, . . . worshipping wood and stone. As I live . . . I will reign over you with overflowing fury* [Ezek. 20:32–33], . . . *and I will bring you into the bond of the covenant . . .'* [Ezek. 20:37], and also *'And what you have in mind shall never come to pass'* [Ezek. 20:32]." From these verses it is clear that even if Israel should change its religion and believe in the idols of the nations, it would not be part of the assembly of nations because they have not been given commands, whereas the Israelites, when they trespass positive and negative commandments, are sinning. That is the meaning of "*and I will bring you into the covenant.*"

As for the idea that, according to the *sages,* the Israelites' possession[like] faith can never become corrupted, it is [discussed] in tractate Qiddushin.[9] [There] Rabbi Yehudah argues with Rabbi Me'ir about the verse *You are children of the Lord your God* [Deut. 14:1]. Rabbi Yehudah said that whenever they [the Israelites] adhere to the ways and customs of *children,* they are included in [the designation] "*children,*" but whenever they do not observe the rules and laws of *children,* they are not called "*children*"; rather, they are strangers and accursed. But Rabbi Me'ir said that they are always *children,* even if they are strangers and are ignorant, for it is written: *For my children are stupid* [Jer. 4:22], even if they reject [their] *faith, They are children with no faith in them* [Deut. 32:21], and even if they should become idolaters, as it is written, *depraved children* [Isa. 1:4].

According to another opinion, whenever Israel embarks on ugly and shameful ways and believes in false ideas, it can remove the *yoke of the Torah* from its neck and leave the community of Israel, as it is said: *There came out . . . one whose mother was Israelite* [Lev. 24:10]. *From where did he come out? He left this world.* But Rabbi Me'ir thinks the opposite, that is, even if he [an Israelite] *profanes the Sabbath in public and becomes an idolater,* he cannot become [part of the] assembly of nations because the Israelite *faith* is joined and strongly attached to his rational soul in such a manner that it can never be separated from him.

Our Master Moses, peace be upon him, explained both of these views in the verses, *And now hear, O Israel, the laws, etc.* [Deut. 4:1], from which it is clear that Rabbi Me'ir's *view* is correct. First, because the Torah which was entrusted to Israel is perfect. Second, it is the most perfect of all Torahs,[10] and the perfect person should follow its perfection. On this subject, it can be explained that the holy Torah is perfect in four aspects. First, in its essence: the Torah is true and just and is not false, for if it were false it would not be perfect; second, because of that person [Moses] who received it, who attained perfection, bodily and spiritual, in both worlds, through all its [the Torah's] parts; third, on account of its comprehensiveness, for every subject that is necessary for the [Israelite] nation is found in it, and there is no need for anything else in addition to it; fourth, because of its arrangement, which is appropriate, intelligible, and well established, so that a person can comprehend it with little trouble and effort. For the Law[11] is for the people, and they by nature abhor difficult things.

The clarification of these four aspects is expressed in the same [biblical] passage. Regarding the first, *You shall not add anything [to what I command you nor take anything away from it], etc.* [Deut. 4:2]. The special virtue of God's religion lies in that it accepts no addition or diminution. Regarding the second, whoever has been commanded and is obedient will reap the reward of this world and the next, [but] he who is rebellious and sinful is guilty: *You saw with your own eyes what the Lord did in the matter of Baal-peor* [Deut. 4:3], that is, you saw with the sense of sight that in the *punishment of Baal-peor* they [the sinful Israelites] were destroyed suddenly. This type of calamity came from God, not from the empyrean heaven.[12] But those who cleaved to God suffered no injury, *[they] are all alive today* [Deut. 4:4]. Regarding the third aspect, namely, that all subjects are comprehended and are complete in the Torah, it is through the confirmation of its positive and negative commandments that those *people* [the Israelites] are deemed *wise and discerning* [Deut. 4:6].

Let me expound on the third[13] aspect, namely, that the *holy* Torah is the most perfect of all Torahs. This is because it is distinguished by three characteristics: first, by its giver; second, by the gift itself; and third, by the means of its transmission [Moses]. Regarding the Giver [we have the proof text], *The day you stood before your Lord* [Deut. 4:10], when the essence of God, *the Exalted,* manifested itself at Horeb, and the souls of all the people became agitated on account of His abundant Grace, and they heard the *Ten Commandments* from Him. Regarding the Gift [the Torah, it is said], *You came forward and stood at the foot of the mountain* [Deut. 4:11], that is, drawing near and standing refer to spiritual knowledge and perceptual difficulties, which are comparable to a mountain. Contrary to nature, their [the Israelites'] souls left them and cleaved to holiness while their bodily strength disappeared. Therefore, *the sages, may their memory be blessed, said, "When Israel heard the Ten Commandments from the mouth of the Holy One Blessed be He, their souls fled, as it is written, 'I was faint because of what he said'"* [Song of Sol. 4:6].[14] And testifying to this is [the fact] that they themselves begged for help, *"Let us not die, then, [for this fearsome fire] will consume us, etc., . . . and we shall die"* [Deut. 5:22]; *[The mountain was ablaze with flames] to the very skies* [Deut. 4:11]. It was in that state that they all perceived all the heavenly forms despite their [the Israelites'] own material state.

Regarding the means [of the Torah's transmission, it is said], *The Lord commanded me to impart to you laws and rules* [Deut. 4:14], that is, the Torah was given through the intermediacy of *our master Moses, peace be upon him, for he is a righteous prophet* of high station, and the Torah was given through him for *he is trusted throughout My household* [Num. 12:7]. To summarize, these three distinguishing characteristics are confined to the Torah of *our master Moses, peace be upon him.*

It was in this manner that Israel was transferred from the material to the spiritual plane and was entered into a covenant with God, the Exalted, *to enter into the covenant [of the Lord your God]* [Deut. 29:11]. Because their souls, through spirituality, experienced and held fast to the divine at the time of the giving of the *holy* Torah, even if they wish to corrupt their faith through their acts and thoughts, they are unable to do so. For it is impossible for them to remove their spiritual powers unless they return to that state of the *departure* of [their] *souls* mentioned above.

Earlier we explained that all souls *in the hereafter* will accept and rejoice in the Torah, [including], *those who are not with us this day* [Deut. 29:14]. From these explanations it is clear that every person, even those who are complete sages, cannot help but agree—through these proofs and demonstrations—that the divine Torah is *true* and real, and that one cannot change one's *faith* and religion. The proofs of *researchers* are like the light of a lamp; it is the true *tradition*[15] like the sun. Moreover, the proofs of the Torah are brighter than the sun, *a lamp in bright daylight, what does it profit you?*[16] *For the commandment is a lamp and the Torah is light* [Prov. 6:23].

Mysticism

10

Siman Ṭov Melammed, who sometimes signed his poems with the nom de plume Ṭuvyah, was one of the most versatile Iranian-Jewish authors. He was born in Yazd and moved to Mashhad sometime before 1793. He became the spiritual head of the Jewish community of Mashhad, where he lived until his death, either in 1823 or 1828. In addition to his communal duties, Melammed was a poet, polemicist, and philosopher, deeply learned in Jewish sources. His surviving works show him at home in Persian, Hebrew, and Aramaic. He wrote numerous poems in all these languages; some have alternate verses in two languages, Hebrew and Persian or Aramaic and Persian. Among these, perhaps his most noteworthy achievement is an *azharah,*[1] a long liturgical poem on the theme of the positive and negative commandments. Melammed's azharah employs all three languages and is a sophisticated literary achievement. His longest and most remarkable work is the mystical-philosophical treatise *Ḥayāt al-rūḥ* (The life of the soul; henceforth ḤR).[2] It is primarily a commentary on Maimonides' Thirteen Principles of Faith and, indirectly, on Jewish life in the Iranian diaspora.

If we recall that the Jews of Mashhad were forcibly converted to Islam in 1839 and that they lived as *anusim,* practicing Judaism in secret, well into the twentieth century,[3] it is reasonable to assume that there were profound tensions in the Jewish community of Mashhad during Melammed's lifetime. In fact, he is remembered as a staunch champion of Judaism who was forced to participate in disputations arranged by the Shiʿi *ʿulamāʾ*,[4] in which he faced apostate Jews as well as Shiʿi Muslims.[5]

Ḥayāt al-rūḥ has not yet been subjected to close scholarly scrutiny, although the scarcity of such works in JP warrants it. It is a highly literate treatise that displays not only Siman Ṭov Melammed's mastery of Persian prose and poetry but also his familiarity with a considerable range of Jewish and Muslim philosophical and mystical sources. Maimonides' influence, especially of the *Mishneh Torah* and *Guide of the Perplexed*, is especially pervasive. It also has a strong Sufi flavor, derived primarily from the influence of *Ḥobot ha-lebabot* (The duties of the heart) of Baḥya b. Paquda (ca. 1050–1156), the famous Spanish Jewish mystical philosopher,[6] as well as from Persian Sufi literature. The originality of ḤR lies less in its content than in its organization and in the poems—some in Hebrew—most in Persian, interspersed throughout the treatise.

Jewish attraction to Sufism is well known to us from other settings, primarily Spain and North Africa. The outstanding example of this inclination was Abraham Maimonides (1186–1237), the son of the famous philosopher, whose profound admiration of Sufism led him to aspire to the (unsuccessful) formation of his own Jewish *ṭarīqah*.[7]

The poem from ḤR translated here clearly expresses the deep inroads that Sufism had made on Jewish life in Iran. Melammed identifies many ascetic aspects of Jewish mysticism with similar trends present in Islam, yet he is careful to see the former firmly anchored in Judaism, and he decries excesses that contradict its precepts. Nevertheless, this Jewish attraction to Sufism raises important questions, such as when, where, and to what extent Iranian Jews were involved with Islamic mysticism.[8] Whether this attraction to Sufism played a major role in Jewish conversions to Shiʿi Islam and, later, to Bahaism, are questions in urgent need of scholarly attention.

That Iranian Jews did not, as a whole, accept Sufism beyond some superficial folk aspects is apparent from the vigorous survival of the community well into the twentieth century. Many pious Jews resisted facile comparisons between Jewish and Sufi ideals and fought against conversion to Islam through the more ecumenical gate of Sufism. The second poem in this chapter exemplifies a form of Jewish protest against this phenomenon through its denigrating description of a Sufi initiation. It also functions, through its refrain, "My life for Moses' life," as a powerful affirmation of the poet's fidelity to Judaism, despite his possible Sufi initiation (see last stanza). We know nothing about the poet other than his name, Jacob.[9]

Siman Ṭov Melammed: *In Praise of Sufis*

Description of the Pious Sufis Roused from the Sleep of Neglect

Godly and radiant like roses[1]
The Sufis are, the Sufis,
Whose carnal soul is dead,
Doused their desires, the Sufis.

Firmly they grasp the straight path,[2]
Leaders benevolent, guides
Of those who strayed are the Sufis.

Godly and radiant like roses
The Sufis are, the Sufis,
Whose carnal soul is dead,
Doused their desires, the Sufis.

Well-spoken, generous
To beggars and kings alike;
Forgiving all sins are the Sufis.

Godly and radiant like roses
The Sufis are, the Sufis,
Whose carnal soul is dead,
Doused their desires, the Sufis.

Drunk with the cup and the soul's sweets,
With love of seeing the Unseen;
Without reins in both hands are the Sufis.

Godly and radiant like roses
The Sufis are, the Sufis,
Whose carnal soul is dead,
Doused their desires, the Sufis.

Dead to the world of the moment,
Alive to the hereafter;
Full of merit and kindness are the Sufis.

> Godly and radiant like roses
> The Sufis are, the Sufis,
> Whose carnal soul is dead,
> Doused their desires, the Sufis.

Clad in threads, drinking dregs,
With their eyes closed and their ears
Silenced by His absence are the Sufis.

> Godly and radiant like roses
> The Sufis are, the Sufis,
> Whose carnal soul is dead,
> Doused their desires, the Sufis.

Lips sublime from the pure cup,
Lacking both food and sleep; their wish
Is granted in bounty of spirit, thus are the Sufis.

> Godly and radiant like roses
> The Sufis are, the Sufis,
> Whose carnal soul is dead,
> Doused their desires, the Sufis.

Their hospices are spacious castles,
Their tables, gardens, and rose beds;
Wounded by separation[3] are the hearts of the Sufis.

> Godly and radiant like roses
> The Sufis are, the Sufis,
> Whose carnal soul is dead,
> Doused their desires, the Sufis.

God's love is their beloved,
God's affection their decoration,
And that which veils Him from the Sufis.[4]

Godly and radiant like roses
The Sufis are, the Sufis,
Whose carnal soul is dead,
Doused their desires, the Sufis.

Enemies of all world worshipers,
Friends to all the intoxicated,
Who break down the carnal self, thus are the Sufis.

Godly and radiant like roses
The Sufis are, the Sufis,
Whose carnal soul is dead,
Doused their desires, the Sufis.

The most contented of beggars,
Avoiding rancor and dispute;
Freed from the Day of Punishment are the Sufis.[5]

Godly and radiant like roses
The Sufis are, the Sufis,
Whose carnal soul is dead,
Doused their desires, the Sufis.

Of pleasant face, of pleasant state,
Good character, right bearing,
Ever praising the Almighty are the Sufis.

Godly and radiant like roses
The Sufis are, the Sufis,
Whose carnal soul is dead,
Doused their desires, the Sufis.

Never electing worldly company,
Eyes set on the hereafter,
Well-mannered and discerning are the Sufis.

Godly and radiant like roses
The Sufis are, the Sufis,
Whose carnal soul is dead,
Doused their desires, the Sufis.

Dark night reigns in their hearts,
With wounded hearts they weep,
With dust upon their heads and feet are the Sufis.

Godly and radiant like roses
The Sufis are, the Sufis,
Whose carnal soul is dead,
Doused their desires, the Sufis.

On the day when from behind the Veil
They ask and take a full account,
The Sufis will flash forth like the sun.

Godly and radiant like roses
The Sufis are, the Sufis,
Whose carnal soul is dead,
Doused their desires, the Sufis.

Jacob: *Against Sufis*

O people of ʿImrān's son,[1]
Let not Satan deceive you,
Lest you forfeit religion and faith;
My life for Moses' life.[2]

Whoever abandons his faith
Becomes a savage like Majnūn,[3]
Roaming about, confused;
My life for Moses' life.

Bravely he is called a friend,[4]
But he turns common instead of chosen,[5]
[Now] what religion can he call his own?
My life for Moses' life.

Quickly he goes to the bathhouse,
At the high point he falls asleep,
He falls, hand and foot, into the snare;
My life for Moses' life.

He dyes his hands and feet with henna,
His beard he colors black,
And thinks of sash and tunic;[6]
My life for Moses' life.

They make him don a golden tunic,
An orange sash over his head,
While all around him they cry "Hū," "Hū";[7]
My life for Moses' life.

They mount him on a saddled horse,
Bewitch him with poems of praise,
And shouts from bloody lips;
My life for Moses' life.

Rascal, dervish minstrels before him
Surround him, front and back,
Leaping around him for his sake;
My life for Moses' life.

In a moment he repents,
Becomes confused and errant
Within himself, about himself;
My life for Moses' life.

They shout around him on every side,
They strike their breasts and clamor,
[He finds no refuge anywhere];[8]
My life for Moses' life.

Sometimes he laments, sometimes
He cries out for justice,
And sometimes he is enraged;
My life for Moses' life.

His foot steps into quicksand;
His hand is paralyzed, resembling
A demon's wing;
My life for Moses' life.

His night and day have both grown dark;
He sighs constantly and groans,
And all his plans are spoiled;
My life for Moses' life.

He has become intimate with grief,
And he is consumed by sorrow,
For having submitted himself;
My life for Moses' life.

Jacob, whose faith is firm,
The more they say his burden is light,
The more his heart is grieved;
My life for Moses' life.

Religious Poems

11

Judeo-Persian manuscripts contain a vast number of short poems, both religious and secular.[1] Some of these are translations with commentary of medieval Hebrew poems. For example, translations of the poems of Israel Najjara (d. ca. 1625), the controversial roving poet who hailed from Damascus, abound and may be helpful in defining his collected poems in an authoritative *Diwān*. The entire corpus of short JP poems is still in need of careful sifting and analysis in order to arrive at an accurate assessment of its originality and literary worth.

Most of the poems translated below come from well-established, if not well-known, Iranian-Jewish poets. The names of Amīnā, Siman Ṭov Melammed, and Bābāī b. Luṭf we have encountered before as authors of other genres. Here we see their great religious fervor, always tinged with, if not explicitly about, Messianic longings.

The works of five new poets, Shihāb Yazdī, Yūsuf Yahūdī, Muflis-i Khwānsārī, Yeḥezqel Khwānsārī, and an anonymous individual also appear in this chapter. "Shihāb" (flame, bright star) may well be this poet's nom de plume. Other than the fact that he came from Yazd, we know nothing about his life; he probably flourished in the eighteenth century. "Almighty Lord

Displaying Might" appears to be his only surviving work. Judging by its lilting meter and the numerous copies of it in JP manuscripts, we can assume that it was a popular religious hymn, perhaps sung to a special melody.[2]

Yūsuf b. Isḥaq b. Mūsā, known as Yūsuf Yahūdī (Joseph the Jew) or as Yūsuf Bukhārā'ī, was one of the better-known Jewish poets of Bukhārā. He lived in the eighteenth century and probably died in 1788. In addition to writing quintets (*mukhammasāt*), as well as a number of *ghazal*s, quatrains, and elegies, Yūsuf Yahūdī was the author of at least two long narrative poems, one based on the famous Jewish legend of Ḥannah and her seven sons and the other on the scroll of Antiochus.[3]

We know nothing at all about either Yeḥezqel Khwānsārī or Muflis-i Khwānsārī (the poor one from Khwānsār), whose moving pleas to the prophet Ezekiel are capped by a wonderful vision of Messianic times. The fact that two poets from Khwānsār wrote on the same theme suggests that they may actually be the same person. The identity of the poet who prayed for the intercession of Ezra is completely veiled. He seems to be speaking for an oppressed community rather than for himself.

These religious poems differ little in tone and aspirations from religious poems written by Jews in other parts of the diaspora. Perhaps one of their most remarkable themes is the veneration of various prophets, especially Moses,[4] Ezekiel, and Ezra, the first for obvious reasons, the last two because their tombs were ancient and fairly accessible pilgrimage sites for Iranian Jews as well as Muslims. By praising the prophets and praying for their intercession, our poets shed light on a specific, primarily folk, aspect of Jewish religious life in Iran. Although Jews from other parts of the world also visited the graves of saints and learned men and prayed for their intercession, I am not aware of a corpus of panegyrics in Hebrew devoted exclusively to this theme. Here we see a "specialization" of the genre among Iranian Jews, perhaps because of the proximity of the two important tombs, and probably under the influence of their Muslim neighbors' paeans in honor of Muḥammad and the twelve Shi'i imams.

Many of the poems translated here convey a powerful longing for the Messiah and describe evocatively the restoration of the Temple.

Amīnā's prayer is a personal supplication, a psalm, composed in a state of distress. He clearly invokes God's wrath upon his enemies (v. 5) and expresses his fervent hope that he will be helped out of his difficulties. Bābāī's prayer[5] is written in the name of a community in distress, one that may have converted to Islam. If this Bābāī is to be identified with Bābāī b. Luṭf—and I am inclined to think so—here is a moving plea to God to remove from the various Jewish communities of Iran the onus of *anusut* (forced conversion).

The purpose of Amīnā's praise of the Twelve Tribes appears to be arriving at number twelve, Benjamin, his namesake.[6] Although he recounts the well-known virtues of each tribe, he invokes them in order that through their merit he, in particular, will obtain God's help.

Siman Ṭov Melammed's love poem for the Messiah evokes the Song of Songs, the poems of the passionate Hebrew poet Solomon Ibn Gabirol (d. ca. 1057), and above all ghazals, lyrical love poems that have made classical Persian poetry famous.

'Imrānī's severely pessimistic view of man's continuous shortcomings in his relationship with God reflects this poet's austere nature and is in harmony with similar Sufi ascetic views.

All the poems in this chapter reinforce the impression that Iranian Jews had a strong Jewish identity that withstood the influences of the Muslim environment even as it was enriched by them.

A Poem in Praise of the Almighty

Shihāb Yazdī: *Almighty Lord Displaying Might*

Almighty Lord displaying might,[1]
Creator of heaven and earth,
Have mercy on us day and night,
Almighty Lord displaying might.

You are One, you lack a peer,
You who cheer our downcast hearts,
Providing us our daily needs,
Almighty Lord displaying might.

The seven-heaven azure dome
Inverted hovers overhead;
Columns it lacks of wood or stone,
Almighty Lord displaying might.

Seven vaults, celestial bows
With angels in their thousands filled;
Each with a name, and all in rows,
Almighty Lord displaying might.

You have created for our sake
Two luminaries in the sky,
And all the stars You elevate,
Almighty Lord displaying might.

You gave us fruit trees of every sort,
In every region myriads
Of pomegranates, grapes, and figs, . . .
Almighty Lord displaying might.

The fish, the crocodile give thanks,
Birds in the air and leopards too;
You care for infidels and Franks,[2]
Almighty Lord displaying might.

In quick succession You brought forth
Four essences to count;
Earth, fire, wind, each is of worth,
Almighty Lord displaying might.

You brought Adam out of clay,
You brought him from a pure abode,
Set in his breast a soul, a ray,
Almighty Lord displaying might.

The Sabbath is the gift of the Lord
Brought by the Veiler's decree.
He made us worthy through His word
Almighty Lord displaying might.

A dragon fierce, Moses' staff
Slew the hearts of infidels.
Light crowned his head, a gaff,[3]
Almighty Lord displaying might.

Like straw that staff devoured
Pharaoh and black-hearted Og,
Blown away by a gust of wind,
Almighty Lord displaying might.

You gave their souls back to the dead,
Unto the living You gave bread,
You cure the pain of those in dread,
Almighty Lord displaying might.

When I can think, I think of Him,
Each moment I call Him to mind,[4]
Gratitude fills me to the brim,
Almighty Lord displaying might.

Almighty Lord, my sole support,
Grant me my wish and I'll proclaim,
"I am called Shihāb," You're my comfort,
Almighty Lord displaying might.

Poems in Praise of the Prophets

Amīnā: *In Praise of Moses, Our Master, Peace Be upon Him*

Pure soul and lamp of faith,[1]
Chieftain and full moon of the worlds,
In lordship you have been chosen
Highest in rank of all the prophets.
Ere you came into the world
You were with God manifest.[2]
O Moses, O God's interlocutor,[3]
O certain knowledge, essence of certainty,[4]
Your station is above the spheres of the sun and moon.[5]
At Resurrection, on the *Judgment Day,*
You will encounter *M*[im] and *H* [a'],[6]
Hearts will incline toward you,
Toward your pure scent and temper.
I am your faithful servant, you

Whose copper visage is well veiled.[7]
You are better than *M*[im] and *H*[a'];[8]
You are made of *M*[im] and *Sh*[in] and *H*[a'];[9]
You are the glory of *face to face,*[10]
The power of our Lord.
This greatness occurred upon Mount Ṭūr,[11]
This *joy* in *Sivan*'s month we found,[12]
This gathering of the *Lord*'s hosts,
When all these fiery words [to us came].[13]

Yūsuf Yahūdī: *A Mukhammas in Honor of Moses*

Out of Your splendid grace this desolate place You made,[1]
Out of a handful of dust such a radiant sun You made,
The nine heavenly spheres,[2] one by one, You made,
Everywhere heaven's wanderers scattered You made,
And over them the moon, shah of shahs, You made.

How can You be described, O Generous Source of Generosity?
If angels and human beings were to do so all the time,
Oceans would turn to black ink, all reed pens would groan.
How can one possibly describe the qualities of the Great Shah?
All the above and more out of Generosity You made.

His creation's four elements for Adam were made manifest,
For a few days within His garden was his dwelling place.
The Most Exalted taught him knowledge's highest mysteries;
Eve was ordained for him from pre-eternity;[3] the pretext,
A grain of wheat,[4] removing him from Paradise You made.

On leaving His garden Adam's heart was full of grief,
Yet he kept company with Eve, and others issued forth from him.
They were both Muslims,[5] but later they trespassed greatly.
To the Incomparable Creator they prayed for a son,
His Excellence Noah in answer to their prayers You made.[6]

Often and much did he admonish those cruel people,
They would reply with blows; Noah despaired of them.
While grieving he became aware of mysteries;

Alone he built a boat and withdrew from everyone,
Saved from the torments of the Flood, him You made.

When the prophet and his three sons left the boat,
All other human beings issued from them.
They were infidels, rebellious, wicked, idolators.
When divine knowledge reached Khalīl[7] from God,
Nimrod's fire into a garden for him You made.[8]

When that graceful cypress left the furnace unharmed,
The light on his forehead amazed the people's eyes.
Then some of them became aware of hidden mysteries.
He sacrificed his son to the Living, Placeless One,[9]
His Excellence Isaac, the noblest of all, You made.

Out of him two rose-cheeked sons came forth:
One Jacob, the other Esau, a lion ready to hunt.
Two tribes without number came out of these two;
His Excellence Jacob feared God in his heart,
For the sage of Canaan the lot of separation You made.[10]

Although that cypress of the plain commanded Egypt as its king,
Better by far is poverty in Canaan in my view:
"Separation from father confounds me; how can I converse with him?
In the end, my brothers' oppression moved me far from my native land."[11]
Almighty God, our destinies from pre-eternity You made.

After a while Joseph was reunited with his father,
The Incomparable Maker heard the wails of Canaan's sage,
His Excellence Moses from their progeny came forth,
On his account the infidel shah killed a hundred thousand babes,[12]
The Egyptians' death at the hand of 'Imrān's son You made.

That falcon of Mount Ṭūr[13] was wondrously bold,
The summons of the Living, Merciful One reached him without
mediation.[14]
Those eyes whose radiant glance could be seen from afar,
Where else in the world can the likes of him be seen?
The leader of prophets, the crown of shahs, him You made.

A sweet singing nightingale was his speech on Mount Ṭūr.
Were it not for God's hand, under His throne he'd have dwelt;[15]
Then the Almighty revealed the Book; through the fervent love
Of his excellence Gabriel, who mediated between them;[16]
You showed him the station of the cherubs that You made.

Better than both worlds is the Torah's register.
Among the cherubs he was busy and rejoiced;
In that hour 'Imrān's son was God's intimate[17]
The world that then existed was destroyed;
Out of gracious generosity new foundations You made.[18]

He was bold at the threshold of the Ancient Judge,
That pure essence longed to see God Himself.
He stood in place firmly, and he was fully conscious,
When suddenly a bright terror passed before him,
The happiness of beholding You for him You made.[19]

From ancient times the cry of distance from the Almighty
Reached Him until Moses drew close to Him two stretches' length.[20]
On seeing his station the cherubs could not help but love him,
None like him was ever born from a mother,
A flame from the brilliant light[21] him You made.

He blessed his excellence Khiżr,[22] who lives forever,
For this, on his arrival, heaven and earth blessed him.
Life in both worlds God bestowed upon him;
Kings and beggars alike long to see his face,
But concealed from everyone's eye him You made.

Seven veils cover the face of that chief of imams,[23]
Day and night are made one by the splendor of his cheeks,
Joy and happiness were had in welcoming that lovely one,
With manna and quails he fed the nation for forty years,
Generosity's treasury, gift and home of goodness him You made.

Out of one stone came twelve flowing paths,[24]
All through the miracles of the Lord of the happy conjunction.[25]
The cloud of mercy was always his parasol,

Whether on the battlefield or killing infidels;
With one blow Og one with the dirt You made.[26]

From among the Lord's servants Aaron was his brother,
He had no other task but offering sacrifices to God;
That rose-cheeked man did nothing but serve God,
He was God's gentlest, most forebearing servant,[27]
A fortunate sage among Your merciful elect, him You made.

Since Moses came into existence from his mother,
He was well-versed in the world's mystery and knowledge.[28]
Alas, that pearl still suffered from fate's vicissitude.
Yusūf Yahūdī composed this quintet for the prophet
Through Your Generosity easing his difficulties You made.

Muflis-i Khwānsārī: *In Praise of Ezekiel*

Confused and longing,[1] my heart and soul
Yearn to kiss your footsteps, O *prophet Ezekiel,*
Longing for you grieves me day and night;
My love makes both repose and patience flee;
My head for ransom of the diadem on yours!
Ready for sacrifice am I to your majesty.
My fainting heart is but a drop of blood;
Would that I could come with ease to kiss your footsteps!
Your name, O *prophet Ezekiel,* is my strength,
And always on my tongue. O Lord,
Grant me the wish to make collyrium
For my eyes out of that dust.[2]
You are our master and we are all your servants;
This is what is proper out of regard for you.
Happy the time when all of us, weaklings,
Will go to *Zion,* to the *holy* mountain,
With our *Saviour.* You are equal to all prophets,
Past and future; as surety you will call them:
Zerubabbel will gladly blow *Resurrection's shofar,*[3]
And at that time we'll move away from hopelessness
And will attain at last our wish;

Elijah will bring forth good tidings,[4]
Bring the community the promised *Resurrection;*
Joyfully all the dead will spring to life,
They'll leap forth quickly from the ground.
Glad and delighted they will gather,
Singing *songs* and *melodies* the while.
From the world's four directions, singly or together,
All will praise God in *song* like nightingales.
Levi's entire tribe will busy itself with *song,*
And over our heads the *priests* will utter *blessings.*
Then all the happy, contented Israelites
Will offer sacrifices to their Lord.
The altar will be adorned; all will rejoice and feast.
The menorah also will be rekindled;
Our hearts' grief will then turn to joy.
The *Tabernacle* will be in the *Sanctuary*'s precinct;
We will light up through joy and melody.
The seven *priests* will don their *pure* garments;
We will perform our pilgrimage on all *three festivals.*[5]
The *righteous, perfect* priests will offer
Burnt sacrifices and *peace offerings.*
They will mix the fragrances of *incense*
And will thereby destroy 'Azaz'el.
The sounds of the *shofar, hallel,*[6] and *songs*
Will brighten twice the *Temple Court.*
It is my hope, [O God], that You
Will extricate me from this whirlpool.
My heart is faint, I lack all strength;
I am sore afflicted and distressed.
Time's hand and the spheres' treachery
Have turned my cheeks yellow from helplessness.
Grant, O Pure Lord, salvation
Until I reach that land [of pilgrimage]!
The day I reach Ezekiel's footsteps
I will join my heart and soul to his.
Lord of Abraham, Sarah, and Isaac,
May we be granted quickly to rejoice!

For the sake of Jacob's sorrow,
For the sake of Joseph's righteousness,
And the honor of all the [Twelve] Tribes;
By the truth of the master of the *urim* and *thummin,*[7]
O Lord, by the honor of Moses, son of 'Imrān,
Release us quickly from this *exile.*
By the truth of that excellent, gentle man[8]
Who was [God's] intimate day and night at *Bet El,*
By the truth of David, the singer of *psalms,*
By the crown and pomp of Solomon's throne,
By the truth and honor due to wise men
For their merit, become our guide,
O *prophet Ezekiel;* send us *Redemption* quickly;
Call us yourself the *treasured people.*[9]
Be our shepherd, and we will be your flock.
Drive us until we reach the realm of *Zion.*
My humble self has come from *God*
To kiss the dust of the *prophet Ezekiel*'s tomb.
O Lord, let the wine of lips flow;
Send the *Redemption* quickly;
Let all *exiles* gather together
To rebuild *God's Sanctuary.*

Yeḥezqel Khwānsārī: *In Praise of the Qualities of Ezekiel*

O prophet Ezekiel,[1] may my heart and soul
Be your ransom!
I am devoted to you heart and soul;
I lack the strength to come to you,
To writhe in your dust, a bird in death's agony;[2]
Give me wings and I will fly to you,
For I have no strength to arrive in stages.[3]
Yearning for you who are distant grieves me;
Only the strength of my heart's fervor endures.
Deem me not distant, for I am near;
Receive me at God's court, O *prophet Ezekiel!*
I have sinned before You, O Living, Universal Lord,

O God, forgive my sins![4]
Day and night I cry for love of you,
My eyes shed tears constantly.
All my work in the world is very hard;
Untie this knot that's in my heart!
Out of your dust I wish to make collyrium,
To make a talisman to ward off every calamity.
My hope rests upon you on *Resurrection* Day,
That you will bring forth my rose from clay.[5]
I have no hope in this state of affairs,
Save coming to kiss your feet, O *prophet Ezekiel.*
You are the candle in all prophets' gatherings,
The bright lamp of the heedless and the blind,
You are the shepherd, and we are your sheep.
Bring us once more to the top of *Bet El;*[6]
Find for us the *Redeemer* on the threshold
Of the palace of the Universal Lord.
Forgive my sins, O Lord,
By the truth of Moses, Aaron, and Samuel.
I have sinned before You, O Living, universal Lord,
O Lord, forgive us our faults.
I have sinned before You, O Living, universal Lord,
Whoever bows down at your threshold,
May he never be troubled by Samael[7]
[O Ezekiel,] be the intercessor, the surety of all Jews,
Especially of your poor servant Ezekiel.

In Praise and Commendation of Ezra

I offer to you my heart and soul,[1]
And come to kiss your footprints on the seashore.[2]
Bestir yourself for the sake of *Israel's exiled,*
That the *Messiah* may appear from Zion's mount.
I weep abundantly day and night, and long
To see the prophet Ezra's countenance.
Happy the hour when I shall see you,
When for your sake I shall rejoice!

You were illiterate,[3] yet you bore good tidings;
Bestir yourself for David and Solomon's sakes!
O Lord, carry us to the seashore,
And let all of us, even me, behold
The countenance of the prophet Ezra.
Happy the day when we will lift our heads
Out of the dust and glance heavenward,
Full of pleasure, delight, and joy!
Bestir yourself for Mordekai and Esther;
Do it, O prophet Ezra, for their sake!
Ever we hope for *Zion* and the *Holy Temple.*
O Lord, let the seashore be my allotted portion,
To prostrate myself before the prophet Ezra
In the dust. Blind and exhausted as we are,
Heedless, infirm; when will we yet behold,
Through miracle, the *Holy Land?*
By Moses, Aaron, and Samuel's Truth,
We beg You, send to us our *Redeemer.*
Don't deem me distant; bring me closer
For the sake of Yekutiel,[4] leader and prophet.
You are our hope on *Resurrection* Day,
When we shall all behold the countenance
Of Ezra.
Save us from their[5] hands,
For we are all distressed[6] and grieving.
Establish once again our House, proclaim
Mercy for us. Let *Judah* rejoice anew,
And we will all rejoice through You.
Let coming to the seashore be my share;
Let me be dazzled by the prophet Ezra.

Bābāī b. Luṭf: *O Elijah, Take My Hand*

This poor man will now declaim[1]
A poem to honor Elijah's fame,
(May he ever protect my name),
O Elijah, take my hand.[2]

Your name is ever my ransom,
Morn and evening it is my custom,
Always through your street to roam,
O Elijah, take my hand.

Peacock of Mercy's oasis,
Sīmurgh[3] of the tower of gnosis,[4]
Toll gatherer on the road to finis,
O Elijah, take my hand.

My head always clamors for you,
My heart's melancholy for you,
Everywhere there's room for you,
O Elijah, take my hand.

Falcon of the Universal Lord,[5]
Faith's builder, the law's Word,
Prophet, certain envoy of concord,
O Elijah, take my hand.

You're His letters "A" and "L,"
His letters "A" and "H" as well,[6]
His appearance you foretell,[7]
O Elijah, take my hand.

The glad news my soul has reached,
The world above it has been breached,
"This is Elijah, he's arrived!"
O Elijah, take my hand.

In the Hebrew tongue you're called Eliyah,
In those of others you are Nāwāyā,[8]
Everyone calls you Khiżr,[9] O Elijah,
O Elijah, take my hand.

A sea of sins is my disgrace,
I drown with a guilty man's face,
Look down on me from your grace,
O Elijah, take my hand.

The four foundations[10] beneath my feet,
Everywhere your presence greet,
All who cry, "O Elijah," sweet,
O Elijah, take my hand.

O you who are light of my eye,
From east to west, under the sky,
Walking 'round through wet and dry,[11]
O Elijah, take my hand.

Glancing at your soles one sees,
Though crossing entire seas,
On wet and dry you are at ease,
O Elijah, take my hand.

O Elijah, O Elijah, you come bright,
Straight from the Almighty's light,
Say, "Mahdī, Guide, come now in sight,"[12]
O Elijah, take my hand.

Because you are our intercessor,
Our pains you heal without rancor,
By the hundreds we obey you, counselor,
O Elijah, take my hand.

You are that last magistrate,
The kingdom's monarch incarnate,
Guide, counselor, and helpmate,
O Elijah, take my hand.

East and west from end to end,
Before your feet are but one bend.
At Resurrection for me you'll send,
O Elijah, take my hand.

King of standard-bearers countless,
Hold firmly to your mount, a fortress
Build for the *exiled* of the universe,
O Elijah, take my hand.

Rebuild the *Sanctuary Great,*
From top to bottom, and we will elevate
To you, morn and night, our only mandate,
O Elijah, take my hand.

O Lord, by the God of Mount Ṭūr,[13]
We live within the grave of Ur,[14]
The world is unjust and impure,
O Elijah, take my hand.

The lovers' candle is your light,
To everyone please show your might,[15]
You're hidden yet visible in the night,
O Elijah, take my hand.

Your dwelling place is Mount Carmel,[16]
A mountain is your citadel,
The world keeps clamoring for El,[17]
O Elijah, take my hand.

O Elijah, enter right now through the door,
Say you forgive your humble suitor,
Bābāī b. Luṭf, who asks for your succor,
O Elijah, take my hand.

Prayers

Amīnā: *A Prayer*

O Lord of Heaven,[1] creator of the sun and moon,
Be my companion lest I stray from the path.
Although I'm not worthy of Your mercy's gift and grace,
I hope not to return black-faced from Your court.
All who come to Your court are freed from Your ire;
Without Your mercy the world would be laid waste.
Take note of my pale face, and afterward deliver me;
Your clemency, like water, washes away all crimes and sins.
Decree my deliverance from ill-wishers' claws;

Be my friend, let the plague fall upon my slanderers.
How can I ever complete the praises of the perfect God?
The Invisible[2] is [All-]Nourisher, the Lord of Hosts.
O dear friends, there is no end to praising God!
How can sweet speech extol the station of the King?
I bow my head in the path's dust of Kalīm's[3] footsteps.
By God's grace, the world gave way before his miracles;
There never was a prophet like him in the world,
Just, brave, and full of wisdom, like the sun and moon;
No messenger ever came between him and the Lord;
God spoke with him face to face,[4] like a friend, a king.
My king is the [All-]Nourisher, Provider of daily needs;
As long as the celestial spheres and firmaments endure,
I will never turn away my face from my King.
O Amīnā, grieve not nor complain of this misfortune,
For in the end you'll be delivered like Joseph from the well.[5]

Bābāī: *A Prayer*

O Lord,[1] by the truth of those whose gaze
Is fixed upon Your threshold, and by the sun,
Jupiter, Venus, and the moon,
By Your exalted, glorious throne,
And by the truth of Your elect of old,
By all the ministering angels,
And by the truth of Heaven and Earth
And Adam's excellence, by the truth of Noah,
Abraham, and all the chieftains,
The prophets *Isaac* and *Jacob,*
By the truth of poor, *righteous Joseph,*
Who was always a candle, faithful,
By the truth of *Moses, Aaron,* and *Phinehas,*
The noblest at Your noble threshold,
[By the truth of] David and Solomon's power,
And by the valor of *Joshua ben Nun,*
By the truth of *Tobiah,*[2] that patient sage,
Remember, Lord, Caesar's oppression![3]

By the truth of *Daniel, Ḥannaniah, Misha'el,*
And also of Ezra, *Mordekai,* and *Esther,*
By the truth of the preferred *Seraḥ bat Asher*[4]
And of all the faithful sages,
By the truth of the wise lovers [of God],
Have mercy on this entire community,
For they are all in *exile,* without strength.
We lack expedience in this *exile;*
There's none to help us in this distress.
We are confused, exhausted, wounded at heart,
For we have turned away from our condition.[5]
All of us, men and women, pray at Your threshold,
That You will provide a salve for our pain.
Perform a miracle again for our sake,
As You once did in Egypt—
Firmly you split the sea in two,
And spoke with Moses openly—
[Do it again] for *Israel,* Your *firstborn;*
Henceforth distance the world's misery from us.
Turn us back from our unbecoming manners,
From the ignoble hands in which You've placed us.
O Lord, pay heed to Your own mercy;
Do not transgress the covenant You made,
Cleave to Your covenant and let the *Sanctuary*
Flourish once again.
Free us at last from this *exile,*
Rescue us from the hands of commoners and kings.
We are all trodden upon like ants,
In this whirlpool we're full of grief and terror.
No one has friends in this affliction,
Neither a beloved nor a comforting companion.
You've been the Protector of the afflicted,
You have ever been the remedy for our pains,
You've freed us every time from every valley
In which we have been held captive.
Why do You fling us now into disgrace,
And make no valley in this whirlpool?

In this sea whose waves are bloodshed,
Our blood fills to the brim a hundred cups.
Is Your threshold bolted against my sighs?
Have You departed to sit safely
In happiness' corner? If not,
Of all these burning sighs, why has not
One wrenching groan reached Your threshold?
You have displayed Your might to kings,
To *Sihon, Og,* and also to *Agag,*
To *Sisera, Sennacherib,* and *Balak;*
You filled the Nile with blood.
The likes of champions, *Amalek* and *Balaam,*
You killed in war just like the kings.
May it please You to neglect us no more;
We have no other God but You.
O Lord, make peace with the Jewish people,
Such as the one that followed the *Broken Tablets,*
As You Yourself declared in the *Torah:*
"*I pardon,*"[6] the *good news* brought by *Moses.*
O Lord, by the truth of Your prophets,
Your beloved, chosen *Samuel,*
Habaqquq, Nahum, Zephaniah,
By the truth of *Jonah* and also *Zekariah,*
Deliver us from this calamity,
Empower once again the Jewish people.
Rebuild the *Sanctuary* quickly,
Let David's harp extol You once again.
Let Bābāī's heart soon rejoice anew,
Let him drink from anticipation's cup.[7]

Miscellaneous Poems

Amīnā: *A Ghazal on the Twelve Tribes*

O Lord,[1] You are herald of all that is secret:[2]
I pray, be the *shield* of this sojourner,
For the *merit* of the firstborn of the *tribes,*

Reuben, his name exalted in the world.
O Lord, You are truly incomparable:
On this sojourner decree no *sin,*
For the *merit* of the secondborn of the *tribes,*
Simon, his name, viceregent of the world.
O Lord, You have no begetter and no cause:
Pledge only good to this sojourner,
For the *merit* of the thirdborn of the *tribes,*
Levi, his name, defender of the faith.
O Lord, You are [All-]Seeing and [All-]Knowing:
Bestow the world to come on this sojourner,
For the *merit* of the fourth of *Jacob's* sons,
The brave lion, *Judah* his name.
O Lord, You are leader and sultan:
Fulfill the wishes of this sojourner,
For the *merit* of *Jacob's* fifth son,
A wise and understanding man named *Dan.*
O Lord, You are life eternal:[3]
Bestow prosperity on this sojourner,
For the merit of *Jacob's* sixth son,
Nimble, light-footed *Naphtali* his name.
O Lord, You've made the world inhabited:
Bestow a happy heart on this sojourner,
For the *merit* of *Jacob's* seventh son,
Named *Gad,* who rose from fortune's constellation.
O Lord, You are present everywhere:
Watch over this sojourner [always],
For the *merit* of *Jacob's* eighth son,
Dipped in oil, *Asher* his name.
O Lord, You are without self and friend:
Be the intimate friend of this sojourner,
For the *merit* of *Jacob's* ninth son,
Gentle *Issachar,* defender of the faith.
O Lord, bestow from Your concealed abundance,
Be the good fortune of this sojourner,
For the *merit* of *Jacob's* tenth son,
King of merchants, *Zebulun* his name.

O Lord, *increase Your community,*
And *increase* the life of this sojourner,
For the *merit* of *Jacob's* eleventh son,
King of the world's kings, *Joseph* his name.
O Lord, for the reverence of the *Shekinah*'s[4] light,
Grant me my portion of *wisdom* and *understanding.*
I have recounted *the [merit of the] Twelve Tribes*
Benjamin's name is also Amīnā's.[5]

Siman Ṭov Melammed: *In Honor of the Lord* Messiah, *His Excellency, the Ruler*

Arise,[1] stand tall, let me caress[2] your stature,
And let me offer you in sacrifice my life.
Let me begin to praise your qualities!
Arise, exalt your countenance, O humble shah,
And let me bow down in the dust at your feet.
If the grace of your excellence will reach
Even one as powerless as myself,
I'll play music and break out into dance.
When that call[3] reaches me in the dark night,
Like a cock I will crow and bring on the morn.[4]
It is evening,[5] glance at these greedy beggars;
Call them from beggary to the table of shahs,[6]
And I will delight in you.
My eyes are shut like the eyes of a falcon
Who yearns for the hunt. I wish that my pinions
Would break open to reveal your face!
If you'd but lie on my pillow,
I'd ask how you were;
Out of love for you, my physician,
I am partial to my body's fever.
If you bestow your friendship on me,
With skirt outspread I'll rise and fly away.
How fortunate that teasing is your virtue's source!
Do tease me, tease me, please,
And I will tease you in turn!

Panegyrics, Lyrical Poems, Quatrains 12

Long narrative poems imitating Persian epics were not the only poetic genre of Persian literature to appeal to Iranian-Jewish poets. The large number of original lyrical poems found in JP manuscripts testifies to the fact that the Iranian Jews enjoyed, copied, and imitated the lighter forms for which Persian poetry is justly famous, especially *ghazal*s and *rubā'īyāt* (quatrains).

Panegyrics in praise of reigning monarchs or wealthy patrons are one of the oldest forms of Persian poetry, derived from the Arabic *qaṣīda* (ode), itself a complex poetic genre. Because Iranian Jews had little or no contact with their rulers, and practically no hope of royal patronage, it is not surprising to find only a few panegyrics among JP texts. They were written in praise of reigning monarchs, as were Shāhīn's two panegyrics for Sultan Abū Sa'īd (d. 1336), one of which is translated below, and Amīnā's poem in praise of Shah Ashraf (d. 1730). I have not found any panegyrics written for Jewish patrons. It is impossible to ascertain whether Shāhīn's and Amīnā's panegyrics had any chance of reaching their objects; panegyrists were usually rewarded for their efforts by the dedicatee. However, Shāhīn and Amīnā, in particular, were both talented poets who may have written their panegyrics simply to experiment in the genre. The two panegyrics of Shāhīn come from the introductory chapters of *Bereshit-nāmah* and *Mūsā-nāmah*. Since all Persian epics open with chapters of praise (for God, Muḥammad, and a reigning sovereign), Shāhīn may simply have been following a literary convention.

The dominant theme of Persian lyrical poetry, which reached its height in the poetry of Ḥāfiẓ (d. 1389), is love. The great Sufi poets, in particular, tended to express love for the divine through earthly metaphors—hence the numerous passionate love poems that have enchanted readers of Persian poetry and driven translators to distraction through their complex double entendres.

The samples of JP love poems included here are of the earthly kind, especially Ya'qov's. Although we know nothing about the circumstances surrounding this poem (more likely, a song), we do know that it was popular, because we find it in many manuscripts.

Amīnā is undoubtedly the greatest Iranian-Jewish lyrical poet. His poems revolve around the theme of obsessive love and tend to reflect his own unhappy experiences in love. "The Story of Amīnā and His Wife" alludes to a deeply unhappy marriage, and it is unusual in its confessional, heartfelt content. It goes a long way to explain the poet's attitude in "On Becoming Cold-Hearted Toward Women."

There are numerous quatrains, usually anonymous, scattered in JP manuscripts. Their themes tend to be Khayyamesque, that is, they bemoan the deceptive pleasures of earthly life and its fleeting passions in a Sufi vein. Unusual among these are quatrains 2 and 3 in the translations below, which have a specifically Jewish content and indicate, once again, the centrality of the figure of Moses in JP literature in general.

Panegyrics

Shāhīn: *In Praise of Bahādur Abū Sa'īd, Monarch of His [Shāhīn's] Realm, He Said*

Upon the great Shah,[1] monarch and son
Of monarchs, Bahādur [A]bū Sa'īd,
Reigning khan, generous lord
Of the universe, let the company

Of victory and good fortune fall.
He is the Farīdūn[2] of the age,
The Alexander of our time;
May the evil eye never glimpse his face!
He is generous to the kingdoms of the world;
He wears Farīdūn's crown upon his brow.
Endless arrays of soldiers, entire armies
He musters through justice and right action.
Kings of the world, from one end to the other,
Bring him tribute from every direction.
Since Jamshīd's[3] time such a radiant sun
Has not been seen in the world.
He made justice and equity abide everywhere;
All creatures rejoice through his good fortune.
If in ages past, in Nūshīrvān's[4] fabled times,
Lambs and wolves drank from the same spring,
Now in this monarch's age, no bloodthirsty wolf
Dares even to appear at the gates of a house.
The shah rids the world of all seeds of oppression;
He tears the hearts of enemies to shreds.
The world flourishes through his good fortune;
Whoever hears his name can't but rejoice.
Through all the regions in which he rides,
He scatters happiness from his stirrup;
Happiness's happiness is Bū Saʿīd;[5]
May his happiness increase daily,
And may the royal crown never depart
From his august brow. May God Himself
Be his friend everywhere, and may misfortune
Never harm his throne and crown.
May those who envy him be fettered hourly;
May Fortune grant him every victory; and may
The sweetness of each moment renew itself
In his embrace. May his life be more plentiful
Than every other earthly thing; and may
His good name endure for all time.
May his nights be auspicious,

His days like the New Year; and may he always
Rejoice, every day of his life. May he
Not see adversity from Time's tyranny; and may
His hand ever clasp goblet and wine. May he
Always be feasting and joined to joy
Forever; and may he need none but the Judge;
May the Lord of the universe be his companion.
O God, keep the evil eye away from his beauty;
May his perfection increase hourly; and may
Calamity never touch his throne and crown.
May his good fortune be as radiant as the sun.
May God ever guard him and keep him; and may
The Lord of the universe be his friend always.
May the winds of calamity blow far away
From his royal parasol; and may
The entire world thrive by his leave.
May slaves, khans, and caesars
Ever attend in service at his gate; and may
Happiness be his friend
Until the Day of Resurrection,
And seal his work in peace.

Amīnā: *O Just Shah Ashraf*

O just Shah Ashraf,[1] your dower will certainly grow,
First Egypt and India second, third Rome, and China fourth.
May God be your refuge and protector; because of you endure
First justice and faith second, third honor, and religion fourth.
Through the blessing of your good fortune, in Iran perished
First war and anger second, third rage, and vengeance fourth.
Your generosity is greater than any source of water, than
First the Tigris and the Oxus second, third 'Oman,[2] and Zan[3] fourth.
Through the intrusion of your spiritual body these appeared in the world,
First fire and spirit second, third water, and clay fourth.
Through contact with your body all these became filled with light,
First the horseshoe, the mount second, third the gallop, and the saddle fourth.

Come, O world-burning shah, consider Amīnā's state,
First look and learn second, third find, and see fourth.

Lyrical Poems

Yaʿqov: *My Lovely Delightful Girl*

My lovely delightful girl,[1]
Dear child, I beg you, please don't tease me.
My pretty face of lovely hues,
Dear child, I beg you, please don't tease me.
Look at my sorry state,
Dear child, I beg you, please don't tease me.
Look at my wounded heart,
Dear child, I beg you, please don't tease me.
Have mercy on my state,
Dear child, I beg you, please don't tease me.
Ask me just once how I fare,
Dear child, I beg you, please don't tease me.
I am nearly destitute,
Dear child, I beg you, please don't tease me.
Beside myself, without myself,
Dear child, I beg you, please don't tease me.
I am bewildered, without help,
Dear child, I beg you, please don't tease me.
I am as wild as Majnūn,[2]
Dear child, I beg you, please don't tease me.
I am nearly at death's door,
Dear child, I beg you, please don't tease me.
My blood will be upon your head,
Dear child, I beg you, please don't tease me.
My love, I have no strength left,
Dear child, I beg you, please don't tease me.
You've drowned me in tears of blood,
Dear child, I beg you, please don't tease me.
Because of you my soul has fled,
Dear child, I beg you, please don't tease me.

Once more, once more, I beg,
Dear child, I beg you, please don't tease me.
My hand clutches at your hem,
Dear child, I beg you, please don't tease me.
You're killing me, you're killing me,
Dear child, I beg you, please don't tease me.
You're stone hearted to one who loves,
Dear child, I beg you, please don't tease me.
My heartfelt sighs are heaven bound,
Dear child, I beg you, please don't tease me.
Answer me just once, dear girl,
Dear child, I beg you, please don't tease me.
Yaʿkov yearns for a young girl,
Dear child, I beg you, please don't tease me.
Love afflicts him in old age,
Dear child, I beg you, please don't tease me.
Answer me just once, dear girl,
Dear child, I beg you, please don't tease me.

Amīnā: *I Wish to Walk in the Rose Garden*

I wish to walk in the rose garden,[1]
I will be you and you will be me.[2]
We'll spite the rival enemy,
I will be you and you will be me.
We'll rest, look into each other's faces
In the shade of the purple Judas tree;
Roses we'll pluck, our hearts carefree,
I will be you and you will be me.
I'll plant a kiss under your chin,
Two and three, two and three,
And four on the corners of your lips;
For two, three days, and the whole night
We'll tumble in each other's arms,
I will be you and you will be me.
My secrets you'll reveal to none,
Nor will you chase after anyone;

Without my leave you'll smell no rose,
I will be you and you will be me.
Sitting together in the rose garden,
We're victim and sacrifice at harvest time;
I'll speak with you, you'll speak with me,
I will be you and you will be me.
There'll be no one else but you and I,
Out of envy the enemy will be in frenzy;
My hand will rest upon your neck,
I will be you and you will be me.
Listen to me, O my lovely idol,
You will get drunk from the azure vault;[3]
But without Amīnā you will not quaff,[4]
I will be you and you will be me.

Amīnā: *She Is the Rose Garden's Cypress*

She is the rose garden's cypress;[1] not so,
For what is then the ravisher's stature?
Her cheeks are the moon; not so,
For what is then this world's sun?
Her curls are a snare; not so,
For what is then a black viper?
Her eyebrows are an arch; not so,
For what is then the people's *mihrāb?*[2]
Her eyes are intoxicated; not so,
For what is then a sick man's illness?
Her ruby lips are sugar; not so,
For what is then the carnelian of lips?
She has a well in her chin; not so,
For what is then the pool of Kawsar?[3]
Her speech is fulsome; not so,
For what is then eternal life?
Her gait is like a gazelle's; not so,
For what is then a swaying box tree?
Her verses are ever so sweet; not so,
For what is then Amīnā's verse?

Amīnā: *Last Night Her Magic Wink*

Last night her magic wink[1]
Confused and maddened me;
From Hindu and infidel alike,
That glance drew forth
Favors galore, last night.
Heedless, the friend sent me
Troubles aplenty and unfriendly,
While her coquettish eyes rested,
Nested within her eyebrows' shade.
A hundred fever-blistered omens
Broke out upon her lip, while she
Kept sighing for the moon's boon.
Sweet from lips to navel,
From navel to knees,
She is pleasing, all teasing.
Roses smile from her cheeks,
Her stature is the reason
For the box tree's gaiety.
With boastful deceit she reduces
Stallions to mousy muteness.
This silver-limbed friend cast
A velvet net upon Amīnā,
Robbed him of his resolve to flee
Her villainy and be free.

Amīnā: *The Story of Amīnā and His Wife*

Listen, my friends, pay attention![1]
Be silent, do not restrain me,
Nor say, "That fellow Amīnā's been unfaithful,
His heart and tongue in two directions pull;
If not, why did he leave his native realm,
Parted from her, a moon of Khotan?"[2]
Listen first and then pass judgment,
Before I slip my foot into the stirrup.
For twenty-five long years a rose I nourished,

Her scent gladdened my every disposition,
And all that time, every day, she showed me
Ten different hues, exasperating mistress!
Yet I kept hoping for her love,
While my heart opened for those rosy cheeks.
Scarce hoping to catch even a whiff of her scent,
I sat in her shade chastely, yet
In the end, caught only the scent
Of hopelessness; in place of sweet liquors
I tasted only blows. Such was that rose.
Yet sure I loved her, heart and soul;
If she had asked me for my head, my soul,
I would have handed those to her.
Over and over I gave proof of my love,
Yet never did I find good faith in that rose.
Her temper was as mean as Time itself:
I said good things and she rejoined with bad;
I would beseech and always be rejected,
Ever and ever I sought her company;
She'd only sting me like a pair of pincers.
I was unprotected from the beauty of her face;
Her gait, her stature, and her hair.
Her entire body was to my liking,
While with every word she hurt me.
When I would try to counsel her,
She held my counsel hateful;
Not one of my words could pierce her ears
Because of her constant cry, her clamor.
My tongue is cleft from so much sweet talk,
Well-worn advice; it never made her well;
No remedy I found for one of her pains.
Then only did I plan wickedness,
Turning from what is right to what is wrong.
(No mother and no father had she here,
Having already dispatched them to hell.)
By this injustice finally incensed,[3]
She finally provided my blow.

It was clear that we were not the same,
That she and I were not one heart and soul.
I tried apologizing, turning myself
Into a humble dervish before her, but
She offered me no cure for all my pains;
That which I suffered was incurable.
I have told the story thus, I have related it
For my heart's sake, in such a manner,
Five hundred times and more.
At times I was a tyrant, and at times
A dervish, yet as a dervish found no cure,
Nor was I cured by my tyranny.
Twenty-five years thus passed
Without a hope of rescue, then,
One evening I caught poisonous words
From those sweet lips: "I do not love you,
I'll never smile at you again."
She swore, "If I remain alive,
I'll drive you to your death."
When I heard these naked words,
I laughed! Yes, it is true:
One hour before it is extinguished,
Lamp's light brightens the house . . .
Thus have I fallen in with strangers,
I've set out for [foreign parts].[4]
Severed my heart from my relations . . .[5]

Amīnā: *On Becoming Cold-Hearted Toward Women*

O my heart, light of my soul, listen to me![1]
If you do not ever wish to be
Buried without a shroud,
Don't tie your heart to a woman.

If her face is like the moon,
And her sugary sweet lips croon,
Listen to me, my own dear soul,
Don't tie your heart to a woman.

If her curls are ambergris,
And she is lovelier than Artemis,
If she is a virgin every night,
Don't tie your heart to a woman.

If her eyebrows are lassos,
Her stature tall, voluptuous,
No matter how pleasing she is,
Don't tie your heart to a woman.

If her lovelocks undulate,
If her eyes intoxicate,
And her scent's from paradise,
Don't tie your heart to a woman.

If her teeth are white as milk,
Her lips like wine, as soft as silk,
Lest she drive you to despair,
Don't tie your heart to a woman.

If at her temple there's a mole,
And her mouth's a honey hole,
Though she's called a Chinese rose,
Don't tie your heart to a woman.

If there's a dimple in her chin,
Her cheeks are round, a sweet jasmine,
And she is as delicate as a thread,
Don't tie your heart to a woman.

If her neck is a long-necked flask,
Her bust is like a marble cask,
If she is Caesar's only daughter,
Don't tie your heart to a woman.

If her breasts are like pomegranates,
Her stature like a plane tree's mate,
Her curls are twisted up like snakes,
Don't tie your heart to a woman.

If she has a silver navel,
And her speech is sweet to unravel,
And her face like a Chinese idol,
Don't tie your heart to a woman.

If her flanks are a silver bait,
Like undulating hills her gait,
Her speech be sweet and sugary,
Don't tie your heart to a woman.

Don't ever walk toward a woman,
Never run, never pursue a woman,
Listen to Amīnā's advice:
Don't tie your heart to a woman.

Anonymous Quatrains

I smell love's rose scent nearby,[1]
Yet seek you, like the moon, up in the sky;
Since coming to you they cruelly bar,
I must pray for your welfare from afar.

We constantly affirm the Lord's exalted essence.
Wary, in creatures we place little credence;
We pass by shrine,[2] mosque, *mihrāb*,[3] and imam,
Accept, with all our hearts Moses' preeminence.

We are this weak and destitute folk,
Mere chaff and straw in the eyes of your folk.
God's interlocutor, Moses, is our prophet,
We are his fellow travelers, do not forget.

This world of double doors, what use is it to man?
Other than pain and death its offers are all wan.

Happy the man no longer among the living,
He's at peace who is not yet a mother's offspring.

O Judas tree, your place is empty,
Sweet-talking rose, your place is empty,
The sweet-talking rose left for the garden;
Sweet lamp of the soul, your place is empty.

Notes

Introduction

1. Utas, "Jewish-Persian Fragment"; Lazard, "Remarques," pp. 205–209; ʿA. A. Ṣadīqī, *The Origins of the Persian Language* [Pers.] (Tehran, 1357 solar), pp. 77–81; and Shaked, "Judaeo-Persian Notes."
2. See Lazard, *Langue,* p. 31; Rypka, *History,* pp. 148–149.
3. The extant catalogues of JP mss. are Spicehandler, "Descriptive List," Rosenwasser, "Judaeo-Persian Manuscripts," pp. 38–44 (Rosenwasser's list has now been updated in Moreen, "Supplementary List"), and Netzer, *Oṣar.* E. Wust is currently preparing a catalogue of the JP manuscripts held in the Jewish National and University Library, Jerusalem, and I am cataloguing the JP manuscripts of the Library of the Jewish Theological Seminary, New York. The core of this collection, to which other manuscripts have been added over the years, consists of the manuscripts purchased by E. N. Adler; see Adler, *Catalogue.*
4. The most recent albeit incomplete bibliography can be found in Netzer, *Oṣar,* pp. 59–69.
5. The word "Persianate" is coined after the definition of "Islamicate," a term proposed by the historian Marshall G. S. Hodgson in his *Venture of Islam,* 1:56–60. "Persianate" encompasses geographic areas to which Persian culture and civilization have spread, beyond the boundaries of present-day Iran (see Barthold, *Historical Geography of Iran*).

   Throughout this book the words "Iran" and "Iranian" are used to refer to the land and inhabitants. "Persian" (*fārsī,* derived from the name of the central province, Fars, whose language became largely synonymous with classical Persian) is used to refer to the language, literature, and arts of Iran. Similarly, I use the term "Iranian

Jews" for the Jewish inhabitants of Iran and confine the use of the term "Judeo-Persian" to the language and literature of Iranian Jews.

6. Fischel, "Region of the Persian Gulf"; idem., "Azarbaijan"; idem., "Jews of Afghanistan"; idem., "Rediscovery"; Brauer, "Jews in Afghanistan"; Netzer, "Yehudim be-meḥozot ha deromit"; Altshuler, *Yehude mizraḥ;* Yehoshua-Raz, *Mi-nedaḥe Yisrael;* Zand, "Hityashavut ha yehudim be-asiyah"; Leslie, "Judaeo-Persian Colophons."
7. Rapp, *Jüdisch-persisch-hebräischen Inschriften;* idem., "Date of the Judaeo-Persian Inscriptions," pp. 51–58. See the more recent photographic reproductions of many of these tombstones, dating from the middle of the eighth to the middle of the thirteenth centuries, in Yehoshua-Raz, *Mi-nedaḥe Israel,* figs. 53–67.
8. The Jewish community of Isfahan dates its origins specifically to this event. See Fischel, "Yahudiyya," pp. 523–526; idem., "Isfahan," pp. 111–128.
9. For a summary and analysis of the ancient phase of Jewish-Iranian history, see Tadmor, "Period of the First Temple."
10. Neusner, *History.*
11. Brody, "Judaism in the Sasanian Empire," pp. 52–62.
12. An overview of this period can be found in Neusner, *Israel and Iran in Talmudic Times,* a more concise presentation of the text that was published in the work cited above, n. 10.
13. Brody, "Judaism in the Sasanian Empire," p. 59.
14. Frye, *Heritage,* pp. 247–249.
15. Brody, "Judaism in the Sasanian Empire," pp. 60–61.
16. Shaked, "Zoroastrian Polemics Against Jews."
17. Frye, *Golden Age,* chap. 4, and Choksy, *Conflict and Cooperation,* chap. 1.
18. Bulliet, *Conversion to Islam;* Choksy, *Conflict and Cooperation,* chap. 3.
19. Goitein, *Mediterranean Society,* 2:201–204.
20. On the exilarchate, see Gil, "Exilarchate." The gaonate continued, with increasingly weakened authority, until the end of the thirteenth century (*EJ,* s.v. "Gaon").
21. Wasserstrom, *Between Muslim and Jew,* chaps. 1 and 2.
22. Ibid., pp. 21–23, 71–89; see also Index, under "ʿIsāwiyya."
23. See Nemoy, *Karaite Anthology.*
24. Wasserstrom, *Between Muslim and Jew,* p. 68; see also his persuasive reconstruction of the "proto-Shiʿi milieu," pp. 82–84; Nemoy, *Karaite Anthology,* p. xii.
25. For an example of this last, see the second part of Shaked's article "Two Judaeo-Iranian Contributions," pp. 304–322; idem., "Some New Early Judaeo-Persian Texts," a lecture delivered in Jerusalem at "Irano-Judaica: Fourth International Conference," July 1998.
26. Shaked, "Persian and the Origins of the Karaite Movement," pp. 7–9.
27. See below, chap. 1. On the Muslim attitude toward mercantilism and the role of the Jews within it, see Cohen, *Under Crescent and Cross,* pp. 88–103.
28. See Goitein, *Mediterranean Society,* 4:2, 192.
29. Fischel, *Jews,* pp. 68–89; Goitein, *Mediterranean Society,* 3:37, 136, 289.
30. See Goitein, *Letters,* pp. 76–78; idem., *Mediterranean Society,* 1:50, 106, 103, 164–165.
31. Commenting on finding some JP writings among the Chinese Jews of K'aifeng as

late as the eighteenth century, Leslie notes, "Persian-speaking Muslims, Arabs and others, were going to China during the T'ang, both by sea and overland. During the Sung, trade was less, but certainly some foreigners were arriving by sea. At this time, Persian was a *lingua franca* of the foreigners in Central Asia, and in China. Persian was one of the languages taught at the Interpreters' College in Peking under the Mongols. It is not very surprising that we find various evidence of Persian spoken and written (in Hebrew script) by the K'aifeng Jews" (*Survival,* p. 118).

32. Cohen, *Under Crescent and Cross,* chap. 3.
33. On the legal position of the Jews in the Muslim world in general and on the Pact of ʿUmar in particular, see Cohen, *Under Crescent and Cross,* chap. 4.
34. See the remarkable careers of Shemu'el ha-Naggid (Samuel Ibn Nagrella; 993–1056) in Eliahu Ashtor, *The History of the Jews in Muslim Spain* (Philadelphia, 1979), 2:41ff., and Saʿd ad-Dawla, in Fischel, *Jews,* pp. 90–117.
35. Bar Hebraeus, *Chronicum Syriacum,* p. 490, f. 575, quoted in Fischel, *Jews,* p. 91n.1.
36. Fischel, *Jews,* pp. 118–125.
37. See Savory, *Iran,* pp. 175 and 187.
38. Ibid., p. 175.
39. See chap. 12, below, for Shāhīn's panegyric dedicated to Sultan Abū Saʿīd (r. 1316–1336) and Amīnā's panegyric in honor of the Afghan ruler Ashraf (d. 1730).
40. See Bausani, *Persians,* p. 130.
41. See Savory, *Iran,* esp. chap. 4.
42. See below, chap. 8.
43. See Benayahu, "Piyyutim," pp. 7–38; Scholem, *Sabbatai Ṣevi,* pp. 637, 640, 752–753.
44. See below, chap. 8.
45. See the discussion of this issue in Cohen, *Under Crescent and Cross,* chap. 10.
46. See Arjomand, *Shadow,* pts. II and III.
47. See Moreen, "*Risāla.*"
48. See Netzer, ed., *Yehude Iran,* p. 8.
49. The Jews of Mashhad recall their move to Mashhad in 1740 as Nādir Shah's recruitment of faithful guardians at the fortress of Qalʿat (about fifty miles north of Mashhad), where he had housed treasures he brought back from his campaigns in India (see Netzer, "Qorot anuse Mashhad," and Patai, *Jadīd al-Islām,* p. 26). On Nādir Shah's general attitude toward the Jews, see Bābāī b. Farhād's accounts in *Kitāb-i sar-guzasht* (below, chap. 12).
50. The name, perhaps derived from the cries of Muslim attackers, certainly represents the Muslim perspective of the event. It was probably adopted by the Jews ironically, in order to conceal their true feelings about what happened.
51. See the detailed account in Yehoshua-Raz, *Mi-nedaḥe Israel,* pt. II, chap. 3. On some of the customs of these *anusim,* see Tobi, "Ha-yahadut ha-iranit," pp. 235–237; Netzer, "Qorot yehude Mashhad," and Patai, *On Jewish Folklore,* pp. 195–275; idem., *Jadīd al-Islām,* chap. 4.
52. Netzer, *Yehude Iran,* p. 8; idem., "Ha-qehillah ha-yehudit," pp. 257–258.
53. See below, chap. 12.
54. On the Jews of Bukhārā, see Zand, *Encyclopaedia Judaica Year Book, 1975–76,* pp. 183–192; idem., *Encyclopaedia Iranica,* s.v., "Bukhārā"; Loewenthal, "Judeo-

Muslim Marranos," pp. 1–11; idem., "Juifs de Boukhara," pp. 104–108; Ben-Zvi, *Exiled,* pp. 54–82.

55. Rodrigue, *Images,* see Index under "Iran."
56. See Gilbert Lazard's summaries in *EJ,* s.v., "Judeo-Persian," and *EI* (2), s.v., "Judaeo-Persian: ii. Language."
57. See De Lagarde, "Persische Studien"; Lazard, *Langue,* pp. 31, 128–134.
58. See Geiger, "Bemerkungen," 1:408–412; Noeldeke, "Judaeo-Persica," pp. 548–553; Salemann, "Zum mittelpersischen Passiv," pp. 269–276.
59. For more detailed presentations, see Lazard, "Judaeo-Persian"; Paper, "Note on Judeo-Persian Copulas"; idem., "Judeo-Persian Deverbatives"; idem., "The Use of *(ha)mē*"; Asmussen, "Jüdisch-persisch *guyan* [gwy'n], Zelt"; Netzer, *Muntakhab,* pp. 64–70; Dick Davis, "Shāhīn, the Father of Judeo-Persian Poetry in the Persian Epic Tradition" (unpublished paper). I thank Professor Davis for sending me a copy of this article.
60. On the dialects of Iranian Jews, see Abrahamian, *Dialectologie iranienne;* Lazard, "Dialectologie du Judéo-Persan"; idem., "Dialecte des Juifs de Kerman"; idem., "Lumières nouvelles"; MacKenzie, "Jewish-Persian from Isfahan"; Sahim, "Dialect of the Jews of Hamadan"; idem., "Guyishhā-yi yahudiyān-i Irān"; Yarshater, "Jewish Communities of Persia"; idem., "Dialect of Borujerd Jews."
61. Paper, "Judeo-Persian," p. 107.
62. Yarsahter, "Hybrid Language," p. 5.
63. Much of this familiarity, however, especially with Persian poetry, need not have been acquired through the reading of texts because memorizing and reciting poetry have always been important elements of Persian culture.
64. Fischel, "Literary Heritage," p. 5.
65. Choksy, *Conflict and Cooperation,* pp. 100, 103.
66. Frye, *Golden Age,* pp. 173, 264n.49.
67. Several general surveys provide an outline of this literary tradition. See Bacher, "Judaeo-Persian Literature"; Fischel, "Israel in Iran"; idem., "Judeo-Persian Literature"; Rypka, *History,* pp. 737–740; Netzer, *Muntakhab,* pp. 17–71; idem., *Oṣar,* pp. 11–49. I shall concentrate on the contents of this anthology.
68. See, for example, Bābāī b. Nuriel's eighteenth-century introduction to his translation and commentary of the Book of Psalms in Grill, *Der achtundsechzigste Psalm,* pp. 223–227; Asmussen, "Judaeo-Persica IV"; Netzer, *Oṣar,* p. 17.
69. For example, Salomon b. Samuel's *Sefer ha-Meliṣa,* finished in 1339 (Fischel, "Israel in Iran," p. 1160), and the fifteenth-century Hebrew-Persian dictionary, *Agron* (Bacher, "Ein hebräisch-persisches Wörterbuch").
70. Fischel, "Judeo-Persian Literature"; on Daniel, see above, n. 25.
71. See the edition by Paper, *Targum ha-Torah;* idem., "Vatican Judeo-Persian Pentateuch: Genesis"; idem., "Vatican Judeo-Persian Pentateuch: Exodus and Leviticus"; idem., "Vatican Judeo-Persian Pentateuch: Deuteronomy"; idem., "Judeo-Persian Translations"; Asmussen, "Judaeo-Persica III"; Schwab, "Une version persane de la bible"; Guidi, "Di una versione persiana del Pentateuco."

    The best-known JP translation of the Pentateuch is that of Jacob b. Joseph Tāvūs (sixteenth century), whose work was included in the polyglot Bible printed in Constantinople in 1546 by Eleazar b. Gershon Soncino alongside the Hebrew text, the Aramaic Targum, and Saadiah Gaon's Arabic version. (See Kohut, *Kritische Beleuchtung;* Fischel, "Bible in Persian Translation.")

72. Bacher, "Ein persische Kommentar"; Asmussen, "Judaeo-Persica IV"; Asmussen and Paper, *Song of Songs;* Asmussen, "Eine jüdisch-persische Version"; Jakab, "Jezsájás könyvének"; Mainz, "Esther en judéo-persan"; idem., "Ruth et le Cantique des Cantiques"; idem., "Livre des Proverbes"; idem., "Livre de Daniel"; Paper, "Proverbs"; idem., "Judeo-Persian Book of Job."
73. See Netzer, *Muntakhab,* pp. 30–31; idem., *Oṣar,* pp. 2–23.
74. Davis, *Epic and Sedition,* p. xxii. This study is a wonderfully perceptive analysis of some of the major themes of the *Shah-nāmah.*
75. Shāhīn's work has survived in several manuscripts and came to be known among Iranian Jews as a *tafsīr* (Arabic for "commentary," "translation") of the Pentateuch; see below, chap. 2.
76. Moreen, "Moses, God's Shepherd"; idem., "Moses in Muhammad's Light."
77. Dan, *Ha-sippur ha-ʿivri,* pp. 20–23 and 133–136.
78. For a recent concise definition of what constitutes an epic, see the new edition of *The Princeton Encyclopedia of Poetry and Poetics,* ed. Alex Preminger and T. V. F. Brogan (Princeton, 1993), p. 361.
79. On the differences between the tragic and romantic forms of the Persian epic, see Amin Banani, "Ferdowsī and the Art of Tragic Epic," and J. C. Burgel, "The Romance," in *Persian Literature,* pp. 109–119 and 161–178, respectively.
80. See Davis, "Shāhīn," p. 3.
81. For a fuller analysis, see Moreen, "'Iranization' of Biblical Heroes."
82. See Moreen, "Legend of Adam"; idem., "Dialogue between God and Satan"; idem., *ʿIshmāʿīliyāt.*
83. On ʿImrānī's life and work, see Yeroushalmi, *Judeo-Persian Poet ʿEmrānī,* pp. 22–41.
84. The JNUL collection of JP manuscripts is especially rich in *derashot.*
85. See, for example, Goodman, *Purim Anthology,* pp. 87–92.
86. See Yerushalmi, *Zakhor.*
87. See Moshe Idel, *Kabalah: New Perspectives* (New Haven, 1988), Index under "Joseph of Hamadan" and his notes ad loc. Professor Idel informs me that more kabbalistic works of Iranian provenance exist in Hebrew.
88. See Netzer, *Oṣar,* pp. 23–25.
89. See Asani and Abdel-Malek, *Celebrating Muḥammad;* Schimmel, *And Muhammad Is His Messenger,* see Index under *naʿt.*
90. An early and unsurpassed example of these are the *munājāt* of the Sufi poet Khwājah ʿAbdullah Anṣārī (d. 1089); see *Ibn ʿAtāʾillah,* pp. 162–224.
91. There is no gender differentiation in Persian in the various pronouns, singular or plural, which leads to gender ambivalence in lyrical poems.
92. For a summary of the history and nature of Persian lyrical poetry, see Heshmat Moayyad, "Lyric Poetry," in *Persian Literature,* pp. 120–146.
93. See the numerous works listed and described in Yaari, "Sifre yehude Bukhārā."
94. See Fischel, "Israel in Iran," pp. 1180–1182. Hakam's unannotated editions are not critical (enough) by modern standards.

95. See Levin's *Hundred Thousand Fools of God.*
96. See Ṭal, *Nusaḥ ha-tefillah.*
97. See, for example, Gutmann, "Judeo-Persian Miniatures"; Moreen, *Miniature Paintings;* Rosen-Ayalon, "Judeo-Persian Amulet"; Sabar, "Decorated Marriage Contract"; Yaniv, "Muʿammā-yi guldastehā-yi towrāt."

Chapter 1 Earliest Judeo-Persian Texts

1. See Lazard, *Langue,* pp. 31–36. In addition to these, there are many fragments from the eleventh century and later that are preserved in the Genizah Collection at Cambridge University (see Netzer, *Oṣar,* pp. 12–13).
2. Henning dated these as early as 752–53 ("The Inscriptions of Tang-i Azao"), but Rapp's redating to 1300 appears to be more persuasive ("Date of the Judaeo-Persian Inscriptions"; idem., *Jüdisch-persisch-hebräischen Inschriften*).
3. See below, n. 7.
4. See Minorsky, "Some Early Documents in Persian (I)," *JRAS* (1942): 183; W. B. Henning, "Mitteliranisch," in B. Spuler, ed., *Handbuch der orientalistik I,* Abt., Bd., *Iranistik,* I (Leiden, 1958), p. 51.
5. See Asmussen, "Judaeo-Persica II: The Jewish-Persian Law Report," which provides a full transliteration of the text.
6. Salemann, "Zum mittelpersischen Passiv," pp. 269ff.
7. Utas, "Jewish-Persian Fragment," which includes a facsimile reproduction, transcription, and annotation of the text, and a detailed bibliography. The quotation is on p. 125. The description that follows is based on this study.
8. See Shaul Shaked, "Judaeo-Persian Notes," *IOS* 1 (1971): 182n.25; ʿA. A. Sādiqī, *Taqvīn-i zabān-i fārisī* (Tehran, 1357 solar), pp. 77–81; Lazard, "Remarques sur le fragment."
9. "A Jewish-Persian Law Report."

A Letter from a Merchant

1. In this selection, italicized words are Professor Utas' reconstructions, bracketed material represents reasonable transitions and conjunctions, words in parentheses are wholly conjectural, asterisks are reconstructions of proper names, and bracketed numbers refer to line numbers of the document.

Chapter 2 Biblical Epics

Introduction to Shāhīn

1. See below, chap. 12.
2. Because "Shāhīn" is a common Persian name, Bacher inclines to the former (*Zwei jüdisch-persische Dichter,* pp. 7–8), whereas modern scholars incline to the latter view (Netzer, *Oṣar,* p. 27).
3. *Kitāb-i anusī* ("The book of a forced convert"; see chap. 8). We still do not have a scholarly edition of this chronicle, but see the introductory chapters.
4. See *Sefer sharh-i Shāhīn,* ed. Hakam, Hebrew Introduction to *Bereshit-nāmah.*
5. This last work has practically no connection with the biblical book.
6. See the Introduction and chap. 6.

7. This edition is inadequate by modern standards. A new edition based on all available mss. is imperative for the study of Shāhīn's epics.
8. See Bacher, *Zwei jüdisch-persische Dichter*, p. 8; Blieske, *Šāhīn-e Šīrāzī*, p. 5; Netzer, *Oṣar*, p. 28. Netzer, *Muntakhab*, p. 37, gives the erroneous date of 1317. A short and comprehensive chronology of Shāhīn (and 'Imrānī's) works is presented in Netzer, "Judeo-Persian Footnote."
9. See Schimmel, *A Two-Colored Brocade*, p. 32.
10. See Bacher, *Zwei jüdisch-persische Dichter*, pp. 9 and 35ff.; Blieske, *Šāhīn-e Šīrāzī*, p. 8; Netzer, *Muntakhab*, p. 39; idem., *Oṣar*, p. 29.
11. The most famous of these in Persian literature is 'Abdū'r-Raḥmān Jāmī's (d. 1492) *Yūsuf and Zulaykhā*. For an exploration of this theme in various literatures, see John D. Yohannan, *Joseph and Potiphar's Wife in World Literature* (New York, 1968).

    Bacher names Firdowsī's *Yūsuf and Zulaykhā* as one of Shāhīn's influential Muslim sources (*Zwei jüdisch-persische Dichter*, pp. 117–124). However, recent scholarship has determined that Firdowsī did not write the work in question. The poem was written by a poet from Khurasan known as Amānī around 1083 (Rypka, *History*, pp. 157–158).
12. See below, chap. 9.
13. See the Introduction and Moreen, "Moses in Muḥammad's Light."
14. Bacher, *Zwei jüdisch-persische Dichter*, pp. 28 and 37.
15. See ibid., pp. 9 and 43–66; Blieske, *Šāhīn-e Šīrāzī*, pp. 5–6; Netzer, *Muntakhab*, pp. 38–39; idem., *Oṣar*, pp. 28–29. See also Asmussen, "Judaeo-Persica I: Šāhīn-e Šīrāzī."
16. *Hazaj-i musaddas-i akhrab-i maqbūż-i maḥzūf*; Blieske, *Šāhīn-e Šīrāzī*, p. 5.
17. See below, *Ardashīr-nāmah*, n. 3.
18. See below, *Ardashīr-nāmah*, n. 50. For Shāhīn's conceptualization of AN, see Moreen, "'Iranization' of Biblical Heroes."
19. See Bacher, *Zwei jüdisch-persische Dichter*, pp. 9, 66–71; Blieske, *Šāhīn-e Šīrāzī*, pp. 7–8; Netzer, *Muntakhab*, pp. 38–39; idem., *Oṣar*, pp. 28–29.
20. See *Ezra-nāmah*, vv. 105ff.
21. I have not retained the Arabic forms in the translations in order to emphasize the fact that these narratives are about well-known biblical figures.
22. See Schimmel, *Two-Colored Brocade*, pp. 37–52. The classic work on Persian rhetoric is Joseph Garcin de Tassy, *Rhétorique et prosodie des langues de l'orient musulman* (Paris, 1873; repr. 1970).
23. See Bacher, *Zwei jüdisch-persische Dichter*, pp. 16nn.2,3,16, and pp. 157–165.
24. See Lazarus-Yafeh, *Intertwined Worlds*, pp. 117 and 121.
25. See Moreen, "Moses, God's Shepherd," pp. 122ff.
26. See Bacher, *Zwei jüdisch-persische Dichter*, p. 41.
27. Bacher posits the intriguing possibility that Shāhīn wrote his epics originally in the Persian script but cannot adduce serious proof for his statement (*Zwei jüdisch-persische Dicther*, p. 74). Most of the available manuscripts contain numerous errors of scansion, implying perhaps different manuscript traditions or even, if Bacher is correct, the possibility that errors crept in through the process of transcription from the Persian into the Hebrew alphabet. Scholarly editions of Shāhīn's epics would help resolve these questions.

Bereshit-nāmah

The Fall of ʿAza'zel

1. This translation is based on [*Bereshit-nāmah*], ed. Ḥakam, pp. 5a–7b, BZI 978, fols. 4v–7r, IV C 43 (unfoliated), and SS Ebp. i. c. 150 (unfoliated). In this episode Shāhīn alternates between the names "ʿAza'zel," "Shayṭān," and "Iblīs," which I retain in the translation to convey Shāhīn's usage. The name "ʿAza'zel" is based on the controversial meaning of Lev. 16:8–10, but Shāhīn uses it primarily in its Muslim connotations. Although this name is not in the Qur'ān, Muslim tradition associates ʿAza'zel with the fallen angels of the Apocrypha, ʿUzza and ʿAza'el, known as Hārūt and Mārūt in Islamic lore (*EI* [2], 1:811, s.v., "ʿAza'zīl"). Some *ḥadīth* (traditions relating to the deeds and utterances of Muḥammad) sources connect ʿAza'zel with the qur'anic Iblīs (Gk. *diabolos*), or Shayṭān (Satan), as does Shāhīn in this episode. For Iblīs, see *EI* (2), s.v., "Iblīs." For a fuller discussion of this entire episode, see Moreen, "Dialogue Between God and Satan"; idem., "Legend of Adam."
2. On the Sufi claim that Satan was the teacher of the angels, see Schimmel, *Mystical Dimensions,* p. 193.
3. Shāhīn derides Satan's useless "capital of obedience" in accordance with the Muslim, especially Sufi, view that tends to blame Satan for his excessive and prideful obedience. See Awn, *Satan's Tragedy and Redemption,* Index, under "Obedience."
4. Here God's celestial court resembles the unpredictable court of an oriental monarch.
5. *Haẓrat-i shāh-bāzī,* lit., "His Excellence the Royal Falcon," is a fairly common Sufi epithet for God.
6. This scene takes place in front of Adam's body, before God endows it with a living soul.
7. Shāhīn appears to have in mind the Jewish idea of commandments, which differs from the Muslim concept in general and from the Sufi concept in particular (*EI* [2], s.v. "'amr," and Chittick, *Sufi Path of Knowledge,* Index under "'amr"). In the rabbinic view and according to such medieval philosophers as Maimonides, the divine commandments, derived and amplified from the Pentateuch through the Oral Law, are regarded as vehicles to shape and elevate human nature rather than as burdens imposed upon it. See Solomon Schechter, "The Joy of the Law," in *Aspects of Rabbinic Theology: Major Concepts of the Talmud* (New York, 1961; repr. of 1909); Urbach, *Sages,* chap. 12; Maimonides, *Guide,* III:27, 31, 35; idem., "Eight Chapters," in I. Twersky, *A Maimonides Reader* (New York, 1972), pp. 372–374.
8. The deep bow is, once again, reminiscent of a gesture of obeisance at the courts of oriental monarchs.
9. See above, n. 3. This and the previous hemistich are not in BZI 978. The Sufi view of Satan's reprehensible act, namely his "reminding" God of his own merits, dovetails here neatly with the Jewish view that also frowns upon the performance of the commandments for the sake of reward. See the references in n. 7.
10. Pers., *aṣl-o vaṣlat; aṣl va-farʿ* (Ḥakam ed.), Arabic for "root," "origin," "source" and "branch," "derivative," are technical terms in Islamic jurisprudence. Ḥakam's choice has the advantage of suggesting that God cuts Satan off sharply by expressing His lack of interest in Satan's legal exposition.
11. See Moreen, "Dialogue Between God and Satan," p. 137. There is a complex Sufi idea embedded in this verse that in Islamic mystical theology is connected with the

concept of Muhammad's light (*nūr al-Muḥammad*): "Adam, as Muḥammad's primogenitor, was the first to have the substantial blaze [of light] on his forehead. . . . Early Muslim sources are already familiar with the view that Adam and Eve were clad in 'clothes of light' in paradise" (Uri Rubin, "Pre-existence and Light: Aspects of *Nūr Muḥammad*," *IOS* 5 [1975]: 96). Although the Sufi veneer of the entire episode suggests that it may form Shāhīn's primary frame of reference, he may easily have received the idea of the special divine light associated with Adam's countenance from Jewish sources (Ginzberg, *Legends*, 5:78, 112–113), which may actually have influenced the Islamic concept in the first place (Moreen, "Moses in Muḥammad's Light," pp. 191–193).

12. These are the four basic elements of Aristotelian physics, which God proceeds to extol (Nasr, *Introduction*, pp. 61–62).
13. Despite the problem of Satan's attitude toward God in this episode, his staunch devotion earned him the admiration of many Sufis, who saw in his refusal to compromise his love for God a sign of his genuine, uncompromising monotheism (Awn, *Satan's Tragedy*, pp. 169–172, and Index under "Monotheist").
14. This hemistich is missing in the Ḥakam edition.
15. Revealing his deviant nature, Satan resorts to "blackmailing" God, demanding recompense for his "debt" of serving God. In a Sufi vein, again, God appears to grant Satan's wish so as not to appear unjust, but He does so for His own reasons, namely, to provide man with spiritual tests. Satan's reproach echoes here a rabbinic expression uttered in an altogether different context, "zu Torah ve zu sekara" (so this is the reward for [the devotion to] the Torah!) (*Babylonian Talmud*, Menaḥot 29; see also the "Ten Martyrs," of n. 20, below). The translation is Judah Goldin's in his "The Death of Moses: An Exercise in Midrashic Transposition," in John Marks and Robert Good, eds., *Love and Death in the Ancient Near East* (Guilford, Conn., 1987), reprinted now in Goldin's *Studies in Midrash and Related Literature* (Philadelphia, 1988), pp. 175–186.
16. The idea of Satan hindering yet not having ultimate power over saints and pious men, present in Jewish sources (Ginzberg, *Legends*, 2:3), is further developed in Islamic legendary lore. As I have shown elsewhere ("Dialogue Between God and Satan," pp. 135ff.), Shāhīn is particularly indebted to the eleventh-century Persian *qiṣaṣ* collection of Abū Isḥāq b. Ibrāhīm b. Manṣūr b. Khalaf al-Nīsābūrī, *Dāstānhā-yi payghambarān* (Tehran, 1961). In his tales, al-Nīsābūrī develops fully the idea of God's ultimate protection of the pious (pp. 10–15). In the Islamic mystical tradition, Satan's stumbling blocks are, of course, the prophets (and, for the Shiʿis, the imams), their descendants, and, especially, the Sufi masters (Awn, *Satan's Tragedy*, pp. 109–121; Chittick, *Sufi Path of Love*, pp. 119–147).
17. Pers., *ḥāl*, a Sufi technical term that denotes a transitory state of mystical illumination (Schimmel, *Mystical Dimensions*, pp. 99ff.).
18. The idea of Satan enticing pious men away from higher spiritual goals and even appearing in the guise of a pious shaykh is well known in Sufi literature (Awn, *Satan's Tragedy*, pp. 79–90). Man's "evil inclination" is often personified as Satan in rabbinic literature (Urbach, *Sages*, pp. 472–483).
19. The Ḥakam edition contrasts *ziyān* (loss) and *sūd* (profit), in place of *gunāh* (sin) and *khūb* (good). In Sufi literature the concepts of profit and loss are earthly meta-

phors for spiritual states (Chittick, *Sufi Path of Love,* Index, under "Profit" and "Loss").

20. Here, again, although similar rabbinic ideas—love to the point of martyrdom—are not difficult to find (e.g., the famous tale of the "Ten Martyrs," the martyrdom of Jewish sages at the hands of the Romans to atone for their ancestors' sin of kidnapping and selling Joseph, immortalized in the "Musaf Service for Yom Kippur" [*High Holiday Prayer Book,* trans. Philip Birnbaum (New York, 1987, pp. 838–844)]), Shāhīn's statement strikes me as primarily Sufi in character. Jewish and Muslim spiritual teachings agree that God tries most those whom He loves best, and His elect, in turn, rejoice in the suffering—even to the point of martyrdom—that represents the summit of this love. (Schimmel, *Mystical Dimensions,* pp. 135–137).
21. See above, n. 11.
22. See Moreen, "Legend of Adam," pp. 166–167nn.23–28. See also Rūmī's verses in the *Masnavī:* "The father of mankind, who is the lord of *He taught the names* [Surah 2:31], has hundreds of thousands of sciences in every vein. / His spirit was taught the name of every single thing, exactly as that thing is until its end" (Chittick, *Sufi Path of Love,* p. 62).
23. See Moreen, "Legend of Adam," pp. 167–168nn.29–31.
24. See ibid.
25. Cf. Gen. 1:28–30. The idea that God created everything for man's sake, although not clearly expressed in the Qur'ān, is also found in the *ḥadīth qudsī* (a divine message not recorded in the Qur'ān), "I have created everything for you" (Schimmel, *Mystical Dimensions,* p. 189).
26. See above, n. 17, although this word can also mean simply "(present) condition, state" in a nonreligious sense.

Jacob and the Wolf

1. This translation is based on BZI 978, fols. 126r–132v, and JTS 8623, fols. 77r–85r. See also BZI 1093 and BZI 4569.
2. Midrashic sources point out that the blood of a kid was used "because its blood looks like human blood" (Ginzberg, *Legends,* 2:25, 5:331n.62). Of course, "there is a touch of subtle irony here since years before, a kid and the garment of his brother had played key roles in Jacob's deception of his father, as told in [Gen.] 27:9, 15, 16. Now his own sons deceive him through the instrumentality of a kid and their brother's garment" (*The JPS Torah Commentary: Genesis,* trans. Nahum M. Sarna [Philadelphia, 1989], p. 262).

   Shāhīn's Persian word for "kid," *buzghāle,* can be found in al-Nīsābūrī (*Dāstānhā,* p. 88). Interestingly, although al-Nīsābūrī is likely the source of many of Shāhīn's Muslim interpolations (see the bibliography, Moreen, "Moses, God's Shepherd"; idem., "Legend of Adam"; idem., "Dialogue Between God and Satan"), he does not include the scene of Jacob's confrontation with the wolf.
3. According to the *qiṣaṣ* version of al-Thaʿlabī (d. 1036), Jacob had a disturbing premonition and was anxiously awaiting his sons in the middle of the road (*ʿArāʾis,* p. 114).
4. This verse could mean "His place is not here" (i.e., he is not here with you) or, in a more hyperbolic fashion, it could show Jacob expressing his extreme love by suggesting that Joseph is a heavenly being who does not belong on earth.

5. Pers., *shāh-i khūbān,* a poetic cliché suggesting supreme physical beauty.
6. The brothers' hypocrisy is especially glaring here because the main reason for their resentment of Joseph, both in the Torah (Gen. 37) and in the Qur'ān (Surah 12:4ff.), is the latter's dreams, which imply dominion over his parents and brethren. Shāhīn inverts the brothers' feelings as these are spelled out in al-Nīsābūrī, "Is it right that we should be inferior to you and you superior to us?" (*Dāstānhā,* p. 87).
7. Cf. Gen. 37:33, where the beast is not identified. Ginzberg (*Legends,* 2:28) identifies it as a wolf, based on *Sefer ha-yashar,* Wa-Yeshev, 85a–85b. The absence of the scene between Jacob and the wolf in midrashic sources leads one to suspect that it entered *Sefer ha-yashar,* a thirteenth-century ethical work, via Muslim sources. Ginzberg suggests this to be the case based on the fact that "in genuinely Jewish legends animals do not talk" (!) (*Legends,* 5:332n.66). In the Qur'ān (Surah 12:13) and in *qiṣaṣ* compilations, as well as in al-Ṭabarī (*The History of al-Ṭabarī,* trans. William M. Brinner [Albany, 1987], 2:151), the beast is identified as *dhi'b,* which means both "jackal" and "wolf." English translators of the Qur'ān prefer "wolf" (see Pickthall, Arberry, and Ali, *ad loc.*). Al-Nīsābūrī uses the unambiguous Persian word *gurg* (wolf) (*Dāstānhā,* p. 86). However, in Knappert's translation of a Swahili account of the Joseph legends, the animal is identified as a jackal (*Islamic Legends,* pp. 89–90).
8. In midrashim the brothers claim, "He came to us not at all. Since we left thee, we have not set eyes on him" (Ginzberg, *Legends,* 2:26), but in the Qur'ān we find, "O our father! We went racing with one another, and left Joseph by our things, and the wolf devoured him" (Sura 2:17; all the *qiṣaṣ* compilations echo the qur'anic verse).
9. A common cliché in classical Persian poetry, referring to the famed beauties of "Chīn[a]" (usually intending Central Asia) and "Rūm," Anatolia, the Byzantine Empire.
10. See al-Thaʿlabī, *ʿArā'is,* p. 115, al-Kisā'ī, *Tales,* p. 170.
11. Jacob's heartfelt lament is fairly long in Ginzberg (*Legends,* 2:26–27), but the qiṣaṣ refer to it only briefly (see n. 10 above, and al-Nīsābūrī, *Dāstānhā,* p. 89). None of these compare with Shāhīn's dirge. Although filled with Persian poetic clichés, the combined effect is moving, even if it reinforces Robert Alter's characterization of Jacob's grief as "histrionic": "Jacob speaks as a prima donna of paternal grief" (*Genesis,* trans. and comment. Robert Alter [New York, 1996], pp. 214, 250).

    It is interesting to note that Jacob's lament has become a prototype for dirges sung at Jewish funerals in Bukhārā, where a dirge called *Yūsuf-i jān-i pidar* (Joseph, [your] father's soul) is still remembered (Elena Reikher, "The Folk Songs of Bukhārān Jews," a paper delivered at "Irano-Judaica: Fourth International Conference," Jerusalem, 1998).
12. Pers., *zandān* (jail) hinting at Joseph's future imprisonment through Jacob's now-turbulent prophetic powers.
13. Pers., *jām-i jahl,* an alliterated expression I was unable to convey in my translation. Persian readers would at once juxtapose it with *jām-i jam(shīd),* the cup of the prehistoric Iranian king Jamshīd (later also of Solomon and Alexander), through which Joseph divined the future. It was immortalized in Ḥāfiẓ's poetry; see A. J. Arberry, *Ḥāfiẓ: Fifty Poems* (Cambridge, 1970), p. 129.
14. Pers./Ar., *qażā* (fate, destiny), a favorite villain of Persian poetry, probably derived from the pre-Islamic Arab concept *dahr* (W. Montgomery Watt, *EI* [2], s.v., "*dahr*").

Pers./Ar., *zamān,* (time), and Pers./Ar., qażā (fate), are inimical to monotheist Muslims who are careful to avoid the pitfalls of theodicy.

15. According to al-Thaʿlabī, Jacob smelled the tunic and rubbed it over his eyes and heart (*ʿArāʾis,* p. 115); in the Swahili account "he rubbed the *kanzu* [long cotton garment] with its stains across his heart" (Knappert, *Islamic Legends,* p. 88), and in al-Nīsābūrī, he placed it on his face and cried until he went blind (*Dāstānhā,* p. 89). Despite the clichés that follow in Shāhīn's version, Jacob's direct address to the garment is most dramatic.
16. Pers., *zībā tamīzam,* suggesting that Joseph was the standard of beauty by which all others were judged.
17. Another poetic instance of Jacob's prophetic insight.
18. The English pun "sun/son" is not found in the Persian *khurshidam* (my sun)/*farzandam* (my son).
19. See Ginzberg, *Legends,* 2:26.
20. Literally, "the men and women of the town."
21. See above, n. 15.
22. See Ginzberg, *Legends,* 2:27. In the Muslim sources the brothers show no remorse.
23. Cf. Gen. 4:10.
24. Pers., *tāzī* (Arab); imputing wiliness to Turks and Arabs is a cliché in Persian poetry.
25. Unlike in Gen. 37:12, where it is Jacob who sends Joseph to his brothers, in the Qurʾān (Surah 12:13) and in the qiṣaṣ Jacob is reluctant to allow Joseph to accompany his brothers to the pastures. He expresses his fear in premonitory fashion ("I fear lest the wolf devour him while you are heedless of him"), appearing to "plant" the idea of the wolf into the minds of his less imaginative sons; in Genesis it is the other way around ("We can say, A savage beast devoured him" [37:20]). Similarly, in the Genesis account and in midrashim, Jacob does not express his suspicion of his sons' foul play. However, in the Qurʾān, he voices his misgivings as soon as the tunic is shown to him ("Nay, but your minds have beguiled you into something" [Surah 12:18]).
26. It seems more appropriate to read this verse as a question, rather than a statement.
27. See al-Thaʿlabī, *ʿArāʾis,* p. 115.
28. These commonsense ponderings belong to Shāhīn, who does not wish his readers to assume even for a moment that the patriarch and prophet Jacob could really be deceived by his sons.
29. This is the description of a typical Persian meadow, also appropriate for vicinity of Shekem, which "is blessed with an adequate water supply and fertile soil" (*Genesis,* trans. Sarna, p. 258).
30. Joseph's unwillingness to join his brothers' games suggests that there was something unseemly about their behavior, just as their hatred of him may have been due not only to his dreams but to Joseph's report to their father about their conduct (Ginzberg, *Legends,* 2:5, 5:326n.8).
31. See above, n. 14.
32. We are not told how the brothers came to this instant conclusion even before they "found" the tunic.
33. See the comments of Rashi and Ibn Ezra at Gen. 37:32.
34. Cf. Gen. 37:31. Jacob's response in the Qurʾān is less extreme: "(My course is)

comely patience. And Allah it is Whose help is to be sought in that (predicament) which ye describe" (Surah 12:18).

35. According to Ginzberg, Jacob ordered his sons to go into the fields to look for Joseph's body, and to "keep a lookout . . . for beasts of prey, and catch the first you meet" (*Legends*, 2:28). In Shāhīn's account the sons fulfill only the second half of the request. In the qiṣaṣ, Jacob orders his sons to find the wolf (al-Kisā'ī, *Tales*, p. 171, al-Tha'labī, *'Arā'is*, p. 115).
36. Pers., *delīrān*, intended, I believe, ironically.
37. See above, n. 13. The epithet is a supreme compliment, often bestowed on heroes in Persian epics. King Jamshīd (Yīmā) is celebrated in Persian mythology as the ruler who organized mankind into various social classes, established the crafts, and reigned over a fully civilized world (Hinnells, *Persian Mythology*, pp. 113–114).
38. In al-Tha'labī, Jacob orders the removal of the ropes with which the wolf is tied (*'Arā'is*, pp. 115–116).
39. "But God caused the wolf to speak" (al-Kisā'ī, *Tales*, p. 171.
40. See above, n. 14.
41. A reference to the seven (planetary) heavens and the abode of fixed stars. Muslim astronomy, following ancient Babylonian, Persian, and Jewish concepts, envisions the universe as consisting of nine spheres, the seven spheres of the planets that are visible to the eye, the fixed stars, and the empyrean or encompassing sphere (Nasr, *Introduction*, pts. I and II).
42. A place in Turkestan reputed for its beautiful men and women.
43. Contrast this soliloquy with al-Tha'labī's terse, "O wolf, you ate my son, the delight of my eye, the beloved fruit of my heart, and caused me to inherit prolonged sorrow and great pain" (*'Arā'is*, p. 119).
44. See ibid.; al-Kisā'ī, *Tales*, p. 171.
45. I was unable to convey in English the pun in this hemistich based on the Persian homonyms *māh*/*māhī* (moon/fish).
46. Cf. Ar., *'alim al-ghayb wa-l shahāda*, "Knower of the invisible and the visible" (Surah 6:73).
47. See above, n. 33.
48. A common Persian epithet for epic heroes, and, in Islam, especially connected with 'Alī.
49. Pers./Ar., *[al-] Shām;* al-Kisā'ī (*Tales*, p. 171) and al-Tha'labī (*'Arā'is*, p. 119), claim that the wolf came from Egypt.
50. Al-Kisā'ī (*Tales*, p. 171) also has the wolf looking for his cub, but al-Tha'labī (*'Arā'is*, p. 119) has him going to visit relatives in Canaan!
51. I am uncertain about the meaning of this hemistich.
52. The wording here is almost verbatim that of Surah 12:18 (see above, n. 34).
53. Cf. Gen. 37:35, "No, I will go down mourning to my son in Sheol."
54. Jacob's grief echoes Joseph's agony in the well.

Mūsā-nāmah

Moses and the Burning Bush

1. This excerpt is based on Exod. 3 and 4; Surah 20:9–47. This translation is based on *Mūsā-nāmah* (Shemot), ed. Ḥakam, pp. 53a–54b and BZI 978, fols. 206v–208r.

As noted before, throughout his epics Shāhīn uses the Arabic names of biblical characters, i.e., "Mūsā" for Moses, "ʿAyyūb" for Job, etc. Occasionally he refers to characters by their qur'anic epithets, i.e., "Khalīl" (God's friend; Surah 4:125) for Abraham, and, as in the present title, "Kalīm Allah" (God's interlocutor; Surah 4:164) for Moses. In most of the translations I employ the biblical nomenclature except when I wish to emphasize either the appropriateness of the qur'anic epithet or, as in the tale of Korah's (Qārūn's) rebellion (see below), the correspondence between the biblical and qur'anic tales and Shāhīn's indebtedness to the latter.

2. A word derived from the Sanscrit *deva* (bright heavenly one) and referring to the nature of Vedic gods. In Zoroastrianism, devas became *daevas* (demons), allied with Angra Mainyu, or Ahriman, the evil deity in mortal struggle with the benevolent god Ohrmazd, or Ahura Mazda. The Indo-European words *deus* (Latin for "god") and *theos* (Greek for "god") also derive from this root (Hinnels, *Persian Mythology,* pp. 42ff.).
3. This foreboding description of night owes a great deal to Firdowsī's description at the opening of the Bīzhan and Manīzhe narrative (*Shāh-nāmah* [Bombay, 1849, 1–2:399]). I thank Dick Davis for drawing my attention to the similarity. However, it may be that at its basis lies the claim of several *qiṣaṣ* compilers that Moses found himself in the desert on a dark, cold, and wintry night, filled with rain and lightning (al-Kisāʾī, *Tales,* p. 224, al-Ṭabarī; *History,* 3:48; al-Thaʿlabī, *ʿArāʾis,* p. 178; al-Nīsābūrī, *Dāstānhā,* p. 159). Unlike them, Shāhīn does not connect the incident that follows with Moses' return from Midian to Egypt in the company of his family (Surah 28:29), after having fulfilled his father-in-law's terms of service (28:28). In al-Kisāʾī's *Tales,* Moses reassures Jethro (called Shuʿayb in Muslim tradition) that he is no longer needed as a shepherd because, "I have made a pact with the wolves and lions that they cause no harm; and I have made this ram with the horns the shepherd" (p. 223)!
4. Moses' solicitude for his flock convinces God that he is to be trusted with leading the Israelites, God's human flock (Ginzberg, *Legends,* 2:300–302, 5:414n.109; Moreen, "Moses, God's Shepherd"). The specific incident between Moses and the kid comes from *Midrash Rabbah,* Shemot, where it is not a direct precursor of the theophany.
5. See al-Ṭabarī, *History,* 3:48; al-Thaʿlabī, *ʿArāʾis,* p. 178; al-Nīsābūrī, *Dāstānhā,* p. 159.
6. "Toward the light," *Mūsā-nāmah,* ed. Ḥakam. Following the Qurʾān (Surah 28:29), all the qiṣaṣ collections maintain that Moses drew near in order to obtain fire with which to kindle his family's fire at the encampment.
7. Cf. BZI 978: "Why are you . . ."
8. Pers., *sar mast o bī-khwish* (intoxicated and beside oneself), is a common phrase in Sufi poetry describing the state of the disciple who achieves union with the Divine Beloved, i.e.: "The dervishes are kings, all of them selfless in intoxication. / Though made of dust, they are shahs and sultans" (from Rūmī's *Diwan,* cited in Chittick's *Sufi Path of Love,* p. 190).
9. "*Ān nūrast ke dīdī nār nīst*" ("what you saw is light [*nūr*] not fire [*nār*]" [al-Nīsābūrī, *Dāstānhā,* p. 159]).
10. Ar., *labayka* (Here am I [God]), part of the *talbīyah,* is the constant recitation of Muslims performing the ḥajj to Mecca, said to have been uttered by the first pilgrim, Abraham. It corresponds to the Hebrew *hinneni.*

11. See above, n. 5. Shāhīn describes Moses' first encounter with God in mystical Sufi terminology.
12. The name of Moses' father, ʿAmram, in Muslim lore.
13. Cf. BZI 978: "Hasten toward Eygpt like an arrow."
14. Instead of the next fourteen hemistichs, BZI 978 has only three: "Carry my message to the accursed Pharaoh, say: / 'O unlucky, accursed infidel, / Let Jacob's offspring leave your realm, / For God's perfect command has come.' / That luminary of earth's pedestal, Kalīm Allah." BZI 978 omits the entire description of the Land of Israel. I am somewhat inclined to believe that Shimʿon Ḥakam, a former Bukhārān and an enthusiastic emigrant to Jerusalem (see below, chap. 6), composed these verses himself. In order to be certain of this, all manuscripts of Shāhīn's *Sharḥ* ought to be consulted. I chose to include the verses because in my view they enhance the narrative.
15. Cf. Deut. 31:20.
16. "Those who believe and do right: Joy is for them, and bliss (*ṭūbā*) (their) journey's end" (Surah 13:29), usually interpreted by Muslim commentators as referring to a unique tree in Paradise.
17. Ar./Pers., *kāfir* (he who conceals [refuses to see the truth] by covering), and, by extension, an "infidel," a pejorative reference to non-Muslims in general and animists in particular. This term appears frequently in classical Persian, especially Sufi, poetry.
18. Pers., *gebr,* a derogatory term for a Zoroastrian ("fire worshiper") and another pejorative designation for non-Muslims.
19. *Mūsā-nāmah,* ed. Ḥakam: "And scattered sugar from his ruby lips."
20. Cf. "Did you not say it was your [staff]? Why do you flee from something that is your own? People don't fear or flee from their own objects!" (al-Nīsābūrī, *Dāstānhā,* p. 161).
21. See above, "Jacob and the Wolf," n. 14; here, this is a strange "dualistic" allusion coming from God.
22. Ar./Pers., *murīd,* a Sufi disciple.
23. See Ginzberg, *Legends,* 2:316; al-Thaʿlabī repeats the Jewish midrashic claim and says that for (unspecified) allegorists (*ahl al-ishārat*) the shoes that Moses is commanded to remove allude to women, that is, to carnal passions (*al-naʿl ʿibārat ʿan al-marʾāt; ʿArāʾis,* p. 179).
24. Lit., "the prophet stood before the Lord," in prayer. See God's lengthy instructions in al-Thaʿlabī, *ʿArāʾis,* p. 180.
25. See above, n. 11.
26. For a discussion of Shāhīn's intimation that the relationship between Moses and Jethro resembles that between a Sufi master and disciple, see Moreen, "Moses, God's Shepherd," pp. 120–121.

Moses' Vision of God

1. This excerpt is a conflation of Exod. 33:18–21, 34:10–11, and 19:10–12. See also Surah 7:143, Ginzberg, *Legends,* 3:137; *Pirqe de-Rabbi Eliezer,* pp. 364–365; al-Thaʿlabī, *ʿArāʾis,* pp. 200–203. My translation is based on *Mūsā-nāmah,* ed. Ḥakam, pp. 156b–157b, and BZI 978, fols. 263r–264r.
2. These first four hemistichs are not in BZI 978.

3. Joshua's mission is not mentioned in any Jewish or Muslim sources.
4. The exception of Aaron is missing from all the sources I consulted.
5. This hemistich is missing in BZI 978.
6. "High mountain made of emerald": hence the emerald tablets hewn from it (al-Kisāʾī, *Tales*, p. 235).
7. This hemistich changes suddenly to the second person plural in BZI 978.
8. This is a typical Sufi statement. Shāhīn's description of Moses' theophanic experience relies considerably on the brief qur'anic account (see n. 1) and on Sufi inspiration.
9. Cf. "And when his Lord revealed (His) glory to the mountain He sent it crashing down" (Surah 7:143); see also al-Thaʿlabī, *ʿArāʾis*, p. 201.
10. According to Sufi interpretations, Muḥammad achieved an even higher state of communion with the divine during his *miʿrāj* (ascension). He is supposed to have attained this state while fully conscious, as opposed to Moses, who, although he spoke with God "face to face" (Exod. 33:11), swooned during his encounter ("And Moses fell down senseless," Surah 7:143); see Moreen, "Moses in Muḥammad's Light," pp. 198–199. On the other hand, losing consciousness ("passing away from one's [sense of] self"), as Shāhīn describes it here, is part of the Sufi's experience of *fanāʾ* (annihilation) (Sells, *Early Islamic Mysticism*, Index), under "Annihilation (*fanāʾ*)," the quintessential (Sufi) mystical experience.
11. This hemistich is missing in BZI 978.
12. Cf. Exod. 33:2ff.
13. Cf. Gen. 10:16ff.
14. This chapter has five more verses in BZI 978 consisting of Shāhīn's personal prayer.

The Killing of the Blasphemer

1. See Lev. 24:10–14. The translation is based on *Mūsā-nāmah*, ed. Ḥakam, pp. 11b–12b, and BZI 978, fols. 271r–272r.
2. In midrashic sources the reason for the enmity is not merely a quarrel between two men. The blasphemer is not only of "unclean" Egyptian stock, he is also the illegitimate son of the Jewish woman raped by the Egyptian whom Moses killed (Exod. 2:11). For further midrashic elaborations, see Ginzberg, *Legends*, 3:239–240, and 6:84n.451.
3. The only Jewish source giving the father's name that I am aware of is the fourteenth-century Persian midrash *Sefer pitron ha-torah*, where he is called "Hapishtokh" (p. 95).

Qārūn's Rebellion

1. Cf. Num. 16; Surah 28:76–82. This translation is based on *Mūsā-nāmah*, ed. Ḥakam, pp. 43b–47a, and on mss. JNUL 180/54, fols. 135v–138v; HUC 2102, fols. 118r–121v. "Qārūn" is the qur'anic version of Korah's name.
2. Cf. Num. 16:3. Some midrashic sources have Korah and his followers say: "Upon Sinai all Israel heard the words of God, 'I am the Lord.' Wherefore then lift ye up yourselves above the congregation of the Lord?" (see Ginzberg, *Legends*, 3:291–292; 6:101n.568 and the sources cited there).
3. Korah's fabulous wealth is acknowledged in rabbinic legends (Ginzberg, *Legends*, 3:286), but it is greatly amplified in all the Muslim sources owing to the different emphasis of the qur'anic account.

4. As the following lines make clear, Korah's party objects as much to Moses' lack of wealth as to his general asceticism; both aspects of behavior are covered by the derogatory (here) term "dervish." The word actually occurs in al-Nīsābūrī's account of this incident (*Dāstānhā,* p. 225), indicating again Shāhīn's reliance on this source.
5. The point seems to be that the commandments that God imposed on the people through Moses appeared excessively burdensome to Korah and his group (see Ginzberg, *Legends,* 3:288–292; al-Ṭabarī, *History,* pp. 106–107; al-Thaʿlabī, *ʿArāʾis,* p. 215).
6. Cf. Num. 16:13; Ginzberg, *Legends,* 3:291.
7. Ar./Pers., *ḥikmat,* lit. also means "science," "knowledge," "philosophy," "mystery." See the references cited in n. 6.
8. Hārūn is the qurʾanic name of Aaron, Moses' brother.
9. This reading is based on JNUL 180/54. The other two manuscripts have *pīr-i afsūn* (HUC 2102: "master of spells") and *por zi afsūn* (*Mūsā-nāmah,* ed. Ḥakam: "full of spells").
10. Cf. Num. 16:5, 16–18; Ginzberg, *Legends,* 3:292–293.
11. A hybrid word composed of Heb. *Miqdash* + Pers. *-i maʿad* (lit., "sanctuary of meeting"), rather than the biblical *ohel moʿed* (Tent of Meeting) of Num. 16:18.
12. In the biblical and rabbinic accounts Datan and Abiram refuse to come to Moses and send him an angry message instead (Num. 16:12–14; Ginzberg, *Legends,* 3:294). Shāhīn heightens the drama by having the two men appear and refuse Moses to his face, despite his attempt to save their lives.
13. Through Moses' soliloquy, not based on any of the sources I consulted, Shāhīn recreates imaginatively the prophet's feelings during the incident.
14. Datan and Abiram.
15. Cf. Num. 16:27.
16. See above, n. 11.
17. This act, as well as the sacrifice that follows, further compound Korah's transgression, for he had not been divinely commanded to build an altar, let alone one exceeding the measurements given to Moses (Exod. 27:1–8), nor was he divinely authorized to offer sacrifices. His doing so here, before the outcome of the trial that Moses proposed, betrays his foolhardy confidence.
18. Heb., *miqdash;* no doubt the Tent of Meeting is intended here.
19. Cf. Num. 16:20.
20. Cf. Num. 16:22, where the plural verb indicates that both Moses and Aaron "fell on their faces" in supplication.
21. The nine vaulted firmaments comprise the seven planetary spheres plus the fixed stars and the empyrean or encompassing sphere. See above, "Jacob and the Wolf," n. 41.
22. *Ki jorm-i hich kas bā kas nagīrī,* lit., "You will not take one man with the sin of another," echoing Num. 16:22, "When one man sins, will You be wrathful with the whole community?" On the complex issue of theodicy alluded to in this verse, cf. Gen. 18:23ff., Exod. 20:5, 34:7, Deut. 5:9, the *Babylonian Talmud,* Berakot 7a.
23. See below, n. 41.
24. Heb., *mishkan;* again, the reference is to the Tent of Meeting.
25. Cf. Num. 16:23.
26. Cf. Ginzberg, *Legends,* 3:297.

27. This verse appears to refer to the amplification of the Jewish Law through the oral tradition handed down by Moses. Objections to the growth of Jewish law beyond its biblical framework were favorite polemical topics of anti-Talmudic Jews and non-Jews beginning with the dissent of the Jewish Sadducees in the Second Temple period, continuing with the arguments of the Karaites (after the eighth century), as well as Christians and Muslims. See Lazarus-Yafeh, *Intertwined Worlds.*
28. Cf. Num. 16:28–30.
29. See al-Thaʿlabī, *ʿArāʾis,* p. 217, and al-Nīsābūrī, *Dāstānhā,* p. 228. The latter was probably Shāhīn's source for this statement.
30. God's reply is not in any of the Jewish or Muslim sources I consulted. It seems to be Shāhīn's imaginative interpretation of Moses' request in Num. 16:30: "But if the Lord brings about something unheard of, so that the ground opens its mouth and swallows them up with all that belongs to them."
31. See Surah 28:81. Rabbinic sources emphasize the destruction of Korah's wealth along with those of his followers: "Not these wicked people alone were swallowed by the earth, but their possessions also. Even their linen that was at the launderer's or a pin belonging to them rolled toward the mouth of the earth and vanished therein. Nowhere upon the earth remained a trace of them or of their possessions, and even their names disappeared from the documents upon which they were written" (Ginzberg, *Legends,* 3:298).
32. I am uncertain about the meaning of this hemistich.
33. The Qur'ān (Surah 28:79) and several *qiṣaṣ* sources (al-Ṭabarī, *History,* pp. 103–104; al-Thaʿlabī, *ʿArāʾis,* pp. 214–215; al-Nīsābūrī, *Dāstānhā,* p. 227) point out that many Israelites were envious of Korah's wealth.
34. Midrashic sources make Korah's death more painful: "Consumed at the incense offering, he then rolled in the shape of a ball of fire to the opening in the earth, and vanished" (Ginzberg, *Legends,* 3:299).
35. Cf. Num. 16:31.
36. I am uncertain about the meaning of this hemistich.
37. That is, from near the divine throne, the abode of Abraham in Muḥammad's ascension (*miʿrāj*) (see *Textual Sources for the Study of Islam,* ed. A. Rippin and J. Knappert [Chicago, 1990], pp. 69–70); see also Nasr, *Introduction,* esp. pp. 132–165.
38. Cf. Num. 18:35; Ginzberg, *Legends,* 3:299.
39. *Yaʿqūbiān,* lit., "Jacobites," i.e., descendants of Jacob, used in many JP texts as a synonym for the biblical Israelites. In all likelihood the verses that follow attempt to explain the number of those who died afterward in a plague (14,700 according to Num. 17:14, "aside from those who died on account of Korah").
40. These last two hemistichs are unclear in the manuscripts I have consulted.
41. The Ar./Pers. word *himmat,* which I here translate as "grace," has many meanings—"desire," "intention," "mind," "thought," "strength." In Sufi parlance it usually denotes strong spiritual power, which is what is intended here (Schimmel, *Mystical Dimensions,* p. 79).
42. The image is startling and beautiful: just as he once physically parted the Reed Sea, Moses now has such spiritual strength that he cuts a path through the "sea" of praise and prayer straight to God.

God's Great Name

1. Shāhīn's text is loosely based on Moses' Second Song, "Ha'azinu" (Deut. 32:1–47; see also Ginzberg, *Legends*, 3:454–455 and 6:153–154nn.912–919). My translation is based on *Mūsā-nāmah*, ed. Ḥakam, pp. 138a–141b and BZI 978, fols. 351v–354v. The titles of the two chapters that follow are in reverse order in BZI 978. I translate *tasbīḥ* (Ar./Pers. for "glori[fies]") in Shāhīn's title as "writes."
2. Cf. Deut. 32:44. Pers., *shah*, obviously a hyperbolic foreshadowing of Joshua's future role, which is not, however, one of king in Jewish sources.
3. BZI 978 adds another distich here: "Words which are signposts of [theological] discourse [*kalām*], / Which the cycles of the world [eternally] serve." (Or "For the cycles of the world serve Him.")
4. Cf. Deut. 32:1.
5. Ar./Pers., *sharṭ* (condition, obligation, stipulation).
6. This reference to Ahrīman (see above, "Moses and the Burning Bush," n. 2) would seem jarringly out of place in Moses' speech were it not for the fact that in Persian poetic language it is simply another name for Satan.
7. This epithet is usually associated with God (see v. 3 above); here it appears to be referring primarily to Moses, perhaps in his capacity as God's interlocutor.
8. Ar./Pers., *sharī'a*, the Muslim term for divine law.
9. Cf. Deut. 32:2.
10. Pers., *rāh-i ḥaqīqat*, a common Sufi expression.
11. Ar./Pers., *ṭarīqa* (way, path), a technical term for the Sufi way of life.
12. Moses is addressing the second generation, those born in the desert, who are untainted by the sins of their fathers.
13. Pers., *yalān*, still gives credit to the strength of the generation that came out of Egypt.
14. Ar./Pers., *shirk* (polytheism, idolatry), that is, associating something with God; in the language of Islam, this is the most serious transgression for monotheists (Surah 4:116) and actually covers a multitude of sins beginning with the polytheistic worship characteristic of animism and ending with atheism.
15. See above, "The Fall of 'Aza'zel," n. 3.
16. This recommendation to rely on present and future sages may perhaps be a touch of anti-Karaite polemics.
17. Pers., *lā makānah*, a Sufi epithet for God.
18. Cf. Deut. 32:15.
19. Lāt is one of the pre-Islamic goddesses of Arabia mentioned in the Qur'ān (Surah 53:19); this is another incongruous reference from the Jewish point of view but not from the perspective of Persian poetical conceits.
20. Cf. Deut. 32:17.
21. Cf. Deut. 32:26–27.
22. The Reed Sea.
23. This distich is missing in BZI 978.
24. Ar./Pers., *wa'ada*, that is, the commandments, the terms of the covenant between God and Israel.
25. See above, n. 11.

The Tale of Job

1. This translation is based on "The Tale of Job," ed. Ḥakam, pp. 92a–94b, and BZI 978, fols. 105v–108v. For a comprehensive treatment of the subject in Jewish and Islamic sources, see *EJ,* vol. 10, s.v. "Job," and *EI* (2), s.v. "'Ayyūb." For more detailed midrashic views, see Ginzberg, *Legends,* 2:226–242 and 5:381–390. The Qur'ān's principal references to Job are in Surahs 21:83–84 and 38:40–43. For post-qur'anic sources, see al-Kisā'ī, *Tales,* pp. 192–204; al-Ṭabarī, *History,* 2:140–143; al-Tha'labī, *'Arā'is,* pp. 153–163, and al-Nīsābūrī, *Dāstānhā,* pp. 254–263. For the location of Job's tale in Shāhīn's epics, see above, "Introduction to Shāhīn."
2. Some midrashic sources consider non-Israelite prophets, such as Shem, Balaam, Job, and his four friends (Eliphaz, Zophar, Bildad, and Elihu), to be descendants of Nahor, Abraham's brother, from his marriage to Milkah (Ginzberg, *Legends,* 3:356, and 6:125n.727).
3. On the confusion regarding the identity of 'Uz in Jewish sources, see Ginzberg, *Legends,* 5:384n.14.
4. A discreet reference to Hamor's rape of Dinah (Gen. 34:1–3).
5. Jacob's sons killed Hamor of Shekem (Gen. 34:25–26).
6. In midrashic sources God punishes Jacob for not allowing Dinah to become Esau's wife by commanding him to marry her to Job, "one that is neither circumcised nor a proselyte" (Ginzberg, *Legends,* 1:396 and 5:288nn.121,122). They also claim that Dinah was Job's second wife (Ginzberg, *Legends,* 1:396, 2:241, 5:386n.27, and 5:388n.35). In most Muslim sources Job's wife is called "Raḥmah," (Mercy); see al-Kisā'ī, *Tales,* p. 195, al-Ṭabarī, *History,* p. 140, al-Tha'labī, *'Arā'is,* p. 156). Al-Nīsābūrī claims that Job had four wives; three were divorced from him during the period of his trials and only the fourth, "Zayna, and some say [her name was] Raḥmah, one of the daughters of 'Iṣ [Esau] b. Isḥāq [remained with him]" (*Dāstānhā,* p. 257).
7. Al-Nīsābūrī takes offense at the view that God gave Satan dominion over righteous Job. Instead, he claims that Job's trials were actually initiated by a conversation between God and the angels. The latter claimed that Job's faithful service was due to the fact that God had bestowed much wealth and many favors on him. God insisted that Job would remain faithful even without these and proceeded to test him. (In effect, al-Nīsābūrī places Satan's general argument against Job in the mouths of the angels.) Citing other unnamed sources, al-Nīsābūrī claims that Job *chose* to be tested by calamity to prove his faith and don the "reward of the patient" (*sawāb-i ṣabīrān*) (*Dāstānhā,* pp. 254–255). See below, n. 22, a Sufi interpretation.
8. Pers., *ṭā'at* (obeying, submitting, worshiping). For Satan's sense of pride in his chief occupations, see above, "The Fall of 'Aza'zel," n. 3. In this translation I tend to translate the word mostly as "worship," except in this verse, where I wanted to point to the cross-reference above.
9. Cf. "The Fall of 'Aza'zel," vv. 292ff.
10. *Mūsā-nāmah,* ed. Ḥakam: "I'll turn treacle into opium in his mouth."
11. Shāhīn omits God's caveat, "See, all that he has is in your power; only do not lay a hand on him" (Job 1:12; 2:6). God's ultimate solicitude for Job is echoed also in Muslim legendary sources: "God gave Iblīs mastery over Job's possessions, though not over his body or mind" (al-Ṭabarī, *History,* 2:141); "You may proceed to rule

over his entire body, but not over his tongue, his heart, and his mind" (al-Thaʿlabī, *ʿArāʾis*, p. 156).

12. Pers., *qahr-i gahhār; al-Qahhār* (the Subduer, the Vengeful), is one of the Muslim names of God (Surah 12:39, etc.).
13. Cf. Job 1:21.
14. Ar./Pers., *shawq*, another Sufi technical term denoting one of the stages of loving God (Schimmel, *Mystical Dimensions*, p. 132).
15. Ar./Pers., *tawḥīd* (to make one, to declare or acknowledge oneness), a complex technical Muslim term denoting one of the most important doctrines of Islam, corresponding to the Jewish concept of divine oneness. For an excellent discussion of *tawḥīd*, see Sachiko Murata and William C. Chittick, *Vision of Islam* (New York, 1994), chap. 3 and the Index under the term.
16. The number of Job's sons and daughters differs in the Jewish and Muslim legendary sources.
17. Ar./Pers., *al-sattār*, is another Muslim (non-qur'anic) epithet for God.
18. Cf. above, "The Fall of 'Aza'zel," vv. 315ff.; Job 2:7.
19. Cf. Job 2:6.
20. This detail is apparently first mentioned in the *Testament of Job*, a Greek pseudepigraphic work, written possibly earlier than 100 CE (*EJ*, s.v. "Job, Testament of").
21. Cf. *EJ*, ibid.; Ginzberg, *Legends*, 2:235 and 5:386n.26.
22. "Eat my flesh until God releases me from suffering" (al-Kisāʾī, *Tales*, p. 195). Al-Nīsābūrī relates an even more curious detail: "Others say that [the reason Job finally cried out to God] was that one day two worms fell off him and he put them back, saying, 'Eat your daily portions and do not quarrel with one another!' When they began to eat, he felt a pain such as he never felt before. He cried out, 'Adversity afflicts me!' [Surah 21:83]. Gabriel, peace be upon him, said, 'O Job, are you [finally] crying out?' He replied, 'O Gabriel, all these years I have not suffered pain and anguish such as I suffer from the stings of these two little worms.' Gabriel said: 'That is because this [test] was your choice [see above, n. 7]. Don't you know that slaves [Pers. *bandah*, in the sense of Ar. *ʿabd* and Heb. *ʿeved* (slave, servant, true [Muslim/Sufi] devotee)] have no business with choice?' " (*Dāstānhā*, pp. 261–262).
23. Like the Qur'ān and al-Nīsābūrī, Shāhīn omits Job's dialogues with his friends and thus keeps the narrative on a mystical-devotional rather than a philosophical plane.
24. Dinah's two disputes with Job are eloquent variations on the solitary verse she utters in the Book of Job, "You still keep your integrity! Blaspheme God and die!" (2:9). Midrashic sources are uncomfortable with Dinah's forthrightness and have her advise Job to pray for death, afraid that he might not be able to endure his suffering (Ginzberg, *Legends*, 2:235 and 5:386n.27). All the Muslim sources I consulted omit this negative aspect of her character, emphasizing Raḥmah's (Dinah) fidelity to Job and the sacrifices she made in order to help him.
25. Again, Shāhīn embellishes Job's solitary reply to his wife: "You talk as any shameless woman might talk! Should we accept only good from God and not accept evil?" (Job 2:10).
26. Far from comforting Job, Dinah undoubtedly adds to his misery with her "reasoning." In Muslim/Sufi terms she represents all that is unspiritual, *dunyavī* (worldly), and *ʿaqlī* (logical), unable to transcend earthly concerns.

27. The following five verses are missing in the Ḥakam edition.
28. The time span differs: "eighteen years[!]" (al-Kisāʾī, *Tales*, p. 199); "seven years and some months" (al-Ṭabarī, *History*, 2:142); "seven years . . . three years" (al-Thaʿlabī, *ʿArāʾis*, p. 163); "seven years and seven months . . . seventeen years" (al-Nīsābūrī, *Dāstānhā*, p. 257).
29. Ar./Pers., *kitāb* (the Book).
30. None of the sources mentions this; Shāhīn's imagination is in high gear.
31. As mentioned before, the Muslim sources emphasize the devotion of Job's wife throughout his ordeal.

Ardashīr-nāmah

1. This translation is based on BZI 980 (its folios are not numbered), JTS Acc. 40919, in which the folios are not properly arranged (the following folios include portions of the narrative; they are listed in the order of the narrative: 9v, 127r, 129r, 129v, 96v, 130r, 130v, 68r), and IV A 129 (unfoliated). For midrashic sources, see Ginzberg, *Legends*, 4:365–390, 6:451–461, and the medieval sources listed and discussed in Walfish, *Esther*, p. 245n.63.
2. The Kayānids are a legendary ancient eastern Iranian dynasty and a probable source of the Iranian epic tradition (Frye, *Heritage*, pp. 58 and 225).
3. The Persian word *bahman* has a multitude of meanings, among them "the supreme intelligence," the pre-Islamic name of the eleventh month of the solar year, and a demon or genius among Zoroastrians (Haim, *Persian-English Dictionary*, 1:296; Steingass, *Persian-English Dictionary*, p. 212). More pertinent here is that "Bahman" is another name of Ardashīr (Ahasueros), the son of Isfandiyār, in Firdowsī's *Shah-nāmah*. It provides the linchpin connecting Shāhīn's epic with Iran's great national epic (Blieske, *Šāhīn-e Šīrāzīs*, p. 6). To understand where Bahman/Ardashīr fits in the *Shah-nāmah*, see the brief summaries in *Epic of the Kings*, trans. Reuben Levy (Chicago, 1967), pp. 218–222. The *Shah-nāmah* connection is, of course, much later chronologically speaking than the traditional scholarly dating that places the story of Esther in the reign of Xerxes I (486–465 BCE; Frye, *Heritage*, p. 29; cf. Bacher, *Zwei jüdisch-persische Dichter*, p. 44).
4. "Rūm" refers, at various times in Islamic history, to Greece, Rome, and the Byzantine Empire. The latter, as a designation of the Anatolian Peninsula, is the meaning most often intended by the medieval poets of Iran.
5. "Arman" refers to the mountainous regions of Azarbaijan, including Armenia.
6. The women in the harem. Calling beautiful females (pl.) *botān* (idols) is a Persian poetical convention with some interesting implications in Sufi poetry.
7. Ahasueros is not known for restraint in midrashic sources, which prefer to emphasize that he was a somewhat foolish monarch (Ginzberg, *Legends*, 4:379–381).
8. In v. 165 we are told that Hegai is a *mobed*, a Zoroastrian priest. Clearly he is not aware of Esther's non-Zoroastrian origins or he would have been less enthusiastic about Ahasueros' marrying her. Midrashic sources identify him only as "chief of the eunuchs of the harem" (Ginzberg, *Legends*, 4:386).
9. These were selected by Hegai earlier as possible candidates to replace Queen Vashti. The number seven symbolizes the planets of medieval cosmology and probably also alludes to the seven beauties courted by Shah Bahrām in Niẓāmī's (d. 1209) fa-

mous allegorical romance *Haft Paykar* (The seven portraits); see Julie Scott Meisami, *Haft Paykar: A Medieval Persian Romance* (Oxford, 1995), pp. 51ff.

10. As we shall see, there are several astrological metaphors in this narrative, but they differ from those found in Jewish sources. For example, in Baḥya b. Asher's thirteenth-century biblical commentary *Kad ha-qemaḥ,* on the section *Purim* (his commentary on the Book of Esther), Ahasueros and Haman are associated with Saturn and Mars, "the forces of evil," respectively, while Mordekai and Esther are associated with Venus and Jupiter, "the forces of good" (Walfish, *Esther,* p. 58).
11. That is, its rays.
12. A poetic reference to Ardashīr's temporary impotence, not mentioned in the midrashic sources.
13. Hegai is volunteering the information without being asked.
14. Pers., *rāz-i Ester,* alluding probably both to her beauty and to her long concealment at the hands of Mordekai (see below, n. 32).
15. Lit., "it is like the letter *dāl,*" which, in the Arabic/Persian alphabet is a line bent toward the left.
16. That is, stop bringing together incompatible elements, such as "pitcher and stone" (*sang o sabū*).
17. That is, Esther was already present among the maidens of the harem.
18. This refers to Esther's modest manners, but it may also hint at her refusal to partake from the food of the court, which is mentioned in midrashic sources (Ginzberg, *Legends,* 4:386).
19. Hegai has presumably been guarding the secret for just such an occasion.
20. The fourth heaven corresponds to the sun, the appropriate royal symbol (Nasr, *Introduction,* p. 204), especially vis-à-vis Ardashīr's pending union with Esther, whom Shāhīn equates with the moon.
21. Needless to say, the courtship of Esther is not detailed in Jewish sources, which view her marriage as a "necessary evil," divinely preordained to save the Jews. Shāhīn's view, perhaps relying on local traditions, sees the union as being *much* more: a happy, fruitful marriage! Unlike the other virgins in the harem, Esther is properly wooed and wed to a monarch, and she gives birth not only to a Jewish savior but to the heir to the Persian throne as well (see above, n. 8, and below, n. 50).
22. Fīrūz is the son of Bishutan, Ardashīr's grand vizier; he is obviously also one of the shah's confidants and high-ranking officials.
23. A mann is a varying weight for measuring dry goods, roughly equivalent to two-thirds pounds avoirdupois, or about three kilograms (Haim, *Persian-English,* 2:988).
24. The Persian word *zar* is used for both gold and money.
25. Qandahar is a famous city in Afghanistan.
26. Kay Qobād was one of the kings of the Kayānid dynasty (see above, n. 2), famous, among other things, for embracing Mazdakism (*Epic of the Kings,* pp. 317–321; Frye, *Heritage,* p. 250).
27. Shush was ancient Susa, the main capital of the Achaemenids after Darius (Frye, *Heritage,* pp. 124–128).
28. Fīrūz was entrusted with organizing the procession of gift bearers, while Hegai was entrusted with the delicate negotiations requesting Esther's hand in marriage.

29. The implication is that Esther lived in royal quarters even before she married Ardashīr, as befitting her descent from the tribe of Benjamin, from which Saul, the first king of Israel, also descended (Ginzberg, *Legends,* 2:146).
30. A royal title originating from, and thus inviting flattering comparison with, the Sasanian king Khosrow Anūshīrvān (Chosroes I), whose reign (531–579) is particularly idealized in Persian poetry and Iranian history (Frye, *Heritage,* pp. 256–264).
31. See above, "Qārūn's Rebellion," n. 3.
32. Pers., *Ester satīrah,* an obvious homonymous pun (*tajnīs*) with practically identical meanings in both Persian (*satīrah*) and Hebrew (*seter*), "concealed," "secret," "hidden." In midrashic sources Esther earns the epithet "she who conceals" through her double concealment, first from the eyes of the king's spies searching for beautiful maidens, and second, by guarding the secret of her Jewish descent from everyone at court (Ginzberg, *Legends,* 4:380, 384). Abraham Saba, a fifteenth-century kabbalistic commentator from Spain, noted in his mystical commentary of the Book of Esther that *El mistater* [Is. 45:15] is among God's names, and that He hid (*histir*) His face from Israel in Esther's time; he identifies Esther with the *Shekinah,* the divine immanence (Walfish, *Esther,* pp. 39–40, and 265n.16).
33. According to some midrashim, Mordekai married Esther, his orphaned niece, when she came of age (Ginzberg, *Legends,* 4:387). Shāhīn ignores this information since it would ruin his tale (see below, n. 50).
34. There is in Persian literature, a definite didactic genre of advice to princes, known as a "mirror for princes." Here we have a small "mirror for princesses."
35. The meaning of the next hemistich is unclear.
36. Deep mistrust of the world is common in Sufism, as indeed in all pietist thought. Cf. Mordekai's soliloquy, below.
37. This extended simile is like a parable describing Mordekai's protective role (oyster shell) toward Esther (pearl), as well as his inevitable loss of her at the hands of a suitor, in this case, the plundering diver (Ahasueros). The oyster shell and pearl are frequently used in Persian (Sufi) poetry as symbols of the original, "organic" love between the lover and the Divine Beloved. For a few examples in Rūmī's poetry, see Chittick, *Sufi Path of Love,* pp. 213, 264, and 303.
38. The proper behavior for Esther—and for Sufi novices.
39. Lit., "act as though you were dead," another advisable characteristic of Sufi novices, especially with regard to complete obedience to the Sufi master (Schimmel, *Mystical Dimensions,* p. 103).
40. For the reason behind Mordekai's apprehension, see Ginzberg, *Legends,* 4:388–389, and Walfish, *Esther,* p. 280n.19. It is interesting to note, as Hava Lazarus-Yafeh has done, that Esther is urged to dissimulate concerning her religious beliefs and conceal her true identity, concepts known much later among Iranian Twelver Shiʿis as *taqiyya* and *kitman* ("Ester ha-malkah," pp. 121–122).
41. Ardashīr's grand vizier.
42. Another of Ardashīr's courtiers.
43. See above, n. 8.
44. Shāhīn's imagination soars even higher in the verses that follow from here on. He ignores the midrashic notion that Esther never consummated her marriage with Ahasueros (how could she, if she was already married; see above, n. 33). Thus,

according to some Jewish sources, the unfortunate king made love merely to "a female spirit in the guise of Esther" (Ginzberg, *Legends,* 4:387–388, and 6:460n.80).

45. Also tokens of gifts?
46. The shah's new marriage appears to be the occasion also for a renewal of his political authority.
47. Badakhshan is a place between India and Khorasan (northeastern Iran) that is noted for its rubies (Haim, *Persian-English Dictionary,* 1:232).
48. A *rūd* is a stringed instrument.
49. A *sāz* (Ar./Pers.) is another musical instrument.
50. As mentioned above, in Shāhīn's epic the purpose of the union of Esther and Ardashīr is not only the immediate deliverance of Iranian Jews but the restoration of Jewish national sovereignty through Cyrus [Pers., Kūresh], the son of Esther and Ahasueros. Some midrashic sources claim that Esther and Ahasueros were the parents of Darius (Ginzberg, *Legends,* 4:366 and 6:452–453n.5). On the confusion in Shāhīn's epic between the roles of Darius and Cyrus regarding the rebuilding of the Temple, see below, *Ezra-nāmah,* nn.4–5. It seems highly plausible that there existed a local Jewish-Persian tradition claiming that Cyrus was the son of Esther, for this is explicitly stated in the fourteenth-century midrashic work originating from Iran, *Sefer pitron Torah,* p. 33.

    Midrashic sources also claim, in a rather contradictory fashion, either that (a) Esther took contraceptive measures to ensure that she would not get pregnant, or that (b) she miscarried on hearing of Mordekai's arrival at the palace "clothed in sackloth and ashes" (Ginzberg, *Legends,* 4:419, and 6:469n.127).
51. See above, "Jacob and the Wolf," n. 37.
52. Full of (thoughtless) enthusiasm, Ardashīr managed to corrupt even ascetics by chasing away their thoughts of penitence with gold.
53. A famous mountain in northwestern Iran, near Hamadan.
54. The greatest hero of the *Shah-nāmah.*

Ezra-nāmah

1. This translation is based on Wilhelm Bacher's edition (itself based on ms. 392 [old numbering] of the Adler collection, JTS), published in his "Le Livre d'Ezra," pp. 249–280; BZI 980 (unfoliated); JTS Acc. 40919, fols. 1–4, 160–164; and IV A 129. See also Bacher, *Zwei jüdisch-persische Dichter,* pp. 66–71. For relevant midrashic sources, see Ginzberg, *Legends,* 4:354–361 and 6:441–449.
2. Pers., *maʿdan-i khāṣ,* in this text a frequent epithet for the First Temple, it is probably related to the Hebrew (mishnaic) honorifics of Jerusalem, the site of the Chosen House (*bayt ha-baḥirah*) (*Babylonian Talmud,* Zeraʿim, Maʿaser Sheni, 5:12).
3. See above, "Moses and the Burning Bush," n. 1.
4. Cf. Jer. 25:11. Jerusalem fell to the Babylonian armies of Nebuchadnezzar in the summer of 586 BCE; the building of the Second Temple was completed in the sixth year of Darius' reign (516/15 BCE). See Tadmor, "Period of the First Temple," pp. 157 and 172. Some Muslim authors were also familiar with the seventy-year count, which is cited by al-Ṭabarī in his *Tāʾrīkh,* 2:690.
5. In Jewish tradition, "Haggai, Zechariah, and Malachi [who is identified with Ezra] were the last representatives of prophecy" (Ginzberg, *Legends,* 4:354–355,

6:441–442nn.33,36), but they were not necessarily, as in Shāhīn's account, contemporaries. Haggai's activities are associated with Darius I (522–486 BCE) and those of Ezra are generally, but not unanimously, connected with Artaxerxes I Longimanus (464–424 BCE). See Tadmor, "Period of the First Temple," pp. 173–174, and Frye, *Heritage,* pp. 147–154. Shāhīn's poetic license is understandable in light of the fact that both prophets were associated with the rebuilding of the Temple.

6. Pers., *rasūl-i akbar,* which can also mean "the greater/est prophet."
7. See Ginzberg, *Legends,* 4:286 and 291 (where Mattatiah is identified with King Zedekiah; idem., 6:382n.1). Mattatiah's role in Shāhīn's account appears to be a conflation of the roles of Zerubbabel, son of Shealti'el, son of Jehoiachim, the last captive king of the Davidic line (Ezra 3:2), and, possibly, Sheshbazzar, "the prince of Judah" (Ezra 1:8). See Ackroyd, *Israel,* p. 204, and Bacher's hypothesis, "Livre d'Ezra," p. 250.
8. Ezra's initiative to go before the monarch resembles here Nehemiah's actions (Neh. 2:2ff.). Shāhīn chose to center his narrative around Ezra, diminishing—or rather neglecting completely—the role of other characters known to have aided in the process of restoration.
9. Here Shāhīn calls Ezra "'Uzayr," the prophet's name in Muslim tradition, for no discernible metric reason, perhaps simply to establish the identity of the two. He appends the epithet *rasūl-i akbar* (see above, n. 6), heedless of its earlier association with Haggai.
10. Presumably the prophet of the Book of Zekariah. For his role in the rebuilding of the Temple, see Ackroyd, *Israel,* pp. 218–233.
11. The bird known as *humā(y)* in Iranian mythological tradition is usually identified with the mythical phoenix, or the real lammergeyer. Its propitious appearance portends kingship to those who sight it (Schimmel, *Two-Colored Brocade,* Index under "Huma"). In the present context it alludes to Ezra's exalted stature over his companions and, indirectly, to the imminent restoration of the Jewish monarchy.
12. Another epithet for Ezra. In Persian literature it is usually associated with 'Alī b. Abī Ṭālib (d. 661), Muḥammad's cousin and son-in-law. Most of the time Shāhīn calls Moses a lion (see Moreen, "Moses, God's Shepherd," p. 117). Here he may be using the epithet consciously, likening Ezra in his capacity of second lawgiver to Moses, as midrashic sources do also (see below, n. 33).
13. Pers., *darbān.* It would appear that the protocol at the Achaemenid, Parthian, and even Sasanian courts required that an usher, who was informed of the purpose of the visit, screen visitors before announcing them to the king (see Shaked, "Two Judaeo-Iranian Contributions," pp. 293ff., where, however, the word *darbān* is not mentioned).
14. Although this Mordekai ought to be identified with the Mordekai in Ezra 2:2, here he is the Mordekai of the Book of Esther, as later parts of the narrative reveal.
15. As Bacher notes, Cyrus addresses himself to Mattatiah, his royal counterpart, rather than to Ezra, the leader of the delegation ("Livre d'Ezra," p. 265n.1).
16. See above, "Moses and the Burning Bush," n. 12.
17. The prohibition on drinking wine touched by a gentile and on eating any kind of cooked food prepared by gentile hands may well be biblical (cf. Joseph's refraining from eating with the Egyptians in Gen. 43:32). It is clearly expressed in the *Babylo-*

nian Talmud (ʿAvodah Zarah, 29b, 34b, 38a). However, it is more likely that the biblical precedent for Shāhīn's account of Mattatiah's test of faith comes, as Bacher notes ("Livre d'Ezra," p. 266 n.1), from Daniel 1:8, where Daniel refuses to eat and drink with the idolatrous Nebuchadnezzar. Bacher suspects that Shāhīn may have been influenced by III Esdras, chap. 3, where the power of wine is extolled at the court of Darius (see *Apocrypha,* pp. 9–11), but the echo of Daniel appears more convincing to me. Such texts of faith are attested in Muslim lands, particularly in Iran, and Bacher cites two examples, one from the Mongol period (late thirteenth century), and the other from the JP chronicle *Kitāb-i Anusī* (see below, chap. 8) from the seventeenth century. He draws attention to the quasi-legendary information related by Israel Levi ("Le tombeau de Mardochee et d'Esther," *REJ* 36 [1898]: 252) that Arghūn, the Il-khanid monarch (r. 1284–1291), offered a bowl of wine to Saʿd ad-Dawla, his Jewish grand vizier (p. 68n.5; see above, Introduction). For a thorough discussion of this prohibition and other aspects relevant to contact between Jews and idolatrous and nonidolatrous nations, see Jacob Katz, *Exclusiveness and Tolerance* (New York, 1975; repr. 1962), chap. 3.

18. See above, "Moses and the Burning Bush," n. 16.
19. That is, the Temple.
20. Shāhīn uses the Arabic word *fatwa,* a Muslim legal term, which denotes the published opinion on a religious matter issued by a recognized Muslim authority. The use of this and other Muslim legal terms by Jews living in Muslim lands is well attested in the Genizah documents; see Goitein in P. Sanders *Mediterranean Society: Cummulative Indices* 6, under *fatwa,* and n. 21, below.
21. Shāhīn's legal terminology in this verse is mixed. He juxtaposes (Ar.) *ḥaram* (prohibited) of the Muslim *sharīʿa* (religious law), with (Heb.) *mutar* (permitted), of Jewish *ḥalakah* (religious law), most likely for the sake of the (still imperfect) rhyme. He thereby demonstrates a tendency apparent already in Saadia Gaon's (d. 942) Arabic translation of the Pentateuch of equating Jewish and Muslim legal terms.
22. Mattatiah's refusal of a royal request could lead to his death.
23. Ezra urges Mattatiah to break customary law (see above, n. 17) in order to achieve the higher goal, returning to the Land of Israel and rebuilding the Temple.
24. Night as malevolent darkness and day as triumphant light are juxtaposed here in traditional Iranian (Zoroastrian) dualistic fashion. Such extended similes are common in Persian poetry, especially, as here, in connection with the passage of (personified) Time, never a positive phenomenon.
25. See above, *Ardashīr-nāmah,* n. 30.
26. For "Rūm," see *Ardashīr-nāmah,* n. 4, above; "Chīn" is China, "Hind" is India.
27. This verse does not seem to refer to Cyrus' returning the vessels of gold and silver that Nebuchadnezzar looted from the Temple (Ezra 1:7–11), nor to the free donations of the Jews (Ezra 1:4) or of the local gentile population (Ezra 1:6). Instead, the verse implies that the gold and silver were donated directly from the royal treasury.
28. The suggestion, or "moral," encapsulated in this verse is that the Jews' fortune improved as a result of their improved ways (Bacher, "Livre d'Ezra," p. 268n.1).
29. Bukhtanṣar is the Persian name of Nebuchadnezzar. This clear reference to Ezra's

mission to restore the Torah because it was burned is found in the Second Book of Esdras (14:20): "For your Law is burnt, and so no one knows what has been done by you or what is going to be done. But if I have found favor before you, impart to me the holy Spirit, and I will write all that has happened in the world since the beginning, which were written in your Law, so that men can find the path" (*Apocrypha,* pp. 95–96). Bacher also draws attention ("Livre d'Ezra," p. 268n.3) to a possible echo here of the persecutions of Antiochus Epiphanes IV in 167 BCE recorded in I Maccabees (1:56–57): "And wherever they found the books of the Law, they tore them and burned them, and if anyone was found to possess a book of the agreement or respected the Law, the king's decree condemned him to death" (*Apocrypha,* p. 378).

30. There are several legendary strands interwoven in verses 115–117. Ezra's fellow Jews urge him to travel to the realm of the "sons of Moses," a group of Levites who were supposed to have survived the destruction wrought by Nebuchadnezzar and who had preserved perfect copies of the Torah. These had been transported miraculously to a distant land cut off by a tumultuous river called "Sambation" (Ginzberg, *Legends,* 4:316–418) and lived in the land of Rekab with the descendants of Jethro, who were not Jewish (idem., 3:76–77). The Rekabites had been rewarded for their ancestor's generosity to Moses with a paradisial dwelling in the "Land of the Blessed," whose access was blocked by an impassable river (idem., 6:409n.57). Bacher adds that the famous medieval traveler Petaḥiah of Regensburg claimed that the Rekabites dwelt beyond the "Mountain of Darkness," which, in Bacher's opinion, refers to the region of the Caucaus ("Livre d'Ezra," p. 269n.4; E. N. Adler, *Jewish Travellers in the Middle Ages: Nineteen First Hand Accounts* [New York, 1930, repr. 1987], p. 83). Bacher amplifies this information by drawing attention to the Muslim legend recorded by the geographer al-Qazwīnī (d. 1283/4), according to whom Muḥammad, carried by his magic steed Burāq, also visited the descendants of Moses; al-Qazwīnī refers to the river Sambation as *wādi al-ramal* (the river of sand) (*Atharu'l bilād,* 2:186), a description that is reflected indirectly in Shāhīn (see v. 115) (Bacher, *Zwei jüdisch-persische Dichter,* p. 69n.2).

According to other Jewish sources, one perfect copy of the Torah, buried under the Temple, was never destroyed and was carried by the prophet Ezekiel into the Babylonian exile from which Ezra returned it to Jerusalem (Ginzberg, *Legends,* 6:220n.24).

31. This time the epithet refers to Moses; see above, n. 12.
32. The reference to writing out the Tetragrammaton, God's Ineffable Name, appears to be to the making of a sort of amulet, although, according to several Jewish sources, Ezra did pronounce the Tetragrammaton, "as it is written" (Ginzberg, *Legends,* 6:445n.49). As a high priest after his return to the Land of Israel, he was certainly entitled to do so (idem., 6:441n.35). The invocation of God by the Ineffable Name for theurgic purposes was a common feature of Jewish life in many places during the Middle Ages (see Joshua Trachtenberg, *Jewish Magic and Superstition: A Study in Folk Religion* [New York, 1977 repr.], p. 83). Its sophisticated use, especially among Kabbalists, is described by Moshe Idel in his *Kabbalah: New Perspectives* (New Haven, 1988), chap. 8, and idem., *The Mystical Experience in Abraham Abulafia* (Albany, 1988), Index, under "Name of God."

33. Shāhīn is alluding here to one of the most important Muslim polemical arguments against Judaism, namely, that the Jews worshiped Ezra (Surah 9:30); see Mahmoud Ayoub, "'Uzayr in the Qur'ān and Muslim Tradition," in *Studies in Islamic Judaic Traditions,* ed. William M. Brinner and S. D. Ricks (Atlanta, Ga., 1986), pp. 9ff. Jewish tradition, although it regards Ezra very highly ("If Moses had not anticipated him, Ezra would have received the Torah" [*Tosefta,* Sanh., 4:7]), stops well short of such veneration (Ginzberg, *Legends,* 6:432n.5, and 446n.50). Nevertheless, perhaps under the influence of some Muslim sources, Shāhīn endows Ezra with superhuman qualities, such as flying by means of writing down God's Ineffable Name and possessing a phenomenal memory. His abilities clearly awe the Jews in Shāhīn's narrative, but they do not "worship" him. Shāhīn uses Ezra's superhuman efforts to transmit the correct form of the Torah as a reply to Muslim charges that Ezra had corrupted the text (see the following note). For a thorough analysis of Ezra's role in Muslim-Jewish polemics, see Hava Lazarus-Yafeh, "Ezra-'Uzayr: Metamorphosis of a Polemical Motif" (Heb.), *Tarbiṣ* 55 (1986): 359–379, and a different version of the same topic in her *Intertwined Worlds,* chap. 5.
34. Shāhīn refutes another of the most important Muslim polemical arguments against Judaism, namely that Ezra transmitted an incorrect version of the original Torah. Al-Ṭabarī had already presented this argument (*Ta'rīkh* [*Annales,* 2:692]), which was quickly adopted by many later Muslim qur'anic commentators and storytellers (*quṣṣāṣ*). Its lasting formulation is found in the works of the famous Spanish scholar Ibn Ḥazm (d. 1064) and of the Jewish apostate Samaū'āl al-Maghribī (d. ca. 1175). They maintain that the various invasions of the Land of Israel resulted not only in the physical destruction of the realm but also in the ruination of the Jews' archives, including their copies of the Torah. In his famous work *On Religions and Sects* [*Al-faṣl fi'l milal wa'l ahwā' wa'l niḥāl*] (Cairo 1928; Beirut 1975), Ibn Ḥazm argues that knowledge of the Torah, which was confined to a few priests (2:149), was lost completely during the oppressive reigns of various kings of Judah and Israel and during the Babylonian exile (1:147–148). According to Ibn Ḥazm, it was Ezra the priest who "concocted the Hebrew scriptures from remnants of the revelation as it was remembered by other priests and from his own additions" (Moshe Perlmann, *Encyclopedia of Religion,* s.v. "Polemics: Muslim-Jewish Polemics"; *Al-faṣl,* 1:148). In *Silencing the Jews* [*Ifhām al-yahūd*], Samaū'āl al-Maghribī claims that Ezra's motive for introducing reprehensible tales (from the Muslim point of view, i.e., Lot's incestuous relationship with his daughters, King David's relationship with Bathsheba) into the Torah was to discredit the Davidic dynasty and prevent it from returning to power after the restoration of the Temple (New York, 1964, Ar. text, pp. 62–63, Engl. trans., p. 60. See also Lazarus-Yafeh, *Intertwined Worlds,* p. 45).
35. Shāhīn uses the terms "'Imrān's people" and "Kalīm's people" interchangeably.
36. Ar./Pers., *dhikr,* another technical Sufi term; see Schimmel, *Mystical Dimensions,* Index under *dhikr.*
37. Cf. above, "Jacob and the Wolf," n. 41.
38. Ar./Pers., *dahr* (time, destiny, adverse fortune, material world), plays the same role in Shāhīn's poetry, and in JP literature in general, as in classical Persian poetry. Derived from a pre-Islamic cosmological and poetic concept, this term alludes to those implacable, adverse aspects of human existence that strict monotheists,

shrinking from the issue of theodicy, are averse to attribute to God and would rather attribute to the workings of "Time" (see *EI* (2), s.v. *dahr;* and above, "Jacob and the Wolf," n. 14).

39. Lit., "Beware, don't fall into the rabbit's sleep." The last four distichs mark the transition to the somber narrative of Esther and Mordekai's deaths.
40. Contrary to Shāhīn's poetic claim, only a small portion of the Jewish population exiled to Babylonia returned to the Land of Israel (Ginzberg, *Legends,* 4:355).
41. See above, n. 14.
42. Shāhīn's indirect source for Mordekai's dream is probably the Septuagint version of the Book of Esther, in which Mordekai's dream is described: "Behold! A din and uproar, thunder and earthquake, and confusion abroad on the earth" (*The Septuagint Bible: The Oldest Text of the Old Testament,* trans. Charles Thompson [Indian Hills, 1960], p. 809); see also C. A. Moore, *Daniel, Esther and Jeremiah: The Additions* (New York, 1977), pp. 153–252, and Elias Bickerman, *Four Strange Books of the Bible: Jonah, Daniel, Koheleth, Esther* (New York, 1967), pp. 171–240.
43. The angel, whose identity is not specified here, addresses Mordekai but uses the second person plural, thus including Esther in his admonition.
44. The Persian words *sarmāyah* (capital) and *sūd* (profit) have many Sufi connotations relating primarily to spiritual "earnings" (cf. Chittick, *Sufi Path of Love,* pp. 114 and 229). Here Shāhīn's angel suggests, rather delicately, that Esther and Mordekai's roles in the divine scheme to restore Jewish national sovereignty have come to an end. As noted earlier, Shāhīn leaves no doubt in *Ardashīr-nāmah* that these roles consisted in bringing about the union of Esther and Ardashīr as the parents of Cyrus, the future liberator of the Jews.
45. Mount Alvand is in a mountain range near Hamadan. Presumably Esther and Mordekai set out from Susa (Heb., *Shushan*), the main winter residence of the Achaemenid rulers of Iran, toward the south, traveling to Hamadan (ancient Ekbatana), the main summer residence of the Achaemenids (Frye, *Heritage,* pp. 124ff.). Jewish tradition maintains that the mausoleum at the center of Hamadan contains the tombs of Esther and Mordekai, but archaeological evidence suggests that the present construction dates no earlier than the end of the thirteenth century (E. Herzfeld, *Archaeological History of Iran* [London, 1935], pp. 104ff.). The site and the tomb have played an important role in the spiritual history of Iranian Jews, particularly the Jews of that region. For a full description of the tomb, the customs, and miracles associated with it as late as the nineteenth century, see R. Menaḥem Halevi, *Maṣevat Mordekai v'-Ester* (Jerusalem, 1932), and Ze'ev Vilnay, *Maṣevot qodesh be-ereṣ Israel* (Jerusalem, 1950), pp. 228–230. Vilnay also mentions a tradition that Queen Esther is buried in Israel, in Kefar Bir'am in the Galil region, near Safed. Curiously, he quotes a certain R. Menaḥem Ḥevroni, who traveled in this region around 1215, to the effect that Queen Esther commanded Cyrus, *her son,* to build this tomb for her (p. 229).
46. Here the homonymous pun *Esther satīrah* projects not only back to the time when Esther hid her Jewish identity at the court of Ardashīr (see above, *Ardashīr-nāmah,* n. 32), but also forward, into the present moment of the tale, when Esther and Mordekai arrive in Hamadan incognito.

47. Although Mordekai's rank is not specified here, his possessing a signet ring implies that he was appointed grand vizier after Haman's execution (cf. Est. 8:2).
48. Bacher cites the *Jerusalem Talmud* (Megillah, 74b) and the *Babylonian Talmud* (Pesaḥim, 101a) in support of the idea that synagogues often served as inns in the talmudic period ("Livre d'Ezra," p. 273n.1).
49. The Hebrew word *parnas* has multiple meanings, all of which relate to the head functionary of a synagogue or a Jewish community.
50. The Ar./Pers. word *raḥīl* (journey) is a poetical and technical term originating in the great *qaṣīda*s (odes) of the pre-Islamic poets of Arabia. It denotes the second section of a *qaṣīda,* the part in which the poet breaks up camp and sets out on a journey, mounted on a favorite camel, and seeks either to be reunited with his beloved or to encounter some formidable adventure (see Michael A. Sells, *Desert Tracings* [Middletown, Conn., 1989]). As the verses that follow show, Mordekai's choice of the word is appropriate, for he is about to set out on the final journey toward the Divine Beloved.
51. See above, n. 38. Mordekai's fatalistic soliloquy reflects many similar passages in classical Persian, especially Sufi, poetry. The Book of Ecclesiastes is one of the earliest sources for this pessimistic outlook.
52. The image of the "cupbearer" is a common cliché of classical Persian, especially Sufi, poetry, where it can denote both the earthly beloved, reflecting the Divine, or the Divine Beloved Himself.
53. "Friend" is another Sufi epithet for God.
54. The Hebrew month Adar usually falls in the rainy season of spring. It is also the month (February or March) in which Purim, the Feast of Esther, is celebrated.
55. Fire and water as independent symbols, and particularly their incompatible relationship, lend themselves to many mystical (Sufi) interpretations, such as the senses for the former and the guidance of the Sufi shaykh for the latter (Chittick, *Sufi Path of Love,* pp. 143 and 240).
56. Pers., *zamāneh,* a synonym of *dahr* (see above, n. 38).
57. Famous kings and heroes in Firdowsī's *Shah-nāmah.* Instead of "Farīdūn," the text actually has *gāv,* which, as Dick Davis suggested in a private communication, may allude to Farīdūn's famous nurturing cow rather than being a repetition or misspelling of the name Gīv (l. 205).
58. See above, n. 45.
59. See Netzer, "Some Notes," pp. 35–52.
60. I thank Dick Davis for correcting the translation of hemistichs 228–230 from the version that appeared in my article "The 'Iranization' of Biblical Heroes," p. 334.
61. According to Muslim tradition, which Shāhīn follows here, Adam's Fall came about through eating a grain of wheat from a wheat tree (Moreen, "Legend of Adam," pp. 159 and 163).
62. Cf. Gen. 6:3; and also Moses' lifespan (Deut. 34:7).
63. The "provisions" referred to in the last two distichs are our good deeds, which are faithfully recorded during our lifetime and carefully scrutinized by specific angels (the "toll gatherers" of v. 244), in both Jewish and Muslim traditions, before we are granted judgment and a resting place in the hereafter.

64. Another Sufi cliché.
65. The extended simile of the jug stands here, as in many other instances in Persian Sufi poetry, for our perishable form, yet this humble object can symbolize even God. Jalāl al-Dīn Rūmī, who is fond of this image, says: "Thou art the wine and I am the jug, / Thou art the water and I am the streambed. / I am drunk in the lane, of my Saki, oh my Water-giver!" and "Sometimes 'jug,' sometimes 'cup,' sometimes 'unlawful,' sometimes 'forbidden'—all art Thou, / for Thou are sometimes the guided and sometimes the Guide." (Chittick, *Sufi Path of Love,* pp. 315 and 308).
66. Ḥātim of Ṭayy, the paragon of traditional Bedouin hospitality and generosity, is celebrated in pre-Islamic and Islamic literatures. See R. A. Nicholson, *A Literary History of the Arabs* (Cambridge, Mass., 1907; repr. 1969), pp. 85–87.
67. Żaḥḥāk, an Iranian mythological figure, is the most evil character in Firdowsī's *Shah-nāmah.* His monstrous deeds made him the paragon of evil in Persian literature. See Levy, *Epic,* pp. 11–25, and Hinnells, *Persian Mythology,* pp. 14–17.
68. See above, "Moses and the Burning Bush," n. 2.
69. Shāhīn's dualistic "theology" is most Iranian.
70. The Sufi concept embedded in the proverb "selfhood is blasphemy even if it be holy " lurks behind this verse. See Javad Nurbaksh, "The Nimatullāhī," in *Islamic Spirituality: Manifestations,* ed. S. H. Nasr (New York, 1991), p. 159.
71. A Sufi cliché that stands for God and Creation, respectively.
72. The delphic maxim "Know thyself" is a cornerstone of Sufism, as of most forms of Western mysticism.

Introduction to ʿImrānī

1. This introduction is based primarily on David Yeroushalmi's doctoral dissertation, "The Judeo-Persian Poet ʿEmrānī and His *Ganj-nāme* (The Book of Treasure)" (Ph.D. diss., Columbia University, 1986), now published under the same title (Leiden, 1995). All references are to the published book; see pp. 3–41. On ʿImrānī and his works, see also Bacher, *Zwei jüdisch-persische Dichter,* pp. 166–206; Netzer, *Muntakhab,* pp. 40–45, 179–260; idem., "Judeo-Persian Footnote"; idem., *Oṣar,* pp. 31–33.
2. Yeroushalmi, *Judeo-Persian Poet,* p. 16.
3. See the Introduction.
4. See below, chap. 8.
5. Yeroushalmi, *Judeo-Persian Poet,* pp. 33–34.
6. Ibid., pp. 24–25.
7. See Bacher, *Zwei jüdisch-persische Dichter,* pp. 166–169.
8. For a complete list of ʿImrānī's works, see Netzer, "Judeo-Persian Footnote"; Yeroushalmi, *Judeo-Persian Poet,* pp. 32–41.
9. Corrupt manuscript copies and more frequent use of Hebrew words which throw off the meter also contribute to this impression (Yeroushalmi, *Judeo-Persian Poet,* pp. 69–77).
10. Yeroushalmi, *Judeo-Persian Poet,* p. 46, quoting Louis Finkelstein, *Mabo' le-massektot Awot we-Awot de-Rabbi Natan* (New York, 1950), p. 5.
11. The authorship remains unclear (see Rypka, *History,* p. 130).
12. See Yeroushalmi, *Judeo-Persian Poet,* pp. 57ff.; and below, chap. 5.

13. Yeroushalmi, *Jewish-Persian Poet,* p. 39.
14. Ibid., pp. 40–41.

Fatḥ-nāmah

1. Cf. Josh. 5, 6. This translation is based on mss. BL Or. 13704, fols. 30v–37v, D fols. 32r–37v, and BZI 4602, fols. 21r–28v. For midrashic sources, see Ginzberg, *Legends,* 4:7–8. Most Muslim legendary accounts do not deal with this episode at length; the most detailed account is in al-Ṭabarī (*History,* 3:89–98).
2. In Sufi terminology, Ar./Pers., *aql-i kull* (Universal Intellect) refers to the first Intellect of the Neoplatonic system, often identified with the Archangel Gabriel, the source of revelation in Islam; the *nous* of Plotinus (Chittick, *Sufi Path of Love,* p. 35).
3. Pers., *zamāneh;* see above, *Ezra-nāmah,* nn. 56 and 38.
4. In this and the verses that follow ʿImrānī employs the Arabic/Persian word *khāṣ* (special, choice, select, excellent, holy), in the full range of its meanings.
5. Cf. Exod. 3:5.
6. Moses' name is not mentioned explicitly in this verse, but the epithet *rasūl-i-ḥaqq* (God's messenger), clearly refers to him.
7. I was unable to find any legendary sources, Jewish or Muslim, for verses 49–52.
8. The Hebrew word *kohen* is joined here to the Persian plural ending *ān.*
9. Heb., *shofar.*
10. The son of the priest Eleazar (Ginzberg, *Legends,* 4:5; 6:171n.10).
11. The priests and the Ark were actually stationed in the middle, between the vanguard and the rearguard of the army (Josh. 6:8, 9, 13).
12. Ar./Pers., *takbīr,* the Muslim formula *Allahu akbar* (God is great), which punctuates the canonical prayer and is used constantly in daily life as a pious exclamation.
13. "The great miracle which happened at Jericho was not that the walls fell, but that they disappeared in the bowels of the earth" (*Babylonian Talmud,* Berakot 54a–54b; Targum Joshua 6.20; Ginzberg, *Legends,* 6:175n.22).
14. Lit., *vaḥdat* (union, oneness), a Sufi term denoting a mystical state of oneness with God. I was unable to find Jewish sources that referred to the priests' mystical experience before the walls of Jericho. For a late seventeenth- or early eighteenth-century JP miniature depicting the priests before the walls of Jericho, see Moreen, *Miniature Paintings,* p. 49 (BL OR. 13704, fol. 31v).
15. Ar./Pers., *tahlīl* (praising God), the first part of the Muslim profession of faith (*shahāda*), *lā ilāha illā-llāh* (there is no god but God). The Islamic term and concept echo the Heb. *hallel* (praise), associated especially with Psalms 113–118 and recited on the New Moon and the festivals.
16. Ar./Pers., *imām[ān]* (leader, model, exemplar), a term laden with meaning for Muslims that ranges from ordinary prayer leader to divinely inspired guide, this latter especially among Shiʿis.
17. Ar./Pers., *wajd* (ecstasy of love), produced by the Divine Presence. This technical Sufi term is derived from the Ar. verb *wajada* (to find), that is, "to find God and become quiet and peaceful in finding Him" (Schimmel, *Mystical Dimensions,* p. 178).
18. Pers., *ṣandūq-i shahādat.*
19. See above, n. 12.
20. This refers to the biblical concept of *ḥerem* (ban, devoted thing), which means

something that is set apart as belonging strictly to God and is forbidden for profane use. War booty in Israel's early wars was devoted entirely to God, and in victory nothing was spared; the idolatrous enemy had to be destroyed utterly (*The Oxford Companion to the Bible,* ed. Bruce M. Metzger and Michael D. Coogan, s.v. "ban"). Here and in the verses that follow, ʿImrānī is playing on the Hebrew term and its Arabic cognate *ḥaram* (forbidden [for sacred reasons]); cf. *EI* (2), s.v. *ḥaram.*

21. This is, of course, anachronistic, as there was no set *miqdash,* cultic site, in Joshua's day (*EJ,* s.v. "Mikdash"). Joshua did not earn unanimous praise for devoting Jericho to the Lord; some Jewish sources thought that he led the Israelites thereby into temptation (cf. Josh. 7; Ginzberg, *Legends,* 6:175n.23).
22. Cf. Josh. 2.
23. A qur'anic epithet for God, Ar., *lā-yazāl* ([He Who] ceases not; see Surah 9:110; 13:31; 22:55).
24. Caleb, the son of Yefuneh, was one of the spies (Num. 13:4–16) whom Moses sent to scout the Land of Israel and who, unlike the majority of the spies, encouraged Moses to proceed with the conquest (Num. 13:30). For this he was rewarded by being allowed to enter the land (Num. 14:24). Some midrashic sources claim that Phinehas accompanied Caleb on this mission (Ginzberg, *Legends,* 3:342, 6:118n.681). Josh. 2:1 does not name the spies. In a midrashic source (*Numbers Rabbah,* 16.1), Caleb is sent to spy out the land again, this time by Joshua, together with Phinehas.
25. Cf. Josh. 2:14.
26. Josh. 6:23 mentions only Rahab and her extended kindred. On whether Rahab was justified in her request, see Ginzberg, *Legends,* 6:174n.23.
27. This and the next two hemistichs are not found in ms. D.
28. Perhaps ʿImrānī bestows this, and other standard Persian epithets, on Rahab tongue in cheek, given that she was a "harlot" (Josh. 2:1). However, he may have been in earnest since Rahab's good deed erased her past and allowed her to join the Israelite tribes.
29. The reason for consecrating everything found in Jericho was, according to some midrashic sources, that it was conquered on the Sabbath: "Joshua reasoned that as the Sabbath is holy, so also that which is conquered on the Sabbath should be holy" (Ginzberg, *Legends,* 4:8; but see the controversy over whether Jericho was conquered on the Sabbath at 6:174n.22).
30. See above, n. 21.
31. According to some midrashic sources, Rahab became a righteous proselyte, the ancestor of prophets and priests (Ginzberg, *Legends,* 4:5; 6:171n.12).
32. ʿImrānī plays here with a common topos of Sufi literature. (Spiritual) drunkenness, usually denoting the mystical state of union with the divine, is used to imply the opposite, the state of spiritual deprivation.
33. See above, "Moses and the Burning Bush," n. 1.
34. According to midrashic sources, Joshua himself married Rahab (Ginzberg, *Legends,* 4:5); Caleb had been married to Miriam, Moses' sister (2:253; 6:185n.25), who died at Kadesh and was buried there (Num. 20:1).
35. See above, n. 31.
36. This and the previous distich are not in BL Or. 13704.
37. ʿImrānī is fond of quoting the poet Saʿdī, but I was unable to find these quotations

in either Saʿdī's *Bustān* or *Gulistān*. Perhaps the reference is to Solomon, traditional author of Ecclesiastes, as these verses are an elaboration of Eccles. 7.1.

38. Muḥammad, his daughter Fāṭima, and the twelve imams revered by Twelver Shiʿis comprise the Holy Family, or the Fourteen Infallible Ones in Shiʿi parlance. Needless to say, this invocation is rather strange here. If indeed this verse exists in *all* extant manuscripts, it may suggest ʿImrānī's hope that his poetry would spread beyond the Jewish community.

The Book of Ruth

1. This translation is based on mss. BL Or. 13704, fols. 97r–100r; BZI 4602, fols. 111r–115r, and BZI 964, fols. 183r–184r. For midrashic sources, see Ginzberg, *Legends*, 4:30–32, 85, 88; 6:187ff. For a lovely poetic rendition of the Book of Ruth based on the biblical and midrashic accounts, see Grace Goldin, *Come Under the Wings: A Midrash on Ruth* (Philadelphia, 1980 repr.).
2. On Ruth's extraordinary beauty, see Ginzberg, *Legends*, 6:192n.57.
3. A *sāz* (Ar./Pers.) is a musical instrument.
4. That is, Ruth shares everything with Naomi, who has been "burned" by the calamities she has endured and who is still in mourning for the deaths of her husband and sons.
5. See Ginzberg, *Legends*, 6:191–192n.55.
6. Boaz's falling in love with Ruth is not mentioned in midrashic sources, but it is a necessary conceit in the Persian romances that served as ʿImrānī's models (see below, n. 9).
7. This is a reference to Tob, Boaz's older brother, who is not actually named in Ruth 4:1. Tob apparently relinquished his right to marry Ruth under the misapprehension that the prohibition against Jews marrying Moabites included females, not just males, as was the case (Ginzberg, *Legends*, 6:193nn.61,64).
8. ʿImrānī omits the entire episode in which Naomi and Ruth "plot" and carry out their plan to have Boaz marry Ruth (Ruth 3). Nor does he mention that according to some midrashic sources, Boaz had been married but that his dead wife had been buried on the day of Naomi and Ruth's arrival (Ginzberg, *Legends*, 4:32 and 6:190n.48).
9. Famous lovers in Niẓāmī's (d. 1209) Persian romance *Khosrow and Shīrīn*, who, like Ruth and Boaz, were of different origins.
10. At the time of their marriage Boaz was apparently an octogenarian and Ruth was in her forties. Since she was past the age of childbearing, the birth of Obed was a miracle vouchsafed to Ruth. Boaz is supposed to have died in the bridal chamber (Ginzberg, *Legends*, 6:194nn.68,69).
11. Heb., for "servant [of God]." According to tradition, Obed was a very pious man (Ginzberg, *Legends*, p. 194n.68).
12. See Ginzberg, *Legends*, 6:194n.69.
13. The musical references in the last three verses form an elegant *tanāsub* (Ar./Pers., harmony of similar things), one of the many rhetorical artifices of Persian poetry (see Schimmel, *Two-Colored Brocade*, pp. 38–40). This particular example looks forward to David's musical skills and back to the fact that his birth could only have come about through an apparently straight arrow (Boaz) "straying" from its path.

Introduction to Aḥaron b. Mashiaḥ

1. This introduction is based on Netzer, *Oṣar,* pp. 33–34; idem., *Yehude Iran,* p. 43; idem., *Ḥobot Yehudah,* p. xi.
2. Netzer, *Oṣar,* p. 34n.57; idem., *Ḥobot Yehudah,* p. xi, Scholem, *Sabbatai Ṣevi,* p. 753n.177.

Shoftim-nāmah

1. Cf. Judg. 11:34–40. This translation is based on mss. BZI 964, fols. 153r–154v and BZI 4571, fols. 102v–105r. For midrashic references, see Ginzberg, *Legends,* 4:43–47. For a perceptive discussion of the quasi-tragic dimensions of Jephthah's vow, see J. Cheryl Exum, *Tragedy and Biblical Narrative* (Cambridge, 1992), chap. 3.
2. In the biblical narrative the daughter's name is not preserved, which is one of the reasons Exum labels the narrative "androcentric" (*Tragedy,* p. 68). Rabbinic tradition not only emphasizes her selflessness but preserves her name as Sheilah (Ginzberg, *Legends,* 4:44–45).
3. A *sāz* (Ar./Pers.) is a musical instrument.
4. A reference to Central Asia, believed to be the home of beautiful Turks in classical Persian poetry.
5. According to Exum, Jephthah's *hamartia* (Greek for "incautious vow") does not render him a tragic hero, primarily because the biblical narrative does not describe an "inner struggle . . . wrestling against his fate" on his part (*Tragedy,* p. 57). Aḥaron b. Mashiaḥ's account attempts to describe such a struggle.
6. Literally, Pers., *kabutar* (dove).
7. According to Exum, Jephthah's daughter also "lacks the development that makes for a genuinely tragic personality. She accepts her fate so willingly and obediently that it is shocking. . . . In the space of a few brief verses, she moves from mirth and celebration of her father's victory to lamentation, and just as quickly she passes into death and celebration in communal memory" (*Tragedy,* p. 58).
8. According to some medieval commentators (i.e., Kimḥi [d. 1235] at Judg. 11:39), Jephthah did not sacrifice his daughter but let her live out her life in seclusion, devoted entirely to God. Early rabbinic sources, however, make no such claim and condemn Jephthah's act (Ginzberg, *Legends,* 6:203n.109). The concept of immurement is not in the Jewish sources I consulted and may well be the poet's original contribution.
9. In some rabbinic sources, the rivalry between Jephthah and Phinehas, the high priest, prevented the former from consulting the latter about the possible annulment of his vow, and this brought about Sheilah's death. Both men were eventually punished for their excessive pride: Jephthah was dismembered in death, and the holy spirit abandoned Phinehas (Ginzberg, *Legends,* 4:46). Rabbinic sources also blame Phinehas for "not having prevented the war between Jephthah and the Ephraimites. He ought to have remonstrated with those proud men who did not intercede in behalf of Jephthah's daughter, though they were ready to go to war over an alleged insult" (Ginzberg, *Legends,* 6:203n.109).

Introduction to Khwājah Bukhārā'ī

1. This introduction is based on Amnon Netzer's doctoral dissertation, "Study of Kh(w)ājah Bokhārā'ī," pp. 1–91, also summarized in idem., "Dāniyāl-Nāme,"

pp. 145–164. My translation is based on Netzer's edition of the text as printed in his *Muntakhab,* pp. 45–46, 261–297, with occasional references to the fuller edition in his dissertation.

2. See Netzer, "Dāniyāl-Nāme," pp. 146–148.
3. See Netzer, "Dāniyāl-nāma and Its Linguistic Features." On the Jews of Bukhārā, see the Introduction. On more literature from Bukhārā, see below.
4. See the entries on Fattaḥ-i Jahūd and Ṭibb-i Ḥāziq, pennames of two Jewish poets living in Bukhārā, mentioned in Muḥammad Badiʿ b. Mowlānā Muḥammad Sharīf Samarqandī's (Maliḥā) *Muzakkir al-aṣḥāb* (The reminder of companions), compiled toward the end of the seventeenth century (ms. 610, Fond Vostochnykh Rukopisei, Akademiia Nauk, Dushanbe, Tadzhikistan, pp. 197–198). I am grateful to Robert D. McChesney for bringing this information to my attention.
5. Netzer, "Dāniyāl-Nāme," p. 155. For chronological inaccuracies within the Book of Daniel, see Bickerman, *Four Strange Books,* p. 93.
6. See Bickerman, *Four Strange Books,* pp. 82–86.

Dāniyāl-nāmah

1. Cf. Dan. 6. This translation is based on Netzer, "Study of Kh(w)ājah Bokhārāʾī," pp. 197–209 and his *Muntakhab,* pp. 284–293. For midrashic interpretations, see Ginzberg, *Legends,* 4:348–349; 6:435; Carey A. Moore, *Daniel, Esther and Jeremiah: The Additions* (New York, 1977), pp. 117–149; Bickerman, *Four Strange Books,* pp. 53–138.
2. See above, *Ardashīr-nāmah,* n. 30.
3. Cf. "A law of the Medes and Persians, which cannot be abrogated" (Dan. 6:13).
4. According to legend, Alexander the Great built a strong wall or rampart of iron and brass in order to stop the incursion of the barbarian "Yājūj" and "Mājūj" on an oppressed people (*EI* (2), s.v. "al-Iskandar").
5. Cf. "All other creatures were instructed to change their nature, if Israel should ever need their help in the course of history. The sea was ordered to divide before Moses, and the heavens to give ear to the words of the leader; the sun and the moon were bidden to stand still before Joshua, the ravens to feed Elijah, the fire to spare the three youths in the furnace, the lion to do no harm to Daniel, the fish to spew forth Jonah, and the heavens to open before Ezekiel" (Ginzberg, *Legends,* 1:50–51; see also *Bereshit Rabbah,* 5.5, and other sources cited in ibid., 5:68n.9. On the primordial nature of miracles already "stamped" upon "the existing nature" of certain things, see Maimonides, *The Guide of the Perplexed,* trans. S. Pines (Chicago, 1974), 2.29, pp. 345–346).
6. Cf. "Darius sets his heart to deliver Daniel (6:15). The king, as Theodotion says, became not Daniel's judge but his advocate" (Bickerman, *Four Strange Books,* p. 85).
7. According to some midrashic sources, a large rock rolled of its own volition from the Land of Israel to protect Daniel against his enemies (Ginzberg, *Legends,* 4:348). Alternatively, an angel assumed the form of a rock to close the pit (6:435n.12).
8. The angel's name is not specified in the rabbinic sources I consulted. Gabriel, one of the four archangels, is an important divine messenger in both Judaism and Islam.
9. See Rashi's biblical commentary at Dan. 6:18.
10. Gabriel's wings are highly symbolic in Sufi lore. When Muḥammad ascended to

heaven (*mi'rāj*) and passed beyond the Lote Tree of the Far Boundry (Surah 53:14) into God's presence, Gabriel could not follow him, for, as the great Sufi poet Jalāl al-Dīn Rūmī had him say, "If I fly beyond this limit, my wings will burn" (Chittick, *Sufi Path of Love*, p. 222).

11. Lit., "dark, night-colored," "dark-bay horse." In the *Shah-nāmah*, Shabrang is the name of Siyāvush's horse; Siyāvush is one of the heroes of the epic. See *The Legend of Siyavash*, trans. Dick Davis (London, 1992).
12. The meaning of this and the distichs that follow to the end of this chapter is not entirely clear, which is probably why Netzer omitted them from his *Muntakhab*, although they can be found in his edition of the text ("Study of Kh[w]āje Bokhārā'ī," p. 201).
13. Royal radiance seems unconnected to sleeplessness . . .
14. This is the principal message of Daniel's ordeal in the Book of Daniel; see Bickerman, *Four Strange Books*, pp. 86 and 95.
15. While he was in the pit, Daniel was being fed by the prophet Habakkuk, who was compelled to bring food from Judea (Ginzberg, *Legends*, 4:348; 6:432n.6; Moore, *Daniel*, pp. 140–141).
16. Cf. "The ferocious beasts welcomed the pious Daniel like dogs fawning upon their master on his return home, licking his hands and wagging their tails" (Ginzberg, *Legends*, 4:348).
17. On the virtues of Daniel, see Ginzberg, *Legends*, 4:326–327, 337–338, 347–348; 6:413–414nn.76–77.
18. I omit the last hemistich, containing the poet's moralizing, which is rather flat after Daniel's speech.
19. Majnūn, Ar./Pers., "[the] demented," the name of the celebrated Bedouin who was the hero of numerous romances written in the Islamicate world. Majnūn's love chained him to Layla, who in Sufi poetry represents the Divine Beloved. See Niẓāmī, *The Story of Layla and Majnun*, trans. R. Gelpke, with E. Mattin and G. Hill (Boulder, Colo., 1978).
20. Pers., *farmān* (command), intended, no doubt, for the Ar. *'amr*. The relation between God's *'amr* (command) and His *'irāda* (will) is complex in Islamic philosophy and mysticism (*EI* (2), s.v. *'amr*, and Awn, *Satan's Tragedy*, pp. 99–108). Here I translate *farmān* as "will" because that is a more idiomatic English expression, though I am aware that in the Islamic context the two terms are not interchangeable.
21. This verse is missing in Netzer's *Muntakhab*.
22. See above, *Ezra-nāmah*, n. 11.
23. Cf. "The hundred and twenty enemies of Daniel, together with their wives and children numbering two hundred and forty-four persons, were torn to shreds by fourteen hundred and sixty-four lions" (Ginzberg, *Legends*, 4:349; for the fantastic numbers, see 6:436n.16).
24. There may be a negative pun in this hemistich that I was unable to capture in my translation: *bi-khunshān panjahārā āl kardand* (lit., "they made red footprints with their blood") plays on the meaning of *panja-yi āl*, or *panj tan*, that is the "five [holy] ones," namely Muḥammad, Fāṭima, 'Alī, Ḥasan, and Ḥusayn, the "holy family" of Shi'i Islam: a thinly veiled polemic against, or perhaps merely descriptive of, this martyr-oriented form of Islam?

25. See above, "Jacob and the Wolf," n. 37.
26. Cf. "The king published the wonders done by God in all parts of his land, and called upon the people to betake themselves to Jerusalem and help in the erection of the Temple" (Ginzberg, *Legends,* 4:349).

Chapter 3 An Apocryphal Epic: *Ḥanukkah-nāmah*

1. This introduction is based on Yeroushalmi, *Judeo-Persian Poet,* p. 36; Netzer, *Muntakhab,* p. 43; idem., "Judeo-Persian Footnote," p. 263; idem., *Oṣar,* pp. 31 and 36.
2. At least two Muslim chronicles from the first half of the fifteenth century bear this title (Yeroushalmi, *Judeo-Persian Poet,* p. 36n.27).
3. ʿImrānī's account is based primarily on the apocryphal *Scroll of Antiochus,* composed originally in Aramaic between the second and fifth century CE, and translated into many languages. I relied on Gaster's translation, *Megillat Antiochus,* pp. 165–183; also *EJ,* s.v. "Scroll of Antiochus." The tale is more remotely based on 1 Macc. 9:13–73 (*Apocrypha,* pp. 408–413). This translation is based primarily on JTS 1411, fols. 65r–73v. JNUL 1183, fols. 22b–51b, and BZI 1075 fols. 1a–61a were also consulted.
4. Khaṭā is northern China; Chīn is China in general; Barbar is Barbary, the north African coast as far as the Straits of Gilbraltar. The point of the verse is that this army was assembled from the farthest corners of east and west.
5. Mangalūs is a place in India famous for its white elephants.
6. Cf. *Megillat Antiochus,* vv. 46–47.
7. This form of the name Bagrīs is from *Megillat Antiochus;* it is "Bacchides" in 1 Macc.
8. Nimrod was a legendary powerful pagan king, remembered in both Jewish and Islamic lore, who persecuted Abraham (see Vera Basch, "Abraham in the Fire," B.A. thesis, Princeton University, 1972).
9. A rather curious spelling for the name Antiochus.
10. Lāt is a female goddess worshiped in pre-Islamic Arabia (Surah 53:19).
11. Cf. *Megillat Antiochus,* v. 50; also, "Then they gathered together and went to Mizpeh, opposite Jerusalem, for Israel formerly had a praying-place in Mizpeh" (1 Macc. 3:46; *EJ,* s.v. "Mizpeh").
12. Ar./Pers., *rukūʿ va-sujūd,* technical terms of Muslim worship.
13. Heb., *ṣom haf[s]kah,* a period of continuous fasting lasting at least two days, interrupted by one meal (E. Ben-Yehudah, *Millon ha-lashon ha-ʿivrit* [Jerusalem, 1914], 2:1158).
14. Lit., "we turned them into *uncircumcised.*"
15. Mattatiah is emulating Jacob's blessing of his twelve sons (Gen. 49) and draws appropriate parallels between namesakes.
16. Cf. Gen. 34:25, 26.
17. Abner is the name of one of King David's captains (1 Sam. 14:50).
18. This verse can refer to Jonathan or, more likely, to Saul's military exploits in 1 Sam.
19. Phinehas, son of the high priest Elʿazar; Num. 25:10–13; see above *Shoftim-nāmah,* n. 9.
20. This detail, in an altered form, may originate in the image of the "heavenly rider" in 2 Macc. 3:25–27.

21. Heb., *mashḥit* (cf. 1 Chron. 21:12).
22. Heb., *esh ve-gafrit* (cf. Ezek. 38:22).
23. In *Megillat Antiochus* (v. 63), El'azar's death is more ignominious: he dies mired in elephant dung.
24. Judah and El'azar.
25. The beginning of the traditional prayer recited when lighting Hanukkah candles.
26. The three patriarchs, Abraham, Isaac, and Jacob.
27. Hebrew for "law court."
28. Cf. *Megillat Antiochus*, vv. 70–75. Hanukkah begins traditionally, on the 25th of Kislev of the Jewish calendar.
29. This couplet is actually written in the third-person singular.

Chapter 4 Didactic Poetry: *Makhzan al-pand*

1. See above, "Introduction to 'Imrānī."
2. This introduction is based on Netzer, *Muntakhab*, pp. 52–53, 369; idem., *Oṣar*, pp. 35 and 183; and Bacher, "Aus einem jüdisch-persischen Lehrgedicht," pp. 223–228.
3. Netzer, *Muntakhab*, p. 52n.55.
4. This translation is based primarily on BL Or. 4731, JNUL 8° 4332, and Netzer, *Muntakhab*, pp. 369–376.
5. The literal meaning of this line is puzzling since it would endorse bad manners in both Iranian and Jewish cultures.
6. Pers., *farzand*, denotes a male or female child, but one is much more likely to have educated one's son in the Islamicate world in general.
7. Ar./Pers., *'adab*, a complex word in these languages denoting politeness, urbanity, propriety of conduct, learning (*EI* (2), s.v. "*'adab*").
8. One's coreligionists are not exempt from character flaws.
9. Cf. Ps. 111:10.
10. Cf. v. 102 above.

Chapter 5 Mishnah and Midrash

Ganj-nāmah

1. In Yeroushalmi, *Judeo-Persian Poet*.
2. See the Introduction.
3. Yeroushalmi, *Judeo-Persian Poet*, p. 44.
4. This text is taken from Yeroushalmi, *Judeo-Persian Poet*, JP text, pp. 411–416; English trans., pp. 269–276. Rabbi Yose was the third of Rabbi Yoḥannan b. Zakkai's prominent disciples, mentioned in Abot 2:8. He was active ca. 80–110 CE. This section comments on Abot 2:12: "Rabbi Yose says: 'Let the property of thy fellow be as dear to you as your own; make yourself fit for the study of Torah, for it will not be yours by inheritance, and let all your actions be for the sake of Heaven.' "
5. Ar., *al-wahhāb* (the Giver, the Bestower, the Munificent), another epithet for God in the Qur'ān (Surah 3:6, 38:8 and 38–34).
6. This couplet is almost a direct quotation from Sa'di's *Gulistān* (The rose garden); see *Gulistān*, ed. N. Iranparast (Tehran, 1976), p. 42, chap. 1, no. 18.

7. Ar./Pers., *kalām,* has at least two meanings. In the Qur'ān (Surah 2:75, 9:6, 48:15) it is used in the sense of the "word of God" in instances where He speaks to Muḥammad. The second usage, *[ʿilm al]-kalām* ([the science of] discourse), is a technical term that designates the scholastic branch of Islamic theology, which flourished between the ninth and twelfth centuries. See Montgomery Watt, *The Formative Period of Islamic Thought* (Edinburgh, 1973), pp. 182–186.
8. Ar./Pers., *ʿilm o ʿamal* (knowledge and works). Throughout GN, ʿImrānī uses these terms as equivalents of Word/Scripture and *miṣvot* (commandments), hence the capitalization of "Word."
9. That is, through Word and deed.
10. Ar./Pers., *nafs* ([the lower, carnal] soul, the flesh); see Schimmel, *Mystical Dimensions,* Index under "nafs."
11. This is not a literal rendition, but rather ʿImrānī's interpretation of, possibly, Prov. 10:21. Similar expressions are found in Prov. 5:23, 15:10, and 19:17.
12. Ar./Pers. *ḥaqq* (truth, justice) is of one of the divine attributes mentioned in the Qur'ān. In Sufi terminology *al-Ḥaqq* (the Real, the Truth) is one of God's most common epithets (see al-Ḥujwīrī, *The Kashf al-Maḥjūb,* trans. R. A. Nicholson [London, 1935], p. 384, and al-Sarraj, *Kitāb al-lumʿa fi'l taṣawwuf,* ed. R. A. Nicholson [London, 1914], pp. 28–35).
13. Ar./Pers., *muqallid,* a technical term in Islamic theology in general and in Shiʿism in particular that designates the follower of high-ranking jurisprudents (*mujtahid*) in matters of religious law (*sharīʿa*) (M. Momen, *An Introduction to Shiʿi Islam* [New Haven, 1985], p. 175).
14. Ar./Pers., *ghusl,* the Muslim term for ritual ablutions before prayer.
15. Muslim legendary lore identifies Khiżr with the prophet Elijah. He is said to have set out in search of the Fountain of Life; after finding it, he guided others to find the source of eternal life. See the definitive study by Wheeler M. Thackston, "The Khiḍr Legend in the Islamic Tradition," B.A. thesis, Princeton University, 1967.
16. Lit., "he will bring the father to God."
17. Num. 11:28; see *The Fathers According to Rabbi Nathan,* trans. J. Goldin (New Haven, 1983 repr.), p. 87.
18. The reference is to Saʿdī, whom ʿImrānī paraphrases in the next couplet ("They will ask you, 'what is your accomplishment?' And they will not say, 'who is your father?' " [*Gulistān,* p. 212]).
19. Ar./Pers., *yaqīn,* a Sufi technical term denoting the "elimination of doubt by virtue of gnostic knowledge and illumination" (R. A. Nicholson, *The Mystics of Islam* [London, 1963 repr.], pp. 50–51).
20. The rose and the nightingale are the most famous cliché characters of Persian Sufi poetry; they symbolize the lover (nightingale) and the beloved (rose), earthly or heavenly.
21. By referring to *amānat* (trust), this verse echoes the opening verses of the section.

A Midrash on the Ascension of Moses

1. This summary, as well as the translation and notes that follow, are based on Amnon Netzer's "Midrash on the Ascension," pp. 105–114 and 134–140.
2. See Ginzberg, *Legends,* 2:304–316.

3. ". . . So is my beloved among the youths" (Song of Sol. 2:3), referring here to Moses.
4. See David Halperin, *The Faces of the Chariot: Early Responses to Ezekiel's Vision* (Tübingen, 1988), pp. 289–313.
5. *Visions of Heaven and Hell,* Eileen Gardiner, ed. (New York, 1989).
6. Cf. Muḥammad's ascension (*miʿrāj*), in Geo Widengren, *Muḥammad, the Apostle of God and His Ascension* (Uppsala-Wiesbaden, 1955).
7. They actually tour only seven spheres. For the number of the heavenly spheres, see above, "Jacob and the Wolf," n. 41.
8. The various redactions give different spellings of the name of the Angel of Hell; cf. Ginzberg, *Legends,* 2:310, "Nasargiel."
9. In the Hebrew version of this midrash published in A. J. Wertheimer, *Batte Midrashot* (Jerusalem, 1980 repr.), 1:281–285, the description of Hell and its classification into seven distinct sections and types of punishment differs from the JP version.
10. Isa. 59:7.
11. Isa. 1:4.
12. Lit., "in the sky."
13. Job 3:21.
14. The various manuscripts are ambiguous about this name; see Wertheimer, *Batte Midrashot,* 1:282. According to the sources cited by M. Gaster, "Hell has seven names: Sheol, Abadon, Beer Shaon, Beer Shahat, Hatzar Maveth, Beer Tahtiyah, and Tit Hayaven" ("Hebrew Visions," p. 602). Or based on Abraham Azulay's *Baraita de-Masseket Gehhinom,* "Beneath the earth is Tehom, under Tehom is Bohu, under Bohu is Mayim, under Mayim is Arka, and there is Sheol, Abadon, Beer Shahat Tit Hayaven, Shaare Maveth, Shaare Salmavet, and Gehinom" (ibid., p. 607).
15. Prov. 30:15. Cf. *Babylonian Talmud,* ʿAvodah Zarah, 17a: "What is meant by 'Give, give,'? Said Mar ʿUqba: 'It is the voice of the two daughters who cry from Gehenna calling to his world: Bring, bring! And who are they? *Minut* (heresy, apostasy) and the government.' "
16. According to Wertheimer, the name of the place is *ṭiṭ ha-yaven* (miry clay; cf. Ps. 40:3; *Batte Midrashot* 1:282). About Dumah as an important section of Hell, see the midrash on Paradise and Hell in *Bet ha-Midrash* (Jerusalem, 1938), 5:44–45.
17. Ruḥiʾel is not mentioned in Wertheimer's *Batte Midrashot.* In Jewish legendary lore Ruḥiʾel is the angel governing the wind (Ginzberg, *Legends,* 1:140).
18. That is, like Aristotle and his followers, they denied creatio ex nihilo.
19. Ps. 3:8.
20. Cf. *Babylonian Talmud,* Berakot, 54b.
21. Perhaps what is meant here is lending money to fellow Jews; lending on interest to strangers (non-Jews) is biblically sanctioned (Deut. 32:21). If the latter is the case, this JP text, emerging from a Muslim milieu, may be reflecting Islam's ban—at least in theory—on lending money on interest (Surah 2:275).
22. That is, they cheated with weights.
23. Isa. 66:24.
24. See above, n. 14.

25. A doxological expression, part of the *kaddish,* one of the central prayers of the Jewish liturgy.
26. Cf. *Mishnah,* Pirke Abot, 4:22.
27. Jer. 17:10.
28. Jer. 32:19.
29. In general, the description of Paradise, with some omissions found in the text, corresponds to the Hebrew versions in Wertheimer, *Batte Midrashot,* 1:283–285.
30. Ps. 144:15.
31. It is interesting to note that in two JP manuscripts ("C" and "G" in Netzer's edition), Moses asks, "Why are my name and the name of my wife not among them?" The theme of this paragraph about the righteous women is not found in Wertheimer, *Batte Midrashot* (cf. *Mishnah,* Shabbat, 2.6).
32. According to the *Zohar* (Num. 154b), Shamshi'el served as one of the two aides of the archangel Uri'el.
33. Seventy thrones in Wertheimer, *Batte Midrashot,* 1:284.
34. According to Gaster, "It is the throne of Abraham the Patriarch" ("Hebrew Visions," p. 586).
35. A verse from the standard Jewish prayerbooks (I. Davidson, *Oṣar ha-shirah ve ha-piyyut* [New York, 1970], p. 4101).
36. Ps. 106:1.
37. JP mss. A, B, F, H: "to those who repented."
38. *Bet ha-Midrash,* 5:47–48; 2:52–53, and 3:131–140.
39. Jer. 32:19.
40. Ps. 31:20.
41. Jer. 32:19.

Chapter 6 Biblical Commentaries

1. See ms. IV D 35; its linguistic peculiarities are described by G. Lazard in *EJ,* s.v. "Judeo-Persian," p. 431.
2. See the Introduction.
3. On the category of *tafsīr* in JP literature, see Netzer, *Oṣar,* pp. 13–14.
4. Ibid., pp. 15–20.
5. See below, chap. 8.
6. See *The Mūsā-nāma of R. Shim'on Ḥakham,* ed. Herbert H. Paper (Cincinnati, 1986), p. xi.
7. See above, "Introduction to Shāhīn," n. 7.

Commentary on Ecclesiastes 4

1. This translation is based on JTS 1403, fols. 53r–54r, 62v–65r; BZI 1045/4 fols. 105r–107v and BZI 4547, fols. 1v–2v, 88r–90r.
2. Ar./Pers., *tafsīr.*
3. We have no way of knowing what commentary Yehudah b. Binyamin is referring to.
4. Obviously, some Iranian Jews found the original Hebrew text of Ecclesiastes difficult to understand.
5. A rather unusual, if noble, motive for the author's undertaking.
6. That is, without gainful employment.

7. The repetition of this phrase, if not a scribal error, is indicative of the author's real intentions. For David Kimḥi, see above, *Shoftim-nāmah,* n. 8.
8. A euphemism for wishing the opposite.
9. Binyamin appears to be creating his own interpretation of this verse in which power is explicitly attributed to oppressors.
10. "He has to eat his own flesh," because either, as Rashi (*ad loc.*) explains, he will eventually behold the reward of the righteous on the Day of Judgment or, as Ibn Ezra claims, he has consumed all his wealth through idleness.
11. Cf. Ibn Ezra, *ad loc., leḥem* (bread).
12. The Hebrew original says simply, "the case of a man who is alone, without companion"; Binyamin is following Rashi's explanation here.
13. See Rashi, *ad loc.:* "He acquires no student [to teach him the Torah] who would be like a son to him, nor does he have a friend [*ḥaver;* someone with whom he could study the Torah] who could be like a brother."
14. Rashi, *ad loc.*
15. Rashi, *ad loc.,* continues to refer to two companions who study texts together and help each other, or elucidate for one another when necessary, the teachings of their rabbi.
16. Both Rashi and Ibn Ezra, *ad loc.,* take this half of the verse to refer to the act of procreation.
17. If I understand the Persian correctly, this differs from the Hebrew text: "If one attacks, two can stand up to him."
18. Rashi, *ad loc.,* adds to the literal meaning again by referring to the strength of the wisdom acquired by three generations of one family (grandfather, father, and son) who have devoted their lives to the threefold learning of Torah, Mishnah, and *derek ereṣ* (ethical conduct).
19. Instead of the Hebrew: "a poor but wise youth," which Rashi, *ad loc.,* says refers to *yeṣer ha-tov* (the inclination toward good).
20. Rashi and Ibn Ezra, *ad loc.,* relate this verse to the previous one, a connection not found in the JP text.
21. Rashi, *ad loc.,* connects the phrase with the generation of the Flood and with Noah. However, Binyamin refers to Noah as "the second son," which is not correct; Noah was the first son of Lemek (Gen. 5:28–30). Perhaps he means that Noah was a "second Adam" because he (re)populated the earth. Ibn Ezra takes the expression to refer back to the two previous verses, to the wise young man who comes to supplant the foolish old king.
22. Rashi, *ad loc.,* gives the same explanation.
23. See Rashi, *ad loc.*

Commentary on Exodus 3–4

1. This translation is based on the text reproduced in Paper's *Mūsā-nāma,* pp. 100–107.
2. Referring to the pre-Islamic *now rūz* celebrated on March 21, the vernal equinox.
3. See Ginzberg, *Legends,* 2:300–305, 316–326; 5:414–416.
4. According to rabbinic tradition, Moses led his flocks deliberately away from inhabited places so that they might not steal, even inadvertently, from other people's

property (*Midrash Tanḥumah*, 12; *Midrash Rabbah*, Shemot 3; *Yalqut Shim'oni*, Shemot 3).

5. See Ex. 3:1, Mount Horeb; *ṭur* (Hebrew for "row," "column"), together with the Aramaic synonym *ṭura*, can also mean "mountain." Muslims refer to Mount Sinai as "Ṭūr" (Surah 52). Cf. Ginzberg, *Legends*, 5:415n.113.
6. Cf. *Yalqut Shim'oni*, 4.172; *Seder 'Olam Rabbah*, 5.2.
7. This is the staff which later becomes the instrument of Moses' miracles (Ginzberg, *Legends*, 2:291–293).
8. It is Moses' solicitude for Jethro's flock that earned him the epithet *ro'eh ne'man* (faithful shepherd) and provided proof that he would be equally solicitous with the Children of Israel (*Midrash Rabbah*, Shemot 2; cf. Ginzberg, *Legends*, 2:301; 5:414n.109: see also Moreen, "Moses, God's Shepherd"). See also above, "Moses and the Burning Bush," n. 4.
9. Pers., *jangalī* (untilled, jungly).
10. Cf. *Yalqut Shim'oni*, Shemot 3.
11. "The first thing Moses noticed was the wonderful burning bush, the upper part of which was a blazing flame, neither consuming the bush nor preventing it from bearing blossoms as it burnt, for the celestial fire has three peculiar qualities: it produces blossoms, it does not consume the object around which it plays, and it is black of color" (Ginzberg, *Legends*, 2:303).
12. An indirect reference to the Persian expression *āyina-yi Iskandarī* (Alexander's mirror), which, together with *jām-i jam*, (Jam[shīd]'s goblet), is a magical object reputed to be able to reveal events all over the world. Both are popular concepts in classical Persian poetry (Schimmel, *Two-Colored Brocade*, p. 109). See above, "Jacob and the Wolf," n. 13.
13. The *Shekinah* is the immanent aspect of God in rabbinic literature and it is usually referred to as feminine. The Hebrew *kaviyakol* is a pious expression intended to allay any intimation of anthropomorphism.
14. Some midrashic sources claim that it was the archangel Gabriel; either angel "served the purpose to indicate the presence of the Shekinah, for it was God Himself, and not the angels, who spoke to Moses" (Ginzberg, *Legends*, 2:415–416n.115).
15. See above, "Moses and the Burning Bush," n. 12.
16. *Midrash Rabbah*, Shemot 3; Ginzberg, *Legends*, 2:305. Ḥakam translates the famous Hebrew expression *hinneni* (here I am) with the famous Arabic expression *labayka*, with the same meaning (see above, "Moses and the Burning Bush," n. 10).
17. Rabbinic sources do not describe how Moses hid his face; the image here is reminiscent of the gestures of hiding and the coquettish modesty often found in Persian miniature paintings.
18. Pers., *shahr* (city, town).
19. Ar./Pers., *muḥaṣṣil* ([tax] collector), for Heb. *noges* (oppressor, taskmaster).
20. Cf. Ginzberg, *Legends*, 2:317.
21. Ar./Pers., *rasūl* (messenger) as opposed to *nabī* (prophet). The former term is associated in Islam primarily with Moses, Muḥammad, and Jesus, who were given divine Scriptures, not just divine admonitions for mankind. On the distinction between the two functions, see Fazlur Rahman, *Major Themes of the Qur'ān* (Minneapolis, 1980), pp. 81–82.

22. Pers., *khodā o nidā,* a rhyming expression.
23. That is, a stranger in Midian. For the chain of arguments between God and Moses that, according to midrashic sources, lasted seven days, see Ginzberg, *Legends,* 2:316ff., and *Midrash Rabbah, ad loc.*
24. Heb., *eḥyeh asher eḥye,* which may also mean "I am who I am," or, "I will be what I will be" (Exod. 3:14; *Tanakh,* p. 88n.a; *Midrash Rabbah, ad loc.;* Ginzberg, *Legends,* 5:421n.128).
25. See Rashi and Ramban, *ad loc.*
26. See ibid.; Aram., *dayah le-ṣara be-sha'tah* (sufficient unto the hour is the evil thereof); *Midrash Rabbah, ad loc.; Yalqut Shim'oni,* Shemot, 3.1; Ginzberg, *Legends,* 5:420–421n.127).
27. Cf. *Midrash Rabbah, ad loc.;* Ginzberg, *Legends,* 2:319.
28. Heb., *adonai* (lord); cf. *EJ,* s.v. "God, names of."
29. Heb., *yeshivah;* see Rashi at Exod. 3:16.
30. Exod. 3:16; *Midrash Tanḥumah,* Shemot 17.
31. See Rashi, *ad loc.*
32. Exod. 3:21; the image of people carrying things off in their up-turned hems appears to be Ḥakam's.
33. Cf. *Midrash Rabbah,* 3.11.
34. See *Babylonian Talmud,* Sanḥedrin, 91a.
35. Ar./Pers., *ḥalāl* (lawful, legitimate, sanctioned by religion), a technical term in Muslim jurisprudence.
36. *The Babylonian Talmud,* Nedarim, 65a, and *Midrash Tanḥumah,* Shemot 17, specifically state that Moses will never return to Egypt.
37. Heb., *hattarah* (loosening, permission, solution), including the annulment of oaths.
38. Cf. Ginzberg, *Legends,* 2:318.
39. Pers., *az man dast bar dār* (take Your hands off me; leave me alone)—not a very polite reply!
40. Cf. *Yalqut Shim'oni,* 3.170.
41. Pers., lit., *bī mazih mī shavam* (I will become vapid, tasteless [to them]).
42. See above, n. 16.
43. Al-Nīsābūrī has an interesting comment on this specific exchange: "Question: God, the Exalted, knew what Moses had in his hand. Why did he ask? Answer: So that Moses would grow froward in his speech and would not be afraid" (*Dāstānhā,* p. 161).
44. I was unable to find the detail of the talking snake in any of the sources, Jewish or Muslim, that I consulted. We are reminded of the talking snake in Gen. 3:4.
45. See *Midrash Rabbah, ad loc.,* and al-Nīsābūrī, *Dāstānhā,* pp. 161–162.
46. Cf. Ginzberg, *Legends,* 2:322.
47. Cf. Ginzberg, *Legends,* 2:325.
48. That is, Aaron. See Rashi, Ramban, and especially Ibn Ezra, *ad loc.*
49. See the sources cited in n. 48.
50. See Rashi and Ramban, *ad loc.*
51. Lit., *imāmat-i kehunah,* an interesting Persian-Hebrew hybrid expression.
52. Cf. Ginzberg, *Legends,* 2:326, 5:422n.139.
53. Ḥakam uses dual verb forms, thus including Aaron in the command.
54. See the sources cited above in n. 23.

Chapter 7 Religious Festivals in Sermon, Commentary, and Poetry

1. See Netzer, *Oṣar,* Index, under "derashot."
2. See the wonderful study, based exclusively on European sources, by Saperstein, *Jewish Preaching.*
3. A movement in Jewish mysticism based on the teachings of R. Issac Luria (d. 1572) of Safed and his followers.
4. See Saperstein, *Jewish Preaching,* pp. 63–79.
5. A non-*ḥalakic* (nonlegal) mode of biblical interpretation.
6. See the sources cited in the notes to the translation.
7. This biographical information is based on Netzer, *Muntakhab,* pp. 50–51, 351; idem., *Oṣar,* pp. 36–37; idem., "Taḥanunim le-rabbi Binyamin b. Misha'el," pp. 48–54; idem., *Encyclopaedia Iranica,* s.v. "Amīnā"; idem., "Rabbi Binyamin ben Misha'el and His Works," a lecture delivered at "Irano-Judaica: Fourth International Conference," Jerusalem, July 1998.

A Derashah on the Hafṭarah for the Ninth of Ab

1. This translation is based on JNUL 28° 5108, which lacks folio numbers.
2. The next word is illegible.
3. Illegible.
4. Pers. *rīzīdeh* can mean both "withered" and "scattered."
5. See, for example, the interpretations of Rashi, Ibn Ezra, and R. Joseph Karo in *Mikra'ot Gedolot: Yirmiahu* (Lublin; repr. New York, n.d.), 6:78–79.
6. On the prophet Elijah's inclination to reveal secrets to mortals, see *Babylonian Talmud,* Baba Meṣia 59b. Khiżr, his Muslim "incarnation," plays a similar role; see Surah 18:61–83, where he is not mentioned by name.
7. Heb., *mishkan* and *ohel.*
8. The verb is illegible in the ms., hence I cannot determine the exact source of the quotation.
9. I have not been able to find a textual antecedent to the author's connection between the verse in Jeremiah and Moses' petition on Aaron's behalf. The association appears to be the author's, based, in all probability, on well-known midrashic suggestions. It is not found in one of the major Persian midrashic collections written in 1328 (*Sefer Pitron ha-Torah,* pp. 23–24, 179–80, 300). However, according to several midrashim, Moses' intercession on behalf of Aaron after the latter helped build the Golden Calf accounts for the fact that God averted his wrath from two of Aaron's four sons (cf. Ginzberg, *Legends,* 3:306, 6:105n.599, and the sources cited there).
10. I am uncertain of the meaning of the next hybrid phrase, *kavod-i jahīmhā* (Heb. [the honor] + Pers. [of hellfire]) in the present context.
11. Heb., *kasher.*
12. *Babylonian Talmud,* Yoma 33a.
13. Heb., *kelippot* (shards, shells), a term associated especially with Lurianic Kabbalah (cf. Scholem, *Kabbalah,* especially pp. 138–139).
14. Aram., *siṭra aḥara* (the domain of dark emanations and dark powers), another kabbalistic term associated especially with Lurianic Kabbalah (cf. Scholem, *Kabbalah,* pp. 123–128).

15. On the different functions of the two Messiahs, see Joseph Klausner, *The Messianic Idea in Israel from Its Beginning to the Completion of the Mishnah* (New York, 1955).
16. A lovely Hebrew pun: *qol ha-tor* (the song/voice of the turtledove), and *qol ha-Torah* (the song/voice of the Torah). The author appears not to subscribe to certain Kabbalistic notions according to which the Torah will change in Messianic times (see Gershom G. Scholem, "The Meaning of the Torah in Jewish Mysticism," in his *On the Kabbalah and Its Symbolism* [New York, 1965]).

Commentary on the Book of Esther

1. This translation is based on JNUL 1388, fols. 323r–330r; JNUL 8° 4332, fols. 99v–104r; BL Or. 4731, fols. 36r–41v and JTS 8616, fols. 145r–153v.
2. Susa.
3. This well-aimed insult seems to have its origins, though not in Amīnā's formulation, in a midrash: "I am Vashti, the daughter of Belshazzar, who was a son of Nebuchadnezzar, the Nebuchadnezzar who scoffed at kings and unto whom princes were a derision, and even thou wouldst not have been deemed worthy to run before my father's chariot as a courier" (Ginzberg, *Legends*, 4:375). According to *Targum Sheni*, Vashti was the daughter of Evil Merodach and grand-daughter of Nebuchadnezzar ("The Second Targum [*Targum Sheni*] to Esther," ed. P. S. Cassel and A. Bernstein, in *The Targum*, p. 295).
4. Vashti is deriding Ahasueros' "lowly origins," as compared with hers! However, according to rabbinic sources, Ahasueros was also the scion of kings, "the son of Cyrus the Persian, who was the son of Darius the Mede" (Ginzberg, *Legends*, 6:451n.4).
5. Midrashic sources identify Memukan with the prophet Daniel and refer to a long-standing antipathy between him and Vashti. Memukan offered his opinion first because "it is customary as well among Persians as among Jews, in passing death sentence, to begin taking the vote with the youngest of the judges on the bench, to prevent the juniors and the less prominent from being overawed by the opinion of the more influential" (Ginzberg, *Legends*, 4:377–378, 6:456nn.41–46).
6. An erotic as well as a martial image, which, however, does not mean that the shah carried out the execution himself.
7. On Ahasueros' name Bahman, see above, *Ardashīr-nāmah*, n. 3.
8. On the relationship between Esther and Mordekai, see above, *Ardashīr-nāmah*, n. 33.
9. "And it was on the third day, after Esther had three successive fasts" ("Second Targum," p. 322).
10. The 15th of Nisan (cf. Ginzberg, *Legends*, 6:472–473n.145).
11. One can't help but hear an echo of the state of mind of Kashan's Jews in Amīnā's time (see below, chap. 8).
12. Lit., "Who is he?"
13. This legend from the *Babylonian Talmud*, Megillah 16a (see Ginzberg, *Legends*, 4:442; 6:478n.181), is the subject of one of the loveliest miniatures found in a JP manuscript (see Moreen, *Miniature Paintings*, p. 34; the miniature is reproduced on the cover).
14. Originally a friend of Haman's, he now tries to switch over to the winning side (cf. Ginzberg, *Legends*, 2:443; 6:478n.182).

15. That is, for Mordekai.
16. Cf. "Second Targum," p. 337.
17. Ibid.
18. A poetic exaggeration.
19. See above, *Ardashīr-nāmah,* n. 2; a famous king in the *Shah-nāmah.*
20. Āṣaf is the name of King Solomon's grand vizier in Islamic literature and lore (see Jacob Lassner, *Demonizing the Queen of Sheba: Boundaries of Gender and Culture in Postbiblical Judaism and Medieval Islam* [Chicago, 1993], Index under "Asaph b. Berachiah").
21. Ar./Pers., "the guided one," a Messiah-like figure in Islam, who is expected to arrive before the Day of Judgment. The concept is more developed among Shiʿi than among Sunni Muslims (*EI* [2], s.v. "al-Mahdī"). Amīnā, like other Jews in the Muslim world going back to Saadiah Gaon, appears to have had no qualms about attaching a Muslim term to a Jewish concept.

Purim-nāmah

1. This translation is based on BZI 1071, fols. 73r–76v; HUC 2167, no. 41 and HUC 2151, no. 13. The first part of this poem in praise of Purim (more likely a song) seems to be a paean on the theme of the well-known saying "When [the month of] Adar arrives, joys increase" (*Babylonian Talmud,* Taʿnit 29). For an edition and translation of a poem on Purim in the JP dialect of Isfahan, see D. N. MacKenzie, "Jewish-Persian from Isfahan," *JRAS* 1968: 68–75.
2. A choice scent in Persian poetry.
3. A harbor in the south of Iran, on the coast of Balūchistān, in one of the bays to the west of the Indus estuary (Barthold, *Historical Geography,* p. 76).
4. A town near Isfahan.
5. That is, Haman. Hanging Haman in effigy used to be customary in many communities. For this and other colorful Purim customs, see Brauer, *Jews of Kurdistan,* pp. 344–362.
6. Haman's wife; see Esther 5:10.
7. The name of one of Haman's sons (Esther 9:7).
8. The (minor) festival of Purim is celebrated in high spirits everywhere. According to a talmudic saying (Megillah 7b), a man is obligated to drink enough wine on Purim to become incapable of differentiating between cursing Haman and blessing Mordekai.
9. Offerings to the dead? See the custom among the Jews of Kurdistan of "distributing cakes among acquaintances and schoolchildren for 'the souls of the dead' " (Brauer, *Jews of Kurdistan,* p. 345).
10. A paste dressed with gravy and milk.
11. Pilaw, a kind of rice dish.
12. Probably alluding to the custom of *mishloʾaḥ manot* (sending portions; Esther 9:22) to friends on Purim and bestowing gifts upon the poor. At least two portions of edibles should be sent to a friend and money should be distributed to at least two paupers.
13. Probably referring to the lax behavior acceptable by *ḥalakah* (Jewish law) only on Purim.

14. An expression of messianic hopes.
15. Heb., "good deeds," a possible reference to procreation.
16. It is likely that Purim merriment often overlapped with the Iranian celebration of *Now Rūz* (New Year), which falls on March 21; Purim also falls, most of the time, in March.

On the Sacrifice of Isaac

1. This translation is based on Netzer's *Muntakhab,* pp. 351–364; JNUL Heb. 28° 3199, fols. 86v–90r and JTS 1403, fols. 62v–65r. There are substantial differences between these manuscripts. According to Netzer, Amīnā relies on a midrash by Yehuda b. Shemu'el b. ʿAbbās, a twelfth-century poet and preacher from North Africa (*Encyclopaedia Iranica,* s.v. "Amīnā"). I was unable to confirm this claim. In the article mentioning this poet and his works, Ḥayyim Schirmann makes no reference to such a midrashic composition ("Ha-meshorerim bene doram shel Moshe b. Ezra ve-Yehudah ha-Levi," *Yediʿot ha-makon le-ḥeker ha-shirah ha-ʿivrit be-Yirushalayim* 6 [1945]: 297–313). For rabbinic views of this episode, see Ginzberg, *Legends,* 1:274–286, 5:249–255, and Spiegel, *Last Trial.* For Islamic aspects, see Reuven Firestone, *Journeys in Holy Lands: The Evolution of the Abraham-Ishmael Legends in Islamic Exegesis* (Albany, N.Y., 1990), pp. 116ff.

   The Arabic/Persian *Khalīl Allah* (the friend of God) is a traditional Muslim epithet for Abraham (Surah 4:125).
2. The thought is based on *Jerusalem Talmud,* Taʿanit 2.4, 65d (quoted in Spiegel, *Last Trail,* p. 90), but Amīnā's wording differs significantly.
3. "A ram . . . which God had created in the twilight of Sabbath eve in the week of creation, and prepared since then as a burnt offering instead of Isaac" (Ginzberg, *Legends,* 1:282). According to al-Thaʿlabī, the bellwether came from the Garden of Eden (*ʿArā'is,* p. 94).
4. See above, "A Derashah on the Hafṭarah," n. 6; "the skin served Elijha for his girdle" (Ginzberg, *Legends,* 1:283).
5. Kings and princes in the Islamic world often rewarded poets who sang their praises with robes of honor.
6. A *sāz* (Ar./Pers.) is a musical instrument.
7. Cf. Ginzberg, *Legends,* 1:283.
8. "And of his two horns, the one was blown at the end of the revelation on Mount Sinai, and the other will be used to proclaim the end of Exile" (Ginzberg, *Legends,* 1:283, 5:252n.246).
9. That is, may this place be the reward of the righteous.
10. Sufi terms are used in this verse.
11. An abbreviated form of "Ibrāhīm," the Ar./Pers. name of Abraham.
12. I was unable to find any legendary sources, Jewish or Muslim, describing such a fabulous earthly paradise.
13. Verses 70–107 are not included in Netzer's text.
14. JTS 1403 ends here.
15. That is, 1710.
16. See above, "Commentary on Exodus 3–4," n. 13.

Chapter 8 Historical Texts

Kitāb-i Anusī

1. This introduction is based on my *Iranian Jewry's Hour of Peril and Heroism.*
2. Since KA is not a chronological account, it is not, strictly speaking, a chronicle.
3. See Felix Tauer, "History and Biography," in Rypka, *History,* pp. 438ff.
4. See Moreen, *Iranian Jewry,* pp. 157–164.
5. Cf. ibid., pp. 27–34.
6. Cf. ibid., pp. 56–107.
7. The translation that follows is adapted with some changes from Appendix C of Moreen, *Iranian Jewry,* pp. 181–207.
8. See above, "Commentary on the Book of Esther," n. 20. Here the name Āṣaf refers to Shah ʿAbbās II's grand vizier; see Moreen, "Downfall of Muḥammad [ʿAlī] Beg," pp. 81–99.
9. Muḥammad Beg is referring to the Shiʿi concept of *najasa* (ritual uncleanliness), attributed by Shiʿis to all non-Shiʿis (*EI* [2], s.v. "nadjasa").
10. The poll tax demanded by Muslims of non-Muslims living in their midst; *EI* (2), s.v. "djizya"; Cohen, *Under Crescent and Cross,* pp. 68–72.
11. For the origins of the Jewish suburb of Isfahan known as Dār al-yahūd or Yahūdīya, see Fischel, "Yahudiyya," pp. 523–526.
12. This statement refers to the periodic prohibition in various Muslim lands against erecting new buildings or repairing old ones, including houses of worship. These prohibitions are based on the so-called Pact of ʿUmar, (see the Introduction), which spells out the conditions imposed on non-Muslim monotheists living in the Islamicate world (cf. Lewis, *Jews,* pp. 24ff., and Cohen, *Under Crescent and Cross,* pp. 54–68).
13. I was unable to identify this location.
14. The grand vizier is obviously punning on Faraḥābād (Abode of joy), the name of a town on the southern shores of the Caspian Sea with a flourishing Jewish community (Moreen, *Iranian Jewry,* Index, under "Faraḥābād").
15. The famous seventeenth-century French traveler Jean Chardin describes the site, southeast of Isfahan, as follows: "Au delà, est la plaine de . . . Hézar dereh. . . . Elle est aride et sèche; et cela vient, dit la légende, de ce que c'étoit un repaire de dragons, de serpens et de toute sorte de bêtes venimeuses, qui s'étoient amassées là en si grand nombre qu'on n'osoit en approcher ni demeurer au voisinage" (*Voyages* [Paris, 1811], 8:99). The area is still, apparently, a Muslim cemetery (Spicehandler, "Persecution of the Jews," 334n.9).
16. A village outside Isfahan which came to be incorporated into it (E. E. Beudouin, *Ispahan sous les grands chahs, XVIIe siècle* [Paris, 1933]).
17. References to Zoroastrianism, the pre-Islamic religion of Iran, are generally negative in classical Persian literature. From KA we note that their status was even lower than that of the Jews and that the latter shared the Muslims' antipathy toward the Zoroastrians (Moreen, *Iranian Jewry,* Index, under "Zoroastrian").
18. Muḥammad Beg is appealing to the Zoroastrians' own well-known adherence to laws of purity. On this complex subject, see Choksy, *Purity and Pollution.*

19. The reference is most likely to Shah ʿAbbās I, rather than to Shah Ṣafī I, Shah ʿAbbās II's immediate predecessor.
20. See the Introduction. Zoroastrian animosity toward Jews climaxed in the third century, under the Sassanids (see chaps. 1 and 2 in Neusner, *Judaism, Christianity, and Zoroastrianism in Talmudic Babylonia* [Boston, 1986], an abbreviation of his *History of the Jews*, vols. 2–5). This animosity appears to have continued through the centuries. It is best encapsulated in the ninth-century polemical text *Shkand-gumanig Vizar* (The doubt-destroying exposition); see ibid., pp. 175–195, and especially J.-P. de Menasce, *Une apologétique mazdéene du IXe siècle: Skand Gumanik Vikar, la solution decisive des doutes* (Fribourg, 1945).
21. A legendary hero of Firdowsī's *Shah-nāmah* and Niẓāmī's romance *Khosrow and Shīrīn*. Shah Khosrow assigned Farhād the impossible task of carving a tunnel through a mountain on the false promise that he would thereby win the hand of Shīrīn, whom the shah also loved.
22. Cf. Moreen, *Iranian Jewry*, pp. 185–186n.12. Seraḥ bat Asher was the daughter of Hadorah, Asher's second wife, by her first husband. She was therefore an adopted grand-daughter of the patriarch Jacob. She is reputed to have lived several centuries and was granted entrance into Paradise while still living as a result of Jacob's blessing (Ginzberg, *Legends*, Index, under "Seraḥ bat Asher"). On the complex history of this tomb, see Ernest E. Herzfeld, *Archaeological History of Iran* (London, 1935), pp. 106–107, and Yiṣhaq ben Ṣevi, *Meḥqarim u-mekorot* (Jerusalem, 1965–1966), pp. 289–291.
23. A veil worn by Muslim women in Iran covering the entire body and most of the face. It was apparently imposed by custom on non-Muslims as well.
24. Ar./Pers., "master," the title of a Muslim learned in Islamic law and, among Iranian Jews, often the equivalent of "rabbi."
25. The statement alludes to the meaning of the Arabic/Persian word *muslim* (one who submits [to the will of God]).
26. This expression is usually associated with ʿAlī and his descendants, the imams, among Twelver Shiʿis. As in n.24, above, a purely Muslim expression is transposed into a Jewish context, referring here, most likely, to Abraham and his descendants.
27. This is probably another reference to Abraham, who separated himself from his father in order to follow God, rather than to the *hijra* (the migration) of Muḥammad (Seligsohn, "Quatre poésies Judéo-Persanes," p. 257n.1).
28. Many JP texts borrow this concept, usually connected with Muḥammad, to refer to Moses (Moreen, "Moses in Muḥammad's Light"). The connection with Abraham is unusual.
29. Like many Persian poets, Ibn Luṭf resorts to cliché epithets even when they seem inappropriate.
30. A way of referring to a person's sudden realization of the "true" religion (here Twelver Shiʿism). Resorting to a night vision was often used by would-be converts of many faiths to explain a sudden, often pragmatic, change of faith.
31. This is ironic in hindsight since Ibn Luṭf later relates Shah ʿAbbās II's displeasure with Muḥammad Beg and the latter's downfall (Moreen, *Iranian Jewry*, pp. 146–148; idem., "Downfall of Muḥammad [ʿAlī] Beg").

32. On the value of this monetary unit, see Moreen, *Iranian Jewry,* pp. 20–21n.8 and the sources cited there.
33. This refers to a *vaqf* (religious foundation), endowed here in the name of Muḥammad, his daughter Fāṭimah, and the twelve imams.
34. I was unable to determine the value of this currency, but it was no doubt less than what the men received.
35. This was Ibn Luṭf's own predicament (Moreen, *Iranian Jewry,* pp. 28–29).
36. Muḥammad Beg's policy of forced conversion is contrary to the Qur'ān's attitude toward the People of the Book, summed up in the famous statement *lā ikrāha fi'l dīn* (there is no compulsion in religion [Surah 2:256]); see Lewis, *Jews,* pp. 13–14; Cohen, *Under Crescent and Cross,* pp. 112ff. The shah's objection is perfunctory, as it is unlikely that he would have been unaware of the methods Muḥammad Beg used to achieve his goal.
37. A long sustained sound made on the shofar.
38. See Moreen, *Iranian Jewry,* pp. 94–107, 208–216.
39. Pers. *zar* means both "gold" and "money." In view of the reference to gilt idols, the first meaning is more appropriate here.
40. *Kadkhudā*s were communal leaders whose precise functions appear to have differed at various times and in various places (Moreen, *Iranian Jewry,* pp. 120–123).
41. A reference to the twelve imams of Shiʿism.
42. Without other evidence, it is difficult to assess the kadkhudās' description of Jewish economic activities in Yazd. The Jews' sizable bribe suggests that they were well off; the kadkhudās' list of their activities shows a considerable range of business.
43. See n. 17 above. The Avesta, the Zoroastrian scripture, gained only grudging Muslim acceptance (Lewis, *Jews,* pp. 17–18; Cohen *Under Crescent and Cross,* pp. 53–54).
44. Duldul was the name of ʿAlī's mule. The shah is, therefore, flatteringly identified with ʿAlī, the first imam of Twelver Shiʿism.
45. See above, "Jacob and the Wolf," n. 37.
46. Zū'lfiqar was ʿAlī's famous double-pronged sword, always victorious in battle.
47. See above, "Moses and the Burning Bush," n. 12.

Kitāb-i Sar-guzasht-i Kāshān

1. This introduction is based on my *Iranian Jewry during the Afghan Invasion.*
2. Cf. Moreen, *Afghan Invasion,* pp. 6–7.
3. Ibid., p. 61.
4. See *Kitāb-i Anusī,* immediately above.
5. See Moreen, *Afghan Invasion,* pp. 7–13.
6. Ibid., pp. 31–37.
7. Maḥmūd never conquered all of Iran; before his accession he had subdued only Kirman and Yazd. Moreover, after the fall of Isfahan, he had serious difficulties trying to conquer the rest of Iran's major towns (Lockhart, *Fall,* pp. 130–131, 195ff.).
8. Bābāī b. Farhād displays clear sympathies toward the Sunni Afghans throughout KS. Iranian Jews may well have perceived the Afghans as "saviors" from the increasingly intolerant Shiʿi regime of the late Safavids (Moreen, *Afghan Invasion,* pp. 26–29). A JP panegyric in praise of Ashraf has also survived; see below, chap. 12, "O Just Shah Ashraf."

9. The favorite slave of Sultan Maḥmūd of Ghazna (r. 999–1030). The sultan's love for Āyāz is a common topos in Persian Sufi poetry, in which Āyāz usually symbolizes the Divine Beloved (see E. Bosworth, *The Medieval History of Iran* [London, 1977], pp. 90–92).
10. Behind the nickname there is a real individual known from Iranian sources as Sultan Amānullah, one of Maḥmūd's closest Afghan generals and rivals (Lockhart, *Fall*, pp. 138, 140, 143, 172–174, 193–197, 204–205, 207, 210).
11. Iranian sources disagree regarding the manner of Maḥmūd's death. Although it is unlikely that Ashraf himself committed the deed, he probably ordered it (Lockhart, *Fall*, pp. 209–211, especially n. 4).
12. Sultan Amānullah's desire for the crown of Iran was already evident during the reign of Maḥmūd, as early as 1723, and Ashraf naturally feared that it might surface again (Lockhart, *Fall*, pp. 204–205).
13. That is, they came forward to lay claim to their share of the inheritance. Sultan Amānullah's wealth was supposed to have been considerable (Lockhart, *Fall*, pp. 276–277).
14. A probable reference to Ashraf's conflict with the Ottoman general Aḥmad Pasha, who was then occupying Hamadan. Ashraf had to repel the Ottomans, and to some extent the Russians, in addition to the forces of Ṭahmāsp Qulī Khan. The encounter with Aḥmad Pasha took place in the fall of 1726 (Lockhart, *Fall*, pp. 288–291).
15. This vague statement is difficult to pinpoint in Iranian sources, for, as indicated in n. 14, Ashraf fought constantly to conquer Iran and to repulse other foreign conquerors as well as Iranian claimants to the throne.
16. Heb. *goyim* (gentile) is probably used here to refer to Shiʿi Muslims, the primary target of the Afghans.
17. Most of the Safavid princes had already been massacred by Maḥmūd in 1725 (Lockhart, *Fall*, pp. 207–208), but it was Ashraf who put to death Shah Sultan Ḥusayn, the last Safavid Shah (ibid., p. 289).
18. That is, to *maydān-i shah* (The royal square), Isfahan's principal site for parades and executions.
19. He was one of Ashraf's *pīr*s, or "[Sufi] religious masters." Mullah Zaʿfarān's death at the hands of Ṭahmāsp Qulī Khan is noted in Muḥammad Marʿashī's *Majmaʿ al-tawārīkh* (Tehran, 1949), p. 80. See also Lockhart, *Fall*, pp. 336–337.
20. Heb., *pasul* (disqualified, ritually unfit [for sacrifice]). I believe that this is an attempt to translate and transpose into a Jewish context the Arabic term *nājis* (dirty, unclean), with which Shiʿis brand non-Shiʿis.

    On the other hand, Maimonides already used the term *al-pasul* (rhyming with *rasūl*, Arabic for "prophet") to refer to Muḥammad, which may indicate that *pasul* is an older term used by Jews to refer to Muslims. I thank Professor E. Spicehandler for drawing my attention to the reference in Maimonides' *Iggeret Teman*, ed. A. S. Halkin (New York, 1952), p. 39, l. 19, in his review of my *Afghan Invasion* (*JAOS* 112 [1992]: 312).
21. Kashan is one of the main roads to the Caspian region, but according to Iranian sources, Ashraf never went that far and reached only as far as Simnan in 1729 (Lockhart, *Fall*, p. 30). It is therefore difficult to determine on which of his several campaigns Ashraf passed through Kashan. But Ibn Farhād's vivid description of

his visit leaves no doubt about its occurrence and shows clearly the restlessness of Ashraf, who was besieged on many fronts.

22. This may refer to Ashraf's rendezvous with the Safavid Prince Ṭahmāsp, somewhere between Tehran and Qum (Lockhart, *Fall,* p. 277). I have been unable to determine the location of Mahsam.
23. See Lockhart, *Fall,* pp. 330–331.
24. This is the first mention in KS of Prince Ṭahmāsp's general, the future Nādir Shah.
25. See above, *Ezra-nāmah,* n. 57.
26. No doubt this refers to the famine that broke out in Isfahan during its siege by the Afghans (Lockhart, *Fall,* chap. 13).
27. The Jewish date 5490 equals 1730 CE, but Ashraf came to power on April 23, 1725, and was killed sometime at the beginning of 1730 (Lockhart, *Fall,* pp. 210–211, 336–338).
28. *Qizilbāsh* (Turkish for "redhead") designates the original tribal supporters of the Safavids (see Kathryn Babayan, "The Safavid Synthesis: From Qizilbāsh Islam to Imamite Shiʿism," *Iranian Studies* 27 [1994]: 135–161). Here it probably refers to Prince Ṭahmāsp and his forces, although it may also include other Safavid claimants to the throne, such as Mīrzā Sayyid Aḥmad and the three men who claimed to be Ismāʿīl Mīrzā, a younger brother of Prince Ṭahmāsp's (J. R. Perry, "The Last Safavids," *Iran* 9 [1971]: 58–59). The "lions" are probably the Ottomans.
29. It appears from what follows that Ashraf's passage through Kashan, as well as his hurried departure to Isfahan, took place toward the end of his reign, when he was already in flight from Ṭahmāsp Khan (Lockhart, *Fall,* pp. 332–333).
30. Ṭahmāsp Khan's rapacious policies continued even after he became Nādir Shah and were among the causes leading to his downfall (Lockhart, *Nādir Shah,* pp. 253, 270).
31. Pers. *dīvār* means both "region" and "house."
32. See above *Kitāb-i Anusī,* n. 40. Ṭahmāsp Khan was probably trying to raise funds from the entire population of Kashan, not just from the Jews.
33. An important *mujtahid* (Shiʿi theologian and legist), probably the famous Āqā Mīr Abū'l Qāsim mentioned in ʿAbd al-Raḥīm Żarrābī's *Tā'rīkh-i Kashan* (Tehran, 1956), pp. 208–209. I cannot be certain because Żarrābī does not indicate his dates, and there were several other prominent individuals, mostly descendants of this *mujtahid,* who also bore the name Abū'l Qāsim. He may also be Mīrzā ʿAbdū'l Qāsim Kāshānī, or Mīrzā Abū'l Qāsim Kāshānī, who occupied the position of *ṣadr* (supreme head of religious institutions under the Safavids), or *shaykh al-Islām* (supreme judge in religious matters), of Iran under Nādir Shah (Lockhart, *Fall,* pp. 102 and 105).
34. The accuracy of this figure cannot be checked.
35. It is not clear who is intended here by "enemies" and "friends." Usually Ibn Farhād intends the Shiʿis by the former and the Jews by the latter, but that doesn't work very well here; nor do other combinations. More likely, it is one of Ibn Farhād's rather lame expressions.
36. Heb. for "prince," "chief"; the title of the leader of a Jewish community.
37. Probably members of Ṭahmāsp Khan's retinue.
38. I thank E. Spicehandler for his correction of my translation here; see n. 20.
39. Probably several thousand *tūmāns*, as the comment on the Hindus below implies.

40. Apparently Ashraf had distributed monetary gifts to the people of Kashan, including the Jews, in order to buy their allegiance. Although Iranian sources do not mention this incident, it is in keeping with the needs and the characters described in this episode.
41. The implication here may be that despair led the men to contemplate suicide.
42. Ibn Farhād's dating appears to be erroneous again. In 1729 (5490), the 8th of Ḥeshwan fell on Monday, October 31, and in 1730 (5491) it fell on Thursday, October 19. Although the second date makes his error somewhat smaller, the pillage must have occurred in 1729 because Prince Ṭahmāsp became shah officially in the winter of 1729. I am indebted to Sidney Becker for these calculations.
43. This statement is probably only partially correct. Although impoverished by Ṭahmāsp Khan's plunder, the Jews of Kashan must have had sufficient funds left, or have been able to raise them, to pay the large sum necessary to regain their religious freedom.
44. No reason for this conversion is mentioned, but the incident is indicative of the Jewish community's sense of insecurity and its divisiveness regarding the available means for survival.
45. Ibn Farhād appears to be supplying a motive for Binyamin's later behavior.
46. It is not clear whether each family head was asked to pay this sum or whether it was a collective amount; the former appears more likely.
47. *Sa'īds* are Muslims who claim descent from Muḥammad and who are held in great esteem by ordinary Muslims. Here they are just another group demanding a "cut" from the Jews.
48. Pers., *ṣāhib-i muqaddam,* an epithet usually connected with the Hidden [Twelfth] Imam. Here it is intended as a flattering title for the absent Prince Ṭahmāsp, Ṭahmāsp Khan's nominal master, or, more likely, for Ṭahmāsp Khan himself.
49. The Muslim profession of faith.
50. This nonsensical phrase is intended to flatter the Muslims present by intimating, inaccurately, that Moses had acknowledged, or as some Muslims believe, had predicted, the prophethood of Muḥammad.
51. This implies that the money plundered from the Jews by Ṭahmāsp Khan was taken in the name of the prince, who later became, very briefly, Shah Ṭahmāsp II.
52. I was unable to find a Muslim source for this legend. In Jewish midrashim Aaron's blossoming rod and Moses' staff are identical (Ginzberg, *Legends,* 6:106n.600). Ṭahmāsp Khan may be improvising his flattery based on the poetic associations of Muḥammad with that flower (cf. A. Schimmel, *As Through a Veil: Mystical Poetry in Islam* [New York, 1982], pp. 76, 207, 183–184, 278n.37). In any case, these "verbatim" dialogues cannot be considered entirely historical.
53. In keeping with the definition of the state of *ahl adh-dhimma* (see the Introduction), Ṭahmāsp Khan advises the Jews to resign themselves to their allotted (by the Qur'ān) state of humiliation and pay up.
54. He seems to be the individual mentioned in n. 45 above.
55. This was a rash, inconsiderate promise, since it was made without consulting the community.
56. See above, "Moses and the Burning Bush," n. 12.
57. See above, *Kitāb-i Anusī,* n. 10.

58. This refers to a gesture signifying the successful[!] accomplishment of their mission.
59. That is, the individuals named above, who were at the banquet.

Khodāidād

1. Salemann, "Chudâidât," pp. i–viii, 1–56.
2. Ibid., pp. iv–v. Based on his study of two additional mss. that were unavailable to Salemann, Bacher agrees only with the likelihood that the author's first name was Ibrāhīm ("Das jüdisch-bucharische Gedicht," p. 205).
3. Salemann, "Chudâidât," p. iv.
4. Bacher, *Jewish Encyclopedia,* s.v. "Judaeo-Persian Literature"; Fischel, "Israel in Iran," p. 1176.
5. Cf. Yerushalmi, *Zakhor;* see Index under "seliḥot."
6. This translation is based on Salemann's edition, "Chudâidât," pp. 1–4, 14–22; IV A 105 (unfoliated), and Bacher, "Das jüdisch-bucharische Gedicht," pp. 197–212. Salemann's edition bears the title "In Memory of Khoidāt, *gadol ha-dor* (Hebrew for "the great [one] of the generation"). The abbreviation of the hero's name from Khodāidād to Khoidāt occurs frequently, for metric reasons, especially in Salemann's edition (Bacher, ibid., p. 200).
7. Pers., *sa'īd-zādah* (from [a] *sa'īd* family); see above, *Kitāb-i Sar-guzasht,* n. 47. Since Khodāidād was clearly not a Muslim, the author may simply wish to endow his family with nobility, which in a Jewish context would imply that he was a *kohen,* a descendant of the priestly tribe of Aaron. But the author did not use the Hebrew word, although he does not hesitate to do so elsewhere throughout the poem. His intention here is unclear.
8. This statement contradicts v. 3.
9. Pers. *maḥmil* can also mean "silk," "satin."
10. Bacher, "Das jüdisch-bucharische Gedicht," p. 200.
11. Pers. *qūsh-begī,* the title of a head of local government in Bukhārā (see M. Mo'in, *A Persian Dictionary* [Tehran, 1984 repr.], 2:2746, and Michael Zand, *Encyclopaedia Judaica Year Book,* 1975–1976, s.v. "Bukhara," p. 185; idem., *Encyclopaedia Iranica,* 3:1988, s.v. "Bukharan Jews," p. 535).
12. If not punished in this world, the perjurers will be punished in the hereafter.
13. Bacher, "Das jüdisch-bucharische Gedicht," p. 205.
14. Cf. below, "The Anguish of the Community of Forced Converts," n. 2.
15. Bacher, "Das jüdisch-bucharische Gedicht," p. 207.
16. Pers. *pādshāh,* more likely the governor, possibly Amīr Ma'ṣum.
17. Pers. *zambar,* also a "handbarrow," or a "leather bag for drawing water."
18. A suggestion of rebirth in the new faith.
19. Pers. *'amal-dār* can also mean "one in command," "official," "functionary."
20. The meaning of this distich, whose first hemistich is defective in Salemann's edition, is not clear to me.
21. Bacher, "Das jüdisch-bucharische Gedicht," p. 208.
22. The royal "we" (Bacher, ibid., p. 208).
23. Pers., *molāim shū, molāim* (be gentle, mild, calm).
24. Pers., *khān o mān* (family and property).
25. I do not understand the second hemistich.

26. Bacher, "Das jüdisch-bucharische Gedicht," p. 208.
27. The meaning of the hemistich is unclear. It appears to refer to a previous decree by a ruler who may have staunchly enforced the prohibition on reneging Islam.
28. Bacher, "Das jüdisch-bucharische Gedicht," p. 208, has *shanān* (dignitaries), instead of Salemann's *shahān* (kings).
29. Bacher, "Das jüdisch-bucharische Gedicht," p. 208.
30. Ibid.
31. In this and the following verse Bacher replaces Salemann's admittedly cumbersome *mo'atal* (kept waiting, detained, delayed), with *maḥtalī*, the meaning of which eludes both him and me (ibid., p. 202).
32. The meaning of the hemistich is not clear.
33. Bacher, "Das jüdisch-bucharische Gedicht," p. 208.
34. Ibid., p. 208, whereas Bacher's ms. A1 and Salemann have *qiyāmat* (Resurrection), instead of *diyānat* (religion, conscience, integrity).
35. Ibid., p. 208; Khodāidād is chosen in the sense of being singled out for the honor of converting to Islam.
36. Ibid., p. 209, has *masnad* (throne, reclining place) instead of Salemann's *maskan* (dwelling, habitation).
37. The word used for "Law" in the section title is the Persian *dat* (Pahlavi, *data*), derived from Armenian, Hebrew, and Akkadian in the Achaemenid period (Frye, *Heritage*, p. 130). It does not occur again in this text.
38. Bacher, "Das jüdisch-bucharische Gedicht," p. 209.
39. See above, "Commentary on Exodus 3–4," n. 5.
40. See above, "Moses and the Burning Bush," n. 12.
41. This is a loose paraphrase of many biblical injunctions.
42. Bacher, "Das jüdisch-bucharische Gedicht," p. 209.
43. Ibid., p. 209.
44. Ibid., p. 209.
45. I am not certain of the meaning of this hemistich.
46. The second hemistich is in the third person singular.
47. Bacher, "Das jüdisch-bucharische Gedicht," p. 209.
48. An intimation of the presence of an angel or, more likely, the Prophet Elijah.
49. Heb., "righteous man"; Bacher, "Das jüdisch-bucharische Gedicht," p. 209.
50. Ibid., p. 202.

The Anguish of the Community of Forced Converts

1. This translation is based primarily on ms. BZI 1071 fols. 3r–7r, with additional consultation of BZI 954, fols. 13r–15r and HUC 2167, no. 43.
2. The refrain that runs through the poem, *īn dīn-i parishānī* is somewhat difficult to translate because the word *parishānī* has several meanings, including "dispersed," "scattered," "confounded," "distracted," "vexed." The poet deviates occasionally from this refrain, mostly by substituting the Ar./Pers. word *shar'* (religious law), for *dīn* (faith, religion); I do not take this change into account in the translation in order to preserve its dirgelike quality.
3. The concept of seventy, seventy-one, or seventy-two nations/languages, to which some seventy sects can be traced, is of ancient origin and is found in many early

Jewish and non-Jewish sources (e.g., Ginzberg, *Legends*, 1:173, 5:194–195n.72, 6:375n.104). Many early Muslim *ḥadīths* (anecdotes from and about Muḥammad) also mention it (see A. J. Wensinck, *Concordance et indices de la tradition musulmane* [Leiden, 1936–1971], p. 135, under "firqatun/firāq").

4. Ar./Pers., *madhhab* (creed, denomination). This is a technical term referring to the principal schools of law in Islam.
5. Pers., *now dīn[im]*, the Persian expression for the more common Ar. *jadīd al-islām* (new Muslim), by which Jewish converts, especially the anusim of Mashhad, were known (Netzer, "Qorot anuse Mashhad," and Patai, *On Jewish Folklore*, p. 200). This may suggest that the poem originates from Mashhad.
6. Of Yom Kippur.
7. The new converts were probably told not to mix Jewish and Muslim practices.
8. Ar./Pers., *murshid*, *ustād*, words that typically designate Sufi masters.
9. Pers., Zoroastrians.
10. Cf. the element of "voluntariness" in the conversions recorded in KS and Mashhad (Introduction).
11. This verse may allude either to the long fast of Ramadan or to the penitential fasts of the community in general.
12. We have no clue as to who is intended here.
13. Perhaps this is a reference to Nādir Shah moving Jews from Qazvin, Gilan, and other parts of Iran, to Mashhad. See Netzer, "Qorot anuse Mashhad," and Patai, *Jadīd al-Islām*, pp. 25–28.
14. Pers., *ākhūnd* (preacher, teacher), of low theological rank.
15. Not to mention the fact that Islam prohibits the drinking of most alcoholic beverages.

Chapter 9 Polemics and Philosophy

On Moses' Prophethood

1. The first person to bring this text to scholarly notice was Asmussen in the appendix to his article "Judaeo-Persica II," pp. 59–60. Asmussen also gave an extract of it in his *Jewish Persian Texts*, p. 16. The text was analyzed, transliterated, and translated into English by MacKenzie, "Early Jewish-Persian Argument," pp. 249–268. It was emended in the same publication by Lazard (pp. 268–269) and by Shaked, "Judaeo-Persian Notes," pp. 178–182. Lazard also discussed it briefly in his "Dialectologie du judéo-persan," 77–98, especially pp. 88ff.
2. Capitals indicate folios, numbers indicate lines of text, words in parentheses are editorial additions. For examples of Jewish responses to Muslim anti-Jewish polemics, see *Ezra-nāmah*. For Zoroastrian anti-Jewish polemics, see above, *Kitāb-i Anusī*, nn. 17–18.
3. Old Iranian, *wăk-* (word, speech). The ritual associated with this term has a wide range of complex usages among Zoroastrians. The most common is that of "a particular essential formula which precedes, accompanies, or follows an action, . . . hedg[ing] the act around with the power of holy utterance"; it is necessary for "most recurring actions, whether of daily life or daily worship" (Mary Boyce and Firoze Kotwal, "Zoroastrian *bāj* and *drōn*," *BSOAS* 34 [1971]: 56–73, 298–313; I am grateful to D. N. MacKenzie for guiding me to this article).

4. Lev. 3:17.
5. That is, by Jews, Zoroastrians, Christians, and Muslims.
6. The "one belief" refers to the truth of Moses' prophethood.
7. Ex. 6:12.
8. Jer. 9:25; Ez. 44:9.
9. Jer. 6:10.
10. I found no biblical expression *ʿarel lashon,* which appears to be synonymous with *ʿarel sefataim.*
11. The commentator's argument is borrowed most likely from the midrash, specifically from *Bereshit Rabbah,* 46.4, later repeated also in *Yalqut Shimʿoni* at Gen. 10:17, where this argument, preceded by a discussion of the expression mentioned in notes 7, 8, and 9, is attributed to Rabbi Akiba.
12. The connection to Joshua 5:3 as well as the linguistic explanation are based on *Vayiqraʿ Rabbah,* 25.7, and on *Midrash Tanḥuma,* "Va-yer'a," 43.22–27. See also the sources cited by Ginzberg, *Legends,* 5:233n.123.
13. Cf. Ginzberg, *Legends,* 4:7, 6:172n.16, and the sources cited there.

Ḥobot Yehudah

1. Originally, my study of this work was based on two mss.: JNUL 8° 5231 and HUC 2007. While I was working on this anthology Amnon Netzer published an annotated edition of the JP text, including a Hebrew translation, introductions in both Hebrew and English, and helpful indexes. My introduction is based on and all references in the translation that follows are to Netzer's *Ḥobot Yehudah,* pp. i–lxxx, 222–225 (JP text), 455–458 (Heb. trans.). I thank Professor Netzer for sending me a copy of his book.
2. There are very few JP texts with a philosophical content in the various collections of JP manuscripts, and they do not, with the exception of Siman Ṭov Melammed's poetic and primarily mystical *Ḥayāt al-rūḥ* (see below, chap. 9), match the depth and scope of *Ḥobot Yehudah* (Netzer, *Ḥobot Yehudah,* pp. ii–v).
3. Three other works may also be attributed to him (Netzer, *Ḥobot Yehudah,* pp. xiiiff).
4. Ibid., p. v.
5. Ibid., p. xxi.
6. Ibid., p. xxv.
7. Cf. *Bereshit Rabbah,* 79.5.
8. *Babylonian Talmud,* Sanhedrin 44.61.
9. *Babylonian Talmud,* Qiddushin, 35.72–36.71.
10. Rabbi Yehudah's comparison is probably intended to highlight the Torah's superiority to other codes of religious law.
11. Ar./Pers., *sharīʿa.*
12. That is, the fate of the Israelites was not determined by astrological forces.
13. The text actually has "second" here and the author refers to himself in this sentence in the third person singular.
14. *Shemot Rabbah,* 29.4.
15. Heb., *qabbalah,* used here in the original meaning of the word.
16. *Babylonian Talmud,* Ḥullin, 60.72.

Chapter 10 Mysticism

1. Heb., "warning," "a category of liturgical poem for the Feast of Weeks (Shabu'ot) in which are enumerated the 613 Commandments" (*EJ,* s.v. "azharot").
2. Published as *Sefer Ḥayāt al-rūḥ, "Ruaḥ ḥayim"* by Natan'el and Binyamin Shauloff (Jerusalem, 1898). I was unable to consult this (uncritical?) edition.
3. See the Introduction; *EJ,* s.v. "Meshed"; Yehoshua-Raz, *Mi-nedaḥe Israel,* Pt. 3, chap. 11.
4. Ar./Pers., "learned divines," "theologians," since Islam has no clergy.
5. *EJ,* s.v. "Melamed, Siman Ṭov."
6. See, for example, Melammed's treatment of the subject of asceticism (JNUL 8° 5760, fols. 82r–95v), which is a close translation/paraphrase of Baḥya b. Paquda's treatment of the same subject (cf. *The Book of Direction,* chap. 9, or the earlier, less precise translation of Moses Hyamson, *Duties of the Heart* [Jerusalem, 1970], 2:288–337).
7. Ar./Pers., "way," "path," refers to an organized Sufi way of life. On Abraham Maimonides, see now the authoritative summary in Goitein, *Mediterranean Society,* 5:474–496 and the relevant notes.
8. Jewish involvement with Sufism appears especially striking in what we know about the life of Sarmad (d. 1661), a fairly learned Jew from Kashan, who became famous for his Sufi-Hindu asceticism, mystical quatrains, and friendship with Dārā Shikōh (d. 1659), the tragic heir-apparent at the Mughal court in India (Lakhpat Rai, *Sarmad: His Life and Rubais* [Gorakhpur, 1978], chap. 2).
9. This introduction is based on *EJ,* s.v. "Siman Ṭov Melamed"; Netzer, *Muntakhab,* pp. 51–52, 365–368; idem., *Oṣar,* p. 38.

In Praise of Sufis

1. This translation from ḤR is based on JNUL, Heb. 8° 5760, fols. 82r–82v. It is a strophic poem (*tarjīʿ band*) characteristic of more popular forms of Persian poetry.

   Pers., *khwāb-i ghaflat* (the sleep of neglect), is a Sufi expression describing those who neglect spiritual quests. The ethos and vocabulary of the poem are Sufi.
2. "The straight path," is a qur'ānic expression; see Surah 9:56, 15:41, etc.
3. That is, separation from the Divine Beloved.
4. Dwelling too insistently on any of God's attributes can become a stumbling block for the mystic striving for union with the Divine.
5. As devoted lovers of God, the Sufis do not tie their worship to concepts of reward and punishment either in the present or in the hereafter.

Against Sufis

1. This translation is based on HUC 2167, no. 29; BZI 1070, fols. 56a–56b, and BZI 1089, fols. 26b–27a. These manuscripts are difficult to decipher and there are serious discrepancies between the various texts.

   Netzer refers to this strophic poem as *shirat ha-anusim* (a poem of forced converts; *Oṣar,* p. 180, no. 32). Although this description is not incorrect, it is incomplete. In my view the poem satirizes the "attraction" of converting to Islam through Sufi initiation, a process with which the poet was obviously familiar but which he was able to resist (see the last stanza); he urges other Jews to do the same.

   'Imrān is the name of Moses' father in Muslim lore.

2. This refrain, which occurs at the end of each strophe, means literally, "[May I be] sacrificed for/instead of Mīm Shīn Ha'," the consonents in MoSheH, Moses' Hebrew name. It obviously expresses the poet's passionate devotion to Judaism. Similar poems praising Muḥammad, using the consonants of his name, can be found in popular Islamic poetry (Moreen, "Moses in Muḥammad's Light").
3. A famous ascetic who lost his sanity in the quest for the Beloved, Majnūn is immortalized in Islamic literature as the paragon of the Sufis' quest.
4. Pers., *yār* (friend), a common Sufi designation for fellow Sufis.
5. An allusion to the biblical, chosen status of the Jews.
6. More customs associated with Sufi initiation, especially the donning of a special mantle (Ar./Pers. *khirqah;* the term used here is the more colloquial Persian word *qabā* [tunic]).
7. An ecstatic Sufi utterance derived from the Arabic *hūwa* (He), referring to God.
8. I was unable to decipher this verse.

Chapter 11 Religious Poems

1. For a list of the poets' names, see Netzer, *Muntakhab,* pp. 53–56; idem., *Yehude Iran,* pp. 54–57.
2. See Netzer, *Muntakhab,* p. 367.
3. See ibid., pp. 49–50, 345.
4. See Moreen, "Moses in Muḥammad's Light."
5. The title of this poem in some manuscripts adds to the Arabic/Persian word *munājāt* (supplications) the Hebrew word *baqashah,* suggesting that the poem was consciously modeled on a specific genre of Hebrew religious verse whose content is supplication and pleading for forgiveness.
6. The poet's real name was Binyamin b. Misha'el.

Almighty Lord Displaying Might

1. This poem has survived in numerous manuscripts, which contain quite a few variants. My translation is based on BZI 1071, fols. 69v–70v, BZI 1070, fols. 56r–56v, BZI 1089, fols. 9r–9v, and Netzer, *Muntakhab,* pp. 377–378. See also Asmussen, "Šihāb," pp. 415–418. The rhyme scheme is aaab, cccb, etc., which I could seldom capture. Nevertheless, I use as much rhyme as possible to try to convey the poem's powerful, entrancing rhythm.
2. Pers., *farangī* (a Christian, a European).
3. That is, a spear or spearhead.
4. Ar./Pers. *dhikr,* cognate of Heb. *zeker,* is also a technical Sufi term meaning "recollection," in the sense of "repetition of divine names or religious formulae" (Schimmel, *Mystical Dimensions,* see Index under "dhikr").

In Praise of Moses

1. This translation is based on JNUL Heb. 8° 5646, fols. 17r–17v, and BZI 1023, fols. 2v–3v. There are considerable variations between these texts. The poem is highly polemical, comparing Moses and Muḥammad, advocating the superiority of Moses even as it endows him with some of the attributes associated with Muḥammad.
2. Although this verse may hint at Moses' nature, "half terrestrial half celestial," which

is how some Jewish sources attempt to explain the meaning of "the designation of Moses as *ish ha-elohim*" (a man of God; Ginzberg, *Legends*, 3:481, 6:166–167nn.965,966), I believe that Amīnā polemicizes here (as have several other Iranian-Jewish poets), arguing that Moses, like Muḥammad, was created out of primordial divine light and thus precedes all creation (see Moreen, "Moses in Muḥammad's Light," and the sources cited there).

3. Ar., *Kalīm Allah*, see above, "Moses and the Burning Bush," n. 1.
4. These two Sufi technical terms refer to the final stages of gnosis in which the mystic acquires *ʿilm al-yaqīn* (knowledge of certitude). True *ʿilm al-yaqīn* leads to *ʿayn al-yaqīn* (vision of certitude or essence of certainty), the station of the gnostics, and it culminates in *ḥaqq al-yaqīn* (real certitude or reality of certainty), the station of God's true "friends" (Schimmel, *Mystical Dimensions*, pp. 141–142). The verse implies that Moses has experienced these highest levels of mystical encounter.
5. Cf. Ginzberg, *Legends*, 3:481.
6. That is, *Muḥammad*.
7. Cf. Exod. 34:29–35; Moreen, "Moses in Muḥammad's Light," p. 192.
8. The polemical intent is clearly spelled out.
9. That is, *Mosheh*, the Hebrew spelling of Moses' name. Amīnā appears to suggest that Moses' superiority is apparent from the fact that his name consists of three consonants. He distorts the name Muḥammad, referring to him only as *MH*, when in fact, Muḥammad's name consists of five consonants!
10. Exod. 33:11. This verse is another polemical thrust at Muḥammad, whose revelation was mediated through the angel Gabriel (Moreen, "Moses in Muḥammad's Light," pp. 197–198).
11. See above, "Commentary on Exodus 3–4," n. 5.
12. Referring to Shabuʿot, the festival commemorating the revelation of the Torah to Moses on Mount Sinai, celebrated in the month of Sivan.
13. The poem appears to be incomplete in both manuscripts.

A Mukhammas in Honor of Moses

1. This translation is based on BZI 4153, fols. 30v–33r, and Bacher's edition in "Der Dichter Jûsuf Jehûdi," pp. 389–427. A *mukhammas* is a poem in five-lined strophes. As I try to show in my translation—at the expense of the poem's literary quality—each strophe ends with the phrase "You made," which is present in all five verses in the first strophe.
2. See above, "Jacob and the Wolf," n. 41.
3. Ar./Pers. *azal*, a concept which in Sufi poetry refers to the Day of *Alast* (Surah 7:171: "Am I not [*alastu*] your Lord"), on which souls of all future beings assented to God's lordship; a shorthand reference to the Muslim concept of primordial covenant.
4. In Muslim legendary lore Eve tempted Adam with ears of grain; see al-Kisāʾī, *Tales*, pp. 40–41.
5. In the literal sense of the word, "one who submits [his will] to God."
6. This is not a full biblical history; the poet skips over generations at will.
7. See above, "Moses and the Burning Bush," n. 1.
8. A reference to the famous legend regarding Abraham's defiance of Nimrod (destroy-

ing his idols) and his miraculous deliverance from a fiery furnace into which Nimrod cast him (see above, *Ḥanukkah-nāmah*, n.8; Ginzberg, *Legends*, Index, under "Fire, Abraham's rescue from, the details concerning"; al-Kisāʾī, *Tales*, pp. 146–150).

9. Interestingly, the poet speaks of the sacrifice as a fait accompli (see Spiegel, *Last Trial*).
10. That is, separation from Joseph. See above, "Jacob and the Wolf."
11. This direct quote is more intrusive in English than in Persian.
12. Exod. 1:15–16; Ginzberg, *Legends*, 2:250–258, which mentions no numbers.
13. That is, Moses.
14. An allusion to Muḥammad's mediated revelation by the angel Gabriel, an important Jewish polemical thrust against Islam (Moreen, "Moses in Muḥammad's Light," pp. 191, 196).
15. I could not find a midrashic source for this claim.
16. Contradicting the concept expressed directly above.
17. That is, when Moses received the Torah on Mount Sinai.
18. Midrashic texts preserve the tradition that God created and destroyed many worlds before the present one (Ginzberg, *Legends*, 1:4) and that a "new world" is His gift to Israel (idem., *Legends*, 3:47, 65, 6:18n.108), but they do not, as far as I know, connect this to Moses' birth or mission.
19. Exod. 33:23.
20. Cf. Surah 53:9ff., the verses that, according to Muslim tradition, allude to Muḥammad's highest mystical experience, his ascension (*miʿrāj*). See also *Al-Qurʾān: A Contemporary Translation*, trans. Ahmed ʿAlī (Princeton, 1990), p. 457n.2.
21. Ar./Pers. *nūr-i tajjalī* (the light of [His] manifestation, an effulgence), a Sufi expression referring to mystical illumination which partakes of God's original manifestation.
22. See above, "A Derashah on the Hafṭarah," n. 6.
23. Ar./Pers. *imām* is used here in the meaning of "model," "exemplar," "leader," rather than in its more complex Shiʿi connotations.
24. The twelve tribes of Israel or perhaps the twelve paths that Moses hewed out of the Reed Sea for the twelve tribes to cross (Ginzberg, *Legends*, 3:21–22). For a lovely depiction of the latter, see Moreen, *Miniature Paintings*, p. 44, no. 5.
25. Ar./Pers. *ṣāhib-qirān*, an epithet given to a fortunate ruler born at the conjunction of the two "happy" stars, Jupiter and Venus. "Officially, only Tamerlane and Shah Jahān were given this high-sounding title, but it was easy for poets to mention it in flattering verses in other contexts" (Schimmel, *Two-Colored Brocade*, p. 212), especially for founders of faiths, like Muḥammad and Jesus; this is probably why Yūsuf Yahūdī attaches it to Moses.
26. Numb. 21:33–35.
27. Ginzberg, *Legends*, Index, under "Aaron, the virtues of."
28. See above, "On Moses' Prophethood," and Moreen, "Moses in Muḥammad's Light," p. 199.

In Praise of Ezekiel

1. This translation is based on a conflation of BZI 4542, fols. 86v–95v, JNUL Heb. 8° 5437, fols. 53v–55r, BZI 1071, fols. 16v–19r, and HUC 2167, no. 42. The poem

describes the strongly messianic prayer of a man who has attained the object of his pilgrimage, the tomb of Ezekiel. The tomb is reportedly in Ḥilla, a small town in Iraq between Najaf and Karbala, two major Shi'i sites of pilgrimage. Muslims identify the qur'ānic prophet Dhū'l Qifl (Sura 21:85; 38:48) with Ezekiel; thus both Jews and Muslims venerate the site. Muslims seized control of the tomb and its surroundings from the Jews in the fourteenth century (*EJ*, s.v. "Ezekiel's Tomb"; Zvi Yehudah, "Mabaqam shel yehude Bavel 'al shelitah be-qever Yeḥezqel ha-navi be-Kifl be-elef ha-sheni le-sefirah," in *Meḥqarim be-toledot yehude 'Iraq u be-tarbutam* 6 [1991]: 31–75). For a purported debate between Shi'is and Jews at this site, see Moreen, "A Shi'i–Jewish Munāẓara [Debate] in the Eighteenth Century," *JAOS*, 119, 4 (1999).

2. That is, the dust of Ezekiel's grave; this is a common conceit in classical Persian poetry.
3. Cf. Ginzberg, *Legends*, 6:438n.25.
4. According to Jewish tradition, Elijah is the forerunner of the Messiah (Ginzberg, *Legends*, Index, under "Elijah, the Prophet, messianic activity of").
5. When the Temple stood, Jews came on pilgrimages to it with special offerings on the three major agricultural festivals of the year, Succoth, Passover, and Shabu'ot.
6. See above, *Fatḥ-nāmah*, n. 15.
7. "A priestly device for obtaining oracles" (*EJ*, s.v. "urim and thummin").
8. That is, Jacob.
9. Heb., *'am segulah* (Deut. 7:6; 14:2).

In Praise of the Qualities of Ezekiel

1. This translation is based on a conflation of JNUL Heb. 28° 1388, fols. 149r–149v; JTS 1411 (unfoliated); JTS ENA 566, fols. 4r–5r; BZI 951, fols. 23v–25v; BZI 1047, fols. 1a–2a and BZI 1071, fols. 7v–9r. There are significant variations between these texts. The poem may have served as a general invocation among Iranian Jews, perhaps on the way—or wishing but unable—to visit Ezekiel's tomb. The poet, who may well be the same as the "Muflis-i Khwānsārī" of the previous poem, seems to be hoping for special help from the prophet whose namesake he is.
2. Pers., *nīm bismil* (half slaughtered), a complex Sufi topos alluding to the mystic's ecstatic throes, which resemble the death throes of a bird that has been ritually slaughtered, that is, upon which the "bismillah" has been uttered (see 'Aṭṭār, *Manṭiq al-ṭayr*, v. 231).
3. Ar./Pers., *manzil* (stages of a journey).
4. This confession of sins in Hebrew forms the poem's refrain but is not present in all the manuscripts.
5. A common pun on *gul* (rose) and *gil* (clay).
6. Heb., "the House of God," that is, the Temple; an allusion to the advent of the Messiah.
7. A Hebrew name for Satan or for the Angel of Death.

In Praise and Commendation of Ezra

1. This translation is based on BZI 4542, fols. 96r–99v.
2. The twelfth-century Jewish travelers Benjamin of Tudela and Petaḥia of Ratisbon refer to Ezra's purported tomb in Babylon (Iraq), specifically in Basra, located on the Shaṭṭ al-'Arab, the delta of the Tigris and Euphrates rivers on the Persian Gulf

(*Jewish Travellers in the Middle Ages,* ed. E. N. Adler, 1930; repr. New York, 1987, pp. 77–79, 84). However, according to Josephus, Ezra was buried in Jerusalem (*Antiquities,* 2:9, cited in Adler, ibid., p. 373n.27). Clearly, among Iranian Jews the first tradition prevailed, and they were accustomed to go on pilgrimages to Ezra's tomb on the Shaṭṭ al-ʿArab; hence the references in the poem to the "seashore."

3. Ar., *jāhil* (ignorant, uneducated, illiterate). This unknown poet also appears to be responding to Muslim polemics alleging that Ezra simply wrote his own version of the Torah (see above, *Ezra-nāmah,* n. 34). The customary word for illiteracy in the Muslim milieu is the Arabic *'ummī,* and it is associated with Muḥammad. Far from being uncomplimentary, its connection with the prophet of Islam is a code word meant to enhance the miracle of the Qur'ān, which, according to Muslim tradition, could not have been created by a human being, let alone an illiterate one (Schimmel, *And Muhammad Is His Messenger,* pp. 71–74).
4. One of Moses' names (*Babylonian Talmud,* Megillah 13a; Sotah 12b, 13a; Sanh. 101b).
5. A reference to difficult, though unspecified, contemporary conditions.
6. Pers. *parishān* also means "scattered" or "dispersed," which would be appropriate here were not the two adjectives adjacent *zar o parishān,* suggesting synonyms that reinforce each other.

O Elijah, Take My Hand

1. This translation is based on BZI 1015, fols. 107v–109v; BZI 4549, fols. 56r–58v; HUC 2151, no. 15 and Netzer, *Muntakhab,* pp. 300–302. See also Asmussen, "Bābāī ben Luṭf," pp. 131–135.
2. I have tried to capture the poem's repetitious rhythmic structure (aaab, cccb, etc.), somewhat at the expense of a literal translation.
3. A mythical female bird in Persian lore, who plays a prominent role in Firdowsī's *Shah-nāmah.* In Sufi poetry she becomes the symbol of ultimate spiritual reality (Schimmel, *Two-Colored Brocade,* pp. 188–189). The topos is most famously developed in ʿAṭṭār's *Manṭiq al-ṭayr* [The conference of the birds].
4. Ar./Pers., *maʿrifa* (gnosis), an important Sufi term and concept.
5. Ar., *rabb al-ʿālamīn* (Surah 1:2).
6. The letters spell "Allah."
7. In Jewish tradition Elijah is the forerunner of the Messiah.
8. "Nāwīyā," in Netzer, *Muntakhab,* p. 300, perhaps a distortion of Ar./Pers., *nabī*/Heb., *navī,* for the sake of the rhyme. BZI 1015 has the equally obscure "Shatīya."
9. See above, "A Derashah on the Hafṭarah," n. 6.
10. That is, the four Aristotelian elements, fire, wind, water, and earth.
11. This verse refers to Elijah's ability to traverse the world with four strides; hence the idea that he is never too distant to help (Ginzberg, *Legends,* 4:203).
12. A plea for the manifestation of the Messiah. For *Mahdī,* see above, "Commentary on the Book of Esther," n. 21.
13. See above, "Commentary on Exodus 3–4," n. 5.
14. Lit., "we are buried alive." Ur was Abraham's pagan birthplace in Mesopotamia.
15. Lit., "Your Essence."

16. 1 Kings 18:20ff.
17. Lit., "the world clamors for you"; "El" is one of the Hebrew names of God.

A Prayer (Amīnā)

1. This translation is based on JNUL Heb. 8° 4332, fol. 1r; BZI fols. 25v–26r and BL Or. 13914, pp. 1–3.
2. Ar./Pers., *lā-makān,* "without place," a Sufi epithet for God.
3. See above, "Moses and the Burning Bush," n. 1.
4. See above, "Moses' Vision of God," n. 10.
5. The poet's heartfelt prayer was obviously prompted by a specific problem, but in the manner of classical Persian poets, he does not provide specific information.

A Prayer (Bābāī)

1. This translation is based on BZI 951, fols. 26v–28v; BZI 1015, fols. 104r–105r; BZI 4549, fols. 51r–54r and JTS 1411, fols. 27r–28r. The poet may be Bābāī b. Luṭf, but we cannot be certain; Bābāī appears to have been a common name for Iranian Jews.
2. A reference to Tobit of the apocryphal *Book of Tobit.*
3. Since no monarch is specified, this may be a general reference to the oppression of rulers in general and of the Romans in particular.
4. See above, *Kitāb-i Anusī,* n. 22.
5. The tenor of the poem suggests that the poet is bemoaning the (forced) conversion of his community. Perhaps this is evidence for identifying the poet as Bābāī b. Luṭf.
6. Numb. 14:20.
7. Ar./Pers., *intiẓār* (expecting, awaiting), a term that Twelver Shiʿis associate with the condition of awaiting the return of the Twelfth Imam (Mahdī). Here, obviously, the term refers to the (Jewish) Messiah.

A Ghazal on the Twelve Tribes

1. This translation is based on BZI 1070, fols. 51r–52v; BZI 4542, fols. 100r–103r; BZI 1073, fols. 9r–9v and JTS 1411, fols. 25v–26v.
2. Ar./Pers., *bāṭin* (interior, esoteric), a Muslim hermeneutical term, frequently used by Sufis and others, which refers to the inward, esoteric meaning of a text. Here the poet uses the term to refer to the traditional symbolic characteristics of each of the twelve tribes.
3. Ar., *lā yazāl* ([He Who] ceases not), a qur'ānic phrase, an indirect epithet for God (Surahs 9:110; 13:31; 22:55).
4. See above, "Commentary on Exodus 3–4," n. 13.
5. Using his *takhallus* "Amīnā," or "the Faithful," the poet puns on the name Benjamin, the name of the progenitor of the twelfth tribe and also the poet's real name, Binyamin b. Misha'el.

In Honor of the Lord Messiah

1. This short lyrical poem (*ghazal*) is from Siman Ṭov Melammed's *Ḥayāt al-rūḥ* (chap. 10). The translation is based on JNUL Heb. 8°, 5760, fols. 142v–143r, and it is somewhat less literal than others in this anthology. In this ghazal traditional Persian love themes are enriched by echoes of the Song of Songs.
2. The rhyme words of this ghazal are *nāz konam; nāz* is a difficult word to render ade-

quately and consistently into English. Its semantic field includes "amorous playfulness," "glorification," "soothing or endearing expressions used by lovers," "fondling" (Steingass, *Persian-English Dictionary,* p. 1371), as well as "coquetry," "mincing air (or manners)," "endearment," and "teasing" (Haim, *New Persian-English Dictionary,* 2:1054).
3. That is, news of the Messiah's arrival.
4. Like a cock, the Messiah himself will proclaim his arrival from the root of the Temple (*Sefer ha-aggadah,* p. 311).
5. A poetic way of referring to the darkness of *galut* (exile) and to the perception of the Messiah's imminent arrival; the night before the dawn.
6. For details of the messianic banquet, see Ginzberg, *Legends,* 1:30, 5:43–44n.127, 47–48n.139.

Chapter 12 Panegyrics, Lyrical Poems, Quatrains

In Praise of Bahādur Abū Saʿīd

1. This translation is based on Shimʿon Ḥakam's edition of Shāhīn's MN, pp. 2v–3r.
2. See above, *Ezra-nāmah,* n. 57.
3. See above, "Jacob and the Wolf," n. 37.
4. Khosrow Anūshīrvān; see above, *Ardashīr-nāmah,* n. 30.
5. A pun on the ruler's name: Ar./Pers. *saʿīd* (fortunate, happy), and *saʿādat* (fortune, happiness).

O Just Shah Ashraf

1. This translation is based on BZI 1044, fol. 13v.
2. The Gulf of ʿOman.
3. Illegible; possibly Zandarūd, a river that runs through Isfahan.

My Lovely Delightful Girl

1. The form, with its frequent refrains, suggests that this may have been a popular song. The translation is based on BZI 1071, fols. 67v–69r and BZI 4579, fols. 83v–85r.
2. See above, *Dāniyāl-nāmah,* n. 19.

I Wish to Walk in the Rose Garden

1. This translation is based on BZI 1070, fols. 3v–4r; BZI 4542, fols. 49r–49v; BZI 1073, fols. 60r–60v and BZI 4549, fols. 77v–78v.
2. Lit., "I will be the friend and the friend will be me."
3. That is, the sky, which resembles a goblet turned upside down.
4. There is a lovely pun here on the Ar./Pers. root *ʾamn* (safety, security, protection) from which "Amīnā" comes, yielding the reading "You will not quaff without safety," that is, "you will be safe drinking [only] with me."

She Is the Rose Garden's Cypress

1. This translation is based on BZI 1044, fol. 11r.
2. A niche in the wall of a mosque indicating the *qibla,* the direction of Mecca.
3. The name of a refreshing body of water in the Muslim conception of Paradise.

Last Night Her Magic Wink

1. This translation is based on JNUL 28° 4435, fols. 27v–28r.

The Story of Amīnā and His Wife

1. This translation is based on HUC 2171, no. 7b.
2. A province in eastern Turkestan famous in Persian poetry for its beautiful men and women.
3. The first half of this hemistich is illegible.
4. Part of the second hemistich is illegible.
5. The text is illegible at the end and the poem appears to be incomplete in this manuscript.

On Becoming Cold-hearted Toward Women

1. This popular poem by Amīnā can be found in many manuscripts. The translation is based on JNUL Heb. 28° 4435, fols. 27v–28r; BZI 4579, fols. 90v–91v and BZI 1071, fols. 65r–66r. I took some liberties with the translation in order to suggest the poem's powerful rhythm.

Anonymous Quatrains

1. These translations are based on JNUL Heb. 38° 5585, fols. 16v, 17v, 22v, 23r.
2. Pers., *bot-khānah* (house of idolatry), that is, any place of worship containing paintings and sculptures forbidden to Muslim pious sensibilities. In Sufi poetry it can refer to a Buddhist shrine or to a Christian church.
3. See above, "She Is the Rose Garden's Cypress," n. 2.

Bibliography

Manuscripts

BL: Or. 4731; Or. 13704; Or. 13914
D: *Fatḥ-nāmah*
FVR: 610
IV: A 105, A 129, A 192, C 43
JNUL: 180/54, 1183, 1388, 8° 4332, 8° 5646, 8° 5760, 28° 4435, 28° 5108, 38° 5585
HUC: 2102, 2151, 2167, 2171
BZI: 978, 951, 964, 980, 1015, 1023, 1044, 1045, 1070, 1071, 1073, 1075, 1089, 4153, 4542, 4547, 4549, 4571, 4579, 4602, 4731
JTS: 1403, 1411, 8616, 8623, Acc. 40919
SS: Ebp. i. c. 150

Published Primary Sources

Apocrypha: An American Translation, The. Trans. E. J. Goodspeed. New York: Vintage, 1959.

Arakel of Tabriz. *Livre d'histoires, collection d'historiens Arméniens*, vol. 1. Trans. and ed. M. I. Brosset. St. Petersburg: Impr. de l'Académie Impériale des Sciences, 1874–76.

ʿAṭṭār, Farīd al-Dīn. *Manṭiq al-tayr.* Ed. S. Gowharīn. Tehran: Tarjomah va nashr-i kitāb, 1963. [*The Conference of the Birds.* Trans. Afkham Darbandi and Dick Davis. Harmondsworth: Penguin, 1984.]

Batte midrashot. Ed. A. J. Wertheimer. 2 vols. Jerusalem: Ketav va-Sefer, 1969.

Bereshit Rabbah. Ed. J. Theodor and Ch. Albeck. 3 vols. Jerusalem: Wahrmann, 1965.

Bet ha-midrash. Ed. A. Jellinek. 3 vols. Jerusalem: Bamberger and Wahrmann, 1938.

Chardin, J. J. *Voyages.* 10 vols. Paris: L. Langlès, 1811.

Chronicle of the Carmelites in Persia, A. 2 vols. London: Eyre and Spottiswoode, 1939.

Della Valle, Pietro. *Viaggi di Pietro Della Valle.* 2 vols. Brighton: G. Gancia, 1845.

Ecclesiastes Rabbah. In *The Soncino Midrash.* Trans. A. Cohen. London: Soncino Press, 1939.

Esther Rabbah. In *The Soncino Midrash.* Trans. Maurice Simon. London: Soncino Press, 1939.

Firdowsī, Abū 'l-Qāsim. *Shah-nāmah.* Ed. E. E. Berthels et al. 9 vols. Moscow: Oriental Institute of the Soviet Academy of Sciences, 1960–1971. [*The Epic of the Kings.* Trans. R. Levy. Chicago: University of Chicago Press, 1967.]

Genesis. Trans. Robert Alter. New York: Norton, 1996.

Ḥamishah Ḥumshe Torah: Miqra'ot Gedolot. Jerusalem: Ma'oz Me'ir, n.d. [*Tanakh: The Holy Scriptures.* Philadelphia: Jewish Publication Society, 1985.]

Ibn 'Ata'illah. *"The Book of Wisdom"* and *Kwaja Abdullah Ansari "Intimate Conversations."* Trans. Victor Danner and Wheeler M. Thackston. New York: Paulist Press, 1978.

Ibn Paqudah, Baḥya. *The Book of Direction to the Duties of the Heart.* Trans. Menahem Mansoor. London: Routledge and Kegan Paul, 1973.

Maimonides, Moses. *Mishneh Torah.* 5 vols. New York: A. Friedman, 1963.

———. *The Guide of the Perplexed.* Trans. S. Pines. 2 vols. Chicago: Chicago University Press, 1963. Reprint 1974.

Mar'ashī Ṣafavī, Mīrzā Muḥammad Khalīl. *Majma' al-tawārīkh.* Ed. A. Iqbal. Tehran: Shirkat-i Sāmī Chāpī, 1949.

Megillat Antiochus. Ed. and trans. M. Gaster. *Transactions of the Ninth International Congress of Orientalists* 2 (1893): 3–32. [= "The Scroll of the Hasmoneans," *Studies and Texts* 1 (1925–28): 165–183; 3 (1925–28): 33–44.]

Midrash ha-Gadol. Ed. M. Margolies. Jerusalem: Mossad ha-Rav Kook, 1967.

Midrash Rabbah im kol ha-meforeshim. 2 vols. Vilna: N.p., n.d.

Midrash Rabbah ha-mevo'ar: Rut, Ester. Ed. Avraham Ṣevi et al. Jerusalem: Makon Midrash ha-mevo'ar, 1986.

Midrash Tanḥuma. Ed. S. Buber. 2 vols. Vilna: N.p., n.d.

Munshī, Iskandar Beg. *Tārīkh-i 'Ālam-ārā-yi 'Abbāsī.* Ed. I. Afshar. 2 vols. Tehran: Chāpkhāna-yi Mūsavī, 1956–57.

———. *Żayl-i Tārīkh-i 'Ālam-ārā-yi 'Abbāsī.* Ed. S. Khwānsārī. Tehran: Chāpkhāna-yi Islamīya, 1939.

Mūsā-nāma of R. Shim'on Ḥakham, The. Ed. Herbert H. Paper. Cincinnati: Hebrew Union College Press, 1986.

al-Nīsābūrī, Abū Isḥāq Ibrāhīm b. Manṣūr. *Qiṣaṣ al-anbiyā' (Dāstānhā-yi payghambarān).* Tehran: Tarjomah va nashr-i kitāb, 1971.

Niẓāmī Ganjavī, Abū Muḥammad Ilyās. *Haft Paykar.* Tehran: Chāpkhāna-yi Sipihr, 1971. [*Haft Paykar: A Medieval Persian Romance.* Trans. Julie Scott Meisami. Oxford: Oxford University Press, 1995.]

Oṣar midrashim. Ed. Yehudah D. Eisenstein. 2 vols. N.p., 1915. Reprint 1980.

Pirqe de-Rabbi Eliezer. Ed. D. Luria. Warsaw: Bamberg, 1852. Reprint 1946. [*Pirqe de Rabbi Eliezer.* Trans. Gerald Friedlander. New York: Sepher Hermon Press, 1916. Reprint 1981.]

Qur'ān. *The Meaning of the Glorious Qur'ān: Text and Explanatory Translation.* Trans. M. M. Pickthall. New York: Muslim World League, 1977.

Sefer ha-aggadah. Ed. Ch. N. Bialik and Y. Ch. Ravnitsky. N.p., 1908–1911. Reprint, 1987.

Sefer pitron ha-torah. Ed. E. E. Urbach. Jerusalem: Magnes Press, 1978.

Sefer Sharḥ-i Shāhīn ʿal ha-Torah. Ed. Shimʿon Ḥakam. Jerusalem: N.p., 1902–1905.

Septuagint Bible: The Oldest Text of the Old Testament, The. Trans. Charles Thompson. Indian Hills, Colo.: Falcon's Wing Press, 1960.

al-Ṭabarī, Abū Jaʿfar Muḥammad b. Jarīr. *Tāʾrīkh al-rusul wa ʾl-mulūk* [*Annales*]. Ed. M. J. de Goeje et al. 15 vols. Leiden: Brill, 1879–1901. [*The History of al-Ṭabarī.* Trans. William M. Brinner. Vol. 2, *Prophets and Patriarchs.* Vol. 3, *The Children of Israel.* Albany: State University of New York Press, 1987, 1991.]

Tales of the Prophets of al-Kisa'i, The. Trans. Wheeler M. Thackston, Jr. Boston: Twayne, 1978.

Tanakh: The Holy Scriptures. Phildelphia: JPS, 1985.

Targum to the Five Megillot, The. Ed. B. Grossfeld. New York: Hermon Press, 1973.

Tavernier, Jean-Baptiste. *Les six voyages de Monsieur J. B. Tavernier.* 2 vols. Paris: La veuve de Pierre Ribou, 1724.

al-Thaʿlabī, Abū Isḥāq Aḥmad b. Muḥammad. *Qiṣaṣ al-anbiyāʾ al-musammā ʿArāʾis al-majālis.* Beirut: Dar al-kutub al-ʿilmīya, 1985.

Thevenot, J. J. *Voyages de Mr. de Thevenot.* 4 vols. Paris: Charles Angot, 1679.

Waḥīd, Muḥammad Ṭāhir Qazvīnī. *ʿAbbāsnāma.* Ed. I. Dehgan. Arak: Chāpkhāna-yi Farvardī, 1951.

Yalqut Shimʿoni. 2 vols. Jerusalem: H. Vagshal, 1990.

Secondary Sources

Abrahamian, Roubene. *Dialectologie iranienne: Dialectes des Israélites de Hamadan et d'Isfahan, et dialecte de Babai Tahir.* Paris: Libraire d'Amerique et d'Orient Adrien-Maisonneauve, 1936.

Ackroyd, Peter R. *Israel Under Babylon and Persia.* New York: Oxford University Press, 1970.

Adler, Elkan N. *Catalogue of the Hebrew Manuscripts in the Collection of Elkan Nathan Adler.* Cambridge: Cambridge University Press, 1921.

———. *Jews in Many Lands.* London: R. Mazin, 1912.

———. "The Persian Jews: Their Books and Their Ritual." *JQR* 10 (1919–20): 584–625.

Altshuler, Mordechai. *Yehude mizraḥ Qavqaz: Toledot ha-yehudim he-haryim me-reshit ha-me'ah ha-teshaʿ esreh.* Jerusalem: Ben Zvi Institute, 1990.

Arjomand, Said A. *The Shadow of God and the Hidden Imam.* Chicago: University of Chicago Press, 1984.

Asani, Ali S., and Kamal Abdel-Malek. *Celebrating Muhammad: Images of the Prophet in Popular Muslim Poetry.* Columbia: University of South Carolina Press, 1995.

Asmussen, Jes P. "Bābāī ben Luṭf's jüdisch-persisches Elija-Lied." In *Festschrift für Wilhelm Eilers.* Wiesbaden: Otto Harrassowitz, 1967.

———. "Classical New Persian Literature in Jewish-Persian Versions." *SBB* 8 (1968): 44–53.

———. "Eine jüdisch-persische Übersetzung des Ben Sira Alphabets." *Ex Orbe Religionum. Studia Geo Widengren oblata* 1 (1972): 144–155.

——. "Eine jüdisch-persische Version des propheten Obadja." *Acta Antiqua Scientiarum Hungaricae* 25 (1977): 255–263.

——. "A Jewish-Persian Munazare." *Iran Society Silver Jubilee Souvenir.* Calcutta: Iran Society, 1970.

——. *Jewish-Persian Texts.* Wiesbaden: Otto Harrassowitz, 1968.

——. "Judaeo-Persica I: Šāhīn-i Šīrāzī's Ardašīr-nāma." *AO* 28 (1965): 245–261.

——. "Judaeo-Persica II: The Jewish Persian Law Report from Ahwāz, A.D. 1020." *AO* 29 (1965): 49–60.

——. "Judaeo-Persica III: Vier ungewöhnliche Worte aus der Genesis version des jüdisch-persische Vatikan-Pentateuchs." *AO* 29 (1966): 247–251.

——. "Judaeo-Persica IV: Einige Bemerkungen zu Baba ben Nuriel's Psalmenübersetzung." *AO* 30 (1966): 15–25.

——. "Jüdisch-persisch *guyan* [gwy'n], Zelt." *Temenos* 5 (1969): 17–21.

——. "Jüdische Hoseastucke." *AO* 4 (1975): 15–18.

——. "Šihāb, a Judeo-Persian Poet from Yazd." In *Memorial Jean de Menasce.* Louvain: Imprimerie Orientaliste, 1974.

——. "Simurγ̌ in Judeo-Persian Translations of the Hebrew Bible." In *Iranica Varia: Papers in Honor of Professor Ehsan Yarshater.* Textes et memoires 16 (= *Acta Iranica* 30 [1990]).

——. "Some Remarks on the Rendition of Geographic and Ethnic Names in Judeo-Persian Bible Versions." *Farhang-i Irān Zamīn* 21 (1976): 1–6.

——. "Some Remarks on the Zoroastrian Vocabulary of the Judaeo-Persian Poet Šāhīn-i Šīrāzī of the Fourteenth Century." In *Sir J. J. Zarathoshti Madressa Centenary Volume.* Bombay: Trustees of the Parsi Punchayet Funds and Properties, 1967.

——. *Studies in Judeo-Persian Literature.* Leiden: Brill, 1973.

——. "Über die Wiedergabe geographischer und ethnischer Namen in einer jüdisch-persischen Jesaia-Version." *Temenos* 10 (1974): 5–9.

——. "Das Verbum, *lebe'im* jüdisch-persischen." In *Hommages et Opera Minora,* 8. *Monumentume Georg Morgenstierne* 1 (= *Acta Iranica* 21 [1981]).

——. "A Zoroastrian 'De-demonization' in Judeo-Persian." In *Irano-Judaica: Studies Relating to Jewish Contacts with Persian Culture Throughout the Ages.* Jerusalem: Ben Zvi Institute, 1982.

Asmussen, Jes P., and Herbert H. Paper, eds. *The Song of Songs in Judeo-Persian.* Copenhagen: Det Kongelige Danske Videnskabernes Selskab, 1977.

Babay, Rephael. *Tovah be'ad tovah: 'Asarah sippure 'am mi-pi yehude Paras.* Jerusalem: The Magness Press, 1980.

Bacher, Wilhelm. "Aus einem jüdisch-persischen Lehrgedicht." *Keleti Szemle* 12 (1911–1912): 223–228.

——. "Der Dichter Jûsuf Jehûdi und sein Lob Moses." *ZDMG* 53 (1899): 389–427.

——. "Elégie d'un poète Judéo-Persan." *REJ* 48 (1908): 94–105.

——. "Un épisode de l'histoire des Juifs de Perse." *REJ* 47 (1903): 262–282.

——. "Un épisode de l'histoire des Juifs de Perse. Livre des evenements de Kachan, par Babai b. Farhad." *REJ* 53 (1907): 85–110.

——. "Ein hebräisch-persisches Liederbuch." *JQR* 14 (1902): 116–128.

——. *Ein hebräisch-persisches Wörterbuch aus dem vierzehnten Jahrhundert.* Strassburg: K. J. Trübner, 1900.

——. "Ein hebräisch-persisches Wörterbuch aus dem 15 Jahrhundert." *ZAW* 16 (1896): 201–241; 17 (1897): 199–200.
——. "Judaeo-Persian," and "Judaeo-Persian Literature." *JE* 7:313–322.
——. "Ein jüdisch-bucharische Gedicht." *ZHB* 3 (1899): 19–25.
——. "Das jüdisch-bucharische Gedicht Chudâidâd." *ZDMG* 52 (1898): 197–212.
——. "Ein jüdisch-persischer Dichter des vierzehnten Jahrhunderts." *Jahrbuch fur jüdische Geschichte und Litteratur* 11 (1908): 88–114.
——. "Jüdisch-Persisches aus Bukhara. 3. Aus Einem Ritualcompendium." *ZDMG* 56 (1902): 729–759.
——. "Jüdisch-Persisches aus Bukhara: Zwei Gedichte." *ZDMG* 55 (1901): 241–257.
——. "Les Juifs de Perse au XVIIe et au XVIIIe siècles d'après les chroniques poétiques de Babai b. Loutf et de Babai b. Farhad." *REJ* 51 (1906): 121–136, 265–279; 52 (1906): 77–97, 234–271. Reprinted as *Les Juifs de Perse au XVIIe et au XVIIIe siècles d'après les chroniques poétiques de Babai b. Loutf et de Babai b. Farhad.* Paris: A. Durlacher, 1907.
——. "Le livre d'Ezra de Schahin Schirazi." *REJ* 55 (1908): 249–280.
——. "Eine persische Bearbeitung des Mischnatraktats Aboth." *ZHB* 6 (1902): 112–118, 156–157.
——. "Ein persischer Kommentar zum Buche Samuel." *ZDMG* 51 (1987): 392–425.
——. "Ein Ritualcompendium in persischer Sprache." *ZHB* 5 (1901): 147–154.
——. "Zur jüdisch-persischen Litteratur." *JQR* 16 (1904): 525–558.
——. "Zur jüdisch-persischen Litteratur." *ZDMG* 65 (1911): 523–535.
——. "Zur jüdisch-persischen Litteratur. Jerusalemische Drucke" *ZHB* 14 (1910): 12–20, 45–51; 16 (1913): 28–32.
——. *Zwei jüdisch-persische Dichter Schahin und Imrani.* Strassburg: Trübner, 1907–1908.
Baron, Salo W. *A Social and Religious History of the Jews.* 18 vols. New York: Columbia University Press, 1958–1984.
Barthold, W. *An Historical Geography of Iran.* Trans. Svat Soucek. Princeton: Princeton University Press, 1984.
Basnage, F. C. *The History of the Jews, from Jesus Christ to the Present Time.* Trans. Tho. Taylor. London: T. Bever and B. Lintot, 1708.
Bausani, Alessandro. *The Persians from the Earliest Days to the Twentieth Century.* New York: St. Martin's, 1971.
Benayahu, Me'ir. "Ketavav shel R. David b. Binyamin Ha-Kohen me-Khunsar: meqor le-toledot Paras bi-me'ah ha-shev'a 'esreh." In *'Iyyunim be-sifrut ḥazal be-miqra' u-be-toledot Yisrael.* Ramat Gan: Bar-Ilan University, 1982.
——. "Piyyutim ve-te'udot 'al ha-shabbtaut be kitve-yad me-Paras." *Sefunot* 3–4 (1960): 7–38.
Ben Sasson, H. H., ed. *A History of the Jewish People.* Cambridge: Harvard University Press, 1976.
Ben Zvi, Yitzhak. *The Exiled and the Redeemed.* Philadelphia: Jewish Publication Society of America, 1957.
——. *Meḥqarim u-meqorot.* Jerusalem: Ben Zvi Institute, 1965–66.
——. "Meqorot le-toledot yehude Paras." *Sefunot* 2 (1958): 190–192, 196–201.
Bickerman, Elias. *Four Strange Books of the Bible: Jonah, Daniel, Koheleth, Esther.* New York: Schocken, 1967. Reprint 1988.

——. *The Jews in the Greek Age.* Cambridge: Harvard University Press, 1988.

Bin Gorion, Emanuel, ed. *Mimekor Yisrael: Classical Jewish Folktales.* 3 vols. Bloomington: Indiana University Press, 1976.

Blau, Ludwig. *Bibliographie der Schriften W. Bachers.* Frankfurt am Main: I. Kauffmann, 1910.

Blieske, Dorothea. "Šāhīn-e Šīrāzīs Ardašīr Buch." Ph.D. diss. Eberhard-Karls-Universität, Tübingen, 1966.

Blochet, Edgar. *Catalogue des manuscrits persans de la Bibliothèque Nationale.* 4 vols. Paris: Imprimerie Nationale, 1905.

Brauer, Erich. "The Jews in Afghanistan: An Anthropological Report." *JSS* 4 (1942): 121–138.

——. *The Jews of Kurdistan.* Ed. and completed by Raphael Patai. Detroit: Wayne State University Press, 1993.

Brody, Robert. "Judaism in the Sasanian Empire: A Case Study in Religious Coexistence." In *Irano-Judaica II: Studies Relating to Jewish Contacts with Persian Culture Throughout the Ages.* Jerusalem: Ben Zvi Institute, 1990.

Browne, E. G. *A Literary History of Persia.* 4 vols. Cambridge: Cambridge University Press, 1969.

Buber, Solomon, ed. *Aggadat Ester.* Crakow: N.p., 1897.

——. *Sifre de-aggadeta ʿal-Megillat Ester.* Vilna: Rom, 1886.

Bulliet, Richard W. *Conversion to Islam in the Medieval Period: An Essay in Quantitative History.* Cambridge: Harvard University Press, 1979.

Carlsen, B. Hj. "Jonah in Judaeo-Persian." *Acta Iranica* 12 (1976): 13–26.

Chittick, William C. *The Sufi Path of Knowledge: Ibn al-ʿArabi's Metaphysics of the Imagination.* Albany: State University of New York, Press, 1989.

——. *The Sufi Path of Love: The Spiritual Teachings of Rumi.* Albany: State University of New York Press, 1983.

Choksy, Jamsheed K. *Conflict and Cooperation: Zoroastrian Subalterns and Muslim Elites in Medieval Iranian Society.* New York: Columbia University Press, 1997.

——. *Purity and Pollution in Zoroastrianism: Triumph over Evil.* Austin: University of Texas Press, 1989.

Cohen, Mark. R. *Under Crescent and Cross.* Princeton: Princeton University Press, 1994.

Costello, V. F. *Kashan, A City and Region of Iran.* London: Bowker, 1976.

Dan, Yosef. *Ha-sippur ha-ʿivri be-me ha-beynayim.* Jerusalem: Keter, 1974.

Davis, Dick. *Epic and Sedition: The Case of Ferdowsi's Shahnameh.* Fayetteville: University of Arkansas Press, 1992.

De Lagarde, Paul. *Persische Studien.* Göttingen: Dietrich, 1884.

Encyclopaedia Iranica. Ed. E. Yarshater. London: Routledge and Kegan Paul, 1982–1990. Continued. Costa Mesa, Calif.: Mazda, 1992–.

Encyclopaedia Judaica. Ed. Cecil Roth et al. Jerusalem: Keter, 1971.

Encyclopaedia of Islam. 2d ed. Ed. H. A. R. Gibb et al. Leiden: Brill, 1960–.

Eshkoli, E. Z. "Mi-piyute yehude Paras." *Mizraḥ ve-maʿrav* 3 (1929): 366–373.

Ethé, Hermann. "Neupersische Litteratur." In *Grundriss der iranischen Philologie,* vol. 2. Strassburg: K. J. Trübner, 1896–1904.

Ettinger, Shmuel, ed. *Toledot ha-yehudim be-arṣot ha-islam.* Jerusalem: Merkaz Zalman Shazar, 1981.

Ezekiel, I. A. *Sarmad: Jewish Saint of India.* Calcutta: Radha Soami Satsang Beas, 1966.

Feldman, Louis H. *Jew and Gentile in the Ancient World.* Princeton: Princeton University Press, 1993.

Finkel, Joshua. "A Judaeo-Persian Tale." *JQR* 21 (1931): 353–364.

Fischel, Walter, J. "Azarbaijan in Jewish History." *PAAJR* 22 (1953): 1–21.

———. "The Beginning of Judeo-Persian Literature." In *Mélanges d'orientalisme offerts à Henri Masse à l'occasion de son 75ème anniversaire.* Tehran: Imprimerie de l'universite, 1963.

———. "The Bible in Persian Translation: A Contribution to the History of Bible Translations in Persia and India." *HTR* 45 (1952): 3–45.

———. "The Contribution of the Persian Jews to Iranian Culture and Literature." *Acta Iranica* 3 (1974): 299–315.

———. "Isfahan: The Story of a Jewish Community in Persia." In *Joshua Starr Memorial Volume.* New York: Conference on Jewish Relations, 1953.

———. "Israel in Iran (A Survey of Judeo-Persian Literature)." In *The Jews: Their History, Culture, and Religion.* New York: Shocken, 1971.

———. *Jews in the Economic and Political Life of Mediaeval Islam.* London: Royal Asiatic Society Monographs 22, 1937.

———. "The Jews in Mediaeval Iran from the Sixteenth to the Eighteenth Centuries: Political Economic, and Communal Aspects." In *Irano-Judaica: Studies Relating to Jewish Contacts with Persian Culture Throughout the Ages.* Jerusalem: Ben Zvi Institute, 1982.

———. "The Jews of Afghanistan" *Jewish Chronicle Supplement.* London, 1937.

———. "The Jews of Central Asia (Khorasan) in Medieval Hebrew and Islamic Literature." *Historia Judaica* 7 (1945): 29–50; 8 (1946): 66–67.

———. "The Jews of Persia Under the Kajar Dynasty (1795–1940)." *JSS* 12 (1950): 119–160.

———. "Judeo-Persian Literature." *EJ* 10: 432–439.

———. "Judaeo-Persian. i. Literature." *EI* (2) 4: 308–312.

———. "The Literary Heritage of the Persian-Speaking Jews." *Jewish Book Annual* 27 (1969–1970): 5–12.

———. "New Sources for the History of the Jewish Diaspora in Asia in the Sixteenth Century." *JQR* 40 (1950): 379–399.

———. "Qehillat ha-anusim be-Paras." *Ṣion* 1 (1935): 49–74.

———. "The Rediscovery of the Medieval Jewish Community at Firuzkuh in Central Afghanistan." *JAOS* 85 (1965): 148–153.

———. "The Region of the Persian Gulf and Its Jewish Settlements." In *Alexander Marx Jubilee Volume.* New York: Jewish Theological Seminary of America, 1950.

———. "Toledot yehude Paras bi-me shalshelet ha-sefevidim." *Ṣion* 2 (1937): 273–293.

———. "Yahudiyya: le-reshit ha-yishuv ha-yehudi be-Paras." *Tarbiẓ* 6 (1935): 523–526.

———. "Zur jüdisch-persischen Literatur der jungsten Zeit." *MGWJ* 77 (1933): 113–127.

Friedman, Dénes. "Pótlás Blau Lajós 'Bácher Vilmós iródalmi munkasága' cimü munkájához." *Magyar Zsidó Szemle* 45 (1928): 143–151.

Frye, Richard. *Bukhara: The Medieval Achievement.* Norman: University of Oklahoma Press, 1965.

———. *The Golden Age of Persia.* London: Weidenfeld and Nicholson, 1975. Reprint, 1993.

——. *The Heritage of Persia.* New York: Mentor, 1963. Reprint, 1966.

——. "Israel und Iran." In *Festschrift für Wilhelm Eilers.* Wiesbaden: Otto Harrassowitz, 1967.

Galanté, Abraham. *Marranes Iraniens, un chapitre inédit de l'histoire Juive.* Istanbul: Société anonyme de papeterie et l'imprimerie (Fratelli Haim), 1935.

Gaster, Moses. "Hebrew Visions of Hell and Paradise." *JRAS* (1925–1928): 571–608.

Geiger, Wilhelm. "Bemerkungen über das Judenpersisch." In *Grundriss der iranischen Philologie.* 2 vols. Strassburg: K. J. Trübner, 1898–1901.

Gignoux, Philipe. "Zoroastrian Polemics Against Jews in the Sasanian and Early Islamic Period." In *Irano-Judaica II: Studies Relating to Jewish Contacts with Persian Culture Throughout the Ages.* Jerusalem: Ben Zvi Institute, 1990.

Gil, Moshe. "The Exilarchate." In *The Jews of Medieval Islam: Community, Society, and Identity.* Leiden: Brill, 1995.

Ginzberg, Louis. *The Legends of the Jews.* 7 vols. Philadelphia: Jewish Publication Society of America, 1938. Reprint, 1968.

Gnoli, Gherardo. "Further Information Concerning the Judaeo-Persian Documents of Afghanistan." *East and West* 14 (1963): 209–210.

——. *Le iscrizioni giudeo-persiane del Gūr (Afghanistan).* Rome: Istituto italiano per il medio ed extremo oriente, 1964.

Goitein, S. D. *Letters of Medieval Jewish Traders.* Princeton: Princeton University Press, 1973.

——. *A Mediterranean Society: The Jewish Communities of the Arab World as Portrayed in the Documents of the Cairo Geniza.* 5 vols. Berkeley: University of California Press, 1967–1988.

——. "Minority Selfrule and Government Control in Islam." *Studia Islamica* 31 (1970): 101–116.

Goldin, Grace. *Come Under the Wings: A Midrash on Ruth.* Philadelphia: Jewish Publication Society of America, 1980.

Goodman, Philip. *The Purim Anthology.* Philadelphia: Jewish Publication Society of America, 1971.

Grill, Julius. *Der achtundsechzigste Psalm.* Tübingen: H. Laupp, 1883.

Guidi, I. "Di una versione persiana del Pentateuco." *Rendiconti della Reale Accademia Nazionale dei Lincei* (1884–85): 347–355.

Gutmann, Joseph. "Judeo-Persian Miniatures." *SBB* 8 (1968): 54–77.

Haim, S. *New Persian-English Dictionary.* 2 vols. Tehran: Beroukhim, 1969.

Halevi, Menaḥem. *Maṣevat Mordekai v'-Ester.* Jerusalem: Ben Zvi Institute, 1932.

Henning, W. B., "The Inscriptions of Tang-i Azao," *BSOAS* 20 (1957): 335–342.

Herzfeld, E. *Archaelogical History of Iran.* London: Oxford University Press, 1935.

Hinnells, John R. *Persian Mythology.* New York: Peter Bedrick, 1985.

Hodgson, Marshall G. S. *The Venture of Islam.* 3 vols. Chicago: University of Chicago Press, 1974.

Horn, Paul. "Zu den jüdisch-persischen Bibelübersetzungen." *Indogermanische Forschungen* 2 (1893): 132–143.

——. "Zu Širvani's hebraisch-persischen Wörterbuche." *Zeitschrift für die alttestamentliche Wissenschaft* 17 (1897): 201–203.

Horowitz, J. "Hebrew-Iranian Synchronism." In *Oriental Studies in Honor of C. E. Pavry.* Oxford: Oxford University Press, 1933.

Huart, Clement. "Quelques observations sur le Judéo-Persan de Bokhara." *Keleti Szemle* 3 (1902): 305–306.

Jakab, Jenö. "Jezsájás könyvének anónymús Perzsa fórditása." *Magyar Zsidó Szemle* 49 (1932): 3–29.

Kashani, Reuben. *Kehillot ha-yehudim be-Paras-Iran.* Jerusalem: R. Kashani, 1980.

Khalid, Adeeb. "The Residential Quarter in Bukhara Before the Revolution (The Work of O. A. Sukhareva)." *MESA Bulletin* 25 (1991): 15–24.

Knappert, Jan. *Islamic Legends: Histories of the Heroes, Saints and Prophets of Islam.* Leiden: Brill, 1985.

Kohut, Alexander. *Kritische Beleuchtung der persischen Pentateuch-Übersetzung des Jacob ben Joseph Tavus. . . .* Leipzig: C. F. Winter, 1871.

Landshut, S. *Jewish Communities in the Muslim Countries of the Middle Ages.* London: Jewish Chronicle, 1950.

Lavī, Ḥabīb. *Tārīkh-i yahūd-i Irān.* 3 vols. Tehran: Kitāb Forūshī-yi Barukhīm, 1956–60.

Lazard, Gilbert. "La dialecte de Juifs de Kerman." In *Monumentum Georg Morgenstierne* II (= *Acta Iranica* 22 [1982]).

———. "La dialectologie du Judéo-Persan." *SBB* 8 (1968): 77–98.

———. "Judaeo-Persian. ii. Language." *EI* (2), 4:313–314.

———. "Judaeo-Persian." *EJ* 10: 430–432.

———. "Le judéo-persan ancien entre le pehlevi et le persan." *Transition Periods in Iranian History* (= *Studia Iranica* 5 [1987]).

———. *La langue des plus anciens monuments de la prose persane.* Paris: Libraire C. Klincksieck, 1963.

———. "Lumières nouvelles sur la formation de la langue persane: Une traduction du Coran en persan dialectal et ses affinités avec le judéo-persan." *Irano Judaica II: Studies Relating to Jewish Contacts with Persian Culture Throughout the Ages.* Jerusalem: Ben Zvi Institute, 1990.

———. "Reconstructing the Development of New Persian." *Al-ʿUṣur al-Wusṭā* 5 (1993): 28–30.

———. "Remarques sur le fragment judéo-persan de Dandān-Uiliq." In *A Green Leaf: Papers in Honor of Professor Jes P. Asmussen* (= *Acta Iranica* 28 [1988]).

———. "The Rise of the New Persian Language." In *The Cambridge History of Iran.* Vol. 4. Cambridge: Cambridge University Press, 1975.

Lazarus-Yafeh, Hava. "Ester ha-malkah—min ha-anusim? Perusho shel Rabaʿ le-Ester." *Tarbiṣ* 57 (1987–88): 121–122.

———. *Intertwined Worlds: Medieval Islam and Bible Criticism.* Princeton: Princeton University Press, 1992.

———. *Some Religious Aspects of Islam.* Leiden: Brill, 1981.

Lazarus-Yafeh, Hava, ed. *Soferim muslimim ʿal-yehudim ve-yahadut.* Jerusalem: Merkaz Zalman Shazar, 1996.

Leslie, Daniel. "The Judaeo-Persian Colophons to the Pentateuch of the K'aifeng Jews." *Abr-Nahrain* 8 (1969): 1–35.

———. "Persia or Yemen? The Origin of the Kaifeng Jews." In *Irano-Judaica: Studies*

Relating to Jewish Contacts with Persian Culture Throughout the Ages. Jerusalem: Ben Zvi Institute, 1982.

Leslie, Donald. *The Survival of the Chinese Jews*. Leiden: Brill, 1972.

Levin, Theodore. *The Hundred Thousand Fools of God: Musical Travels in Central Asia and Queens, New York*. Bloomington: Indiana University Press, 1996.

Levtzion, N., ed. *Conversion to Islam*. New York: Holmes and Meier, 1979.

Lewis, Bernard. *The Jews of Islam*. Princeton: Princeton University Press, 1984.

Lockhart, Laurence. *The Fall of the Safavi Dynasty Under the Afghan Occupation of Persia*. Cambridge: Cambridge University Press, 1958.

——. *Nadir Shah*. London: Luzac, 1938.

Loeb, Laurence. "The Jewish Musician and the Music of Fars." *Asian Music* 4 (1972): 3–14.

Loewenthal, Rudolf. "The Judeo-Muslim Marranos of Bukhara." *Central Asian Collectanea* 1 (1958): 1–11.

——. "Les Juifs de Boukhara." *Cahiers du Monde Russe et Sovietique* 2 (1961): 104–108.

MacKenzie, D. N. "Ad *Judaeo-Persica II* Hafniensia." *JRAS* (1966): 159–170.

——. "An Early Jewish-Persian Argument." *BSOAS* 31 (1968): 249–269.

——. "Jewish Persian from Isfahan." *JRAS* (1968): 68–75.

Mainz, Ernest. "Esther en judéo-persan." *JA* 258 (1970): 95–106.

——. "Le livre de Daniel en judéo-persan." In *Irano-Judaica: Studies Relating to Jewish Contacts with Persian Culture Throughout the Ages*. Jerusalem: Ben Zvi Institute, 1982.

——. "Le livre des Proverbes en judéo-persan." *JA* 268 (1980): 71–106.

——. "Ruth et le Cantique des Cantiques en judéo-persan." *JA* 264 (1976): 9–34.

——. "Vocabulaire judéo-persan." *Studia Iranica* 6 (1977): 75–95.

Margoliouth, D. S. "An Early Judaeo-Persian Document from Khotan in the Stein Collection, with Other Early Persian Documents." *JRAS* (1903): 735–760.

——. "A Jewish-Persian Law Report," *JQR* 40 (1899): 671–675.

Margoliouth, George. "Persian Hebrew Manuscripts in the British Museum." *JQR* 7 (1894): 119–120.

Melammed, Ezra Z. *Shir ha-shirim: Targum arami-Targum ʿivri. Tafsir be-lashon yehude-Paras*. Jerusalem: N.p., 1971.

Minorsky, Vladimir. "Early Hebrew-Persian Documents." *JRAS* (1942): 181–194.

Mizraḥi, Ḥanina. *Toledot yehude Paras u-meshorereihem*. Jerusalem: Reuben Mas, 1966.

Moore, Carey A. *Daniel, Esther and Jeremiah: The Additions*. Garden City, N.Y.: Doubleday, 1977.

Moreen, Vera B. "A Dialogue Between God and Satan in Shāhīn's *Bereshit [-nāmah]*." *Irano-Judaica III: Studies Relating to Jewish Contacts with Persian Culture Throughout the Ages*. Jerusalem: Ben Zvi Institute, 1994.

——. "The Downfall of Muhammad [ʿAlī] Beg, Grand Vizier of Shah ʿAbbās II (r. 1642–1666)." *JQR* 72 (1981): 81–99.

——. *Iranian Jewry During the Afghan Invasion: The Kitāb-i Sar Guzasht-i Kāshān of Bābāī Ibn Farhād [1721–1731]*. Stuttgart: Franz Steiner Verlag, 1990.

——. *Iranian Jewry's Hour of Peril and Heroism: A Study of Bābāī Ibn Lutf's Chronicle [1617–1662]*. New York: American Academy for Jewish Research, 1986.

——. "The 'Iranization' of Biblical Heroes in Judeo-Persian Epics: Shāhīn's *Ardashīr-nāmah* and *Ezra-nāmah*," *Iranian Studies* 29 (1996): 321–338.

——. "Ishmāʿīliyāt: A Fourteenth Century Judaeo-Persian Account of the Building of the Kaʿba." In *A Festschrift in Honor of Prof. William Brinner,* forthcoming.

——. "Jewish Responses to Anti-Jewish Muslim Polemics in Two Judaeo-Persian Texts." *Irano-Judaica IV: Studies Relating to Jewish Contacts with Persian Culture Throughout the Ages.* Jerusalem: Ben Zvi Institute, forthcoming.

——. "The *Kitāb-i Anusī* of Bābāī ibn Luṭf (Seventeenth Century) and the *Kitāb-i Sar Guzasht-i Kāshān* of Bābāī ibn Farhād (Eighteenth Century): A Comparison of Two Judaeo-Persian Chronicles." In *Intellectual Studies on Islam.* Salt Lake City: University of Utah Press, 1990.

——. "The *Kitāb-i Sar Guzasht-i Kāshān* of Bābāī ibn Farhād." *PAAJR* 52 (1985): 141–157.

——. "The Legend of Adam in the Judeo-Persian Epic *Bereshit [-nāmah]* (Fourteenth Century)." *PAAJR* 57 (1991): 155–178.

——. *Miniature Paintings in Judaeo-Persian Manuscripts.* Cincinnati: Hebrew Union College Press, 1985.

——. "Moses, God's Shepherd: An Episode from a Judeo-Persian Epic, *Mūsā Nāmah.*" *Prooftexts* 11 (1991): 107–130.

——. "Moses in Muḥammad's Light: Muslim Topoi and Anti-Muslim Polemics in Judaeo-Persian Panegyrics." *Annemarie Schimmel Festschrift* (= *Journal of Turkish Studies* 18 [1994]).

——. "The Muslim Vocabulary of the *Kitāb-i Sar Guzasht* of Bābāī b. Farhād." *JQR* 75 (1985): 375–384.

——. "The Persecution of Iranian Jews During the Reign of Shah ʿAbbās II (1642–1666)." *HUCA* 52 (1981): 275–309.

——. "The Problems of Conversion Among Iranian Jews in the Seventeenth and Eighteenth Centuries." *Iranian Studies* 19 (1986): 215–228. Reprinted in *Studies in Islamic and Judaic Traditions II.* Ed. William Brinner and S. D. Ricks. Atlanta, Ga.: Scholars, 1989.

——. "*Risāla-yi sawāʾiq al-yahūd [The treatise lightning bolts against the Jews]* by Muḥammad Bāqir b. Muḥammad Taqī al-Majlisī (d. 1699)." *Die Welt des Islams* 32 (1992): 177–195.

——. "Salmān-i Fārisī and the Jews: An Anti-Jewish Shīʿī Ḥadīth from the Seventeenth Century?" *Irano-Judaica II: Studies Relating to Jewish Contacts with Persian Culture Throughout the Ages.* Jerusalem: Ben Zvi Institute, 1990.

——. "The Status of Religious Minorities in Safavid Iran between 1617 and 1661." *JNES* 40 (1981): 119–134.

——. "A Supplementary List of Judaeo-Persian Manuscripts of the British Library," *The British Library Journal* 21 (1995): 71–80.

Moreen, Vera, B., and Joseph Gutman. "The Combat Between Moses and Og in Muslim Miniatures," *Bulletin of the Asia Institute,* 1 (1987): 111–122.

Moreen, Vera B., and Michel M. Mazzaoui, eds. *Intellectual Studies on Islam.* Salt Lake City, Utah: University of Utah Press, 1990.

Nasr, Seyyed H. *An Introduction to Islamic Cosmological Doctrines.* Boulder, Colo.: Shambhala, 1978.

Nasr, Seyyed H., ed. *Islamic Spirituality: Manifestations.* New York: Crossroad, 1991.

Nehmad, Moshe. "The New Garment." In *Five Folktales from Jewish-Persian Tradition.* Haifa: Ethnological Museum and Folklore Archives, 1966.

Nemoy, Leon. *Karaite Anthology: Excerpts from the Early Literature.* New Haven: Yale University Press, 1952. Reprint, 1980.

Netzer, Amnon. "Dāniyāl-Nāme: An Exposition of Judeo-Persian." In *Islam and Its Cultural Divergences: Studies in Honor of Gustave E. von Grunebaum.* Urbana: University of Illinois Press, 1971.

———. "Dāniyāl-nāma and Its Linguistic Features." *IOS* (2) (1972): 305–314.

———. *Ḥobot Yehudah le-Rabbi Yehudah ben El'azar.* Jerusalem: Ben Zvi Institute, 1995.

———. "An Isfahani Jewish Folk Song." In *Irano-Judaica: Studies Relating to Jewish Contacts with Persian Culture Throughout the Ages.* Jerusalem: Ben Zvi Institute, 1982.

———. "A Judeo-Persian Footnote: Šāhīn and 'Emrānī." *IOS* 4 (1974): 258–264.

———. *Judeo-Persian Literature.* 1. *A Chronicle of Bābāī b. Farhād.* Jerusalem: Akademon, 1978.

———. "A Midrash on the Ascension of Moses in Judeo-Persian." In *Irano-Judaica II: Studies Relating to Jewish Contacts with Persian Culture Throughout the Ages.* Jerusalem: Ben Zvi Institute, 1990.

———. *Muntakhab-i 'ash'ār-i fārisī az āsār-i yahudiyān-i Iran.* Tehran: Intishārat-i farhang-i Irān, 1973.

———. *Oṣar kitve ha-yad shel yehude Paras be-makon Ben Ṣevi.* Jerusalem: Ben Zvi Institute, 1985.

———. "Ha-qehilla ha-yehudit be-Tehran me-reshitah 'ad ha-mahpekah ha-ḥuqatit." *Shevet ve-'am* 4 (1981): 257–258.

———. "Qorot anuse Mashhad le-fi Ya'qov Dilmaniyan," *Pe'amim* 42 (1990): 127–156.

———. "Redifot u-shemadot be-toledot yehude Iran be-me'ah ha-17." *Pe'amim* 6 (1980): 33–56.

———. "'Shazadah o sufi' me'et Elisha' b. Shemu'el." *Pe'amim* 35 (1988): 24–45.

———. "Some Notes on the Characterization of Cyrus the Great in Jewish and Judeo-Persian Writings." *Acta Iranica* 2 (1974): 35–52.

———. "The Story of the Prophet Sho'ayb in Shāhīn's *Mūsānāmeh.*" In *Iranica Varia: Papers in Honor of Professor Ehsan Yarshater.* Textes et Memoires 16 (= *Acta Iranica* 30 [1990]).

———. "A Study of Kh(w)ājah Bokhārā'ī's *Dāniyāl-Nāme,*" Ph.D. diss. Columbia University, New York, 1969.

———. "Taḥanunim le-rabbi Binyamin b. Misha'el me-Kashan." *Pe'amim* 2 (1979): 48–54.

———. "Yehudim be-meḥozot ha-deromit shel ha-yam ha-kaspi." In *Society and Community: Proceedings of the Second International Congress for Research of the Sephardi and Oriental Jewish Heritage 1984.* Jerusalem: Misgav Yerushalayim, 1991.

Neusner, Jacob. *A History of the Jews in Babylonia.* 5 vols. Leiden: Brill, 1965–70.

———. *Israel and Iran in Talmudic Times: A Political History.* Lanham, Md.: University Press of America, 1986.

———. "Jews and Judaism Under Iranian Rule: Bibliographical Reflections." *History of Religions* 8 (1968): 159–177.

———. "Jews in Iran." In *The Cambridge History of Iran,* vol. 3. Cambridge: Cambridge University Press, 1983.

Nöldeke, Th. "Judenpersisch." *ZDMG* 51 (1897): 669–676.

——. Review of *Chudâidât, ein jüdisch-bucharisches Gedicht,* by Carl Salemann. *ZDMG* 51 (1897): 549–668.

Paper, Herbert H. "Judeo-Persian Bible Translations: Some Sample Texts." *SBB* 8 (1968): 99–114.

——. "A Judeo-Persian Book of Job." *Proceedings of the Israel Academy of Sciences and Humanities* 4 (1976): 313–365.

——. "Judeo-Persian Deverbatives in *-sn* and *-st*." *Indo-Iranian Journal* 10 (1967–68): 56–71.

——. "A Note on Judeo-Persian Copulas." *JAOS* 87 (1967): 227–230.

——. "Proverbs in Judeo-Persian." In *Irano-Judaica: Studies Relating to Jewish Contacts with Persian Culture Throughout the Ages.* Jerusalem: Ben Zvi Institute, 1982.

——. *Targum ha-Torah le-parsit-yehudit.* Jerusalem: Ben Zvi Institute, 1972.

——. "The Use of *(ha)mē* in Selected Judeo-Persian Texts." *JAOS* 88 (1968): 483–494.

——. "The Vatican Judeo-Persian Pentateuch. Genesis." *AO* 28 (1965): 263–340; 29 (1965–66): 75–181, 253–310.

——. "The Vatican Judeo-Persian Pentateuch: Deuteronomy." *AO* 31 (1968): 55–113.

——. "The Vatican Judeo-Persian Pentateuch: Exodus and Leviticus." *AO* 29 (1965): 75–181.

Paper, Herbert H., ed. *Jewish Languages: Theme and Variations.* Cambridge, Mass.: Association for Jewish Studies, 1978.

Patai, Raphael. *Jadīd al-Islam: The Jewish "New Muslims" of Meshhed.* Detroit: Wayne State University Press, 1997.

——. *On Jewish Folklore.* Detroit: Wayne State University Press, 1983.

Rapp, E. L. "The Date of the Judaeo-Persian Inscriptions of Tang-i Azao in Central Afghanistan." *East and West* 17 (1967): 51–58.

——. *Die jüdisch-persisch-hebräischen Inschriften aus Afghanistan.* Munich: J. Kitzinger, 1965.

Rodrigue, Aron. *Images of Sephardi and Eastern Jewries in Transition: The Teachers of the Alliance Israélite Universelle, 1860–1939.* Seattle: University of Washington Press, 1993.

Rosen-Ayalon, Miriam. "A Judeo-Persian Amulet." In *Irano-Judaica II: Studies Relating to Jewish Contacts with Persian Culture Throughout the Ages.* Jerusalem: Ben Zvi Institute, 1990.

Rosenwasser, J. "Judaeo-Persian Manuscripts in the British Museum." In *Handlist of Persian Manuscripts, 1895–1966.* London: British Museum, 1968.

Rypka, Jan. *History of Iranian Literature.* Dordrecht: Reidal, 1968.

Sabar, Shalom. "A Decorated Marriage Contract of the Crypto-Jews of Meshed from 1877." *Kresge Art Museum Bulletin* 5 (1990): 23–31.

——. *Ketubah: The Jewish Marriage Contracts in the Hebrew Union College Skirball Museum and Klau Library.* Philadelphia: Jewish Publication Society of America, 1990.

Sabar, Yona. *The Folk Literature of the Kurdistani Jews: An Anthology.* New Haven: Yale University Press, 1982.

Sahim, Haideh. "The Dialect of the Jews of Hamadan." In *Irano-Judaica III: Studies Relating to Jewish Contacts with Persian Culture Throughout the Ages.* Jerusalem: Ben Zvi Institute, 1994.

——. "Guyishhā-yi yahudiyān-i Irān," *Teruā* 1 (1996): 149–170.

Salemann, Carl. "Chudâidât: Ein jüdisch-bucharisches Gedicht." *Memoires de l'Académie Impériale des Sciences de St. Pétersbourg* 42 (1897): 1–30.

———. "Zum mittelpersischen Passiv," *Bulletin Académie Impériale des Sciences de St. Pétersbourg* 52 (1900): 269–276.

Saperstein, Marc. *Jewish Preaching, 1200–1800: An Anthology.* New Haven: Yale University Press, 1989.

Savory, Roger. *Iran Under the Safavids.* Cambridge: Cambridge University Press, 1980.

Schimmel, Annemarie. *And Muhammad Is His Messenger: The Veneration of the Prophet in Islamic Piety.* Chapel Hill: University of North Carolina Press, 1985.

———. *Mystical Dimensions of Islam.* Chapel Hill: University of North Carolina Press, 1983.

———. *A Two-Colored Brocade: The Imagery of Persian Poetry.* Chapel Hill: University of North Carolina Press, 1992.

Scholem, Gershom S. *On the Kabbalah and Its Symbolism.* New York: Schoken, 1965.

———. *Sabbatai Ṣevi: The Mystical Messiah, 1626–1676.* Bollingen Series no. 93. Princeton: Princeton University Press, 1973.

———. "Te'udot shabbtaiyot ḥadashot me-sefer To'e Ruaḥ." *Ṣion* 7 (1942): 172–196.

Schussman, Aviva. "Sippure ha-nevi'im be-masorat ha-moslemit." Ph.D. Diss. Hebrew University, Jerusalem, 1981.

Schwab, Moise. "Une version persane de la Bible." *REJ* 58 (1909): 303–306.

Seligsohn, M. "The Hebrew-Persian Manuscripts of the British Museum." *JQR* 15 (1903): 278–301.

———. "Quatre poésies judéo-persanes sur les persecutions des Juifs d'Ispahan." *REJ* 44 (1902): 86–103, 244–259.

Sells, Michael. *Early Islamic Mysticism.* New York: Paulist Press, 1996.

Shaked, Shaul. "Judaeo-Persian Notes." *IOS* 1 (1971): 178–182.

———. "Persian and the Origins of the Karaite Movement." *Association for Jewish Studies Newsletter* 18 (1976): 7–9.

———. "Two Judaeo-Persian Contributions: 1. Iranian Functions in the Book of Esther. 2. Fragments of Two Karaite Commentaries on Daniel in Judaeo-Persian." In *Irano-Judaica: Studies Relating to Jewish Contacts with Persian Culture Throughout the Ages.* Jerusalem: Ben Zvi Institute, 1982.

———. "Zoroastrian Polemics Against Jews in the Sasanian and Early Islamic Period." In *Irano-Judaica II: Studies Relating to Jewish Contacts with Persian Culture Throughout the Ages.* Jerusalem: Ben Zvi Institute, 1990.

Soroudi, Sorour. "The Concept of Jewish Impurity and Its Reflection in Persian and Judeo-Persian Traditions." In *Irano-Judaica III: Studies Relating to Jewish Contacts with Persian Culture Throughout the Ages.* Jerusalem: Ben Zvi Institute, 1994.

———. "Judeo-Persian Religious Oath Formulas as Compared with Non-Jewish Iranian Traditions." In *Irano-Judaica II: Studies Relating to Jewish Contacts with Persian Culture Throughout the Ages.* Jerusalem: Ben Zvi Institute, 1990.

———. "Shirā-ye Ḥatanī: A Judeo-Persian Wedding Song." In *Irano-Judaica: Studies Relating to Jewish Contacts with Persian Culture Throughout the Ages.* Jerusalem: Ben Zvi Institute, 1982.

Spicehandler, Ezra. "A Descriptive List of Judeo-Persian Manuscripts at the Klau Library of the Hebrew Union College." *SBB* 8 (1968): 114–136.

———. "The Persecution of the Jews of Isfahan Under Shah 'Abbās II (1642–1666)." *HUCA* 46 (1975): 331–356.

———. "Shāhīn's Influence on Bābāī ben Luṭf: The Abraham-Nimrod Legend." In *Irano-Judaica II: Studies Relating to Jewish Contacts with Persian Culture Throughout the Ages.* Jerusalem: Ben Zvi Institute, 1990.

Spiegel, Shalom. *The Last Trial.* Philadelphia: Jewish Publication Society of America, 1967.

Steingass, F. *A Comprehensive Persian-English Dictionary.* Beirut: Libraire du Liban, 1892. Reprint, 1975.

Stillman, Norman A. *The Jews of Arab Lands in Modern Times.* Philadelphia: Jewish Publication Society of America, 1991.

Sunderman, W. "Zum Judenpersisch der Mas'at Binyamin." *Mitteilungen des Instituts für Orientforschung* 11 (1966): 275–300.

Sunderman, W., J. Duchesne-Guillemin, and F. Vahman, eds. *A Green Leaf ["Bargi-Sabz"]: Papers in Honour of Professor Jes P. Asmussen.* Leiden: Brill, 1988 [= *Acta Iranica* 28 [1988]).

Tadmor, Ḥayim. "The Period of the First Temple, the Babylonian Exile and the Restoration." In *A History of the Jewish People,* pt. 2. Cambridge: Harvard University Press, 1976.

Ṭal, Shlomo. *Nusaḥ ha-tefillah shel yehude Paras.* Jerusalem: Ben Zvi Institute, 1980.

———. "Siddur tefillah nusaḥ Paras le-fi kitve ha-yad Adler." Ph.D. Diss. Tel Aviv University, 1973.

Tobi, Yosef. "Ha-yahadut ha-iranit." In *Toledot ha-yehudim be-arṣot ha-islam.* Jerusalem: Merkaz Zalman Shazar, 1981.

Urbach, Ephraim E. *The Sages: Their Concepts and Beliefs.* Cambridge: Harvard University Press, 1987.

Utas, B. "The Jewish-Persian Fragment from Dandān-Uiliq." *Orientalia Suecana* 17 (1968): 123–136.

Walfish, Barry D. *Esther in Medieval Garb: Jewish Interpretation of the Book of Esther in the Middle Ages.* Albany: State University of New York Press, 1993.

Wasserstrom, Steven M. *Between Muslim and Jew: The Problem of Symbiosis Under Early Islam.* Princeton: Princeton University Press, 1995.

Weissenberg, S. "Zur Anthropologie der persischen Juden." *Zeitschrift fur Ethnologie* 65 (1913): 108–119.

White, W. C. *Chinese Jews: A Compilation of Matters Relating to the Jews of Kaifeng Fu.* Toronto: University of Toronto Press, 1942.

Widengren, Geo. "The Status of the Jews in the Sassanian Empire." *Iranica antiqua* 1 (1961): 134–154.

Wust, Efraim. "Yehude Iran ve sifrut parsit—iyyunim be-kitve yad." *Kirjath Sepher* 58 (1983): 605–621.

Ya'ari, Avraham. "Sifre yehude Bukhara." *Kirjath Sepher* 18 (1941–42): 282–297, 378–393; 19 (1942): 35–55, 116, 139.

Yaniv, Bracha. "Mu'ammā-yi guldastehā-yi towrāt dar sharq-i Irān." *Pādyāvand* 1 (1996): 169–220.

Yarshater, Ehsan. "The Dialect of Borujerd Jews." In *Archaeologia Iranica et Orientalis: Miscellanea en Honorem Louis Vanden Berghe.* Gent: Peters, 1989.

———. "The Hybrid Language of the Jewish Communities of Persia." *JAOS* 97 (1977): 1–7.

———. "The Jewish Communities of Persia and Their Dialects." In *Memorial de Jean de Menasce.* Louvain: Imprimerie orientaliste, 1974.

Yarshater, Ehsan, ed. *Persian Literature.* New York: Persian Heritage Foundation, 1988.

Yehoshua-Raz, Ben Zion. *Mi-nedaḥe Yisrael be-Afganistan le-anuse Mashhad be-Iran.* Jerusalem: Bialik Institute, 1992.

Yeroushalmi, David. *The Judeo-Persian Poet ʿEmrānī and His Book of Treasure.* Leiden: Brill, 1995.

Yeroushalmi, Yosef H. *Zakhor: Jewish History and Jewish Memory.* Seattle: University of Washington Press, 1982.

Zand, Michael, "Bukhara." In *Encyclopaedia Judaica Year Book, 1975–76,* pp. 183–192.

———. "Bukhara. VII Bukharan Jews." *Encyclopaedia Iranica* 4: 530–544.

———. "Hityashavut ha-yehudim be-asiyah ha-tikonah bi-me qedem u-bi-me ha-beynayim ha-muqdamim." *Peʿamim* 35 (1988): 4–23.

Index